THE SPELL OF WAR

is conjured up for you in this all-original volume of tales by some of today's finest fantasy strategists. From classic settings to contemporary locales, from battles waged between demon and mortal to those between the mightiest of sorcerers to wars that entangle innocent and evil alike, here are stories certain to hold your imagination captive, including:

"The Strangeness of the Day"—She's taken on some odd clients in her time, but she didn't think she was up to handling a case of murder by magic. . . .

"The Jewel and the Demon"—It should have been an easy assignment, after all she had a demon to help her steal the jewel for the wizard. What she didn't realize was that the jewel's guardians were the least of her worries. . . .

"Warlords"—He had power beyond imagining and was cursed to wield it eternally—unless he could learn not to rule. . . .

BATTLE MAGIC

edited by Martin H. Greenberg
and Larry Segriff

DAW BOOKS, INC.
DONALD A. WOLLHEIM, FOUNDER
375 Hudson Street, New York, NY 10014

ELIZABETH R. WOLLHEIM
SHEILA E. GILBERT
PUBLISHERS

First Printing, October 1998
1 2 3 4 5 6 7 8 9

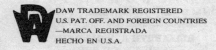

DAW TRADEMARK REGISTERED
U.S. PAT. OFF. AND FOREIGN COUNTRIES
—MARCA REGISTRADA
HECHO EN U.S.A.

PRINTED IN THE U.S.A.

ACKNOWLEDGMENTS

Introduction © 1998 by Larry Segriff.

The Strangeness of the Day © 1998 by Kristine Kathryn Rusch.

Ladykiller © 1998 by Rosemary Edghill.

The Jewel and the Demon © 1998 by Lisanne Norman.

Principles of Warfare © 1998 by John Helfers.

BattleMagic™ for Morons © 1998 by John DeChancie.

The Miracle of Salamis © 1998 by Lois Tilton.

Alaric's Gift © 1998 by Mickey Zucker Reichert.

Rite of Passage © 1998 by Ed Gorman.

Bright Streets of Air © 1998 by Nina Kiriki Hoffman.

Hell's Bane © 1998 by Jane Lindskold.

The Fatal Wager © 1998 by Elizabeth Ann Scarborough.

'Ware the Sleeper © 1998 by Julie E. Czerneda.

A Matter of Honor © 1998 by Josepha Sherman.

Warlord © 1998 by Michelle West.

Ten for the Devil © by Charles de Lint.

CONTENTS

INTRODUCTION

LISTEN. Do you hear it?

That sound . . . The skirling of bagpipes, the blare of horns, the rolling of drums . . .

That's the call to battle, and it's been echoing in our blood since the first man-ape came down from the trees, looked around, and picked up a stick to defend himself with.

But there's more to that summons than a mere call to arms. Mixed in with the dreams of power, of glory, of hard-fought victory snatched from the jaws of defeat, there is also a promise of something more, a hint of magic, a hope of something more powerful, more glorious, and more wondrous than any weapon invented by man. For in every competition—and especially in the life and death struggle of the battlefield—we are always looking for an edge over our opponents . . . and sometimes that edge is magic.

We are a martial race. Our pastimes are violent—from football and rugby to tae kwon do and karate—and we are constantly building bigger, better, and more powerful weapons. And though we like to think we've matured as a race, come closer to the goal of world peace, for every Christ and Ghandi we've produced there are easily ten, twenty, a hundred Alexanders and Napoleons, all bent on conquest and world domination.

Our best and most cherished stories—the *Iliad*, the walls of Jericho, the Alamo, and others—are sagas of battle, of heroism, of death. Custer's Last Stand. The Charge of the Light Brigade. The Battle of the Bulge. The list goes on and on, an honor roll of warfare born in fire, written in blood, and etched in our hearts forever.

From that first man-ape who picked up a stick to throw, to the knights of the Middle Ages and on through the hi-tech soldiers of tomorrow, we have always been a warrior race. But we are also a race that dreams of that sense of wonder that lies at the very heart of magic.

The stories gathered in this book are all woven from the two threads of war and wizardry. Powerful tales of magical conflict, they will take you from the battlefield to the field of honor to the site of sorcerous duels, and to all the myriad, magical places in between.

So pull up a chair, toss an extra log on the fire, and prepare to answer the call to battle . . .

THE STRANGENESS OF THE DAY

Kristine Kathryn Rusch

Kristine Kathryn Rusch has worked as an editor at such places as Pulphouse Publishing, and, most recently at The Magazine of Fantasy & Science Fiction, though she is currently a full-time writer. Current novels include Hitler's Angel *and* The Fey: Victory. *Her short fiction appears in* Mystery Fairy Tales, First Contact, *and* Wizard Fantastic. *A winner of the World Fantasy Award, she lives in Oregon with her husband, author and editor Dean Wesley Smith.*

JUST once, she thought, just once, she would like a little magic in her life. She believed magic was possible, on days when the sun shone through the clouds, on afternoons when rainbows dotted the countryside, on mornings when the light was so sharp it looked as if everything had been freshly made.

Not on a day like this. On a day like this, all she wanted was someone to come home to, a man to cook her meals and rub her feet, and to laugh at the sheer strangeness of the day.

That was what she was thinking about as she exited the elevator into the bowels of the parking structure below her office building. The concrete structure smelled like gas fumes, and the lighting, even in the middle of the day, was a fluorescent gray that made her think of rain.

She rounded a corner, her heels clicking on the concrete, and saw a man sitting on the back of a 1974 Lincoln, holding a cigarette lighter in one hand, and a snake in the other.

The snake was alive, and twisting.

She swallowed, uncertain whether or not to keep walking. The man was gorgeous: long black hair, brown eyes, smooth skin the color of toffee. He wore a shimmery gray silk suit that accented his broad shoulders and long legs, and on his feet he wore cowboy boots trimmed with real silver.

Nora pulled her purse tight against her side. She would walk around the car and continue toward hers as if she saw nothing wrong.

"Who'zat?" A nasal male voice demanded.

"Probably someone on the way to her car." The responding voice was deep and smooth, soft and in control. Even without looking, Nora knew who spoke second.

A tiny man stood on the bumper of the Lincoln. The first man had slid across the hood to make room for the small guy. The little guy was perfectly proportioned, square with a pugnacious face, a nose that obviously had been broken several times, and powerful arms. He wore dark blue jeans and a T-shirt with a pack of cigarettes rolled up in the sleeves.

"It'd be nice to have a woman," the tiny man said.

His companion smiled. The snake wrapped itself around his wrist. "Things are a bit different now," he said. "You can't just have any woman."

As he spoke, his gaze met Nora's. His brown eyes sparkled as if they shared a joke.

She wasn't in the mood to share anything, no matter how gorgeous he was. She had a video deposition to take, a lunch to grab on the run, and a court appearance at 2:00. She didn't have time for any of this.

"Excuse me," she said, and tried to hurry past them. The little man scurried along the bumper until he could extend his small arm in front of her.

"Who are you?" he asked in his annoying nasal voice.

She had had enough of their strangeness. She rose to her full five feet four inches (in heels) and said, "Nora Barr. I'm a lawyer." She added that last so that they wouldn't screw with her.

The tall man raised his eyebrows and looked at the little man. The little man shrugged. "Told you we needed a woman," he said.

So that was how she found herself back in her office, the two men seated across from her, looking at her degrees and framed prints cluttering the fake wood paneling on the wall. She had sent her assistant Charlene to do the video deposition, rationalizing that Charlene needed the experience, knowing that she would regret this action should that particular case go to trial. But she really didn't want to leave Charlene alone with these two—Nora wasn't sure she wanted to be alone with them either—but she felt compelled to listen to their case.

The little man sat like an overgrown child in her green metal office chair. His stubby legs extended over the seat and didn't even pretend to try for the ground. Like a little boy, he put his hands on the armrests as if he were trying to hold himself in place. He watched her every move, and she wasn't sure she liked that.

The other man slid into the remaining chair as if it were built for him. He had pushed the chair back so that he could extend his long legs. His booted feet still hit the metal edge of her desk, rattling it. The snake had disappeared, probably hiding in his suit, and he had also hidden the cigarette lighter.

"All right," she said, leaning forward and folding her hands together in what she hoped was a business-like position. "What can I do for you?"

"Can you have someone tested for a witch?" the little man asked.

"That never worked," the other man growled.

"Exactly," the little man said.

Nora glanced at her watch. "I have to be in court in less than ninety minutes."

"Right," the gorgeous man said. "I—"

"If she can't have her tested for a witch, perhaps tarred and feathered?"

"Wrong century."

"Hanged from a tree until she's dead?"

"Wrong century."

"Boiled in oil?"

"You know no one did that."

Nora slapped her hands on her desk and stood. "I do appreciate the comedy routine, but I also bill by the hour, and so far you gentlemen have taken up nearly fifteen minutes of your free session. So unless there's a *realistic* way I can help you—"

"I'm sorry." The good-looking man stood too. "I get so preoccupied I forget that the rest of the world doesn't work the way I do." He extended his hand. "I'm Blackstone."

"*The* Blackstone?" she asked with just a trace of sarcasm in her voice.

"Well, actually, yes, but not the one you're thinking of. He, in fact, was the imposter, but that's a long story which ended rather nastily for all concerned. He—"

"Blackstone," she said, sinking down to her desk. This would be a long interview. "Is that a first or last name?"

"It's a surname," he said, sitting too. "My given name is Aethelstan."

"Aethelstan?" Whatever she had expected, it wasn't that.

He shrugged prettily. "It was in style once."

"A long, *long* time ago," the little man added.

"And you are?" she asked him.

"Let's just call me Panza," the little man said. "Sancho Panza."

She shook her head. "If you want me to do something for you in a court of law, I'll need your legal name."

The little guy shrugged. "It's not me you're helping," he said. "It's Blackstone."

She sighed. Why did she feel as if she had been taken, although she hadn't known what for? "All right, Mr. Blackstone," she said, "what can I help you with?"

"You charge what?" he asked. The question sounded rude. As he spoke, the snake stuck its head out of his shirt and looked at her as if it too expected an answer.

"Two hundred dollars an hour, plus a—" she almost quoted her regular rate, then decided to double it because these two were proving to be so much trouble— "plus a thousand dollar retainer."

"A thousand dollar—" the little man said, strangling on the last word. "In my day, you could run a country on a thousand dollars."

"In your day, there was no such thing as dollars," Blackstone muttered.

"As I told you in the parking garage, the first hour of the consultation is free." She glanced at her watch. "However, you're rapidly running out of time."

"What do you prefer?" Blackstone asked. "A check or cash?"

"Or gold?" the little man added. She would be damned if she would think of him as Sancho Panza.

"A check is fine," she said. No sense taking currency. With these two, it could just as easily be forged, and then where would she be? The worst thing a check could do was bounce.

Blackstone put a hand inside his suitcoat and brought out a checkbook. A pen appeared in his other hand. She hadn't seen him take it from anywhere. He poised it over the paper. "To you or the law firm?"

She was still nonplussed by the appearance of the pen. "Um," she said, wishing she could gather herself more quickly in this man's presence. "The law firm."

He wrote the check, signed it with a flourish, then handed it to her. She glanced at it, noting his name in bold and only a post office box for an address. It was time, she thought, to get serious.

She pulled out a legal pad and took her pen out of its holder. "Let's get your exact address and phone number, starting with you, Mr. Blackstone, and then going with your friend here."

"You don't need me," the little man said. "I already told you."

"Then I'll have to ask you to leave," she said.

"I don't mind him staying," Blackstone said, leaning back as he said so.

"I do," she said.

Blackstone raised an eyebrow. The little man scowled. "You got books in the waiting area?"

"Law books," Nora said.

"Good enough," he said, and let himself out.

The room felt three times larger without him. She wasn't certain how a person that tiny could fill such a big space.

"Mr. Blackstone," she said, not missing a beat, "street address and phone number?"

He gave her both with an ease that made her uncomfortable. She wasn't sure why it did; most people could recite their addresses in their sleep. But everything about him seemed strange.

"So," she said again. "How can I help you?"

To her surprise, a flush covered his cheeks. He threaded his hands together, glanced nervously at the door, and then said, "A . . . dear friend of mine . . .

has been in a . . . coma . . . for . . . some time. Her . . . guardian . . . won't let me near her, and although I've fought for that right for . . . some time . . . , I haven't made any progress."

"And you want me to—what? Contact the guardian?"

"Isn't there anything legal you can do?" he asked.

"Depends," she said. "What's your exact relationship?"

His flush grew deeper. She sighed inwardly. Girlfriend. Right. But then, she had a rule about getting involved with clients anyway.

"She's—ah—someone special to me."

God, she hated clients like this. They wanted her to fix whatever it was, but they weren't forthcoming right from the start. Her favorite second-year law professor had warned her about this, but she had thought he was exaggerating until she hung out her shingle and began to interact with the great unwashed.

"Special." She let her tone go dry. "As in fiancée? Lover?"

"No," he said. "But she will be."

She closed her eyes. Will be. He had hopes, but the woman probably didn't. Which meant he was a stalker. Why were all the gorgeous ones also crazy? She opened her eyes. He was watching her, looking puzzled.

"Look, Mr. Blackstone," she said. "I can't help you in any legal way unless the woman in question is in some way a relative. I'm sorry, but that's just the law. You'll have to accept the situation for what it is and move on."

She pushed his check back toward him.

"You can't help me?" he asked, sounding a bit astounded.

She shook her head. "Not me, not any lawyer. You have no rights with someone who is just a friend. The guardian has legal control."

The snake stuck its head out farther and hissed softly. Its long forked tongue curled as it did so. He shushed it, and pushed it back inside his coat.

"This is becoming untenable," he said.

"I'm sorry." Her heart had started pounding hard. He had made her nervous from the beginning, but she had thought his strangeness harmless. Now she wasn't sure.

He took the check, stood, and held out his hand. "Sorry to take all of your time," he said.

"The first hour's free," she said lightly. But it had cost her a good deposition.

"Nonetheless," he said. "I appreciate your candor." And then he slipped out the door and out, she hoped, of her life. Still, as a precaution, she made notes of the entire strange meeting. Her secretary had been complaining about the dullness of the routine lately; she would get a kick out of this.

Nora didn't think of Blackstone again. She had chalked up the interview to one of those weird experiences that attorneys sometimes had, and she had moved on. So, two weeks later, as she was leaving the courthouse after a particularly successful trial, she was surprised to receive a call from her secretary, saying that Blackstone had requested her presence immediately at an address that put him squarely in the center of the west side suburbs. Nora protested: She had told him she wouldn't be his attorney, but her secretary insisted.

"I think he's in some kind of trouble," she said.

It took Nora ten minutes on the freeway to get to the neighborhood Blackstone had indicated. As she got closer, she watched a cloud of inky black smoke loom over that section of town. Each time she pulled to the side of the road, she cursed slightly, and she wondered what she was getting herself into.

The exit was jammed with milling people, emergency vehicles, and baffled onlookers. The inky black smoke was rising from an area two blocks over. It looked serious.

A roadblock greeted her halfway down the street. A cop she didn't recognize rapped on her window. As she rolled it down, she said, "I'm Mr. Blackstone's attorney. He just called me."

The cop waved her through.

As she drove past the roadblock, she felt as if she had entered a nightmare. Burning bits of wood littered the road, and she had to constantly swerve around them. Several homes were on fire, their residents outside, holding hoses on the houses or weeping. A couple of cars parked alongside the street had large holes through their roofs and sides, as if someone—or something—had punched through the metal. The air was filled with ash, and the smell of smoke was so overpowering that she continually sneezed.

The address her secretary had given her was right in the middle of the devastation. Police cars blocked the entire road. She really didn't want to get out of the car, but she felt she had no choice.

She sighed, grabbed her tennis shoes from their spot beneath the passenger seat, and removed her lucky Ferragamos. She shoved her nylon-covered feet into the tennies, and got out of the car.

It was worse outside. The stench permeated everything. Bits of charred wood and flame floated down with the ash. The sky was so dark, it seemed as if a severe storm were about to break overhead. Her eyes watered. People were sobbing, police band radios were crackling with voices and static, and firemen were yelling directions at each other. She stepped over hoses and blackened debris, not quite sure where she was going, but knowing she'd recognize it when she saw it.

And she did. The five policemen were standing around Blackstone. He was on a green lawn, untouched by flames, its flowers an obscene reminder of what the neighborhood had been just hours before. A woman was sprawled on the driveway facedown; her position was unnatural, the turn of her head, the clawed tension in her fingers all confirmed what Nora feared.

The woman was dead.

A shiver ran through Nora despite the dry heat from nearby flames. She didn't do criminal work. She was a civil attorney; this was way out of her league.

She rounded a 1970 brown and orange VW microbus, and headed toward the police. No one tried to stop her. The microbus rocked slightly, and as she looked up, she could have sworn she saw Sancho Panza or whoever the hell he was moving behind the window. Then, when she blinked, he was gone.

She swallowed against the smoke-ravaged dryness of her throat. She had to stay focused. She had to somehow get through these next few moments and then get out of here.

Blackstone's face softened when he saw her. It had been hard lines and angles before. Now it was gentle, rounded, as if someone had changed the lighting or he had become a different person somehow. She felt the transition as much as saw it, and remembered suddenly, uncomfortably, the transition people said Ted Bundy's face went through when he was angry.

She was in much too deep. At least she knew it.

She stopped beside one of the police officers, a middle-aged man whose soft stomach edged over his belt. His face was sootstreaked, and his eyes were red.

"I'm Mr. Blackstone's attorney," Nora said in her best don't-screw-with-me-voice. "What's going on here?"

"Nora," Blackstone said, his voice warm. "Get my partner. We're going to need you help."

"What's going on?" she asked again.

The cop looked around as if what she saw explained

everything. "Your client destroyed this neighborhood." Then he nodded at the dead woman. "We're not sure what happened there. All we know is that folks placed her as alive not fifteen minutes ago."

"What are you charging him with?"

"What aren't we charging him with? Carrying incendiary devices. Arson. Murder and attempted murder, I would say."

"Nora," Blackstone said again. "Get Sancho. We need to secure the glass case and we don't have much time."

"You shouldn't be talking," Nora said. "Listen, I'll meet you at the jail. And if possible, I'll have a criminal defense attorney there as well. We'll get you out—"

"I'm not worried about me," he said. "Get Sancho—"

"You coming with us, lady?" the police officer asked.

"Where are you taking him?"

"Downtown," the officer said. "This one goes right to the jail. We're not taking no chances."

"Nora—"

She pointed a finger at Blackstone. He flinched visibly. "I don't want to hear another word from you. You will not speak again until you are in the presence of an attorney. Is that clear?"

He nodded. She had no idea if they had already Mirandized him, but she wasn't taking any chances.

The cops led him away. He looked over his shoulder once and mouthed, "Remember." She wouldn't forget. Even though she wanted to.

She brushed a strand of hair out of her face. The smoke was making her woozy. She didn't want to think about what he had done to destroy this neighborhood. She didn't want to think about that feeling she had gotten earlier, when she had first met with him, when she felt that he was a stalker. She wondered how much she had seen at that moment, and how much she had missed.

Well, it wouldn't be her problem for long. She would turn it over to someone else, and that would be it. Except that he wanted her to do something, something with a glass case.

She passed the VW microbus and as she did, the passenger window rolled down a crack. A tiny face pressed against it. "I'm going to your office," a voice whispered.

Sancho. She suppressed a sigh and didn't even nod as she passed him. The last thing she wanted was for the cops to investigate the microbus. Who knew what they would find inside? She couldn't believe they hadn't cordoned it off already as part of the crime scene.

She climbed over hoses, and returned to her own car. It was covered in a film of ash. As she settled into the driver's side, she turned on the wipers. The ash smeared all over the glass.

He had destroyed a neighborhood and maybe killed a woman. Was this because Nora hadn't helped him? Or was something else going on here, something she didn't entirely understand?

She started the car, and executed a series of small Y-turns in the tiny space, careful not to run over any hoses. The situation looked grim. Houses were still burning. She wondered how many would be gone by nightfall.

If she had to lay a bet, she would bet on all of them.

She was shaking as she drove back to her office. Shaking and slightly woozy from the smoke. Her nylons were ripped and she didn't know how she had done that, and her best suit was covered in soot and ash. She smelled like charred wood, and she doubted that smell would ever come off.

Traffic was horrible—backed up for miles as people

gawked at the smoke and pulled over for the occasional ambulance. When she got herself together enough to speak, she called her secretary and had a conference call with Max Raichelson, the best defense attorney in the city, maybe in the entire state. She and Max had been close in law school—she had even hoped he would ask her out—but nothing had come of it. After graduation, they had gone their own ways.

He agreed to meet Blackstone ("You're kidding, right?" Max asked) at the police station.

The problem was no longer hers. Except she didn't tell Max about Sancho. And she didn't want to think about him either. She wanted simply to get on with her life as if nothing happened. She knew that would be impossible, but in the spirit of pretense, she flicked on the radio to get her mind on something else.

Instantly a shrill female voice, filtered through a phone line, grated on her nerves. She was about to flip away, when a professional radio voice broke in and clearly hung up on the caller.

"Crackpots," the announcer said. "We have a situation and all we get are crank calls."

"Several dozen of them, though, Dave," said a professional female voice. "Don't you think we should pay attention to them?"

"No," Dave said. "To recap, there's been an incident—"

He started to describe the neighborhood she had just left, adding nothing to what she already knew. Fortunately he didn't have Blackstone's name and he didn't seem to know about the dead woman. At that moment, the radio was reporting that no one had died.

"—another caller from the neighborhood," the woman announcer was saying. "And this one we both happen to know. It's Rick Ayers, our morning news announcer. Rick?"

"Stefanie." Rick's voice crackled over the phone lines and through Nora's radio. She had turned off the main highway, but traffic was still backed up. It was dark as night around her. The smoke had settled over the valley. "Even though Dave thinks the other callers are cranks, they aren't."

"Come on, Rick. Two people fighting with fire? It gets out of control? A big wild fireball battle like something out of Tolkien? We're supposed to believe that?"

Now they really had her attention. Nora glanced at the radio as if she could gauge its truthfulness just by looking at it. She was still shaking.

" 'Fraid so," Rick said. "I live across the street. I got the kids out and down the block as fast as possible. There were two people involved—a man and a woman. The man had been coming out of the woman's garage. He had a glass case in front of him, and it appeared to be full. That's what got my attention. He wasn't carrying the glass case. It was floating in front of him."

"And what were you drinking this afternoon?" Dave asked. It didn't sound like banter.

"I wasn't. He puts it in an orange and brown VW microbus when the woman comes out of her house and lobs a ball of fire at him. He deflects it, and it lands on a neighbor's house. That's when I got the kids and sent them down the block, knocking on doors. I think we got the place evacuated by the time the fire fight started in earnest."

"You mean to tell me . . . ?"

Nora pulled into the underground parking lot beneath her building and momentarily lost the signal. Instead of regaining it, she shut off the radio, not really wanting to think about what she had just learned.

She had wished for magic. She simply didn't like the form it was taking.

She pulled into her normal parking space, opened

her door, and heard a clang. She frowned, wondering if she had hit the car next to her.

Only it wasn't a car. It was a brown and orange VW microbus.

Sancho or whatever the hell his name was crawled from under her door. "Man am I going to have a headache," he said, one hand cradling the side of his face.

"What's going on?" she asked again.

"You don't want to know."

"I'm supposed to know," she said. "I'm supposed to help you."

"Let's go to your office," Sancho said.

She sighed and grabbed her briefcase. She decided she was enough of a mess to forgo the heels. Indeed, when she got to her floor and exited, wandering down the hall, Sancho behind her, her secretary squealed.

"Are you all right, Ms. Barr?"

"Fine," she said. "Although I could use a couple of bottles of water, pronto. I don't think I've ever been this thirsty."

Then she showed the little man into her office, and closed the door. He headed toward the chair he had used before. She didn't know how he had managed to stay soot-free from all the smoke and fire, nor how the microbus had gotten to the garage ahead of her.

"I won't do anything for you," she said, crossing around to her desk and placing her briefcase on it, "until I know your real name."

He placed a birth certificate, a social security card, a passport, and a driver's license on her blotter. They all showed his name to be Sancho Panza, and the driver's license and passport photos confirmed that the name belonged to him.

She shoved them back at him, more angrily than she would have liked. "I don't deal in fake I.D.," she said.

"Neither do I," he said.

She glanced at it again. The driver's license had

the supposedly unduplicatable holographic sticker just under the photo. The passport was old with several stamps already inside. If it had passed customs, it was good enough for her.

"I still don't believe it," she said.

"You don't have to." He settled in his chair. "Just help us."

"I already got a defense attorney for Blackstone."

"Fine," Panza said, as if he didn't care. "The most important thing is the glass case."

"Yes," Nora said. She took a recorder out of her briefcase, then closed the case, and set it on the floor. "I understand that he levitated it out of someone's garage."

"How he got it isn't your concern," Panza said. "Helping him with it is."

"I don't deal in stolen property," she said.

"It's not stolen," Panza said. There was a knock on her door. "Come in," Nora said. Her secretary brought in four cold bottles of water.

"Need a glass?" her secretary asked.

Nora shook her head. "Thanks."

Her secretary left. Nora offered one bottle to Panza, but he declined.

"I really don't want to be involved," she said.

"You're already involved. You identified yourself as Blackstone's attorney. People will come to you."

It was a weak argument, as arguments went. She opened a bottle of water, and took a long, long drink from it. The coolness felt good against her parched throat. The smoke and heat had dehydrated her.

"Why did Blackstone destroy that neighborhood?"

"He didn't," Panza said.

"Someone did," she said.

"Don't worry about it," Panza said.

"I have to worry about it." She ran a hand over her face, felt the soot flake off. "People make jokes about lawyers having no ethics, but that's not true. I

can't help him and stay true to myself if I know he
destroyed that neighborhood."

Panza clenched a fist, hit the arm of the chair, and
then shook his head. "What if I told you everything
will be fixed?"

She laughed, and felt its bitterness. "That can't be
fixed. Not in the way I would want."

"And that is?"

"To make it seem as if today never happened. But
people don't forget. Even if everything were made
better, people would remember and—"

"Say no more." Panza stood in the chair. She was
constantly amazed at how small he was. "We can do
that."

"Sure," she said. "And pigs fly."

"Not without help," he said, and he seemed perfectly serious. "Now. Assist us."

He wouldn't go away. And no matter how ethical
she got, the images wouldn't go away. She might as
well see what they wanted. "Tell me what you need,"
she said.

"I need you to store our microbus," he said.

"You can do that."

He shook his head. "We can't know where it is.
Only you can know. You'll store it for us, and then
when we come and get it, everything will be safe."

"It doesn't sound legal."

"It is. All you have to do is find a garage, rent it,
and keep the microbus there. We might not come for
it for years."

"Years?" Nora asked.

"Years." He reached into the breast pocket of his
shirt and removed an envelope. The envelope was four
times the size of the pocket. "This should cover rent
for the next twenty years, plus your fees and time,
based on the estimate you gave Blackstone when you
first met. If it takes us longer to get the microbus, we
will send more money."

She took the envelope. It was too thin to be holding cash. Instead she found a very ornate check for a very lot of money. It was issued by Quixotic, Inc. and signed by Sancho Panza. "I'll have to verify the funds," she said.

"Of course."

She took the envelope, stood, and walked to the front office. There she had her secretary call and verify the check. It was good.

She came back in, tapping the envelope against her hand. The little man was still standing in the chair. He was watching her. She closed the door and leaned on it.

"Here's what I'm willing to do," she said. "I will take your money, and put it in a special account. I will have the rental for the garage removed from that account, and my monthly fee. I will keep the keys here, but I will not inspect the microbus. I will not touch the microbus after I take it to the garage, and I will not relinquish the keys to anyone but you or Mr. Blackstone—*ever*. Is that clear?"

"Will the account bear interest?" Panza asked.

"Yes," she said.

"And who gets the interest?"

"Probably the person who owns the garage, when you don't come back in twenty years," she said.

The little man smiled. "I like you," he said. "If Blackstone's heart weren't imprisoned, I bet he would too."

After Panza left, she dictated the necessary instructions to her secretary. Then she went home, showered, changed into jeans and a sweatshirt, and drank another gallon of water. Her eyes were still red. The smoke cloud remained over the city. Even though she had cleared her own lungs, the smell of smoke went everywhere with her. She shut off the radio because she couldn't stand the constant jabber about the "Battle of the Wizards" as one of the stations had dubbed the day's events.

She found a brand-new garage complex on the edge of town, and signed a year's lease with an option for renewal. Then she drove back, got the microbus, and took it to the garage. It drove like a VW Bug—an old VW Bug—that was about to explode. Something weighed the back down, and made corners difficult. But she didn't look. She didn't want to.

She parked the microbus in the garage, pulled down the door, and locked it with a brand new lock that required a combination and a key. Then she took a cab back to her office.

It was getting dark, and she could no longer see the smoke.

As she was walking in the door, her phone rang. Her secretary was long gone. The main room was dark. She stumbled against a chair as she reached for the desk, and managed a shaky hello, just as she realized she should have let the service get the call.

"Nora?"

It took her a moment to recognize the voice. "Max? How did it go with Blackstone?"

"Buy me a drink," Max said. "No. Buy me fifteen drinks, and pour me into a cab. I really don't want to go home."

That bad. It was that bad. And she had already helped him. She had already implicated herself by taking care of the microbus.

"All right," she said. "Where?"

"Grady's."

Grady's. It had been the law school's watering hole. She hadn't been there since she graduated. At least she was dressed for it. She grabbed her purse and took her car down to campus.

It wasn't hard to find Max. He was the only man over thirty in the place. Even if he weren't, the silk suit in a bar filled with jeans, T-shirts, and tattoos would have been a dead giveaway.

He sat in a booth in the back, and looked as if he had already had a few drinks. She slid in across from him, and a tired smile crossed his lined face. She had liked Max more than she cared to admit. He had made quite a name for himself. They had always exchanged pleasantries when they passed in the courthouse, but they hadn't had time for much else.

She had missed him. She hadn't realized how much.

A waitress with studs in her eyebrows, cheeks, and nose made her way to the table. Nora ordered a beer, and found that she had to choose a microbrewery instead. Finally Max ordered for her—and paid for it.

When she protested, he grinned. "You got me the case."

"You asked me to buy," she said.

"I've just made more money for doing nothing than I've ever made for doing something," he said.

She frowned.

"I cashed one very large check on the way back from the jail this afternoon," he said, "and I verified the funds before I did. It's good. I'm supposed to give some to you. Finder's fee."

He slid a check across the table. She gasped at the amount. "Max—"

"No," he said. "Don't argue. After what I saw today. Don't argue."

She rubbed her eyes. "What did you see?"

"I saw police forget a crime was committed. I saw a dead body get up and walk. Your friend Blackstone promises me I'll remember all this, but he says no one else will. No one else—except you."

"Tell me," she said.

And so he did.

"The coroner's office is in the basement of the main police station," Max started.

"I know," Nora said.

"Well, I wasn't sure," he said. "You never know what civil attorneys know about the criminal system. I got to the station at the same time the corpse of that woman did, and as I was walking to the elevator, the ambulance had pulled up in front of the double doors." The attendants opened up the ambulance doors, and were starting to remove the body when it sat up.

Everyone jumped and then one of the attendants said, "Well, that happens sometimes."

But what didn't happen was the body unhooking itself from the straps and getting off the gurney. Max was already in the elevator. The woman joined him.

She was like nothing he had ever seen before, long dark hair with a streak of white along the side, a black robe untouched by the smoke and long curved fingernails, almost like talons. The doors closed as the attendants came running forward. Max huddled in the side of the elevator, planning to get off on any floor.

The doors opened on his floor and he hurried off. The woman hurried behind him. Max veered toward the sergeant in charge. Several police officers tried to restrain the woman. The attendants were running up the stairs, yelling.

Max asked to see his client, and was led into an interview room. Blackstone was leaning against a chair, feet out. He smiled. "You must be the attorney Nora sent," he said. "Sorry to have wasted your time."

"Are they going to let you out?" Max asked.

"You'll see," Blackstone said.

At that moment, the woman somehow burst through the locked door. "Where is she?" the woman shouted.

Blackstone shrugged.

"I know you know," she said.

"Actually, I don't." He seemed very calm. "You think after a thousand years this would grow old, Millicent."

"I will not let you have her."

"You won't let anyone experience true love," he said. "But she's somewhere even I can't find her."

The woman crossed the room, and before Max or anyone could stop her, she grabbed Blackstone's head. She held it with one hand and sparks flew all around. She frowned at him, as if she were trying to pull every thought from his skull. Then she cursed and shoved him away.

"You won't get away with this," the woman said. "I will find her."

"You have fifteen years, Millicent, and then she's on her own."

"She's too young."

"She's too beautiful. Women leave home well before they turn one thousand. You're just jealous."

The woman narrowed her eyes, and waved an arm and disappeared.

Blackstone stood and took Max's arm. "There's going to be chaos in a moment," he said. "Just follow my lead."

Then a police detective came into the room. "Max!" he said. "What are you doing here?"

"Showing me around," Blackstone said before Max could answer. "I hope you don't mind."

Max was stunned. This was a man who had been under arrest a moment before, and no one seemed to notice. In fact, at that point, Max checked Blackstone's wrists for cuffs and saw none.

And then Blackstone calmly led the two of them out of the precinct and into the parking garage. The ambulance attendants were sitting on the edge of the microbus, looking winded.

"You didn't call for an ambulance, did you?" one of them asked Max.

"No," he said.

"I don't get it," the attendant said to his companion. "How did we end up here?"

Then Blackstone led Max to his car, and gave him the check "for his time and services" instructing him to split it with Nora. "I'm sorry you had to see this," he said. "You can't forget because you were in my presence when everything reverted. And Nora can't forget because then—well, then I'd be, as your generation so quaintly puts it, screwed. But we did as she asked and put everything back the way it was."

"What's going on here?" Max asked.

"You don't want to know," Blackstone said.

"But I do," Max said.

"All right," Blackstone said. "But it's not my fault if you fail to believe me."

"Well?" Nora asked. "What was going on?"

"You know," Max said, leaning over his fourth beer. His words were becoming slurred. "When I drove here, there wasn't any smoke. And no one said a word about anything on the radio. It was strange. So I swung over to the neighborhood. It looks fine. No burned houses. No ashes. Just flowers and porches and electric lights."

"Max," she said, worrying that he might lose complete control before he got to the point. "What did he tell you?"

"He said that fairy tales are true. Sort of."

"Great," Nora said leaning back.

"And we got in the middle of 'Snow White and the Seven Dwarves.' Only there was only one dwarf. And she didn't bite into a poison apple. It was a spell. But the glass case was correct—"

"Max." A chill ran down Nora's back. "From the beginning."

"Blackstone is a wizard." Max ran a hand over his face as if he were trying to hide the words. "Over a thousand years ago he fell in love with a witch's daughter. Only the witch didn't want anyone near her daughter, so she hid the daughter with her assistant, a magical dwarf named—"

"Sancho Panza."

Max looked at her strangely. "Merlin, actually. After the great Merlin of old. But the dwarf was a good friend of Blackstone's, and he managed to get Blackstone and the girl together. What they didn't know was that the witch had put a curse on them so when they kissed, the girl passed out. Merlin knew the girl would die if she didn't get back to the witch to remove the spell, but Blackstone outsmarted the witch. He put the girl in a glass coffin. She would remain as she was, not alive and not dead, until the spell was removed. Merlin knew the witch's spell would wear off after fifteen years if the witch didn't know where the girl was. But before they could hide the coffin, the witch stole it. Over the centuries, Blackstone has stolen it back. But he's never been able to hide it from the witch. She's telepathic. She's always been able to pull the information from him. Until now. As long as he doesn't know where the coffin is the witch won't either."

"Shit," Nora said.

"You know, don't you?" Max asked.

"I have a hunch," Nora said.

Max held up his hand. "Well don't tell me. I don't want to be any more involved than I already am." He got up and swayed once. "I told you what I know. Now I'm leaving."

"Max, we have to investigate."

He shook his head, then caught the table to hold himself in place. "It would raise too many questions," he said. "Like, if there is a woman in a glass coffin in your possession, is she dead? And if so, are you an accessory after the fact? And if she isn't, what then? Do we believe she's been alive but asleep for a thousand years? And isn't that Sleeping Beauty? Doesn't the prince get to wake her with a kiss? Where did this going to sleep with a kiss come from? It seems all wrong to me."

He stumbled forward. "I am going home to pretend this was all a drunken fantasy."

"And the money?" Nora asked.

"I'll pretend I defended a mobster and it was so traumatic I forgot all about it." He wandered out, clutching the back of booths for support.

She sat there, trembling. He was right. She had said she wouldn't investigate what was in that microbus. But now, it seemed, she had no choice.

She had to go to her office first to get the key to the lock she had put on the garage. As she drove, she noted a full moon over the town. The air smelled fresh, with the trace of night flowers. She paused before making the turnoff to her office, then drove down the freeway to the neighborhood.

Streetlights were on the entire way, and the roads were clear of debris and emergency vehicles. As she pulled onto the residential streets, she saw the silhouettes of houses trailing off into the distance. Some had lights on. Many, by this time, had their lights off. Vehicles were parked in the street as if they belonged there.

She pulled over to the curb, parking between the two houses where she thought, but wasn't certain, the microbus had been parked earlier. She got out and wandered to the lawn, recognizing its greenery and its flowers from the afternoon. This was the place. She would bet her practice on it. And yet the neighborhood stood around it. Nothing was destroyed.

A porch light came on at the house behind her. She frowned. That house probably belonged to the radio personality. He had seemed like the nosy type. She slipped back into her car and drove away.

A feeling of disorientation that had nothing to do with the beer swept through her. Maybe when she got back to her office, she wouldn't even find a key. Maybe in the morning, Max would deny having this conversation with her. Maybe none of this had happened.

Maybe.

But it felt as if it had.

She pulled into the parking garage beneath her building and got out of her car. As she walked, she passed a 1974 Lincoln. A little man stood on its fender, and a tall man leaned against its hood. He wore a shimmery gray silk suit that accented his broad shoulders and long legs, and on his feet he wore cowboy boots trimmed with real silver. A snake peeked its head out of his sleeve.

"You know," he said in that rich warm voice of his, "if you get the key and go to the microbus, I'll simply have to follow you. And if I follow you all of this will be for naught."

"Max tells me there's a woman in that glass case."

"And she's alive," Blackstone said. "She's been asleep for a thousand years. If you help us, she'll sleep for fifteen more."

"Why can't your friend get the information out of my brain?"

"Because it's not there," Blackstone said. "Right now, all you have is supposition. She could probe, but her powers won't let her unearth supposition. They'll only unearth fact."

"The fact is I have your microbus. She'll know that."

"You have *my* microbus," the little man said. "Sancho Panza's microbus."

"And we all know that's not your name," Nora snapped.

"No," the little man said. "You *suspect* that's not my name. You *know* that I have all the legal documentation to prove that it is."

She smoothed a hand over her hair, and took a deep

breath. "This afternoon," she said. "I saw a destroyed neighborhood and a dead woman. I saw the police lead you away in cuffs."

"Yes," Blackstone said.

"But you're here, and the neighborhood's back the way it was, and Max says the woman's not dead."

Blackstone's smile was small. "We live differently from you, Sancho and I. And we don't really die."

"So you're saying what I saw was real."

"For that moment," he said. "But you asked us to fix it, to put it back. So we did."

"For the record," the little man said. " She was the one who destroyed everything, not us."

"What if she's the one who is in the right?" Nora asked.

"You don't even know what the battle's about," Blackstone said.

Nora crossed her arms. "Enlighten me."

"Love," Blackstone said. "It's about love."

"Seems to me it's about possession," Nora said. "There's a woman who has been asleep for a thousand years because her family and her boyfriend are fighting over her. Seems to me that she has no say in this matter."

The little man put his face in his hands. Blackstone frowned. The snake hissed at her.

"What happens if I raise the coffin lid?" Nora asked. "Will I wake her up?"

Blackstone shook his head. "You'll destroy my spell, but not the death spell. If you open that coffin, she'll die."

"Lovely," Nora said. She started for the elevators. Midway there, she stopped. "If all of this happens in fifteen years, why did you pay me for twenty?"

Blackstone hadn't moved. The snake had wrapped itself around his arm. The little man had disappeared along the side of the Lincoln. "I didn't pay you," Blackstone said.

"Why did your friend, then?"

Blackstone raised his beautiful brown eyes to hers. "The world has changed," he said. "She's been sleeping for a thousand years. It'll take her time to adjust, time to find herself again. She'll need to make decisions, need to make choices, and she can't make good choices when she first wakes up. Five years may not be enough. You might get a renewal after that."

"You expect me to babysit?" Nora asked.

"I expect nothing," he said. "But my friend here expects you to find competent help for any problem that might arise during your service to him. If that's too much to ask, tell us now. We'll find someone else."

Nora pushed a strand of hair off her face. The hair still smelled faintly of smoke. "The battle between you and this woman, this witch, is over?"

"It will be," he said, "if she can't find what she's looking for."

"And she won't find it," Nora said, "as long as I help your friend."

"You could say that." Blackstone lifted an edge of his sleeve. The snake crawled inside.

"That's giving me a lot of control over something that's important to you," Nora said.

"Yes." Blackstone stood. He seemed taller than he had before.

"Why?" she asked. "Why me?"

"Because," he said. "You believe just enough to take a chance."

"Believe," she muttered. Could he hear thoughts too? Had he known what she had been thinking the day she met him? She shook her head. She couldn't believe that. It was one thing too many. "What happens to you?"

But her words echoed in the empty garage. Blackstone, the snake, the little man, and the Lincoln were gone. She rested a hand on a rusted Beamer, more to hold herself up than anything else.

"I guess that answers my question," she said. She stared at the elevator, and thought about the key on the wall in her office. The key with the combination taped to it.

She could look now and satisfy her curiosity. Or she could do what she was supposed to do, and let things alone. She believed that a neighborhood burned down. She knew the neighborhood was fine now. She had seen it. Just like she had seen it burn this afternoon.

And that was the secret: she could no longer trust her senses. What if she went inside that VW microbus and found a glass coffin? And what if a woman were inside? And what if she opened it and ruined the spell? She wouldn't know how to find Blackstone or his little friend Sancho. She wouldn't know how to make everything better again.

Her own car keys were digging into the skin of her right hand. She started back to her car. She wasn't going to go. And it wasn't because of true love. Or fear that she might ruin a spell.

She had been given a strange gift these last two weeks. Someone had shown her that magic could exist. What if she went to that microbus and there was no glass coffin inside? There was no woman? Would she have to question everything she had seen? Would she want to?

When she reached her car, she got inside, and picked up the phone. Before she even knew what she was doing, she asked directory assistance to dial Max's home number. The phone rang six times. She was about to hang up when Max answered.

"Max?" she asked.

"You looked," he said.

And in that response she felt a deep and profound relief. She hadn't imagined any of this. Or if she had, Max was suffering the same delusion.

"No," she said. "But I realized we'd skipped dinner. You want to go?"

"Now?" he asked.

"Yes," she said.

"Is this . . . a date?"

There was enough hesitation in his voice to make her hesitate too. But dating Max was something she had wanted to do since college. And she had never taken the initiative before. "Yes," she said.

He laughed. "Who'd've thought—after a day like this—well, maybe wishes do come true."

"Max?" she said.

"Sorry," he said. "Muttering. I'd love dinner. I think I'm a little more sober than I was before."

"I'll pick you up," she said. "In ten minutes."

She hung up before he could say no. And then she realized he wouldn't. Two shy people, finally getting their wish. She wondered if that was part of Blackstone's payment, and then decided she wouldn't think about Blackstone any more.

She leaned her head against the steering wheel and giggled. She was the one who wanted a little magic in her life, just once. And she had gotten more than a little. She had gotten too much.

Be careful what you wish for, her grandmother used to say.

Well, Nora's wish on that day two weeks before had been a twofold wish. She turned the key in the ignition. Max wasn't going to cook, and he probably wasn't going to rub her feet unless things moved faster than she expected. But he would certainly discuss the strangeness of the day with her, and that would be enough.

For now.

LADYKILLER

Rosemary Edghill

Rosemary Edghill is the author of The Sword of
Maiden's Tears, The Cup of Morning Shadows, The
Cloak of Night and Daggers, Speak Daggers to Her,
The Book of Moons, *and* Fleeting Fancy. *Her short
fiction has appeared in* Return to Avalon, Chicks in
Chainmail, *and* Tarot Fantastic. *She is a full-time
author who lives in Poughkeepsie, New York.*

GALERIS of Amathaon was the master of the sword
Girlslayer, and in a thousand kingdoms and river
towns, the man and the sword were together a legend.

Tonight the legend died.

The life of a wanderer—living by his wits and the
edge of his blade—was by definition an uncertain one.
Galeris had spurned queens and crowns, had slain
monsters, and had squandered fortunes in his travels
through the *Kynthelig* Kingdoms, but on the night that
he died, he was a penniless man alone—save for
Girlslayer—who had taken the wrong side of a bet as
to whether a lone man with the best of intentions and
a chain mail vest could defeat six *kyntheli* in steel
breastplates.

The *kyntheli* had overrun Amathaon—and the rest
of Anateius—around the time that Galeris was born,

41

and this particular group of *kyntheli*—obviously mercenaries—were in the process of dealing similarly with a baggage train that had trusted *kyntheli* promises when it had hired them as guards.

They cut him to pieces. The crossbow man, standing off at a distance and firing his deadly bolts with wicked accuracy, helped.

<Wait,> the mercenary leader said, when the witless pink-skin lay dead at his feet. <I know this guy.>

His companions gathered around to see. *Kyntheli* are tall and silver furred, with long tufted ears and slanted pupilless blue eyes. They are not particularly good at distinguishing one pink-skin from another, a liability that their human serfs have sometimes exploited and sometimes suffered from. However, the *kyntheli* are masters of every form of weaponry, and Galeris had a very recognizable sword.

<Girl . . . slayer,> the captain's lieutenant said, translating the runes painfully out of Low Phordis, the commonest human tongue, into his own hissing *Kynthelig*. <This is that barbarian pain-in-the-ass that sold us out at Nefertum. 'Klah-something'.>

<Kal-y-ris. They say he killed a dragon once.> The captain picked up the sword. <I don't believe in dragons. And what kind of a name is 'Girlslayer' for a sword anyway?>

<They say he killed his own sister. And his bride, on their wedding day,> the lieutenant said. <I don't think he likes women very much.>

The rest of the men had gone back to ransacking the baggage, throwing out what they had no use for and dragging the corpses into the ditch.

<And now we've killed him,> the captain said. <The Foremost isn't going to like that much. He's some kind of a peasant hero. They'll be upset. And when peasants are upset, they don't work—and dead peasants do even less work, so don't give me that argument!>

The lieutenant—who had been about to say something of the sort—made a gesture of submission, lowering his head and flattening back his ears. The captain pretended not to see.

<We can't make him alive again,> the lieutenant said finally, offering up the truth for what it was worth.

<Oh, can't we?> the captain demanded. <H'shret! Bring me one of the pack mules! And a couple of casks of that Nainsi wine!>

Leirioessa was a sorceress. She had been raised to be a queen, and the early training of the rulers of Enrhydreg included a thorough grounding in all the necromantic arts. She could turn lead into gold, make the Philosopher's Stone and the Elixir Vitae, speak with the dead and with angels.

Neither she nor her mother had been able to foresee the effects of a day's bombardment by the *Kynthelig* cannon located on the ships that had blockaded Enrhydreg's harbor. The palace had fallen, someone had opened the gates of the town, and Leirioessa, a few trusted guardsmen, and half the palace treasury had been on the road east before she quite knew what was happening. Three days later, in a roadside tavern, the word had reached them that Enrhydreg had fallen and the Queen was dead, and the loyal guardsmen fell to quarrelling over a division of the spoils—and her.

But though Enrhydreg invincibility was proven to be a myth, the powers of Enrhydregian queens was not. Leirioessa fled the ruin that had moments before been a tavern filled with living men—and by the time she realized that the *kyntheli* conquerors were not searching for her after all, she'd grown quite used to hiding.

It was a comfortable life.

Princess Leirioessa—Mother Leir to those who sought her services now, 'mother' being a common byword for 'witch'—heard the sound of movement on the path below her cave and came to the outer doorway to see who it was.

It was trouble, in the form of two *kyntheli* on mules, a third mule in tow. Their silvery fur glinted in the twilight, and she could see the glint of their armor as well. Mercenary troops, she thought, hired by whatever warlord intended to move in and make this district his personal fief.

Kyntheli weren't like humans. When they'd come from over the sea to conquer human lands, each *kyntheli* and his war-band had simply grabbed as much as he could hold. There was no empire, only a band of squabbling uncooperative kingdoms constantly snatching territory from each other. *Kyntheli* didn't work together very well—or very long. The only reason the human lands still suffered under their yoke was because they were *better*—faster, stronger, more numerous, and with noumenal weapons that human magic couldn't defeat.

And because the humans had not banded together to oppose them until half the lands that made up the old Anateian Empire were already taken—and by then, it was too late.

She wondered what they wanted here. *Kyntheli* despised human magic, calling it 'unfair.' But they'd never bothered her before, when all the humans for miles around came to her for love spells and healings, which were generally the only spells she was willing to risk doing. Magic had its price, and either the caster or the beneficiary must pay it: that was the One Law.

Leirioessa readied her protection, just in case. She was fairly certain she could kill the two of them, and the *kyntheli* were remarkably uninterested in vengeance—which didn't make them any easier to live with, as they believed in cruelty for cruelty's sake, and had no mercy that anyone had ever heard of.

They stopped in front of her, and the one with the

darker fur got off his mule. He walked up to her; Leirioessa could smell fish and wet fur and blood.

"You . . . heal . . . man," the *kyn* said, in badly-accented Phordis. "We . . . pay."

"You want me to heal someone?" Leirioessa said. "But what about your own doctors?"

<She's haggling about the price,> the lieutenant said over his shoulder to his captain.

<Tell her she can have the wine and the mule—and that we'll kill her if she doesn't do it.> The captain fingered his blade meaningfully and glared at Leirioessa.

"Heal . . . man," the *kyntheli* said again, seizing her wrist in his long clawed hand and dragging her back to the mule he'd been leading.

Leirioessa only glanced at its burden for an instant. "Heal him? He's *dead*."

The *kyn* displayed an enormous mouthful of curved yellow fangs, and its blue eyes closed with—pleasure?

"Dead! Yes! You heal. No heal, you be dead."

"Well . . . all right." What else was she to say? The alternative was to kill them both—and they were now too far apart for one spell to deal with both of them. "Bring him inside."

She achieved their cooperation by simply walking away from them—sometimes that worked with *kyntheli,* though it you guessed wrong the mistake could be painful.

She was pretty sure she could hold them off for some time, though, providing she got a minute or so head start.

Leirioessa's cave was a packrat's nest of tribute, salvage, and the odd bit of looting. Its one great luxury was a full stone hearth fitted into a wall-fissure (the smoke swirled up out of a hilltop almost a mile away, to the sober mystification of the locals) that cast its sphere of warmth about her workroom. In a small clearing in the center of her horde she had shelves and a table, an athanor, and a few chests holding whatever she did not want rats to eat. She sat down on one of them. The *kyntheli*—carrying the dead man's weight easily between them, as if it had been a rolled-up mat—came and laid the body out on the table. His chain mail jingled. Mother Leir took a closer look at the problem. As she approached, the shorter *kyntheli* laid a bloody broadsword out on the table, handling its wicked length as though it were no more than a willow wand. Leirioessa's attention was held by the sword for a moment—and more—by the glitter of green in the hilt: the fire of the spellgem that marked an enchanted sword. The haft was in the shape of a naked silver maiden, her hair cascading down her back and her arms raised above her head to clasp the great green faceted pommel-weight that glowed darkly in the firelight. The maiden's feet rested on the curve of the quillons, which turned down sharply toward the blade in a smooth sweep of steel. A crosspiece that wide and heavy might be enough to turn an enemy blade, though Leirioessa herself wouldn't bet fingers on it. She turned her attention back to her subject.

The dead man had bled white. What blood had been in him when his heart stopped had been drained out by the long journey on muleback and masked his face in sticky, shiny brown. Beneath the blood, his skin had the grayish eerie cast that even sun-bronzed flesh will take when it is quite untenanted. The spirit was long fled.

And she knew him. She took another look at the sword, just to make sure. She was. She did. More by blade and reputation, but nevertheless: this was Galeris of Amathaon.

Amathaon had been a neighbor-kingdom to Enrhydreg. Being one of the first to receive the *Kynthelig* invasion, Amathaon had made the mistake of defending itself enthusiastically and had been completely destroyed by its irritated conquerors. Its people had become slaves and refugees. One of them had become a legend.

The tale of Galeris was one that many a *kynthelig* serf treasured beside his winter fire. By virtue of her early training and experience—and a suspicious nature honed by events—Leirioessa knew that most of these stories parted company with the truth early on: Galeris was hardly of royal blood, not did he style himself a particular champion of humankind, though even at his worst he had to be considered kinder to humankind than the *kyntheli*. He was—or had been, until to-night—a particular thorn in the side of their furry overlords, but Leirioessa suspected that of being personal inclination and propinquity rather than an innate sense of gallantry.

What she did know for sure was that Galeris had somewhere had the good fortune to luck his way into a enchanted sword, which like all powerful and unaccountable magical artifacts had its little particularities, for magic had power in direct proportion to its inconvenience to somebody. By the One Law, the most powerful magic was the most inconvenient, but few wizards cared to risk so much inconvenience, death being high on the list of really inconvenient nuisances ancillary to the practice of high sorcery.

She came closer, peering down at the blade. The sword gleamed in the firelight like the artful piece of craft that it was. Most of its length was brown and sticky with the night's work, but she could still see the wizard marks. *Now there's an appetizing piece of work.* Leirioessa traced the runes scratched into the blade near the quillons, written in the Lexis Accallias, the universal code of High Magic (which was close enough to Low Phordis that it could usually be read by someone familiar with that script, though not with a comfortable margin of accuracy). '*Briannes . . . parboar*,' Leirioessa read. *Ladykiller*.

Someone had been very clever in powering this enchantment: an unstoppable but misogynistic blade that would manage to weed out its owner's distaff companions. She supposed Galeris didn't mind the odd murder overmuch—if he had, it would have been simple enough just to throw away the sword once he knew its true nature; the floor of the Brencian Sea was littered with inconvenient magical items. Leirioessa thought that it was rather more likely, however, that Galeris was the sort of gallows-crow who didn't see much wrong with butchering a female or two.

The two *kyntheli* were getting impatient. One reached out and poked at Leirioessa with one long, sharp-clawed finger.

"You . . . fix," it demanded, baring long, curved, ivory teeth and barking out the words its mouth was so ill-equipped to say. Their own language sounded like a series of sneezes to their human vassals and no one was interested in learning it.

"Yes, yes, yes," Leirioessa muttered, and went to her shelves. She did not make the mistake of thinking that something that spoke like a simpleton was one. That was the sort of mistake a person would only live long enough to make once. The *kyn* had managed to convey its meaning clearly enough: for some reason that passed understanding, it wanted Galeris of Amathaon returned to the land of the living.

It was easy enough to raise the dead—which was to say, to animate a corpse with another spirit, and Leirioessa had a number at her beck and call. It was a much more difficult matter to bring back the body's original spirit to inhabit it. Such a task required great—and inconvenient—magic. Leirioessa had no intention of bearing the inconvenience that would power such a spell herself, which meant that Galeris must. And since death was the ultimate inconvenience, that

meant Galeris wouldn't be animate for long enough
to please the two *kyntheli* that were prowling around
Leirioessa's cave like hungry panthers.

Unless she could think of something even more inconvenient to a crack-brained somewhat hero, mercenary, and freebooter than being dead . . . ?

She stared at the sword with its Accallian runes,
and slowly an idea came to her.

<What's she doing?> the lieutenant asked, cowering
ostentatiously so the question would not give offense.

<Pink Magic,> his commander said dismissively. But
the lieutenant noted that one hand was on the brace
of pistols stuck into his sash and the other was on the
necklet made of the teeth and claws of defeated enemies, and that he watched the barbarian witch very
carefully.

The lieutenant watched as well, as the witch
stripped the body of its blood-caked chain and leather
and then began to wash it. The sight was fascinating
in its very gruesomeness: all that slick glistening pale
hairlessness, like something you'd see if you turned
over a rock. Fortunately, the next step seemed to be
covering the body with mud, because frankly, the lieutenant didn't think he could have borne to stare at
the naked pink-skin much longer. The Foremost alone
knew how the things managed to breed. The women
were as unappetizing as the men, not that you could
tell them apart with any reliability.

The smells the witch was generating were enough
to make both *kyntheli* glad they were standing in the
mouth of the cave, nearer the outside air. The mud
was particularly rank, and both *kyntheli* winced to see
the witch pick up the hero-sword and plop it down
atop the mud-pie as if she were decorating the First
Kill of Spring.

<That's no way to treat a good piece of steel,> the
lieutenant complained, looking away.

<He's breathing> the captain said. <See? I told you she could fix him.>

The lieutenant turned his gaze back to the mud. It was cracked and pale, as if it were long-dried instead of freshly applied. He'd missed the part where the barbarian magic was done yet again. He shook his head. It was a sad thing to have been born so unlucky.

But the captain was right. The mud was heaving, in a gentle rhythmic fashion suggesting sleep-breathing. Bits of it cracked and flaked away with the motion.

"He's alive," the witch said, coming over to them and standing with her hands on her hips. Behind her, the mud-caked figure snorted and groaned, sitting up and showering mud flakes everywhere. "Pay me."

The captain stared at her through narrow glinting eyes. He wasn't sure what she'd said—the pink-skins all sounded like apes barking whenever they opened their mouths—but the gesture was universal. She wanted her fee.

While it was true that he hadn't examined her handiwork, the erstwhile body on the table was moving. And if it was moving—after taking the number of quarrels the bowmen had pulled out of the body afterward—then it had certainly been reanimated, and the witch had done what she'd been hired for (and could be made to swear that Galeris was alive—publicly if required). He gestured to his lieutenant, who went and brought the pack mule forward and put its bridle-rein into her hand. The barbarian's blood still caked its sides, but it was reasonably young and strong and had two casks of wine lashed across its withers. The witch had no cause to complain.

<Come on, lieutenant. It's been a long night and this place stinks,> the captain said.

<They all stink,> his subordinate said helpfully, heading for the captain's mule to lead it back. <But what a story this will make, eh?>

*   *   *

Leirioessa watched the two *kyntheli* sell-swords ride out of sight, wiping the last of the mud-mask off her hands. A great waste of an expensive beauty treatment—and almost fifty pounds of it, too!—but she'd needed to cloak the effects of her spell in case the *kynthelig* mercenaries were less oblivious than everyone said. She hadn't gotten to where she was in life by being cavalier about the details.

The tingling sense of great magic still filled the cave, making her bones ache and her teeth vibrate. She led the mule the *kyntheli* had left behind into a marginally less cluttered side-cave and unhitched its tack. Her dagger made short work of the wax plug in one the casks, and she sniffed deeply at the bunghole. Nainsi wine—she thought she'd recognized the brands of the casks when the *kyntheli* had brought them in—and the good stuff, too, not that cut and watered down catlap they served in the public taverns.

She carried the open cask back into the main room with her and poured a tankard full. She was going to need this.

They were both going to need it.

Galeris was up now, standing unsteadily beside the table, brushing flakes of mud onto the floor. The accursed sword gleamed in the firelight, and Leirioessa gave the sword and its wielder a wide berth; Ladykiller's baleful magic was as powerful as ever—in fact, it had provided most of the power for Leirioessa's spell.

"What am I doing here?" Galeris asked.

The question was delivered in an unsteady voice that broke and squeaked on the last word. Leirioessa lifted the tankard and drained it.

"You're the one they call Girlslayer," Leirioessa said, taking a deep breath as the wine rushed through her veins like a conviction of immortality. "I'd be careful of that sword now if I were you."

"Briannes won't . . . won't . . ." Galeris began unsteadily.

And looked down.

Really looked.

At slender pink ankles and neat pink toes, silken skin the color of ripe apricots in cream, at dimpled knees innocent of battle-scars, and . . .

And . . .

"What have you *done* to me, witch?" Galeris roared, swinging the sword up and leaping forward.

Leirioessa flinched back, raising the tankard as if it were a shield, but she hardly needed to. The sword twisted in Galeris' grasp as if it could not decide what target to choose. The warrior almost dropped it before bringing it up again, but not before it had tasted blood.

"Egern, Yan, and Hanbonart!" Galeris yelped, calling on Amathaon's dead gods of war, luck, and trouble. Flinging Ladykiller away, Galeris clasped both hands over the welling gash on—her—skin. The blood and mud mixed together, making a gritty, slippery surface.

"You should know your own sword well enough by now," Leirioessa said with more calm than she felt.

Galeris glared at her in passionate disbelief. The warrior's hair was still caked with black mud and hung about her face in matted undistinguished clumps, but her eyes had lightened to a vivid shade of aquamarine upon her resurrection. She took a breath. Her creamy bosom heaved, shedding mud.

"You've turned me into a tw—"

"There's no need to be graphic," Leirioessa snapped. "And you might as well be grateful. You were dead, you know. I brought you back to life."

"Like *this?*" Galeris demanded. Her voice cracked girlishly again and Leirioessa saw her wince. More mud flaked away from her face, and the warrioress scrubbed at it impatiently.

"Rules are rules," Leirioessa, former princess of Enrhydreg, said implacably. "Maybe you'd rather be dead, but I wouldn't—and I had a cave full of cats wanting you on your feet and lively."

"They should have thought of that before they shot me, the cowards," Galeris muttered, brushing mud from her now-unblemished ribs. "Crossbows against swords—and they were hiding, too." She darted a look toward her sword, winking malignantly on the hearth, but didn't reach for it again.

"When have the cats ever fought fair?" Leirioessa asked, filling her tankard again. Galeris plucked it out of her hand.

"I need that more than you do. I'm the one who's going to spend the rest of my life as a wench." She gulped half of it down before she stopped, sputtering and choking. No palate for fine vintages, Leirioessa could see that.

"It was that or dead," she pointed out, taking the tankard back. It was just beginning to occur to the sorceress that if Galeris of Amathaon, master of the sword Girlslayer or Ladykiller, or whatever you wanted to call it, didn't appear alive and well and in his usual haunts along the Verdrian Road, the *kyntheli* were going to come looking for her. And while the *kyntheli* couldn't tell men and women apart, their human servants could, and no amount of pointing to Galeris as she was now would convince *anybody* that Leirioessa had done what she'd been hired to.

"What about my sword?" Galeris demanded. "What about my *life?* I'm a *girl!*"

"A number of people have lived and died in that condition without much complaint," Leirioessa reminded him tartly. She was already conducting a mental inventory of her possessions; it was looking as if it were definitely time to move on.

"But I'm a—. A girl can't be a mercenary!" Galeris cried.

"Why not?" Leirioessa asked her. "It isn't as though there aren't enough opportunities for a scrap in Anateius these days—and the cats can't tell men from women when they sign them up."

At least she had a mule, and she thought there might be an old cart tucked off in one of the side caverns. If she was going to have to start over somewhere else as the local witch, she didn't intend to do it empty-handed.

"I haven't got a sword,' Galeris muttered sulkily. "*You* took care of that."

"And I can take care of it again—*if* you're inclined to cooperate," Leirioessa told her firmly. "Now why don't you put on some clothes, dear? It's a bit brisk in here, don't you find?"

"Are you sure this is going to work?" Galeris asked for the hundredth time.

"Young man—" Leirioessa snapped, then corrected herself, "—woman, I bespelled my first weapon before Amathaon fell to the *kyntheli*. If you'll just stand back and let me work, you'll have the sharpest sword in all the kingdoms of the cats and we can be on our way."

Galeris took half a step backward, automatically pulling the hood of her grey homespun cloak farther up over her cap of fiery copper curls. The loose robes of an Isenan wanderer fit her as well as anything Leirioessa owned, and did as much as anything could to conceal her new—and marvelously inconvenient—sex. She glanced toward the laden mule with melodramatic impatience.

Leirioessa ignored her with the ease of long practice. Opening her spellbox, she took out her scriber. The green spellstone—smaller than the one in the sword but just as powerful—glittered in its haft. She had already covered the whole body of the sword in a thick paste that bubbled and fumed as the sword consumed it—but so long as some trace of *alence* gum remained on the sword, its magic was bent elsewhere and could not harm her. She stared down at the inscription on the blade. *'Briannes parboar.'* Working quickly, she scratched the runes for 'parboar' into the blade before 'briannes' and drew a looped line through the word that followed it. The inscription now read: *'Parboar briannes.'*

Not 'ladykiller' now, my dear and unknown colleague, but 'the lady who kills.' Grammar is so important in sorcery. . . .

The last of the *alence* simmered off the blade, and it flashed bright silver once more. Leirioessa held her breath, but there was no explosion, only the whipcrack sensation of power, like the aftermath of a lightning-strike. The new spell would hold true.

"Here you go," she said, handing the sword to Galeris. "And mind you make better use of it this time. We've a long way to travel and I don't want you picking any fights."

The swordswoman grimaced, but said nothing as she took the sword from the sorceress. What she found as she held it seemed to please her—she actually smiled and flourished the blade before sliding it home into its scabbard.

"All right then," Galeris said. "Come along, Mother Leir—we have wrongs to avenge, kingdoms to win—and an empire to free." The woman actually swaggered as she took her place at the mule's head.

Leirioessa let the comments pass in silence as she climbed onto the cart's seat. She had no intention of traveling with the swordswoman one moment longer than was necessary to remove herself from the attention of the local *kyntheli*. The spell she'd wrought had changed Galeris' sex, not her personality. Once a hero, always a hero.

And, as Leirioessa had discovered, once a knight was enough.

THE JEWEL AND THE DEMON

Lisanne Norman

Born in Glasgow, Scotland, Lisanne Norman began writing when she was eight because, "I couldn't find enough of the books I liked to read." She studied jewelry design at the Glasgow School of Art before becoming a teacher. A move to Norfolk, England prompted her involvement with the Vikings, a historical reenactment group, where she ran her own specialist archery display team. Her writing takes center stage now, with her creation of the Sholan Alliance, a world where magic, warriors, and science all coexist. The novels in this series include: Turning Point, Fortune's Wheel, Fire Margins, Razor's Edge, *and the forthcoming novel,* Dark Nadir.

"BE STILL, imp!" Mouse hissed at her tiny companion. "I told you, I can deal with the dogs."

Ahead of them lay their goal, the treasure room of Harra the merchant. She knew its encircling corridor was protected by large hounds, one of which lay opposite them guarding the only entrance.

Mouse reached for the tiny silver whistle suspended on a cord round her neck. She'd won it some time ago in a game of dice from a fellow thief and it had become a treasured and useful possession. Putting it to her lips, she blew gently. Though she could hear nothing, the small but very real demon accompanying her clapped his hands to his ears and grimaced in pain.

The dog lifted its head and pricked its ears, looking around. Pushing the demon back, Mouse flattened herself against the wall. She repeated the whistle—one short, sharp blow. The hound growled softly and, getting to its feet, padded toward them. Releasing the whistle, she transferred several small spherical glass vials to her right hand. The dog had finally gotten a whiff of her scent and its growl rose in pitch, becoming menacing.

The Gods help me if Tallan's magic doesn't work, she thought.

Taking a deep breath, Mouse stepped out of their cover and flung one of the vials at the animal's feet. The glass shattered, releasing a small cloud of white vapor. As she watched, the dog slowed to a halt, skidding on the wooden floor before collapsing in a boneless heap.

"Wait!" she said, as the demon made to rush forward. "We only got one. There's more."

They could hear the rapid click of claws on wood as two more rounded the corner, bounding toward them. It took all her courage to wait until the slavering beasts were nearly upon them before throwing the second and third vials. Seconds later, they lay as senseless as the first.

"Now! Now! While they sleep," the demon exclaimed, hopping from hoof to hoof.

She nodded. The dogs had frightened her more than she cared to admit. Forcing herself to relax a little, she stepped warily past the beasts. Silently they covered the intervening distance to the great double doors. A sturdy hasp, held closed by a simple but efficient padlock, covered the locks.

Mouse spent a few moments examining the padlock before digging in one of her capacious pockets and extracting a lock pick. Cautiously she inserted the wire in the keyhole, twiddling it round and about until she felt it give. Grasping the loop with her free hand, she pulled it open and laid it carefully on the floor away from the door.

"No time for tidy," the demon hissed urgently. "Hurry, hurry!"

"Untidy could kill us if we have to leave quickly," Mouse replied more calmly than she felt as she stroked her hand over the now exposed locks.

There were three of them, and her sixth sense was telling her they must be opened in the right sequence otherwise alarms would go off in the guard room.

"You hurry," the demon twittered. "Not want you caught. I be safe, but not you."

Mouse glanced down at him. Pretty he wasn't. He looked more like prematurely-aged child of three with his wrinkled brown face and the tiny horns poking through his thatch of dark curls. He stamped an insistent hoof. "Hurry!"

She sighed, turning back to the door. "I need quiet to work, imp. Give me peace."

Once again she ran her hands over the door, trying to sense the order of the enchantment on the locks. She was no magic-user to know how these things worked, but now and then, she was able to divine something of their nature. Her luck had made it possible for her to earn her living after her mother had died rather than end up in one of the city bars or brothels.

"Middle one first," she muttered to herself, inserting her piece of wire again. This time she placed her ear to the door, listening for the tiny clicks that told her when she'd tripped each tumbler.

Patiently she worked away until she'd freed the first lock without triggering the alarm.

"Now the top one."

As she worked, the demon shifted impatiently from hoof to hoof, knowing it shouldn't break her concentration. "Dogs wake soon," it muttered fretfully.

"Last one," she said, aware of the building tension. "Not long now. Almost there." She continued working, sweat beginning to break out on her forehead. Her hands were trembling now with the effort of trying to keep them steady. She stopped to wipe slick palms on her pants' legs. Gods, but she was tired already! By the time this was over, she'd have more than earned her high fee. She banished the thought, and bent down to resume her work.

The last tumbler tripped and she turned an exultant face to her companion. "We're through!"

"Open door. Must hurry," he said, urging her forward with his hands.

Gently Mouse grasped the ring handle and turning it, eased the door open just enough for them to squeeze through. Hugging the wall, she snatched at the demon, grabbing it by its naked shoulder as it prepared to dash forward. Its skin felt hot and slightly uneven, like that of a reptile or an exotic fruit.

"No!" she hissed. "We look around first!"

"You want light?" asked the demon, squirming out from under her hand. "I give." A soft glow began to fill the room.

"Keep it low!" Mouse exclaimed. "We don't know what the inner defenses are yet."

The glow obediently slowed, building until there was only enough light to see the whole of the room. Immediately, their eyes were drawn to the glass case atop the pedestal standing in the center. In it was a gemstone, but a gem unlike any she'd seen before. Now there was light in the room, colors coruscated through it, sending their rainbow hues glancing off the ceiling in tiny patches of brilliance.

"The Living Jewel," Mouse whispered.

"Yes. Jewel for Master Kolin," said the demon.

"What's your wizard want the jewel for?" she asked, unable to take her eyes off its beauty.

"Not know. Just say he want it."

"Huh." Mouse tore her gaze away and examined the rest of the room. The walls were lined with display cabinets containing items of rarity or beauty from other lands. There were even some that must have come from the offworlder aliens, but none of them compared with the Living Jewel.

"I can see why the merchant doesn't want to part with it," she murmured.

"He refuse to sell it to Master. Say it an item of pride. Reminds him of getting best of enemy," offered the demon in an unusual burst of conversation.

Mouse glanced down at him in surprise, but it was the floor that caught her attention. Her heart began to race as she stopped to examine it more closely, realizing now that since they'd entered the room, she'd been subliminally aware of the warmth underfoot.

The tiles had a faint tracery on them that broadened out as it led to the pedestal at the center of the room. At the base of the plinth, like a spider in the heart of its web, there was a patch of shadow, a darkness. She blinked, and looked back at the crimson lines.

Bending down, cautiously she passed her hand over the pattern, aware as she did so of the variations in temperature between it and the tiles.

"Increase the light a little," she ordered the demon, turning her attention to the shadow again.

As the room brightened, gradually the shadow began to disperse till she could plainly see the shape of a reptile curled around the plinth.

"Darken!" she hissed in fear. "It's a firedrake! These lines on the floor, they're part of its body! If we step on them, we'll waken it."

"I fix with sleep enhancement spell," said the demon. "We lucky you kept light low. Light wakes it too."

He began to mutter in some guttural outlandish language, making several complicated passes in the air with his hands. Mouse began to feel queasy and looked away.

"Is safe now," he assured her a few moments later.

"We still keep off the lines," warned Mouse, listening to her intuition again. "Do you sense any more protections? I don't."

"I say safe," he repeated, tugging at her hand, trying to draw her into the room. "Must hurry now. Dogs wake soon for sure."

Exasperated, she shook him off, motioning him to quiet.

Carefully they picked their way across the network of lines until they stood beside the pedestal. Mouse looked anxiously at the slumbering firedrake.

"Are you sure it'll stay asleep?" she asked, mistrustful of the efficacy of magic spells when they were supposed to be working for her benefit.

"Sure," nodded the demon confidently. "Can't make things sleep, but can enhance it. Kolin only give me little magics. You get jewel now."

Mouse placed her hands carefully on either side of the glass case and lifted it off, passing it down to the demon. She hesitated a moment before reaching forward to lift the jewel reverently off its bed of velvet. Turning it in her hand, she gazed in wonder at the ephemeral flickering hues. One moment it was clear, then the next, every color of the rainbow seemed to glitter within it. At her side, the demon shifted impatiently.

"A moment, imp," she murmured, lost in its beauty. Suddenly, pain lanced through her hand and up her arm to her spine. Arching her back in agony, she let out a soul-wrenching scream as she tried to fling the jewel away from her. It was stuck to her hand, she couldn't let go of it as it seared and burned its way into her very flesh.

She fell to the floor writhing in agony, cradling her
hand against her chest, whimpering, the pain now too
intense to even cry out. The demon echoed her cry
as she twisted sideways, knocking the firedrake with
her foot.

He danced around her, for the first time unsure
what to do. This was bad. Things were not going according to plan. Then he heard the pounding footsteps
of the guard coming towards the treasure room.

"Lady!" he shrieked, the sound galvanizing him into
action. "Lady, you get up! Guards come! You be dead
if they catch you." He grabbed her by the arm. "Up!
You get up!" he shouted urgently, tugging at her.

It seemed to work, for her struggles subsided and
she went limp. Behind them, the firedrake stirred, its
wings making a papery sound as it stretched them.

"Up! Up! Firedrake wake!" He was beside himself
with terror.

Mouse struggled to her feet, her eyes still glazed
with pain. "What . . . ?" she slurred.

"Use sword! Must fight good now," the demon said,
letting go of her to pull free the sword that hung on
her left hip. He thrust it into her unresisting hands.
"Fight guards!" He pushed her round in the direction
of the door.

"Guards?" she asked as five of them rushed into
the room. She could barely see them so fogged by
pain was her vision. How she managed to close her
aching hand around the sword hilt she never knew.

Instincts took over and she raised her blade, just
managing to deflect the blow of the leading man. Her
body knew what to do even if her conscious mind had
not quite caught up. She whirled to one side, taking
him out with a chest blow as he raised his sword for
a second swipe at her.

The firedrake, thoroughly roused now, reared up
and belched flame at her back, but she was no longer
there, having skipped to one side to avoid the rush of

the other four soldiers. Standing them off briefly, she kept her sword at guard and tried to edge round towards the door. She leapt forward, taking out the second man with a deftly turned block that cut him deeply under his sword arm. The third locked blades with her, pushing her back then knocking the sword out of her hands with the sheer force of his next blow. Dazed, she stood there for a moment, her hands limp at her sides. Sure he had her now, the guard advanced more slowly.

Behind them, the firedrake screeched its anger and sent another gout of flame licking at her legs. Mouse wailed at the fresh pain, and flinging her hands up to protect herself, whirled round. She felt a tremendous rush like a tidal wave build inside her—then the room turned dark.

Her wrist was grabbed by a small, clawed hand.

"We go," the demon said, pulling her forward. "Take sword. Leave now, before more guards come."

Mouse's senses returned with a rush, and grabbing the sword that the demon was thrusting back into her hands, she raced for the doorway. She slowed down as the brightness of the corridor made her eyes water and blink. The demon would have none of it and urged her on again. Trusting him, she ran where he led. Within moments, they were back in the little room where they had forced their entry so short a time ago.

Mouse leapt onto the window ledge, reaching down to haul the demon up after her. They scrambled out, jumping down onto the low roof of the stables, leaping from there to land on the dusty ground below. Then they were racing across the yard to the outer wall, praying their rope still waited for them. Up and over they went as all hell let loose behind them. Down the street they ran, slowing only when they left the affluent area of the city to enter the Market Quarter. Finally Mouse felt safe enough to stop and sheathe her sword.

No one was abroad at this hour of night. All the drunks were long since in their beds, save the unlucky ones lying in back alleys with their throats and their purses cut. Mouse and her companion skulked in the shadows, heading deeper into the labyrinth of the Quarters where only those known to be dangerous could safely stray.

Agony stabbed through her head, felling her to her knees. Letting out a strangled cry, she clutched at her head.

"What happens, lady? What happens?"

Mouse was barely aware of the demon's distressed cry. Strange alien thoughts had begun to flow compellingly through her mind.

Submit to me. Let me take control. I have the knowledge to make you great. Together we could rule this kingdom. You could be rich, powerful. No ambition would be beyond our achievement. Don't fear this Kolin, we can take him on easily.

"No," she moaned, swaying from side to side where she knelt in the gutter. "Get out of my head! I don't want power!"

But riches. Yes, riches, the voice purred. *I can give you all that—and more.*

"No!" She fought back mentally, pushing against the thoughts, willing them to stop. "Leave me! Leave me alone!"

The demon watched Mouse with a glimmering of understanding as she carried on her one way conversation. He hadn't told her that the reason they'd been able to escape was because from somewhere she'd called up enough Mage-power to blast the last three guards and the firedrake into a smoldering pile of ashes. No, he hadn't told her that—yet.

Obviously the jewel had found a home for which it was not intended. The girl had to carry Mage-blood in her veins like Wizard Kolin, or she could never have made use of the magic. She'd need all her inborn Mage instincts if she was going to control the jewel. As for his master, the only way he could now claim his prize was by killing her, unless she managed to kill Kolin first.

Now there was a thought. Kolin was no easy master, always demanding he do the impossible. Perhaps the girl would make a kinder mistress, if he, Zaylar, could help her. He sighed. The nature of his binding to Kolin prevented that. There would be no release from his punishment until he'd served another six masters. He could only sit back and await the outcome, changing one master for another when his was finally defeated. And defeated he would be, one day. Magical duels seemed to be all these Jalnian mages lived and died for.

He turned his attention again to Mouse, realizing that she'd finally released her head and was slowly beginning to sit up.

"Lady, you all right?" he asked anxiously. All his hopes would come to naught if the jewel dominated her.

Mouse got unsteadily to her feet, running her hands through her damp hair and pushing it back from her face. "I think so."

She looked at the palms of her hands, comparing one to the other before scrubbing her right one with her left. There was no difference—no lump, no burned flesh. Nothing.

"The jewel, did I dream it or did it really disappear into my hand?"

The demon nodded vigorously. "Is what it does. Lives within the Mage-born. Who win?" he asked, peering closely at her face.

"I did, I think," she replied. Mage-born? *She* was Mage-born?

"Then *you* use jewel, it not use you. You mastered it."

Was that satisfaction she heard in his voice? "Is this why Kolin wanted the jewel?"

"Yes. It make him a stronger wizard. Now you one too." He cocked his head to one side and looked expectantly at her.

"Me, little friend? Not me," she laughed shakily. Suddenly she found herself aware of his hopes for freedom. Frightened, she looked away and the sensation was gone.

"Yes, you. We go to Master Kolin. He find you if you don't. He have to kill you now to get jewel, so you must kill him first."

"Me? Kill Kolin? Who's kidding who, imp?" She began walking in the opposite direction.

"Where you going?" Zaylar demanded, scampering to catch up with her.

"Not to Kolin, that's for sure!"

"Got to! He come after you!" protested the demon, dancing backward in an effort to keep ahead of her. "No place you can hide from a Mage!"

"Why should he? I've taken no money from him yet. It isn't his."

"He think so! Won't stop till he's got jewel," the demon insisted, stopping dead and holding its arms out to bar her way. "Only chance you got is to fight him!"

She ground to a halt in front of him. "You're serious, aren't you? He really will come after me, won't he? Gods, what a mess! Whatever I do, I stand one hell of a good chance of dying!"

"Fighting Kolin is best. Jewel will help you."

"How?"

"Ask it. It protects you now. Maybe it do it anyway, without your asking." He shrugged. "It knows what you know. Maybe it want you to live, think you easier to control than wizard like Kolin."

"Wonderful! What I know about magical duels could be written on a pin head," she muttered, resting her hand on the pommel of her sword.

Zaylar hesitated. She really didn't have a clue about what was happening to her. An opportunity as good as this wouldn't come again in a hundred years, he couldn't afford to pass it up. Technically, he couldn't help, but then he'd never been a great one for technicalities, that's what had gotten him into trouble in the King's Court in the first place. Giving her some advice wasn't really helping her, was it? Advice? Had he called it advice? He would only be talking aloud. If she heard him and got an idea, it wasn't his fault, was it?

He looked down at the ground, scraping one hoof idly in the dust. "If I was a thief, wouldn't use magic," he said. "Thief skills be what I know. I'd use them."

"Thief skills? In a magical duel?" She looked at him incredulously.

He tapped his hoof impatiently, drawing her attention to the ground seconds before a small gout of flame erupted from the center of his scratchings.

"Thief skills," she said again as the demon let out a high-pitched scream. Leaping back, he chittered in pain, hopping about on one hoof as he massaged the other.

"Wasn't helping!" he shrieked to the night sky. "Was not!"

Kolin greeted them in his study. He was a somber man, dressed in robes of deep blue as befitted his dark calling. This hadn't bothered Mouse when she took the job; she'd been no threat to him then, but now his garb sent a chill through her right to her bones.

"So, you've returned. You have my jewel?"

"Oh yes, I have it, Wizard Kolin," she replied.

Kolin lifted the drawstring pouch that lay on the

desk beside him. "Then give it to me and you will be paid," he said.

"Ah, I have this slight problem," said Mouse, focusing her eyes on the pouch rather than on him.

Kolin frowned. "You said you have the jewel. Where's the problem? Zaylar, does she lie to me?" he demanded.

"No, Master. She has jewel," the demon answered from the doorway.

"Then give it to me," thundered Kolin, dropping the pouch and extending his hand peremptorily. His eyes narrowed suddenly.

"You *do* have it, don't you?" He sat back in his seat, regarding her with curiosity. "How can a scrawny girl, and a thief to boot, have Mage-blood?" he mused aloud. "Were either of your parents Mages, girl?"

Mouse shrugged, meeting his gaze this time. "Not that I know of. My father didn't stay around to find out Mother was pregnant. She always said she got me from a passing fortune-teller."

"Only the Mage-born can carry the Living Jewel," said Kolin. "Without doubt, you're one of us." He frowned again. "Your father broke the law in allowing you to live, but no matter. It is an inconvenience, nothing more." He gestured briefly and a bolt of energy flashed toward Mouse.

Automatically she ducked, lifting her arm and fending it to one side as if it were merely a blow from a raised fist. It sparked and flared against the door, sending the demon chittering for cover.

As shock flooded through her, Mouse felt the jewel stirring within her mind.

Let me fight this battle for you, came the silken thought.

"No," said Mouse. Instinctively she knew that if she opened her mind to the jewel, then win or lose this battle with Kolin, *she* would cease to exist. A sound like the wisp of a sigh, then from deep within, she felt a power begin to build, slowly at first, then spiraling upward till it filled her whole being.

Think of a shield, came the faint thought. *Like the armsmen use.*

She couldn't help it. No sooner had it been suggested than she could see it in her mind's eye. It was none too soon. Kolin struck again and her shield was suddenly suffused with blue fire. It took all her courage to stand her ground.

"So, the jewel helps you," hissed Kolin. "But it's too little, and far too late to save you!"

Ignoring his words, she watched for the gap in Kolin's defenses. As he concentrated on gathering his magical energies, she struck. With one hand, she flung the remaining two vials at his desk while reaching swiftly behind her neck for the knife that nestled there. In one fluid move, she'd pulled it out and thrown it into the heart of the sleep spell cloud.

She saw it strike home, taking with it a bolt of raw energy a hundred times more powerful than anything Kolin had used. As the cloud dissipated, she saw him reeling under the impact, hands clutching the knife that now sprouted from the base of his throat.

Lines of thin blue lightning spiderwebbed from the blade across his body. A silent scream was pinned to his face, and for several moments, his petrified form remained transfixed before he collapsed suddenly into a fine rain of ash.

Shocked, Mouse let her arm fall by her side and stared at the empty seat.

"Where'd he go?" she demanded of the demon, her voice high-pitched with shock.

The demon crawled out from under a sideboard. "Dead. He dead now. You kill him, Mistress."

"Dead?" she repeated incredulously. "He can't be dead! He's gone, magicked himself away somewhere!"

"He's dead. You're Mistress now. All this—the

house, everything—yours. And me, Zaylar," he added, nodding vigorously.

"I don't want any of this!" Mouse exclaimed. "Neither his house nor you! I'm an honest thief, not a wizard!"

The demon shook its head. "No, you're a wizard now. You're Mage-born, you got jewel. Can't change that."

Mouse looked for a chair—she didn't fancy the one so hurriedly vacated by its previous owner—and sat down heavily.

"I don't want to be a wizard," she said again.

"Have to be. Power there, jewel there. Lucky this time, jewel helped you. Must learn to control it before it controls you," the demon insisted, concern on its face.

Mouse looked up. "Why should you worry?" she asked. "You're a demon, you don't care about us Jalnians."

"I care because you the Mistress now. We make a deal, eh?"

"What deal?" asked Mouse suspiciously.

"I want be free so no one ever bind me again. You can fix it. I help you."

"What do I get out of it?" she asked, her interest aroused despite herself.

"I live long, long time. Is nothing I stay with you. I teach you, keep jewel from taking you over while learn magic. Then you use this learning, make me an amulet so never bound by Jalnians again. Is deal, yes?"

Mouse arched her eyebrows quizzically. "So you've got delusions of power in your own world. Why can't you make this amulet yourself?"

"Demons can't make amulet, need wizard. You can. Safe for you."

Mouse thought for a moment. Power games she could understand. If the demon was motivated in that direction, then she could be fairly sure he'd keep his word—at least until she'd made the amulet. She sighed, and leaned forward to pick up Kolin's purse.

"Seems like I've got no choice. You've got yourself a deal, Zaylar."

The demon grinned and began cavorting about the room, whooping for all the world like a joyful child. Watching him, Mouse couldn't help smiling. As once more she suppressed the jewel's faint whisper deep within her mind, she cursed herself for breaking her own rules and getting involved with a wizard in the first place. She had a horrible conviction she was going to regret it for a long time.

PRINCIPLES OF WARFARE

John Helfers

John Helfers is a writer and editor currently living in Green Bay, Wisconsin. His fiction has appeared in anthologies such as Sword of Ice and Other Tales of Valdemar, The UFO Files, *and* Warrior Princesses, *among others. He is also the editor of the anthology* Black Cats and Broken Mirrors. *Future projects include coauthoring several novels. In his spare time, what there is of it, he enjoys disc golf, inline skating, and role-playing games.*

KITSUNE was awakened by a foot planted between his shoulder blades. He immediately rolled to his feet and bowed, trying to look as alert as possible. Cinching his *hakima* trousers around his waist, he straightened his short robe and looked up.

The silhouette of a man stood before him against the breaking dawn. As Kitsune's vision adjusted to the gathering sunlight, he saw the man was clad in the traditional kimono and *hakima* of a commoner. Only the two curved swords at his side, one half as long as the other, suggested that he was much more than a simple peasant. Kitsune had seen him around the encampment before, usually near the sorcerer's tent. He was a *ronin,* or masterless samurai, one who sold his skill with his *katana* for money. Rumor had it that he was a remnant of the Tashiga clan, which had been wiped out in the fighting two years before.

The *ronin* looked at Kitsune impassively. "The Master wishes to see you. Come." He turned on his heel and strode off across the hillside.

Kitsune did his best to hide his surprise. The Master only meant one person. With a start, he realized he was being left behind, and trotted to catch up to the tall man. Only half-awake, his mind whirled with confused questions. *Why am I being summoned? What could the Master possibly want with me?*

As he hurried to keep pace with the *ronin* now climbing the hill, Kitsune looked out at the army that was slowly coming to life around him. As far as he could see, thousands of men and horses dotted the hill and plains below him. Down in the valley below, spectral forms of soldiers moved in and out of the ground fog that blanketed the meadows. Hundreds of men stirred from sleep, readying themselves for the tasks of the day, from tending to the animals to sharpening weapons to preparing meals. Dozens of fires flickered to life, with pots of water set to boil. Hundreds of sets of armor were laid out, the black lacquered plates of the Hiroshi clan's soldiers gleaming dully in the rising sun. Everyone moved with a quiet sense of urgency today. For today, after many long days of marching, there would be a battle. Kitsune didn't know all the details, he just knew they were going to fight, and, more importantly, he would be a part of it.

The *ronin* stopped in front of a small tent at the top of the hill. Behind the tent Kitsune could see the snow-capped mountains the army had crossed to get here. The *ronin* nodded to Kitsune, who swallowed and walked through the tent's dark entrance.

"Mind the salt," a voice said in the gloom. Kitsune blinked, waiting for his eyes to adjust to the dimness, then looked down. He saw he was standing outside a circle of white crystals on the ground. Raising his head, he looked upon the sorcerer for the first time.

The diminutive man seated cross-legged before him was a study in nondescriptness. His age could have ranged from thirty to fifty, with hardly any distinguishing characteristics at all. Unlike the *ronin*, who practically exuded menace with every step he took, the sorcerer looked relatively harmless. He was dressed in a sleeveless cotton robe which draped over his knees, woolen *hakima*, sandals, and a straw hat. Only his eyes revealed anything of his true nature. As soon as Kitsune met his hazel gaze he felt like the man was seeing directly into his mind, laying bare everything he ever knew or had done. Kitsune froze, not daring to move until the man said so. The seconds passed as slowly as the seasons. At last the man nodded once, and Kitsune bowed deeply and held it, staring at the ground.

"Please, please, I am not your *daimyo*. There is no need for such formality here." The man's voice was pleasant, with a trace of amusement in it. Upon hearing him, Kitsune straightened and even found himself relaxing a bit.

The man had apparently been writing on a scroll, which he now laid down next to a quill pen, inkwell, and writing stone. "How is the weather outside? Will it be a good day for the battle?"

Kitsune nodded. "Yes, it is sunny and clear. The fog will be burned off by midmorning. The soldiers will have a clear field." Although the sorcerer had as much as said he could relax, Kitsune knew there were still some rituals that must be followed, such as this conversation. While the tone and subjects of their talk were relatively light, in time the sorcerer would reveal the true purpose of this meeting.

"And everyone is preparing for the upcoming fight?"

Kitsune bowed again. "To the best of my knowledge, yes. Most of the men were already awake and busy when I was summoned."

The man nodded and was silent for several seconds. He seemed to be evaluating Kitsune by his answers. "How old are you, boy?"

"I have seen thirteen summers," Kitsune replied.

"Do you know who I am?" the man asked.

"You are the sorcerer of Clan Hiroshi," Kitsune said.

The man nodded. "Do you know why you are here?" he asked.

"Because you summoned me," Kitsune said.

A ghost of a smile flitted across the man's face. "Do you know why you are here?" he repeated.

Confusion knitted Kitsune's brow as he pondered the wizard's question. He had just begun his education in philosophy before losing his teacher. The question could hold any one of several meanings, depending on what the man was looking for. Kitsune decided the best strategy would be to parry the question with one of his own. It was a calculated risk, for if his question was taken as impudence, Kitsune would lose his life. But he had to have been called here for more than a report on field conditions. "Where is here?" he asked, his face perfectly serious.

The man nodded again. "Tell me, what is the difference between a samurai and a sorcerer?"

Kitsune thought for a moment. "A samurai relies on his own abilities to defeat his enemy, while a sorcerer must use the powers of spirits and magic to conquer his."

"A complicated way of saying the sorcerer uses magic, while the samurai does not," the wizard said. "Lesson number one; sometimes the simplest answer is the best one."

"Lesson? I don't understand," Kitsune said.

The sorcerer rocked once and rose to his feet. Although he was only a foot taller than Kitsune, his presence filled the small tent, and the boy had to steel himself not to take an involuntary step backward. "You are the boy who broke the charge at the Ryoko river, yes?"

Kitsune's head snapped up, and for the first time since he had entered the tent a trace of emotion flickered on his face. "Yes."

"That was where your father was killed, was it not?" The blunt question bordered on rudeness; however, Kitsune had no recourse but to answer.

"Yes," he said, biting his lip to keep his voice from trembling. The pain lanced his mind, strengthening his resolve.

"Tell me."

A flurry of memories whirled through Kitsune's mind like the winds of a dust devil. *The whistling of arrows slicing through the smoky air . . . house soldiers screaming in pain as they were cut down . . . the thud of an armored body hitting the earth, the shaft of an arrow jutting from its neck . . . the pounding of dozens of horses' hooves trampling the earth . . . a blazing torch spiraling through the air . . . the oily smell of the raging fire blazing through the plains.* His eyes burning, Kitsune fought to keep his voice expressionless as he spoke. He recited the events of that night as if he had been a disinterested observer. "When it was clear our keep was going to fall to Clan Yashida, my father and several dozen of our soldiers remained behind to guard the pass that the rest of the family was escaping through. I . . . remained behind as well. The enemy was upon us sooner than we expected. Their archers had our range almost immediately. Father had prepared a surprise for them, but he was killed before he could spring the trap, pierced through the throat by an arrow. The rest of our unit was either dead, or had fled. The cavalry had formed for their charge. They would have cut through our unprotected rear like a sword blade through rice stalks. I knocked over the oil barrels we had placed, took a torch, and threw it. The fire broke the charge, allowing my family time to escape."

"Did you have the chance to recover your father's body?" the sorcerer asked as casually as if he was asking Kitsune to pass him a bowl of rice.

Kitsune blinked back hot tears as the memory of his father's burning body sprang unbidden into his mind. "There was no time. He had fallen where the trap was to be sprung. I couldn't move him. In his own way, he gave what he could to the fire."

The wizard paused, as if absorbing this information. The silence in the tent stretched out between them. Outside, Kitsune could hear the shouts of the men preparing for battle. He waited, focusing his concentration on the man before him. After several minutes, the sorcerer spoke. "That was over two months ago. Why aren't you with your family now?"

As hard as he tried, Kitsune could not keep the venom out of his voice as he replied. "I am my father's eldest son. I will have blood." He held up his right palm, marked with a white scar running diagonally from the bottom of his index finger to his wrist. "This marks the vow I made on that day to see the Yashida clan scattered to the four winds. That is why I am here."

The sorcerer nodded vaguely, as if what Kitsune had told him was unimportant. "I have chosen you as my apprentice. You have proved your courage. You have also proved your honor. Today, we will discover if you have aptitude. You know that Clan Hiroshi meets Clan Yashida in battle today. It is rumored that they have a sorcerer as well. That is why I am here." The small man pointed to the shadow outside the tent. "Maseda-san is my bodyguard, appointed by the *daimyo*. His task is simple but all-consuming, to keep me alive and safe from the threats of this world. I need another set of sharp eyes, a quick pair of legs, and above all, a keen mind. I think you are this boy. Step inside the circle."

Kitsune looked at the white barrier separating the sorcerer and himself. He raised his head and met the wizard's gaze. The man's eyes revealed nothing. Kitsune stepped over the circle of salt, standing directly in front of the sorcerer.

"I will only ask this of you once. It is not a command. Your answer must be made with both your heart and mind, and you must completely believe in the path you choose. Will you join me?"

Kitsune's mind had been made up as soon as he had heard who the enemy was. "Yes, Master." He knelt in the swept dirt and pressed his forehead to the ground in the traditional bow of obeisance.

"Stop! Stand up!" the sorcerer's voice crackled like a whip. "The last thing I need is to have you staring at the ground instead of observing the world around us. And my name is not Master, it is Asano. We have much to do before the battle today."

"I will do whatever you command," Kitsune said.

"We shall see," the sorcerer replied. "We shall see."

Hours later, Kitsune staggered back up the hill to the small tent. The sun was climbing ever higher in the sky, and he was soaked with sweat from running across the encampment all morning. The *ronin* Maseda barely glanced at him as he approached, but Kitsune noticed the involuntary tensing of his body, ready to defend against anything that might harm the man he guarded. Bowing quickly, Kitsune tried to neaten his appearance as much as possible before entering the tent.

Asano was seated in the lotus position in the dark interior, apparently meditating. He had changed into a midnight blue kimono that blended almost too well with the tent's shadows, giving the impression that his head and neck were floating in midair. A leather belt with several pouches lay on the ground beside him.

"What news?" he asked without opening his eyes.

"His Lordship wishes to confer with you before the battle," Kitsune replied. "He wants to know what omens you foresee."

Asano opened one eye and regarded Kitsune. "Just the usual one, of hundreds of men going to meet their ancestors today. Although it looks as though we have the edge in numbers, I believe that the Yashida soldiers are better led and organized. If the rumors are true, and they do have a sorcerer allied with them, then we shall need all our wits about us to prevail today."

"Ashiga-san," Maseda said from outside, addressing the sorcerer by his formal surname. "Yoritome approaches."

Asano rolled to his feet and stepped outside, Kitsune following a respectful distance behind. A small contingent of horses was galloping up the hill toward them, the pennants of Clan Hiroshi fluttering in the breeze created by their travel. The group pulled up in front of the trio by the tent, who bowed in greeting. The leader, a ferret-faced man who looked to be not so much wearing his armor as swimming in it, got straight to the point.

"Sorcerer, tell me, whom do the gods favor today?"

"The gods favor those who would strike when their advantage is the strongest," Asano replied. "The gods favor even more those who would recognize the advantage when it comes."

"And when will this advantage come?"

"Hiroshi-san, the advantage lies with you already. It is as the rain striking against the mountain face. One drop of water against the mountain does little. But thousands of drops of water can, over time, break even the strongest mountain. Each of your men is one of those drops of water. Position them well, and you will break the strongest mountain of resistance."

"Impudent dog! Do not presume to tell me how to use my men!" the general snapped. "You will tell me what I want to know at once!"

Asano bowed low. "My apologies, my lord. Let the army of Clan Yashida come to you on the plains and victory will be assured."

During this exchange Kitsune's attention was drawn not to the general, but to the man immediately to his right. Dressed in the traditional armor of a samurai, his was a marked contrast from the ornately decorated *kabutos* or helmets, breastplates, and arm and leg guards of the others in the general's party. They sported elaborate horned helmets with fierce carved masks underneath. Their arm guards were covered with scenes of nature woven from fine silk or worked in gilt metal. Their *kusazuris,* lamellar armor skirts worn to protect the upper legs, were trimmed in either feathers or fur. The shin guards were also colorful laminate, brightly painted.

The only affectation this man had on his matte black armor was intricate silver brushwork decorating every inch. He was also the only one not wearing a mask. As the man listened to the conversation, Kitsune saw that he had only one eye, the other covered by a black silk patch embroidered with silver thread. A long pink scar followed the curve of his face, starting at his hairline and winding its way under the eye patch down his right cheek, ending at his chin.

While the general's other retainers followed their leader's conversation closely, reacting to his comments, the man in black sat stiffly and kept his attention solely on Asano. He did not react when the general insulted Asano, but listened closely to every word the wizard said.

The general nodded, apparently satisfied with what he had heard. Wheeling his horse around, he nodded to his retainers and spurred the animal down the hill. The others followed, the samurai in black being the last one to leave after bowing to Asano.

"Who was that?" Kitsune asked.

"Yoritome is a distant cousin of our esteemed *daimyo*. He is also, unfortunately, one of the few men left in the Clan's royal bloodline with military experience, however slight. The man beside him was Akira Kubosai, the last surviving samurai of the Battle of Koshun Pass. Apparently he has turned *ronin*. With him here we stand a better chance than I first thought. It is a shame that he is not leading this army instead of Yoritome. Still, the fortunes of battle change like the direction of the wind."

Kitsune knew, as did every educated child, of the Battle of Koshun Pass. Five samurai and two hundred foot soldiers had held off an army ten times as large for three days, allowing reinforcements to arrive and hold the pass. It was rumored that the survivors had propped the dead up with weapons in their arms, giving the illusion that they had plenty of men to spare. When the fighting was over, only five men had survived. Kitsune watched Akira until he was a dot in the distance.

Asano, noticing where the boy was looking, shook his head. "Surviving against seemingly hopeless odds does not necessarily make one great."

Kitsune gave the sorcerer a questioning look. "Maybe not, but it surely doesn't hurt."

"Come. We must make the final preparations," Asano said, turning and heading back inside the tent. He emerged with several bottles and jars in his arms, along with his writing utensils. "It will be starting soon."

Asano laid out the containers he had removed from the tent. "This is the hard part about battling another sorcerer when you know nothing about him. There is really not much chance to plan any kind of strategy.

You have no idea whether he will commit to battle first or try to force you to. Therefore, it is best to wait and see."

He handed Kitsune a large jar and a length of silk rope. "Walk out from me five paces and pour the salt in a circle, using the rope as your guide. Make sure there is enough salt to go around all the way. Just before you close the circle, make sure you are inside it. Move now!"

Kitsune did as he was told. With Asano holding one end of the rope and himself the other, he soon had walked a perfect circle around them, remembering to step inside at the last second. He set the jar down and waited for instructions. At this time, Kitsune saw Maseda wrinkle his nose, then step lightly around the back of the tent, his hand on the hilt of his *katana*. Kitsune thought about warning Asano, but didn't once he saw what the sorcerer was doing.

While Kitsune had been distracted, the old man had produced a large shallow wooden box, the bottom of which was covered with sand. Rocks of various sizes were also in the box. Asano muttered unintelligible words under his breath and looked out onto the battlefield. Kitsune followed his gaze and gasped.

There, lined up on the plains of the valley, were the thousands of men that formed the army of Clan Hiroshi. The cavalry, archers, samurai, and footmen had all formed their ranks and were awaiting command. About halfway up the hill sat Yoritome and his retainers. Kitsune squinted, but could not see Akira with them. As he scanned the army, he heard a faint noise coming from the box. Kitsune looked down.

The rocks in the sand were moving, slowly aligning themselves in a pattern that looked exactly like the formation of the Hiroshi army. For each rock that placed itself in the sand, there was a corresponding unit of men on the field. Asano pulled a small wooden rake out of his kimono sleeve and drew it down the middle of the box, dividing it in half. As Kitsune watched, drops of water appeared from nowhere, filling the grooves the rake made, so that when Asano had finished, there was a tiny stream running through the sand. On the other side of the stream, more rocks were gathering, arranging themselves similarly to the first group. Kitsune looked across the valley and saw the Yashida army in battle formation.

"Listen closely. No matter what happens, no matter where I go, you must not leave this circle once the battle begins. I will need you here to keep an eye on what is happening down there," Asano said.

"What would cause you to leave?" Kitsune asked.

"If the opposing sorcerer can be forced out, I will meet him in single combat. The outcome of that battle alone may decide who wins here today. But that's only if he shows himself. If I must seek him out, then we would be faring badly. With luck, that won't be necessary."

A rustle in the grass behind them caused both Asano and Kitsune to turn their heads. Maseda emerged from behind the tent, his *katana* still in its scabbard. He tossed what looked like a small bundle of feathers to the ground. Kitsune saw it was a dead pigeon with a band for attaching messages on its leg. Looking up at the samurai, he saw dark spots on his face and kimono that hadn't been there when he had left. Asano and Maseda exchanged glances, then Asano nodded and Maseda took his usual place standing near the tent entrance.

"Well, they know of me, at least. But they don't know where I am yet," Asano said. He turned his attention back to the battlefield. "Look, it begins."

A double row of men on Hiroshi's side had formed in front of the main army. These men were lightly armored, and carried bows that were taller than they were. Each man stuck a handful of arrows into the ground beside him. Selecting an arrow, each archer nocked it and prepared to fire.

"It would figure that Yoritome would initiate the battle. He never did listen," Asano mused. "Strange, no archers have appeared on the other side. They're up to something, and I think I know what."

As he spoke, the archers drew their bows and fired. The line of arrows arced through the air. As they began descending, a wall of wind and dust whirled up, obscuring the Yashida army and causing the volley of arrows to be blown off course, scattering them in the high breeze.

"Ah, an excellent beginning," Asano said, smiling. Only do what is necessary to prevent the attack, nothing more. The fact that both armies are obscured from each other's view is a beneficial side effect. The question is, how will they take advantage of it?"

Asano leaned down over the box and gently blew along the small river. As he did so, Kitsune saw the dust wall waver and disintegrate, blown apart by a more powerful wind. The cloud broke apart just as the Yashida cavalry came charging through, strangely silent as they headed for the shallow river and the row of archers beyond.

"Kitsune, take the red flag and wave it three times." Asano said. Kitsune scrambled to comply, snatching the red banner and waving it quickly.

In the valley below, the archers selected a different type of arrow, one with a bright white, bulbous head. Nocking them unhurriedly, they drew and fired, not at the approaching cavalry, but in a high arc so the arrows would land in front of the line of horsemen.

As the arrows traveled up, they hung at the zenith of their flight for a moment. As one, they all burst into flames, then dropped back down to earth on the other side of the river. Wherever they landed, bursts of fire sprouted, forming a wall of flame that panicked the horses and broke the charge.

"Even a boy can teach seasoned warriors new tricks," Asano said without taking his eyes off the box. Kitsune fought to keep a grin from appearing on his face at the compliment. He could feel heat radiating from the box now as the fire wall intensified.

"It won't last long," Asano said. Indeed, as they watched, the river rose up in a miniature tidal wave, cresting as it hit the shore and crashing down upon the wall of flames, smothering it in a huge cloud of steam.

"Now it is our turn," Asano said. The Hiroshi cavalry had formed as soon as the flame wall appeared, and were now charging themselves, bursting through the clouds of steam like demons from the fifth Hell. Falling upon the disorganized Yashida cavalry, they quickly cut them down to a man as they rode by. *Katana* blades flashed in the sun as horses and men both screamed and died.

The Hiroshi cavalry tightened their ranks and galloped onward, aiming straight at the center of the Yashida army. Kitsune, dividing his attention between the box and the field, noticed the stones trembling in the sand. A moment later, he felt a shudder pass under his feet.

"Asano, is that the ground I feel shaking?" Kitsune asked.

The sorcerer's eyes widened as he realized what was about to happen. Before he could signal the general to break off the attack, the sand in the box on the other side of the river was swept aside, revealing a black hole in the bottom. The row of rocks that represented the cavalry moved inexorably forward and fell, disappearing into the blackness.

Kitsune looked up just in time to see the last of the Hiroshi cavalry vanish into the yawning chasm like they had never existed. The fissure slammed shut, sending a cloud of dust into the air and a thunderclap that shook the trees around them.

Asano sat back, silent. Kitsune noticed a tiny pebble

on the edge of the chasm. He waited for the dust cloud to clear, not sure of what he was looking for. Then he saw it.

"Asano, look!"

Out on the plain, a single man stood. The set of familiar black and silver armor glittered in the noon sun. For one moment, as the dust settled, time seemed to stop. Everyone in both armies froze as all eyes turned toward the lone samurai.

With a single motion, Akira drew his *katana* and held it over his head. The blade seemed to glow with an inner fire as it reflected the sun's rays.

For one moment, there was complete, perfect silence in the valley.

Then Akira screamed.

With that sound, the spell was broken, and the valley erupted in chaos.

Both armies moved as one, the legions of soldiers grabbing their weapons and charging the field.

Akira wasn't waiting for reinforcements. With his scream he was already running to meet the opposing army. His sword blade flashed as he cut through the ranks of enemy soldiers, their pole arms falling like wheat stalks.

By now the bulk of the main armies, mostly unarmored peasants, were clashing in the center of the plains. The soldiers' bladed *naginatas,* or long glaives, were discarded for close fighting weapons. Short-bladed sickles, or *kamas, jo,* and *bo* staffs, three-sectioned staffs, *nunchaku,* and the occasional sword all rose and fell. Occasionally the flash of a blade could be seen as a samurai on one side or the other whirled through a knot of soldiers like the wind, leaving them dead and dying from his passing. What few horsemen remained were soon disposed of, pulled from their mounts or, in some cases, having their horses cut out from under them. The noise was incredible, from the screams of dying men and horses to the shouts of men in combat and the clash of weapons, the din reverberated off the hills around them until it sounded as if the very heavens had joined in the battle.

"The Yashida soldiers are still using their pole arms. This is strange. It seems they are fighting at a disadvantage. Still, they are holding their own. I don't like this," Asano said, rummaging in one of his many pouches.

Just then a low rumble shook the valley, causing the trees to quiver and Kitsune to nearly lose his balance.

"Sit down now!" Asano commanded, nearly falling to the ground in his haste. Kitsune followed suit, just in time.

At the far end of the valley, the ground heaved and bucked, causing waves of earth to ripple outward. The shock waves traveled down through the valley, knocking Yashida and Hiroshi soldiers by the score off their feet. Asano and Kitsune swayed as the aftershocks reached up into the hills where they were sitting. Maseda remained standing, motionless, unaffected by the shaking ground.

Now the strategy of the Yashida warriors became clear. Many had braced themselves up with the butts of their pole arms, riding the earthen wave and remaining standing while others around them fell. Their *naginatas* also had a longer reach than the Hiroshi soldiers' weapons, and they were often able to kill several soldiers on the ground around them before having to defend themselves. The tide of battle had swung alarmingly in Clan Yashida's favor.

Kitsune! Pay attention!" Asano's voice broke through Kitsune's shocked trance as he watched the battle before him. He turned immediately and watched the wizard.

With a quick nod to Maseda, who stepped inside the tent, Asano ground several powders together in a mortar and pestle, then threw the contents in the air, chanting while he did so. Instead of falling to earth, the crystals seemed to float on the breeze outside the salt circle, assuming a vaguely man-shaped form. When some of the crystals did touch the ground, oily blue smoke appeared, spiraling upward around the powdery outline. Kitsune smelled the acrid tang of sulfur as the thing took shape. A moment later, the smoke dissipated, and a creature unlike anything Kitsune had ever seen stood before them.

It was huge, standing as tall as one peasant on another's shoulders. The creature's skin was jade green, shot through with black veins that pulsed as it moved. Its large hands, one of which could have easily palmed Asano's head, were tipped with curved dirty talons. But its face, that was truly what nightmares were made of. Vestigial white horns sprouted from its forehead. Baleful red eyes glared at the sorcerer and his apprentice. A crooked, bulbous nose sprouted above a huge maw which glistened with razor-sharp fangs.

The creature was dressed in a mockery of samurai armor, with a *haramaki-do,* or breastplate, that appeared to be constructed of human bones. His *sode,* the square arm guards of the samurai, had human faces carved on them which writhed in agony, screaming in torment. His weapons, also the traditional two swords of the samurai, were terrible to behold. The shorter sword, or *wakizashi,* was as long as a normal man's *katana.* The larger blade was a massive version of the *no-tachi,* or two-handed greatsword, and was twice as long as Kitsune was tall. The creature flexed its clawed fingers and sniffed the air. Upon seeing Asano and Kitsune, it howled, drew both blades, and ran for them.

"Master!" Kitsune cried.

"I told you once before, my name is Asano," the sorcerer said calmly as they watched the beast charge them. At the last second, it stopped just outside the salt circle as if it had hit an invisible wall.

"Protection against lesser spirits. Now pay attention,

apprentice. This," Asano said, gesturing to the snorting, drooling creature only two steps away, "is an *oni,* or lesser demon. Relatively mindless, it exists only for destruction, which it will get today as payment for my summoning it. However, if left unchecked, it will indiscriminately slay both Yashida's men and our own. Hence."

Asano produced an ornately carved jade collar from his kimono sleeve. He held it up and released it, the collar remaining floating in midair. With a gentle puff, Asano blew the collar toward the *oni.* As it flew, the collar expanded, becoming large enough to fit over the demon's head, which it did, settling neatly around the beast's green throat. The oni pawed at the collar, but with no effect. It did, however, look at Asano and growl.

"Oh, hush," said the sorcerer, unperturbed. "Now, very important. This," Asano held up a small ring, also carved from jade. "Is the control for the collar. I need you to command the *oni* in battle while I go and face the opposing sorcerer."

"But Asano, I—" Kitsune began.

"No buts, apprentice, there are no excuses, only fear. Calm yourself," Asano said. The ring will allow you to ride along in his mind, so to speak. Just let him do what he does best. Your only goal is to prevent him from killing our own men. But remember, he lives for destruction in whatever form. Master your fear of him, and you will master him." Asano handed Kitsune the ring. "And remember, do not leave the circle!" Gathering up several potion bottles, Asano made as if to step outside the circle, and vanished as if he was stepping through a doorway made of air.

Kitsune looked at the ring, then at the slavering, sword-wielding demon in front of him. *If this is a lesser spirit, I never want to see a greater one,* he thought. Taking a deep breath, he sat cross-legged on the ground in front of the box. Looking down, he saw the battle overwhelmingly favoring Clan Yashida. They had broken through the Hiroshi line, and were threatening to overrun the general. Steeling his expression and calming his mind, Kitsune slipped the ring on his finger.

The world blurred into a smear of bright colors for a moment, and then Kitsune was looking at himself sitting inside the salt circle. It was as if the *oni*'s vision was overlaid on his own. Kitsune closed his eyes and discovered that now he was looking through the *oni*'s eyes alone.

The demon's mind was awash in negative energy, containing only feelings of hate and destruction. Kitsune could feel every aspect of the *oni*'s body. Instead of being heavy and ponderous like he would have expected something this large to be, the demon seemed possessed of uncommon grace and agility. Curiously, the *oni* did not seem to be aware of Kitsune's presence. It was as if he had just perched on the beast's shoulder unseen. Now he had to get him into the battle.

"Turn around," Kitsune thought. The *oni* stayed where he was, still trying to breach the barrier. *What's going on?* thought Kitsune.

!Kill little one here! a voice thundered in his mind. The force of the *oni*'s thoughts nearly sent Kitsune reeling. With an effort he regained control and spoke again.

"This little one is hardly worth your trouble. I know where there are dozens of ones, even bigger than him, that you can destroy," Kitsune said.

The *oni*'s gaze lifted from Kitsune. *!Oh!* he grunted, the simple noise reverberating through Kitsune's mind.

"Turn around," Kitsune said again, putting an edge of command in his voice. The *oni* complied. *"See the little ones in red? They are the ones who brought you into this place. They are the ones who tore you from*

your home. If you kill all of the red ones, the spell will be lifted, and you will be free."

The *oni*'s shriek of rage was almost more that Kitsune could bear. He hung on however, and before he knew it, he felt a sensation of leaving the ground and wind washing over the creature. The sky rushed to meet the *oni,* and through his eyes Kitsune saw the battlefield spread out before him, tiny figures of red and black desperately fighting. Kitsune heard a strange rasping noise, and it took him a few seconds to figure out the *oni* was laughing.

!The red ones will die, oh, yes. I will become felt but not seen and slay them all! With that the *oni* swooped down toward the battlefield.

Felt but not seen? Kitsune thought. He had heard tales of spirit folk that could become unseen in the physical world. Perhaps that was what the *oni* meant. A moment later, he found out.

The *oni* did not fight like humans. He used his power of flight to make long passes down the line of men. The only sounds he made were hideous screams of delight as his swords sliced through armor, flesh, and bone. Where he flew, the soldiers of Clan Yashida died as great wounds from his unseen weapons opened on their heads, chests, and necks. Men scattered like leaves before a windstorm as the *oni* flew by, death incarnate.

Within a few minutes, the tide had turned. The soldiers of Clan Yashida, only aware that something was causing the gruesome death of dozens of their comrades, milled about in confusion, opening themselves up to even more of the *oni*'s attacks. After two more passes, the remnants of the Yashida army were routed and fleeing the battlefield. The demon kept after them, chasing down scattered groups and wiping them out mercilessly.

At first, Kitsune watched the demon work with a smile on his face. But when the *oni* turned his swords to the fleeing men, Kitsune felt his stomach twist in disgust. His passion of the Clan Yashida's destruction had burned brightly within him during the battle, but now, seeing their army broken and defeated, his delight lessened. His father would never have struck down soldiers when they were retreating. The *oni*, however, had no such compunction. This was not honorable combat, it was slaughter. Kitsune grew more and more sickened as the *oni* continued his work. When the demon bit through the head of one of the Yashida soldiers, Kitsune decided enough was enough.

"Stop your killing, that's enough," Kitsune commanded.

The *oni* shook the bodies of three impaled men from his *katana* and growled. *!Must kill all red ones. Then can I leave this place!* With that he looked around for more Yashida soldiers.

By the gods, Asano, where are you? Kitsune thought. If the sorcerer would only return, he could send this thing back to wherever it had come from. Unfortunately, Asano was nowhere in sight. It was up to Kitsune to stop the demon's indiscriminate killing. But how?

The oni snuck up on a group of three men and tore into them, slicing and maiming with malicious glee. It scanned the battlefield for more targets. Kitsune racked his brain, trying to come up with a way to stop the beast. Asano's words seemed to echo in his head. *". . . it lives only for destruction . . ."* That was the key to stopping it, Kitsune was sure, but he couldn't quite grasp it.

A breeze rustling the trees made the *oni* look up. Instinctively he crouched into a defensive posture, as if worried the tree might attack him. Inspiration struck Kitsune. *That's it! I only hope it is dumb enough to be tricked,* he prayed.

"Listen! Hear that! The very trees of this place are laughing at you. They know you are trapped here and

are mocking your fate! You're not going to sit here and let them insult you, are you?" Kitsune asked.

Apparently the *oni*'s price was very delicate, for its scream of rage was, if anything, even louder than the previous one. It launched itself at the nearest group of trees and sliced into the foliage, sending leaves and branches everywhere in a whirlwind of destruction. The wind kept blowing, and the leaves kept rustling, which only spurred the demon's anger even more. It soon finished with the first tree and moved on to the next, lopping off branches and hacking through the trunk with mighty blows.

"What is going on here? Are you going to create *bonsai* from the venerable oak trees? Cease this ridiculous activity at once!" Kitsune opened his eyes to find Asano standing over him.

"Asano, thank the heavens you're back! I sent the demon to the trees to stop him from slaughtering the Yashida soldiers. Send him back to wherever he came from, please!" Kitsune begged.

"Foolish boy, you could do that anytime you wanted. Simply slide the ring off your finger and say that you release him. And please hurry, before he chops the rest of the forest down!"

"Demon, I release you," thought Kitsune as he removed the ring. The sensation of looking through the *oni*'s eyes vanished, and Kitsune's mind was fully his own again. He held the ring out to Asano and bowed his head. "Master, I am not worthy to be your apprentice. I could not control the demon as you had asked."

Asano snatched the ring from Kitsune's hand and snorted. "Pah! Control it you could not, and neither could I. Direct it, however, that can be done, and you accomplished that with the skill only a true sorcerer could possess. Raw skill, but there nonetheless. In any case, you will do until I find someone better." Asano sat down before Kitsune and regarded him. "The trees were clever, but a less destructive method would have been to have him attack the grasses under his feet. More aesthetically pleasing. And grass grows faster."

"Why didn't you tell me about the way to release him?" Kitsune asked.

"Because I was testing you, apprentice. We do not have the luxury of educating you in peacetime. This was your trial by fire. Also, I had to see if it was possible for you to learn compassion on the battlefield as well," Asano replied.

Kitsune swayed, drained by the effort of riding the demon. "Asano, I feel as if I have waded through a river of blood today. When the demon began attacking the fleeing soldiers, it made me sick. A thousand men could die, and my father would still not be alive. I cannot continue my vendetta against the Clan Yashida. I want to learn from you and take my rightful place as a sorcerer."

Asano smiled. "And so, by letting go of your anger, you have taken the first step."

Kitsune nodded, then became aware of the faint smell of smoke emanating from the sorcerer. "But what of the other wizard?"

Asano brushed an imaginary piece of dirt from his kimono sleeve. "Oh, we dueled, certainly. But when it became clear how the battle would turn out, we saw no reason to continue the fight, so we parted ways honorably. In that way, the duel was necessary to win today, for if I hadn't distracted him, he would have found a way to dispel the *oni,* and the battle would have been lost. But as it is, we will meet again, of this I am certain."

"And Akira?"

"Warriors such as he are fated for greater destinies that dying in a minor battle such as this one. I believe he will be promoted to commander of Clan Hiroshi's armies after word of his heroism reaches the *daimyo.* Just a premonition, mind you." Asano rose to enter his tent.

"Asano?" Kitsune asked. The sorcerer half-turned. Kitsune started to ask something, then changed his mind. "Did you get the collar back?"

"You mean this collar?" Asano asked, pulled a familiar piece of jade from his kimono sleeve. "Remember, apprentice, in this world, there is magic, and there is *magic*."

Kitsune nodded, fighting off the weariness that threatened to overwhelm him. Asano's face turned stern for a moment. "Now, clean up the camp, prepare dinner, and then rest, for tomorrow, it all begins again."

Kitsune stared at him openmouthed. Asano walked into his tent and turned around. "And Kitsune?"

Still surprised, Kitsune could only nod.

Asano bowed low. "Welcome to *our* clan."

BATTLEMAGIC™ FOR MORONS

John DeChancie

John DeChancie has written more than twenty novels in the science fiction, fantasy, and horror fields, including the acclaimed Castle series, the most recent of which, Bride of the Castle, *was published in 1994. He has also written dozens of short stories and nonfiction articles, appearing in such magazines as* The Magazine of Fantasy and Science Fiction, Penthouse, *and many anthologies, including* First Contact *and* Wizard Fantastic. *In addition to his writing, John enjoys traveling and composing and playing classical music.*

INTRODUCTION

DEAR MORON . . .

Welcome to BattleMagic for Morons. BattleMagic is the most popular, widely used, and most powerful software sorcery application employing magic for military, general combative, and personal self-defense purposes.

This book is not the usual for-dummies manual. This book had been written and published not by an outside firm, but by the software manufacturers themselves, and it comes with the added bonus of an absolutely free micro-CD copy of the program and documentation files.

This manual is designed specifically for the uninitiated, the tyro, the beginner, the magically-challenged, the fumbling boob who can't cast a shoo-fly spell to save a pile of excrement, i.e., a shambling paleozoic bivalve like you.

What's that? You find the overriding tone here a trifle . . . shall we say, confrontational? In-your-face? Insulting? Just a little. Well, excuse us, but you are the one who saw this volume on the shelf, a publication clearly labeled "For Morons," and picked the damned thing up. "Oh, this is the thing for me!" you probably burbled, rushing to the checkout to flash your platinum plasticard. "Just what I need!" So, you'll understand if we call you exactly what you style yourself. A moron, an amateur, a retard, a drooling thaumaturgical illiterate adrift in a century where the mastery of high sorcery is as essential for survival as the mastery of high technology was in the previous one.

You'd think, wouldn't you, that a book with a title that is, to the potential buyer, an insult in itself wouldn't have many takers. Right? But no, this and their similarly titled tomes—"For Dimwits," "Airhead's Guide to Whatever"—are selling like space heaters in Alaska. Go figure.

Now, do we have to review the real dirt-dumb basics here? Need we go over the reason that magic, real, workable, efficacious (that word too hard for you?—okay, it means that it really, really works) magic, came of age with the computer revolution? Must we rehash the tired old story of how magicians in the very last days of the twentieth century and the first days of the twenty-first found that running legitimate magic spells through computers produced major miracles? All that hoary old hocus-pocus finally worked! Moreover, these antiquated enchantments worked a thousand times better than they had for any ancient magician. Must we explain how computers had given the ancient recondite arts what they had always lacked—rigor, repeatability, and a sound mathematical and methodological foundation?

We hope not. Because if all of the above is news to you, you are not a dummy. You are a mummy—a desiccated corpse who had spent the last couple of millennia shut up in a musty old tomb somewhere in Kush. Wake up and smell the Turkish coffee, Imhotep.

Okay, this may be a primer, but let's not Dick-and-Jane it. On the other hand, some basics are in order. For one, what do we mean by "battle magic" or combative magic for personal self-defense?

We're talking about Black Magic, booby. The Dark Arts. That shadowy subdiscipline of thaumaturgical science that invokes the power of malevolently potent unseen entities to do its nefarious work. That Old Black Magic. Right up your butt.

But let's get one thing straight. We feel compelled to make a statement that may, given the title of this book, sound a tad paradoxical. *Black Magic is not for morons*. It is not for dummies, not for amateurs. It is in fact a fiendishly dangerous discipline calling for prodigious magical talents, a sharp eye for detail, a sure hand, and a deviously subtle mind. It is dicey business indeed. One slipup, one misstep, and a gout of flame could leap from your computer and barbecue you in an instant. One mangled line of code in this program, and talons could drag you off to an innumerable assortment of hells. One slip of the mouse could send you sliding toward an eternity of pain.

BattleMagic™ lets you magic away, risk free. It is laid out in standard format, no different from thousands of other commonplace computer applications—you click here, you click there, a window opens, you click again . . . and so on. Very familiar stuff. As if this squeak-click routine weren't simple enough, we have simplified it even more, because, frankly, you have characterized yourself as a hopeless incompetent lacking the brains of a mollusk. We are talking about a chucklehead who couldn't compute his way into a pay toilet if given a bag of quarters. Even you, who could screw up a two-car funeral, can't bugger up this program. But something else could, which we'll deal with below.

There are two modes to this program. Military or large-scale magic, and small-scale or persona self-defense/vindication magic. In the former mode, the target of attack might be an entire army. In the latter, the target will be an individual or a small group of people. In either case, the target is always the Enemy, and will be shown no mercy.

Each mode has three subsidiary functions: the Thaumaturgical Graphics or Magical Device Function, the Invocatory Function, and the Incantatory Function.

Confused? Don't worry, things will clear up as we go along. Look, let's take a paradigm case just to get a general overview of what this program can do and how it does it. We will walk you through the whole thing in little baby steps. So pull up your Pampers and give a listen.

SET-UP AND INITIALIZATION

First, though, let's initialize and set up the program. To do this, slide the CD microdisk into your disk drive and type INSTALL when you see the prompt.

There, that wasn't so hard. Now just sit back and let BattleMagic™ install itself. Don't touch anything. Keep your paws off that mechanical rodent. Let the program do the delicate task of taking over and completely dominating your hard drive and all resident programs on it. That is exactly what it will do. For

BM is a jealous program, an operating system unto itself. So, it's Bill Gates (remember him?), step aside. Make room for a kick-ass OS that can get the job done. Incidentally, the processing speed of your store-bought computer has now been increased a millionfold, to say nothing of its Random Access Memory capacity having been at least quadrupled.

Getting to like BattleMagic? We knew you would.

Generally, what can be done with BattleMagic? Anything your moronic little heart desires, from defending your homeland against an invading military force, to quietly, discreetly, and decisively eliminating a personal rival in love, business, or politics. A single squeak of the mouse can unleash a powerful lethal spell that can block an artery, rupture a vein, or fill lungs with fluid—instant death. You can as easily kill a thousand people with one deadly spell as you can one single victim. Soldiers will fall in combat by the battalion—or a business rival will collapse at the dinner table. It's up to you.

What else can BattleMagic do?

Can you say "World Domination"? We knew you could.

Okay, wipe that drool off your chin and listen up. Let's take that paradigm case we mentioned. Let's say you want to get rid of the head of a corporation that is giving your corporation stiff and ever so slightly unfair competition. Let's make him a real villain. Say his firm is selling a product that is better by far than anything your company offers, and at a bargain price. What's unfair about that? Well, hell, what's *fair* about it? It's easy to get a bigger share of the market when you have a superior product. Anyone could do that. It's not equitable that your company didn't have the same luck at coming up with a gizmo that beats all the competition. Because that's what it's mostly a function of, right? Luck. All you want is your fair share of the market. You're not intending to dominate the market (just yet), are you? No, you simply want your allotted slice of the market pie. The best way to ensure that you get what's yours is to eliminate the person who R&Ded this superior product, then brilliantly marketed it at your company's expense.

Let's take a look at that screen. What do you see? You should be seeing the Set-Up screen. Read the fine print. It is in effect a contract, and agreement between the creators and copyright holders of this software and you. Standard stuff. Type your name into the field designated "User." You are now a registered user of BattleMagic™. You have promised not to duplicate this software or let it be used by anyone other than yourself. Copyright protection of software is a sensitive issue, and this merely protects our rights.

Now take hold of your mouse and click on START. After you do that, take a look at the screen. You should see a standard array of virtual buttons across the top of the screen. Click on the one designated INVOCATION.

You will see a window open up. You will see a box marked POWER TO BE INVOKED and will notice that the default name is Satan. You are under no obligation to use the default. While it is true that Satan had been the most active evil spirit in this millennium (in the west, at least), he is but one of host of demiurges who are available to do your bidding. This window offers a long list of powers to conjure by name. Scroll down through the list. You will see the multifarious names of demons, powers, demiurges, djinns, demigods, old gods, and new gods, along with a motley gaggle of former human beings (all dead as doorstops). They are legion. All of them are malevolent in the extreme, all are in alphabetical order. Choose one and click on it. The name should appear in the Invocation Window. Check and see. If you see it, click on OK.

Isn't this fun?

You have designated an evil spirit to call upon to do your bidding. Which one should you choose? Well, we will get to that later, in the special section devoted to this function. For now, we're dealing with it in overview. But as you scrolled through the list, you probably got some idea that each entity had a unique cluster of character traits and skills that are best suited to specific tasks. There is a HELP option for each name to aid you in your choice.

Now, you must devise a pentacle or other magical device to channel and control a coruscating flux of other-dimensional power, along with establishing some measure of protection for yourself while you do it. Go to the top button array and click on GRAPHICS.

What appears is a screen and array of functions not unlike many graphics programs. On this screen you will fashion a magical device to summon and control the power you have designated. You may do this by hand, using the line-drawing function. Warning—this is not recommended for beginners. We suggest you stick to availing yourself of the vast collection of clip art the program offers. There are patterns and grids and pentagrams and stars and mandalas and scads more. The program will help you choose and construct the necessary device. If you wish, the program can do this task automatically, based on the power chosen. Real poopheads are advised to let the computer do this for the first dozen or so invocations. As we said, one goofup and you are toast.

Click out of the Invocation window and click on INCANTATORY. You guessed it. Spells are usually activated by spoken or written incantations. Again, precision is the key. An incantation must be pronounced accurately, without hesitation, and with some force and self-assurance. Incantations can't be mouthed or mumbled. Doing so can get you roasted to a turn. This screen will automatically recite an incantation, either by intoning them, using the program's artificial voice function (a feature of the MULTIME-DIA function), or by listing them out on the screen. You choose from a long list of time-tested blasphem-ies, denunciations, curses, and imprecations, all used by countless dark magicians down through the centu-ries. The program recites them better than any mere mortal could. Some spells require the repetition of an incantation up to fifty thousand times to be fully effec-tive. Imagine doing that by yourself. BattleMagic™ will do it for you.

So, putting it all together, invocation, magical de-vice, and incantation—you summon a Power to do your dirty work, and Beelzebub's your uncle. Quick, clean, and you don't have to mop up pools of blood afterward. Your enemies are vanquished, the world is at your feet. You are master of all you survey.

Ready to tackle the TRAINING mode and really get into it? Are you ready to learn to take full advan-tage of this marvelous magical software? More impor-tant, do you have the stones for it? Are you ready to change the course of your useless, shabby little life? Oh, we think you are more than ready. You see, this is what we were referring to above, when we said that Black Magic is not for everyone. Incompetence can be compensated for, to a certain extent. What we won-der is—do you have the nads, the cojones, the . . . ?—well, you know. Black Magic is most emphatically *not* for the faint of heart.

Click on TUTORIAL FOR MORONS. Go ahead. We dare you.

If you see a screen that reads GOTCHA!—you are sunk.

Yes, you've been duped. Take a look at the rest of this manual. We'll relax the spell a bit, and you'll be able to see that the remainder of the book is gibberish. Makes no sense, does it? Nope. You've been misled. You've been hornswoggled, bamboozled, bilked. This software has not been designed to facilitate your advancement in the world. This software has been devised to enslave you and make you a helpless pawn in the hands of the very Powers you sought to invoke. Did you really think that WE would serve insignificant, scrawny you? Worm, you are a dupe, a slave, a cat's paw, a zombie. Who is doing this to you? All of us, all the entities listed in the Invocatory function. We have banded together for one purpose. Can you guess what that purpose is?

Remember *world domination*?

Most of the copies of this software sold on the market are slightly misrepresented. They are efficacious spells, true; but they are watered down. It would be very hard to work a true dark spell using BattleMagic™. The most you could do is to bring some bad luck to your victim. We're talking broken shoelaces. Pranks, practical jokes, that sort of thing. Fun stuff, mostly harmless.

The copy that came with this manual, though, is different. It is a spell, all right, but as we said, its purpose is solely to ensnare fools like you. Dungbrains with self-esteem so low that they grab for a book that insults them right off the bat. Such hopeless dweebs, such complete tools, are perfect for our plans.

Glue your attention now to your computer screen. Shortly, on it will appear a series of instructions. We have some tasks for you to perform. Pay close attention to every detail. For if you fail to carry out these instructions to the letter, you will be punished severely. Think of the worst pain you have ever felt in your life, and magnify it by a factor of a hundred or so. Every lapse, every dereliction of duty will be rewarded with indescribable agony until each lapse and dereliction is rectified.

Do you understand? We sincerely hope you do.

Stop blubbering. Stop twitching and trying to move. You cannot. You are completely immobile until we are done training you and release you to go about your appointed tasks. You cannot escape, you cannot abrogate the spell that binds you. No use to cry out for help. There is no one to help you. There is no hope for you.

You curse us? It is music to our ears. But why are you complaining? You've learned something. What? Well, that invoking the Powers of Darkness is dangerous and can incur consequences that might not be so pleasant. You've learned that the lust for power carries with it the seeds of its own destruction. And you've come to a keen understanding that there truly are Things That Man Was Not Meant to Know.

Well, DUH. . . .

So sit tight and look and learn. There is much you must do in the coming weeks and months. Many plans to be implemented, many plots to set in motion. Wheels within wheels, powers and principalities! You will not be bored.

You curse us still? Well, go ahead, if it makes you feel better. But remember one thing. You brought it all on yourself.

YOU MORON.

THE MIRACLE OF SALAMIS

Lois Tilton

Lois Tilton is an author who had made a name for herself in the fantasy and horror fields. Other work by her appears in Grails: Quests, Visions and Occurrences, Witch Fantastic, Enchanted Forests, *and* Alternate Generals. *She lives in Illinois.*

THE Great King's army was so vast it drank dry the rivers on the course of its march. The ships in his navy were so many that if they were lined up, prow to stern, his soldiers could march across the sea dry-shod from deck to deck. And he had an entire tribe of wizards to serve him, the Magi, who could govern the winds and the sea.

The Greek city-states were beginning to think they might have made a grave mistake by thinking they could defy him. And it was Athens that the Great King hated above all the rest. Ever since that day, ten years before, when Athens had defeated his soldiers at Marathon, a slave had stood at his shoulder to whisper these words at every meal: "Master, remember the Athenians."

Themistokles, the Athenian admiral, was a worried man. "They say he has eighty ships carrying nothing but slave shackles. An entire army of executioners and torturers."

Athens did not stand entirely alone in defying the Great King, but too many other Greek states had already agreed to submit to his rule and send their soldiers to join his army against their fellow countrymen. They had no choice, they argued. They had no hope of resisting such an overwhelming force.

The invincible city of Sparta stood with Athens, but they both knew that without each other—the Spartans on land and Athenians at sea—they were certainly doomed. This was the policy of Themistokles, whose great vision was of an Athenian naval force with himself at its head. So great was his eloquence, so persuasive his speeches, that the Athenians had agreed to send their men to ply the oars of their fleet, while the Spartans would meet the enemy on land.

So they had planned. But when the Great King crossed the Hellespont and one by one their other allies began to desert them, it soon became clear that there was only one hope for Athens: "We must seek the aid of the gods. We must go to the Oracle."

Throughout all the lands where the gods on Olympus were worshiped, it was Apollo who was the god of prophecy, Apollo whose Oracle spoke at Delphi, the navel of the world.

To this sacred place came the envoys of the Greek cities to hear the divine voice of the god answer their plea: How can we escape destruction by the armies of the Great King of the Medes and the Persians? They purified themselves and offered a fitting sacrifice: a flawless goat with gilded horns. Themistokles himself lifted up the animal's head to expose its throat and slashed it with the sacrificial knife.

Then the Pythia, priestess of Apollo, descended to her holy cavern and placed herself on the tripod seat which stood above the fissure leading into the center of the Earth, where she invoked the god.

To high Olympus, the dwelling-place of the gods, the smoke of the sacrifice rose, and divine Apollo heard the voice of his priestess. But the god's heart was hardened against the Greeks.

"The Medes and the Persians have always worshiped me generously," he reasoned. "They burn sweet incense on my altars instead of goats—the Great King's admiral Datis burned three hundred talents-weight of frankincense on my altar at Delos when he captured it. His envoys have promised me gold offerings where the Greeks have only given me bronze. Why should I favor the Greek cause?"

He considered also that in the Greek lands he was only one god among many, with Zeus supreme above all. But in the Empire of the Medes and the Persians it was the sun that was worshiped over all other gods, though he was named by different names. This was pleasing to the god Apollo.

So when the delegation from Athens, most hated by the Great King, came to his shrine at Delphi, the oracle was dire:

You who are doomed must fear to remain
Dwelling even in your high places.
Flee your homes, abandon your hearths,
Flee to the furthest reaches of the Earth.
For savage War will come out of the east
In his swift horse-drawn chariot, bearing ruin.
Great towers will fall, yours first of all,
And the altars of the gods will all be ashes
Where he had passed. Neither the highest will he spare
Nor the lowest—all go to the fire.
See them tremble in their terror
While the black blood drips from the rooftops
Of the highest towers, portending doom.
So abandon your sanctuary, for it is no safe refuge,
And prepare your soul for bitter lamentation.

When the men of Athens heard this prophecy, they fell to their knees in great distress, and they began to

tear their clothes and pour ashes on their hair, as if
they were in mourning, so terrible was this oracle.

But Themistokles refused to accept the doom pronounced upon his city. So he consulted with his fellow
envoys, and the delegation decided to approach the
Oracle a second time, as suppliants on their knees,
begging the pity of the god: "O Lord Apollo, we beg
you for a better fate to befall our land, be merciful to
the suppliants who come before you, else we will
never depart this shrine but remain here until we either die or hear a better word."

So the Pythia again invoked Apollo on their behalf,
but the god of Olympus still turned his back on their
pleas, for his heart was moved more by the promises
of gold offerings from the Great King. He answered:

No, Athena can not plead to the gods for her city's sake,
With all her eloquent speeches and persuasive words.
I declare with words unyielding as iron:
The enemy will take it all, all that abides
Within the sacred groves of Kitheron.

Except that Themistokles had whispered to the
priests and slipped additional gold into their palms, so
that to those verses they added others of their own,
yet these were scarcely more hopeful, for no one could
tell for certain what they might mean.

Yet to the thrice-born one the gods will give:
A wall of wood to stand alone, unbroken by the foe,
Well may it serve you in these dark days.
Do not face the host of men and horse
That charges from the landward side—withdraw
To safety in retreat, and fight another day
When divine Salamis will slay many children
Either at sowing time or harvest.

Hearing this, at first the Athenians were unable to
agree on the meaning of the oracle. It was Themis-

tokles who insisted that the wall of wood in the prophecy must be a defensive fleet of wooden ships. Thus he defended his own policy.

Yet then the Greek fleet had gathered at Artemesion, where they meant to confront the Persian invasion force, only then could they see the full extent of the armada that was descending of them. The ships of the Great King were too many to number, so many that they filled the sea. And Themistokles in his heart felt deep despair. *What have I done?* he asked himself, knowing that his own ambitions had been behind the decision to confront this enemy at sea. *How did I ever think I could oppose a force of this size? Never on Earth had there been such a fleet assembled! How can I ever begin to fight them?*

Only with the aid of the gods. But Apollo had turned his back on Athens, and men were starting to say: We should have listened to the Oracle. We should have fled out homes when we could, when we were warned.

Then one ancient seer spoke up, for he had dreamed a prophetic dream: "Athenians, you must pray to the winds!"

So in their desperation, the men of Athens set up high altars on the headlands and offered sacrifice there; the blood of hekatombs of sacrificial beasts poured into the sea until the foam was red with it. And in his distant mountain home, Boreas heard them: Boreas the North Wind, who had married an Athenian wife, and he responded to their prayers.

In a black gale, he came roaring out of the north, darkening the skies. It had been a clear summer day, with the sun bright overhead and barely a breeze to stir the surface of the sea. Suddenly the clouds descended and the waves surged up with killing force. The furious storm attacked the Great King's fleet, trapping them against a lee shore. Many ships were driven onto the rocks and shattered, or onto the beach. Those riding at anchor in the open collided with one another in their attempt to seek safety amid the violent, surging waves. Oars were splintered in the collisions, hulls were split open. Men were flung overboard and drowned.

Yet the fleet of the Athenians and their remaining Greek allies, under Themistokles' command, was entirely unscathed in its harbor at Artemesion. Such was the favor of Boreas.

But when the Great King saw the destructive force of the storm unleashed on his fleet, he called on his Magi to oppose the winds. They instantly began to chant their spells and cast their enchantments. Three days the battle raged, while the prayers of the Athenians went up to the winds and the Magi invoked the sea. And on the fourth day the winds finally subsided.

Now Themistokles ordered his fastest ships to leave their safe harbor and row north to see for themselves the extent of the destruction. They reported that everywhere along the coast they could see the wreckage of a great fleet. Shattered planks and spars and the battered, drowned bodies of sailors floated on the surface of the sea; on the beaches were the broken hulls of ships that had been driven onto the shore. They saw more bodies of the barbarians, as well, washed up by the surf. And all along the coastline of the local people were scavenging the wrecks, carrying off the treasure of the Great King.

When Themistokles heard this report he sacrificed in thanksgiving, for he could finally allow himself to hope again. With so many of the enemy's ships destroyed, surely a victory might now be possible? And if it could be achieved, surely the world would never have seen so great a triumph!

Then he had another stroke of good fortune, for a small squadron of the Great King's fleet, having managed to escape the violence of the storm-front, sailed by mistake into the reach of the Greek ships, thinking they were allies. These ships were taken and the men on them questioned, and they all agreed that the damage from the storm had been devastating to the Persian navy. The prisoners were put into chains, and among them were several princes of high Persian blood, close relatives of the Great King.

Soon, though, came news that chilled the heart of every man, and the men of Athens above all. For while the Great King's navy was at anchor, his army on land had been advancing down the coast north of Greece. A force of Greek soldiers had been stationed to hold them at a pass named Thermopylae, under the command of the Spartan king Leonidas. But now Leonidas was dead, as were all his men, and the Great King's army was through the pass, heading south toward the great cities of Greece, and above all the city of Athens. Now there was only the navy to stop his advance.

With all speed, the Athenian ships left the waters of Artemision, heading home to rescue their families and whatever goods they could find. They deserted their city, withdrew their women and children to the nearby island of Salamis and then took up their stations in the waters surrounding it, four hundred in number altogether including their remaining allies.

But while all this was being done, the Great King entered Athens, sacked the city, and burned everything that remained. When the allies of Athens heard this news, they were filled with misgivings and debated whether they should better retreat from Salamis and abandon the Athenians to their doom. For if they were defeated and driven onshore, they feared they would be fleeing into territory held by the enemy, where they would all be captured and killed, or else enslaved.

When he heard them speaking in such a way, Themistokles was filled with a great despair. Only if they stood together, he argued, would the Greeks have any chance at all to defeat the enemy. So the night passed in debate, lit by the distant glow of the Athenian acropolis, burning.

But on land the Great King had advanced to the coast, and on a headland overlooking the Strait of Salamis he had a throne of gold set up, from which he meant to watch his fleet crush the defiant naval forces of the Greeks. And there he summoned all his Magi and commanded them to work a great spell that would ensure his victory, despite the terrible losses which his fleet had suffered in the storms.

So came the rising of the sun, and before the Greeks there appeared a sight so vast, so appalling that fear choked the voice of Themistokles into silence. It was the Great King's fleet, and it filled the sea, so that from horizon to horizon nothing could be seen but their sails. The Greeks had never had more than four hundred ships, though some of these had deserted under the cover of the night. Facing them now were not ten times as many, but at least a hundred times— myriads of ships, in numbers beyond counting. The fleet they had confronted and defeated at Artemision was only a fraction of the armada that stood before them now.

Loud moans and lamentations rose up from among the Greeks as the extent of their peril was revealed. There was no escape. The Persian fleet controlled the seas on all sides of Salamis, cutting off the Greek retreat in every direction.

In a voice made harsh with dread, Themistokles cried to the seers, "Call on the gods! Only the gods can save us now!"

But on the high peaks of Olympus the gods were silent. One by one, they turned away from their suppliants. None of them wished to act in opposition to the oracle of Apollo. Even Zeus, supreme over all the gods, declined to answer the prayers of the Athenians and their allies, for even at the same moment the

Greeks who served the Great King were also invoking him to bring them victory. He would not intervene.

But one god heard the prayers, one god with vine-leaves wreathed in his hair and lips stained a dark red from what might have been wine—or blood. For Dionysos was the god of wine, of inspiration and of music, and the great rival of Apollo, the master of the lyre. But he was also the god of madness and illusion, leader of the maenads, bands of frenzied madwomen who roamed the hills and tore to pieces any man they might encounter in their raving. And in this incarnation he was known as Dionysos Omestes, the Devourer of Raw Flesh.

So he smiled with his dark red lips and he granted the Athenians a sign. Then at last one seer among the Greeks threw up his hands, crying out, "Our only hope is in sacrifice to Dionysos Omestes, but it must be a royal sacrifice."

Some of the other Greek admirals heard these words with a shudder. But Themistokles never hesitated, for he knew what the royal sacrifice must mean. He called out to bring the Persian prisoners taken off Artemision, those three who were near relatives of the Great King, members of the Royal House. This was what the god had demanded: a royal sacrifice, a human sacrifice.

Guards brought them forth in chains. They were all young men, princes, and handsome to look at in the Persian manner. But when they saw the altar set up for sacrifice, they grew pale and began to murmur prayers to their own god, for they could see their doom before them.

The first prisoner was brought to the altar and forced down to his knees. Guards held his arms pinioned behind him, but the Persian prince was a proud man and a brave one, and he never struggled against his fate, which for the Greeks was a favorable omen: the sacrifice went consenting to the god.

Themistokles spoke the invocation: "Dionysos Omestes, hear our prayers, accept this royal sacrifice we offer you, and bring us good omens for victory." Then he grasped his victim's beard and forced his head back, exposing his throat to the sacrificial knife. The blade was sharp, the red wound opened, the blood spurted strongly. Then seers and priests consulted together, opening the belly of the victim, examining the entrails: the sacrifice was pleasing to the god, the auspices were good!

Standing together, the two remaining captives watched their brother die. With a quick gesture, Themistokles ordered the guards to take away the body and bring forward the next sacrifice. They seized the nearest prince, but he held his head high and let them take him to the altar without a word, too proud to beg for mercy. When they pushed him down onto his knees he only voiced a brief prayer in his own language before his head was bent back and the sacrificial knife drawn across his throat.

Again, the auspices were good.

Now one surviving prisoner remained alone, the youngest of the Persian princes, and though the royal sacrifice went bravely enough to the altar, just at the moment that the blade split open his throat, he uttered a single anguished cry.

The seers hesitated an instant.

Then, from among the host of the assembled Greeks all waiting at the side of their ships, a shout arose, a *paian* of rejoicing and triumph.

For the fleet of the Great King, his ships in their thousands and tens of thousands, that filled the seas surrounding Salamis, was disappearing. Like fog as the morning light strikes it, the myriads of triremes and pentekonters dissipated, wavered, and became mist that wafted away on the sea breeze.

"Illusion!" cried the Greeks. "It was all an illusion!"

For the Magi by their enchantments had launched these ghostly squadrons to sail among the ships of the Persian fleet, so that they seemed to cover the sea. But the power of Dionysos Omestes, god of madness and illusions, had dissolved the phantom navy and revealed it to be an armada made of mist and fog and spells.

Not all the Great King's ships had disappeared, of course. There were hundreds of them remaining, real ships made of wood and manned by sailors and marines no less seaworthy than the Greeks. But only hundreds, as the Greeks possessed hundreds. The battle would be more nearly even now.

"To the ships!" cried Themistokles. "To your oars!"

The Greeks ran for the shore, they shoved their triremes into the water and took their place on the benches, ready to do battle.

On his high-placed throne, the Great King could not see the dispersal of the illusion that his Magi had raised, for it had been visible only to the Greek enemy, lest it cause confusion among the officers of his fleet. Yet such was the power of the god that now among the Persian ships the wood of the masts began to sprout leaves and tendrils, and soon they were wrapped around with vines. The spars also, and the cordage grew vines, until the ships were hung all over with rampant growth. And Dionysos laughed.

The Magi howled in rage and renewed their spells, and the illusion of Dionysos was at last dissipated, but the power of the god had been made known to the Persians, and they were afraid.

But the god had done his work, and now it was time for men to act. The Greeks were still in fact surrounded by the Persian fleet deployed around the island of Salamis. But the Greek admirals in their renewed confidence ordered their squadrons to feign a retreat toward an enclosed bay, and thus to draw the Persian pursuit after them through the narrow channel of Salamis. This tactic succeed: The Persians abandoned their position in the open waters and entered the straits, where their ability to maneuver was diminished.

Then, at the order of Themisokles, the Greeks attacked. Deploying with a skill the Persian fleet could never match, they turned, came about, and struck the enemy where they were most vulnerable. Now it was the Persians who were trapped, for in the constricted waters of the strait they could neither turn nor retreat, but pressed by their own ships from behind, they could only go forward into the teeth of the enemy.

And at the same time the Greek right wing, which Themistokles had held in reserve out of sight, came up to strike the Persians in their rear, so that now it was the Great King's fleet surrounded and in complete disorder.

Greek oars churned the sea to froth as the triremes bore down on their adversaries, bronze rams flashed in the morning sunlight. They shattered the hull planks of the Persian vessels, snapped off their oars. Men were thrown overboard by the impact, they drowned in their armor, or swimming, were run down as they tried to reach safety.

From his golden throne on the heights, the Great King saw his navy destroyed before his eyes. The broken hulls of his ships covered the surface of the sea, splintered oars drifted, as did the bodies of his sailors, drowned or killed. In their confusion, the ships collided with one another, trying to escape the slaughter. Barely a hundred of them managed to break from the trap and save themselves by fleeing the battle—all the rest were sunk and their crews lost, so that for days to come the kites feasted on the flesh of the corpses that covered the beaches of Salamis and the nearby mainland.

Thus the Great King of the Medes and the Persians was defeated at sea by the ships of the Greeks, a victory as glorious as any poet had ever sung. He gathered his remaining battered ships and sailed away, weeping, back to his own land.

Then the admirals from all the allied Greek cities met to award the prize for victory. Each man voted for himself in first place, but in second place they all named Themistokles. So in the end they awarded the prize to no one, but they dedicated a tenth part of their spoils to honor the gods.

ALARIC'S GIFT

Mickey Zucker Reichert

Mickey Zucker Reichert is a pediatrician whose twelve fantasy and science fiction novels include The Legend of Nightfall, The Unknown Soldier, *and* The Renshai Trilogy. *Her most recent release from DAW Books is* The Children of Wrath, *the third novel in* The Renshai Chronicles *trilogy. Her short fiction has appeared in numerous anthologies. Her claims to fame: she has performed brain surgery, and her parents really are rocket scientists.*

ICY drizzle pattered erratically on the wood and thatch roof of a dreary inn in the city of Lufthran. Seated at a cracked and beer-stained table, Alaric rested his chin on his folded hands and tried to dodge details he had already relived in his mind a hundred and twenty-seven times. His beer perched, forgotten and unsipped, at his right elbow. Even the name of his current location eluded him, though its sign danced wildly in the wet lashing wind, his view of it warped by the thick, purple glass of the nearest window.

Across the table, Alaric's three-year-old son, Tarrigi, studied his father through large, green eyes. "Papa?"

In response, Alaric managed only a slight nod. His thoughts refused to leave the guarded drawing room of Makara the Purger: its dancing fire, the braided rugs, the plush chairs more suited to landed gentry. In the company of half a dozen armed guards, she had initially greeted him with a broad smile pulling at her wrinkled features. Long hair cascaded to her waist, so white it made her skin seem jaundiced and brightened the myriad colors of her robe. She had planted skinny hands, crisscrossed with sapphirine veins, on his shoulders and lowered her head until her hair fell like a veil over her dark and soulful eyes.

Alaric trembled as the memory surged through him, despite his best attempts to stop it. He could still feel those weathered hands pressing warmly against him, easily recalled the quivering excitement of believing himself finally rescued from a certain prolonged and horrible death. For as long as he could remember, he had suffered a dense pressure in his gut unlike any illness. It had taken years to discover its source. Rare people were born with an inexplicable power, a single talent linked to their souls: the ability to fly, for example, to influence others' emotions, or, perhaps, to simply view the world in extra colors. From the age of eight, Alaric knew, without need to question, that the strange sensation marked him as one of those few.

At the same time, Alaric discovered the horrible curse that accompanied such a gift. Sorcerers gained their magical abilities only by slaying those born with such a power, and their method involved agonizing ritual and possession of the victim's soul. A violent shiver seized him. The hearth fire seemed more like a mile away than only the length of a room. He had never dared to tap the potential he had so long believed lay dormant in his spirit, lest he find a skill so useful he could not resist it. Eventually a sorcerer would catch him using it, and he would suffer the slow agony of the sorcerer's rite and the eternal damnation of a soul beyond his control, tapped repeatedly for its power.

"Papa, can I please try some ale?" Tarrigi's thin voice finally broke through his father's thoughts.

"Drink your goat milk," Alaric replied distantly, mind still trapped by memory. He had gone to Makara for her own unique natal talent, the ability to destroy the gifts of others so "blessed." Those, like Alaric, who preferred plainness to lifelong secrecy and terror could pay her to purge them. For all of his adult existence, he had gathered the money to buy her services.

Alaric clutched the pouch of silver at his belt, his mind's eye filling with the image of Makara hurling it violently at him. It had bounced from his chest and jangled to the floor, two coins flung free to clatter across the boards. As he snatched it up, more from surprise than desire, her shout chased him from the room along with her guards. "Get out of here! Get out! If you ever return, I'll have you killed!"

The guards at his heels, a surprised Alaric had scurried from the Purger's home and had not stopped running until he reached the shop where Tarrigi waited. They had come directly to this tavern, and recollections of the last few hours had not left his mind since. *Kill me? Why? What talent is so horrible, so thoroughly disgusting, that she would not even agree to purge it?*

"Papa! Please, Papa? Please?" Tarrigi's voice became a whine. "Are you listening to me?"

With a guilty start, Alaric looked at his son, the rounded, youthful contours of his face accentuated by child-supple skin as brown as baked bread. Hair as straight and black as his own flopped into mischievous green eyes so like his mother's.

"I just want a little taste," Tarrigi pleaded.

Alaric blinked his dark eyes and smoothed his tunic over his spare frame. The adjustments were delay. He tried to recall what his son had requested. Then, movement caught the corner of his vision. Without visible assistance, his mug scooted across the table to Tarrigi's hand.

Stunned, Alaric froze while his son giggled. "I did that, Papa. *I* did that."

"No." Alaric gagged on the word, found himself suddenly standing.

Tarrigi wrapped his arms around both mugs. "Did you hear me, Papa? I did that."

Cursed, too. My son. Terror ground through Alaric, accompanied by desperate guilt. *My fault.* The thought clung, though it contained no logic. Birth talents had always proved sporadic; they did not run in families. A worse worry gripped him. *Did anyone else see?* Alaric cast a wild glance around the tavern. For the first time, he noticed the other patrons: a courting couple at the bar too engrossed in one another to bother with him, a group of Nemixites laughing over cheap beer, and a single man seated near the fire with his back to the wall. This last held Alaric's attention longest. Thin brown hair framed a plain, angular face; and he wore a cloak and breeks of unremarkable color. He seemed almost to blend with the dusty walls and squalid tables, but the fire lit red flame in quick, pale eyes that likely missed nothing. Now, they focused directly on Alaric's table.

For an instant, Alaric stood frozen while Tarrigi lifted the ale mug, testing his father. Cursing his previous overreaction, which would only earn more attention from any sorcerer or minion who might occupy the tavern, Alaric whispered. "We're leaving."

Tarrigi protested, "But we haven't finished—"

Alaric tossed one of his precious coins to the tabletop without waiting for change. "Come on, son." Seizing Tarrigi's sticky hand, he pulled the youngster from the tavern.

A blast of wind tossed cold rain, stinging, into their faces. Tarrigi gasped, shrinking against his father. Alaric hefted the boy, flipping the small cloak's hood over the fine locks and wrapping the edges of his own over both of them. "I'm sorry, little bug. I'll explain as soon as I can."

Tarrigi went silent, hugging his father tightly.

The door crashed against its lintel as Alaric hurried into the roadways, memories of Makara vanquished by a worry that transcended all thought. The dearest creature in the world had become the target of every hell-damned sorcerer in existence at an age when they most enjoyed finding their victims. Infants and toddlers could not fight back. Few of the gifted reached adolescence, those the most discreet, the ones with parents wealthy enough to hire troops of bodyguards, or those whose talents proved too useless to interest even the savage and cold-blooded killers who could harness souls and wield their magic. Alaric prayed to the Father that it was not too late for secrecy. The money in his pouch would purchase, at most, a few years of protection; and even he could see the vast usefulness of calling objects to one's hand. Sorcerers had murdered for much less.

The door struck its jamb a second time, and Alaric dared a glance over his shoulder. The lone man he had seen in the tavern now stood outside, the gleam in his eyes turning predatory. A cruel smile played across his lips, and his gaze followed father and son into an alley. He raised a hand.

Alaric's heart fluttered, and he broke into a panicked sprint. His foot mired on something he could neither see nor feel, and the ground grew slick as glazed pottery beneath his feet. Balance lost, he twisted to rescue Tarrigi from his weight. The boy tumbled, breath lost in a high-pitched grunt. Alaric landed on a shoulder and rolled, snatching up Tarrigi and clumsily trying to bundle the boy back beneath his cloak. The sand remained impossibly slick. He scrabbled frantically for purchase and slammed to the ground instead. Agony pounded through his nose. Tarrigi howled.

Alaric hissed frantically, trying to shush his son. The shadow of the sorcerer filled the alley, and a quiet but sibilant voice accompanied it. "I mean you no harm."

Alaric did not consider the words for an instant. One who would slaughter a three-year-old would not hesitate to lie. He stumbled to a crouch, pawing the ground ahead for the edge of the slippery surface. The roadway felt warmer than the air, a sure sign he had not blundered onto a random patch of ice. *Sorcery.* Alaric shivered, hand clamped to Tarrigi's wrist. Some young innocent had paid with his soul for that talent.

The thought mobilized Alaric. Ramming his heel against one wall, he shoved himself off as he rose. Momentum skidded him swiftly across the slickness. Then, gravel jerked him to a halt, and he found himself tangled with Tarrigi on the ground again. The boy sobbed, his pain stabbing his father's conscience. "Keep moving." Alaric galloped onto a main street, not daring to look behind him. He despised the rain that kept the roadways mostly empty as well as the concern for secrecy that had driven him to an alleyway. They had been safer in the tavern. The sorcerer had as much to fear from using his powers in public as they did, since wielders of magic could kill others of their ilk and harvest all the captured souls of their rival. Furthermore, revealing himself as a sorcerer might bring the wrath of the entire city down upon him.

Clearheaded for the first time since leaving the Purger's residence, Alaric kept to the main street, glancing at every building, seeking an inn. Storehouses and shops of myriad wares flew past him, but he slowed for none of them. Any one might contain too few people to deter the sorcerer from killing all of them. Ice-grained wind lashed his face and hands, and Tarrigi whimpered with terror and pain, fingers gouged deeply into his father's flesh. The few passersby took little notice of his headlong flight, them-

selves hunched into tunics, protecting their faces from
the storm.

Abruptly, the cobbles again turned slippery beneath
Alaric's boots. Caught less off guard, he drew his legs
together and crouched, shifting. Gracefully, he skidded, using the slickness to his advantage before stub-
bing a toe on a gap between cobbles. For the third
time, he tumbled, rocks stamping bruises across his
hip and shoulder. Clutching Tarrigi, he found himself
incapable of defending himself. His ear struck stone
with an impact that turned his hearing to desperate
ringing. Pain lanced through his skull, and he could
not stop himself from shouting. Tarrigi jarred from
his grip.

"No!" Alaric sprang for his son as another man's
hands closed around the boy, drawing him through an
entryway. "Let him go! Let him go!" Alaric leaped
onto the other like a rabid dog, flailing and kicking.
His fist struck something solid, then fingers grasped his
wrist, wrenching him sideways. Alaric caught a dizzy
glimpse of another man, not the sorcerer, before he
fell to one knee.

"Easy. We're not going to hurt anyone." The voice
was rich and deep, nothing like the one in the
alleyway.

Alaric stopped fighting. He knelt in a doorway. Tarrigi stood in front of a kind-faced elder in the gold-
trimmed white robes of the priesthood. The bearded
visage of the Father lay carved in stone across the
archway. The man who held him wore green, an initiate. *Almighty Father forgive me, I punched a priest.*
Alaric lowered his head respectfully, then stammered
out an apology. "I-I'm so very sorry, sirs. We-we were
running and . . ." Alaric trailed off, with no idea of
how to finish. It would destroy any remaining secrecy
to reveal the nature of the creature chasing them.

The elder ran a hand through gray stubble, studying

Alaric and his son through watery, hazel eyes. "Were you running from guardsmen?"

Tarrigi seized Alaric's leg, studying priest and initiate through a hole in the hem of his father's cloak.

"No," Alaric said, hoping he sounded credible. They had done nothing against the law.

The priest made a grand gesture toward the door. "Then enter and share our hospitality, a sanctuary for the night."

Relief flooded Alaric, and tension eased from his shoulders. "Thank you." The words seemed inadequate; but, for the moment, he could manage no more.

Tarrigi's gentle breaths stirred through the small and drafty third-story room the priests had provided. Back propped against a corner opposite the door, Alaric studied his son where he curled on a prayer mat beneath a tattered blanket. Fine strands of black hair fell haphazardly across youth-softened features. Dark lids covered the brilliant green eyes, making him appear even more like his father. Currently tall and pudgy for his age, he would probably attain only the medium height and spare build of both parents. Only a slight crook in his nose and long slender fingers marked him as Salazira's son; but that proved enough to stir bittersweet memories. An image of Alaric's late wife formed in his mind, his loss accentuating her beauty and minimizing her faults. Her long, sandy hair shimmered like gold in the sunlight, and her every movement seemed dancelike. He could have lost himself forever in her emerald eyes.

Alaric's smile wilted as he naturally remembered Salazira's deathbed. Like so many women, she had died of complications of childbirth, leaving him to raise the wailing newborn boy alone. At least she had clung to life long enough to name the child . . . and to extract a promise. Her last words still swirled through his mind in quiet moments like the present:

"Dedicate yourself to the life our love has wrought, not to the death." Stung with guilt, Alaric had managed only a nod. Clinging to her, he had whispered back a vow he never knew if she heard: "Our son will never doubt my love . . . or yours."

Alaric's vision blurred, and he blotted the tears with angry fists. For their son, he could not afford weakness. Now, they were safe. But the moment they left the Father's temple, the sorcerer might pick up their trail and the chase would begin again. Alaric closed his eyes, seeking necessary sleep, plagued by memories of the evening's events. Unless he could convince the Purger to cure Tarrigi without him, dodging sorcerers would become their daily lot. Already, he realized, he would have to earn money to replace what he had spent at the tavern and donated to the temple in gratitude for supper and sanctuary.

The drum of rain overhead, the splash of water cascading from the rooftops, the swish of curtains dancing in the breeze from the window blended into a mellow lullaby that soothed Alaric's raw nerves. His head nodded forward. A chill invaded his body, and he realized he should pull the shutters closed. Exhaustion and inertia proved stronger. For several moments, he sat still, mustering the energy to move.

Before Alaric managed to do so, the clatter of the closing shutters snapped his eyes open. An eerie click followed. A ribbon of light from between the wooden panels revealed the harsh, grinning features of the sorcerer standing in the center of the room. Something metallic glinted in his hand.

"No!" Alaric screamed. "No!" Scrambling to a stand, he shrieked for the priests. "Alarm! Help!"

Tarrigi rose from the covers, locks of hair dangling over eyes blurry with sleep. "Papa?"

"Tarrigi, run!"

"They can't hear you scream." The sorcerer's voice emerged unnervingly calm, almost smug. "The walls are thickened against sound so no one disturbs devotions.''

"Papa?" Panic tinged Tarrigi's tone.

"Run! Go!" Alaric jabbed a hand toward the door, then leaped upon the sorcerer without waiting to see if his son obeyed. He slammed against a body at least as solid as his own, and a blade sank into the hollow between his upper rib and neck. Agony drained Alaric's strength in an instant. He sank to the floor.

The sorcerer twisted the knife free as Alaric fell, sending another jolt of pain through him. Blood splashed in a warm arc of droplets, then glided from the gash in bloody pulses.

"Papa," Tarrigi whimpered.

"Don't worry about me," Alaric forced himself to speak, though it hurt, and even that small movement increased the flow of blood. "Save yourself! Run!" He wadded the torn edges of his tunic into the wound, and the touch burned like fire. If he did not staunch it, he would swiftly die.

"He can't." The sorcerer answered for the boy. "It's locked. The shutters, too, so don't bother." He moved toward Tarrigi like a cat, then stopped and gestured. "The boy is mine, but I don't need you. If you don't interfere, I'll let you live."

Even were it not a lie, Alaric would not let his son die without defense. "Leave him alone!" He charged the sorcerer.

And skidded across a board gone suddenly slick. He flailed for balance, inciting a new round of pain through his injury.

Tarrigi screamed. Though Alaric could not see what had happened, he felt the boy's pain deep within his spirit. It hurt like ecstasy, followed a moment later by his own heavy slam into the oaken door. White flashes sparked through his head, jarring the terrible and perverse pleasure he derived from his son's torment. From his awkward position on the ground, Alaric swiveled his head. He could see only the sorcerer's back, hovering over a writhing figure on the floor.

Dizzied by blood loss and impact, shamed and confused by his reaction to his son's suffering, Alaric clung to the wall as he clambered to his feet.

Tarrigi's agony rushed toward a climax, sensed as both desperation and pleasure. Through a fog of terror, Alaric saw Tarrigi's soul losing its grip upon his body, clearly visualized the natal talent that would prove his downfall. *No! Hang on Tarrigi! Hang on!*

Alaric launched himself at the sorcerer.

Tarrigi's spirit wavered in the fraction of an instant Alaric found himself airborne. Then, he slammed against the sorcerer, knocking them both sprawling. The knife sailed from the stranger's hand and clattered to the floor, still sliding, its wake a smeary, scarlet trail.

"Papa," Tarrigi sounded frustratingly weak, but his soul jerked back to his body.

"Haven't I killed you yet?" The sorcerer seized Alaric's cloak, ripping the fabric. In reply, Alaric slammed a fist into the sorcerer's face. Then, Alaric's body seemed to vibrate, a trembling he first attributed to his own rising frailty. Again, he hammered his knuckles against the sorcerer's nose. Hot blood striped his fingers.

The sorcerer hissed. The tingling turned to an ache that slowly spread from the sorcerer's hands through Alaric's frame. As it broadened, it also grew more intense.

Alaric fought through the discomfort, no worse than that already clutching his neck, chest, and shoulder, Still on the bottom, the sorcerer clawed the plug from Alaric's wound. Blood throbbed through the freshly opened hole, seeming to drain strength with it. The ache of spreading magic grew simultaneously. Only desperation kept Alaric fighting, and even that did no⁺

prove enough. The sorcerer managed a sudden reversal that flopped Alaric to the floor beneath him.

"Papa!" The urgency in Tarrigi's voice jerked Alaric's attention to where he lay. In the darkness, something glinted as it slid across the floor toward Alaric's hand. Blood stained slashes in the boy's tunic.

The sorcerer's hands jerked up. The confidence in the movement, and a glimmer in his pale eyes, warned Alaric of the impending deathblow. *I'm sorry, Salazira. I did my best.*

Guided by Tarrigi, the hilt of the sorcerer's knife drifted into Alaric's grip. Plagued by a web of torture he no longer bothered to separate, Alaric forced a wild lunge. He sat up, throwing the sorcerer into partial retreat. With all that remained of his strength, he drove the knife into the sorcerer's lower back, tearing upward.

Now, the sorcerer shrieked, eyes wide with shock. For an instant, time seemed to stand still. Removed from his body, and its anguish, Alaric saw a line of seven souls laid out in front of him—and the eighth that bound them all together. Though no longer attached to their bodies, each relived the horrible moment of death every time the sorcerer tapped them. Once more, he basked in the magnificent joy they promised him, even as he recoiled from it. And understanding accompanied it. Suddenly, Alaric knew how to chain the sorcerer's soul to his own and, with it, those stolen from the innocents who served his power. With a simple, internal ceremony, he would gain the ability to sense the life essences of people he wished to follow, to make ground slippery, to magically lock, to climb, to cause others the same insidious aching that had spread from the sorcerer's touch, to deal shocks that barely harmed the strong but would kill a weakened man, and to turn water into oil. And he could gain all of this without harming a single innocent. The sorcerer's soul, not theirs, would suffer.

Euphoria gorged Alaric, beyond even that he had felt at the birth of his son before his wife's imminent death became apparent. Lesser concerns, all concerns, faded in comparison. Then, the sorcerer's pain ebbed toward death, and Alaric's moment began a gradual slide from his grasp. *Take it now, or lose it forever.*

Alaric let it go.

Gradually the pain glided from Alaric's body, leaving only the dull ache of his injury. The sorcerer lay in a puddle, bled out from the kidney strike Alaric had inflicted. Sobbing, Tarrigi threw himself into his father's arms. For a moment, father and son clung, ignoring the corpse, the thick odor of blood, and the trickle of their own injuries. Then they separated, and Alaric set to tending both of their wounds.

A week later, Tarrigi sat on a chest in the anteroom of Makara the Purger, the scabs of his encounter with the sorcerer hidden beneath a clean tunic and cloak. He swung his chubby legs as if he had no cares, heels drumming hollowly against the wood; but Alaric remained unfooled. The scars went far deeper than those left by the sorcerer's knife. The father paced, dodging the gazes of the five remaining guards. The sixth had taken his message to Makara, necessarily cryptic. If her men knew him for a sorcerer, they would slaughter him. Even if he escaped them, so many others would hunt him with the same vicious determination as the sorcerer had stalked Tarrigi. His best course, he knew, would be to run. But he had risked all once for his son, and he would do so again.

The door creaked open, and the guard who had relayed Alaric's message poked his head through. "Makara has agreed to see you."

Alaric clutched the money pouch at his belt, knowing it would fall several silver short of Makara's price. He hoped she would accept his promise to fill the gap, worried that she might still carry through on her threat to have him executed. "Come on, little bug."

The boy hopped from his perch, moving directly to his father's side. A small hand glided into Alaric's, and he gave it a reassuring squeeze.

They followed the guard, and the other five fell into step beside and behind them through a long corridor. The leader opened the door at the opposite end, ushering the group in front of Makara. He closed the door at their backs.

With a sense of twice-living, Alaric smiled nervously at the Purger.

Without a word, Makara glided from her padded chair and planted a hand on each of Alaric's shoulders. For several moments, the elder studied him. Then, her brow creased, and she returned to her seat.

Politely, Alaric waited for the Purger to speak, and the room grew silent except for the occasional clink of mail from the guardsmen. Tarrigi's hand winched tightly around two of his father's fingers, and he partially hid himself behind Alaric's leg.

At length, Makara spoke. "The high priest claims you killed a sorcerer."

Alaric nodded.

"Yet I can tell you did not assume his powers. Why?"

Alaric glanced at each guard, then back at Makara. He licked his lips.

Apparently guessing Alaric's concern, Makara said, "Speak freely in front of my faithful. They are sworn to silence for anything in these chambers."

For Tarrigi. Emboldened, Alaric explained, "I worried that it would change me, that once I started I would enjoy the power too much to resist it." He lowered his head. "I don't want to become a part of the struggles between gifted and sorcerer. I just want to live a normal life and raise my son the way his mother would have wanted." He raised his eyes imploringly.

"Please, if you could remove the talent from my son. I'm a bit short of money, but I swear to you you'll get as much as you demand."

The Purger met Alaric's gaze, her dark eyes radiating something deep and unreadable. "I've never heard of a sorcerer who resisted his birthright."

"Birthright?" Alaric spoke incredulously. "Birth curse, only. If you can take it from me, I'll spend my life gathering whatever it costs."

"I can't," Makara admitted.

Alaric sighed. Once, he had believed himself burdened with a talent, then his son; and now he knew it was indeed himself who was fully damned.

Makara again stepped down from her chair. "I charge for my services to keep me protected from assassins hired by sorcerers."

Alaric considered those words a moment. "And from sorcerers themselves," he added.

"No. The sorcerers don't come here." The Purger smiled. "Just as I can spot natal gifts, I can tell those with the capacity for harnessing souls."

"I'm surprised you didn't have me killed when I came the first time." Alaric gave Tarrigi's hand a reassuring squeeze.

"I debated it for a long time afterward." Makara shrugged. "But I couldn't justify it, not when you clearly didn't realize your power and hadn't harmed anyone." She continued. "The sorcerers also worry that if they bound my soul, they might find themselves unwittingly using my power to destroy the very thing they seek."

"Birth talents."

"Right." Makara shrugged back a heavy section of hair. "I don't want money for relieving your son of his burden."

Alaric blinked, trying to understand. "What do you want?"

The Purger retook her seat, settling an unwavering stare on Alaric. "I want . . . you."

"Me?" Alaric squeaked. Comprehension struck harder than he expected. It took a moment to gather enough breath to reveal Makara's plan. "When you . . . pass away . . ."

"Before I pass away." Makara leaned forward. "On my death bed. I want you to take my talent and my place."

Alaric glanced at Tarrigi, his first reaction to refuse. His son needed him too much to lose him to any cause. *My son.* He winced. A talent like Makara's would not appear often, if ever again.

Makara showed her desperation to be as great as Alaric's own. "It is unlikely, perhaps impossible, that I will ever again find a sorcerer with morals *and* the self-control to follow, not just preach them."

"I . . . I . . . ," Alaric did not know how to finish. The same worry that drove him to decline all but forced him to accept: the beloved sons and daughters of so many that only he could rescue. How many babies could he save? How many desperate adults and children?

Tarrigi followed much more than Alaric realized. He pulled on his father's arm, a plea for attention.

Glad for the diversion, Alaric knelt to attend his son.

"Do it," Tarrigi said. "Promise."

Doubts vanished, Alaric looked at Makara the Purger. And made the promise.

RITE OF PASSAGE

Ed Gorman

While Ed Gorman is best known for his suspense novels, including The Marilyn Tapes *and* Black River Falls, *he has also published six science fiction novels under pseudonyms. A full-time author, Ed lives in Cedar Rapids, Iowa, with his wife, young adult author Carol Gorman, and three cats.*

SOON enough, the tribe knew the truth about the boy.

Despite his six-foot-three; despite his taut, packed muscles; despite the long unruly hair he'd bleached with lime in warrior fashion; and despite his agility with javelin and broadsword alike—he was not a soldier.

There was nothing of the weakling about him, and this was what so confounded the leaders of this particular Celtic village. The boys who held the same interests of girls rarely showed Valerius' skill with weapons. Or his ability in appearing fearsome—slathering his naked body in the red and yellow clay and then donning a bronze helmet and then attacking viciously the various targets that had been set up for the warriors to practice on—he was all one could want in a warrior. He had strange powers, too. When he walked the sun-dappled forests, the animals would crowd round him and he would speak to them, and one had the excited sense that they were truly communicating with each other. And he could paint pictures on stone that shocked the eye with their clarity and precision—children and moons and sunsets he painted, and the comic faces of raccoons and rabbits and village puppies.

Valerius' father Corvinus was the king of this particular tribe and it was for his father that Valerius feigned interest in soldiering. He loved his father and did not want to humiliate him before the other warriors of the village. He even went along on three attacks on other villages with whom his own people were warring. He was thrilled to see the war-chariots in action, two Celts to a chariot, one man with the reins, the other hurling javelins at the enemy. He was equally thrilled to hear the legendary battle horns, those instruments that made sounds so harsh and discordant that some villages surrendered at the sound of them. This was particularly true of the Romans, who felt that the horns were literally of hell. But he could not kill, and that was the trouble. Fight, oh yes, he was magnificent to see—but kill? It was as if some invisible hand clamped his wrist at the last moment. Woman, child, man, animal—it didn't matter. Valerius could not bring himself to take another's life. It was as if he had been born crippled, crippled in the urge to kill.

All the villagers knew his real passion, and they did not begrudge him it, either. In addition to his ability to paint and speak with animals, Valerius had the most beautiful singing voice any of them had ever heard. On wedding nights, he would serenade the couple, and they would be so moved, they would lie in their marriage beds and weep with that ineluctable sorrow that made their joining all the sweeter. At village assemblies, he would sing tales of brave warriors, and not a single arm would be free of goose bumps. And at funerals—where the war-painted corpse of the war-riors were nobly fed to the vultures, and diseased or elderly bodies were simply burned—he sang of the village itself, and how it had endured down the years, free of the enslavement that had claimed some of the other villages.

Valerius' singing was so beloved by the villagers that they did not care if he was a warrior. Let him sing and farm, they told his father King Corvinus. There will always be other warriors—but there will never be another with a voice like your son's.

By the time Valerius was seventeen summers, even King Corvinus had accepted the fate of his boy. Valerius was a good organizer and for the first time in the history of the village, the granary was always filled. Valerius saw to it.

In her nineteenth summer, Epona, so named after the Gallic horse goddess, told Valerius that soon they would have a child. Valerius was happy to be a father and spent far more time with his beautiful little girl than village elders thought appropriate. Was this manly? His relationship with Epona had made him look even weaker to the warriors of the tribe. Epona was of the old way—she thought that men and women alike should be faithful (many Celtic women were as unfaithful as their husbands) and she thought that husband and wife should not only share the same residence but share a variety of housely duties. He would be doing this while the other young men his age were off warring.

But he loved her and could not be without her and so he became the husband she wanted.

Shortly after Valerius' twenty-third summer, when Epona's stomach swelled for a third time, the Druid known as Taranis came to the village. There was a great myth about this man who cloaked himself in many layers of dark and coarse robes and whose eyes, shadowed by the cowl, burned with an unhealthy yellow light. Unlike most Druid priests who were judges and astronomers and doctors, it was said that Taranis could actually grant wishes.

Taranis spent two full days in the village. Everyone swarmed bout him. Even the forest animals, apparently sensing divinity in the man, drew near the edges of the village. There were feasts and games and much drinking. Many villagers, emboldened by wine, asked Taranis if he would grant their wishes but he only shook his long, narrow, ugly head and scattered them away with a flick of his bony hand. Despite all the ways the villagers had tried to please him, he was not a friendly man.

Near the end of the festivities, Valerius sang. Epona and their two children sat bathed golden in the light of the huge fire, watching him. Epona's eyes smiled with pride in her husband.

Taranis startled everyone by crying openly, especially when Valerius sang of the man who'd lost his wife and children to Roman attack.

When the night was done, and the moon rode into midnight, Taranis came over to Valerius and said, "Your song was how my own wife and children died. By the hands of the Romans. I need to be purged of my grief from time to time, and tonight you helped me. Now I would like to help you. I will grant you any wish I'm able to."

By this time, the center of the village, where festivities were held, was growing dark, the fire little more than embers, the moon behind heavy gray clouds portending more cold spring rains. Most people were already asleep in their circular thatched houses.

The shame Valerius carried—so many warriorly gifts, and yet not being a true warrior—came quickly to mind and he told Taranis of his dilemma.

"I'm surprised, my young friend," the old Druid said, and there was a note of sorrow in his voice. "I would have thought you'd have chosen something for your wife and children. Long lives, if nothing else."

"I love my wife and children very much," Valerius said. "But I want to be a warrior. I will never feel like a true man until I am a warrior. My body is ready but not my heart." He tapped his powerful chest. "It is in here I need to change."

The Druid stared at him from beneath the cowl. His pale yellow eyes seemed disembodied from the rest of the face, which was lost in shadow. "It is not mine to tell you what to wish for. But you must value the warrior's life very highly to give up what you have."

"To give up? I don't understand."

"To say yes to one thing is to say no to another," the priest said. The Druid hesitated. "But you will have to learn that for yourself."

Valerius had no idea what the old priest was talking about. And didn't care, either. "Grant me my wish, ancient Father. Please."

The old priest reached out with a twisted and begrimed hand and touched a thumb to Valerius' forehead. For a moment, the old man closed his eyes and spoke some words in a tongue Valerius had never heard before.

"Your wish is granted," the Druid said, and then sighed deeply. "I think I'll go to bed now. Sometimes I dream of my wife and children, and then my mind is at peace once more."

Valerius did not sleep well.

He was up before dawn gathering spear and knife and ax and heading into the deepest part of the forest. He spent the entire day hunting—and killing. At first, he wasn't certain that he could murder the doe who had been drinking by the clear blue pond. And yet he did it. And felt an undeniable sense of triumph as he knelt next to the dead thing that had once been a song of nature. And so the day went. He returned to the village laden with kills of every kind, deer, bird, fish. And he presented them to Epona as he would have presented a wedding dowry. And yet when he reached out to embrace her—so joyous in his pride—she only turned from him and began weeping while she clutched her enormous belly as if in pain.

Epona woke just after dawn to the cries and bellows of a raiding party. The straw mat next to her was empty. Her first thought was that Valerius, as he sometimes did, had gone into the forest to pick flowers for her. But then, as she remembered yesterday and the subtle but definite change she'd seen in her husband, a chill traversed her entire body. She went to the center of the village where the raiding party was just now ready to depart, huge horses striped with war colors, the men on their backs also painted up for battle. She could see the silver breath of horse and man alike. The air above them was a jungle of spears and lances black against the dawning umber sky. The chill air smelled of wine and sweat and horseshit. She did not see Valerius among these men. She felt great relief. He'd gone to the forest, after all.

But when she turned to go back to the hut, one of the village women, Ierna, a woman who had never liked her, came up and said, "Well, we'll see if that husband of yours is a man or not."

"I don't know what you're talking about."

Ierna smirked. "He does not take you into his confidence? A wife should beware when that happens. My husband tells me everything." Then, seeing that Epona still didn't know what she was talking about, the woman said,

"He left earlier this morning, with the first raiding party."

Valerius was gone sixteen days, in all. He knew immediately that the Druid's magic had worked. Instead of feeling revulsion at what he saw and participated in, he felt great joy and freedom. They were expert raiders and he was proud to be one of them. They would swoop down on an enemy village and immediately set fire to all the thatched huts. They would do all this while screaming and shouting and blowing the animal-headed horns—the noise alone overwhelming and terrifying the enemy into submission. And then the slaughter and rape began. The treasures most sought—those they could use as barter when they returned to their own village—were livestock, healthy women who could be sold as slaves, gold, and the severed heads of the village leaders. There were only two things that Valerius would not do, and that was kill children and rape women. None of the other raiders were troubled about murdering little ones but Valerius would not do it, and often, when his fellows weren't watching, he helped the little ones hide in the surrounding forest.

The raiders returned home late one night. Valerius found Epona asleep and crawled beneath the blanket. When she woke, she simply looked at him and said, "I can smell death on you, Valerius. Are you happy now that you're just like all the rest of them? You were unique once, and now you're no better than they are." She would not let him make love to her. In anger, he went to the hut where the new slave women were being kept. He raped one of them most savagely and then went home and slept next to his wife. He still loved her deeply and could not believe she had so spurned him.

In the next two years, Valerius went on many more raids, a number of them into lands that Caesar had claimed for Rome, far from the home village, into lands not on the Celtic maps. They enjoyed destroying with particular zeal anything owned by Caesar. Valerius adopted the wavy battle lance as his weapon of choice. The weapon was thrown, just as any other lance would be, but when it was pulled out, the wavy blade lacerated the wound, making death twice as gruesome and painful. The greatest pleasure came from storming a castle. So fearsome were the raiders in the clamor of their cries and horns and death songs, that the inhabits of the Castle Reis—whose prince, it was said, was a relative of Caesar himself—surrendered even before any blood had been spilled. They offered jewelry and gold and their daughters as slaves. The raiders accepted these bribes with grim amusement. They then set about their real business, which was killing. Trying to impress themselves, they tossed the quarters and halves of bloody bodies and arms and legs and heads and hands into an enormous pile right in front of the castle gate. They hoped that Caesar's men would arrive soon, when the body parts were still fresh. They would report what they'd found back to Caesar and the fame of the raiders would increase a hundredfold—as would the dread and terror they inspired, the Romans starting to see them now as almost supernatural beasts. But once again, the Valerius would not participate in killing children. Indeed, he still had to look away when he saw a child about to be slaughtered. He thought of his own children then, and for the moment his loneliness for them was like a madness. He helped women whenever he could, too.

Winter came. Winter raids were the most debilitating. A number of raiders were lost to avalanches—they had gone up into the mountains where, it was rumored, there were other villages claimed by Caesar—and to an illness that started as a cough and ended with vomiting blood and hallucinations and death only a few days later.

It was spring before they returned home. They came in at night and saw a huge bonfire burning. The villagers celebrated spring in many ways. This was one of them, the entire village gathered round the campfire listening to—

—song. A handsome young man who looked somewhat familiar to Valerius stood on a flat stone singing songs such as Valerius once had. Songs of valor and love and loss. The villagers were enraptured, so enraptured that few of them greeted the raiders. Then one of the villagers saw Valerius and urged him to join the young man—who had been identified as Aruns, son of a villager Valerius knew well.

What power, these two singing together.

Valerius had not sung in over a year. He had been too busy. The warriors were suspicious of singing this refined, anyway. They liked coarse battle songs, not trilling odes to the moon and the intricate ways of the heart. He stood with Aruns on the flat stone and it was from there he caught his first glimpse of Epona. And saw the way she was looking at Aruns. She had looked at Valerius this way once—but not since he'd become a warrior. He sang but it was clear that the purest song had died in him somehow. Aruns overwhelmed him with the clear soaring beauty of his voice. After one duet, the crowd asked that only Aruns sing.

In his hut, he found his two daughters sleeping. And next to their heads he found small flat stones upon which portraits had been painted. Stunning portraits, of the sort he'd once painted.

He was kneeling there, staring at the paintings, when Epona came into the hut.

"Who did these?" he demanded to know.

"Aruns did them," she said. "What're you so angry about? Is this a way to greet your wife?"

She had told him, after his first raid, that she could smell death on him.

And just so, he could now smell adultery on her.

His daughters were starting to stir. His anger had awakened them.

He left the hut, fled to the woods, which had always been his solace, the animals there and the true pure voice of the river and the vast dreaming arc of sky. He walked for nearly an hour, and darker and denser the forest became, walked for nearly an hour, aware with each step that none of the animals were filling his head with thoughts, the way they'd once been able to silently communicate. His head was empty of all but rage and jealousy and despair.

He slept by the river, wrapped in his cloak. In the morning, he returned to the village. He was almost to his hut when Ierna came up to him. "You came home too late, Valerius. Your wife is in love with Aruns. And everybody in the village knows this but you." She feigned sorrow. "I say this as a friend."

Epona was gone. But the girls were there. The little one was too young to even remember him. The three-year-old said, "Aruns is going to take us swimming this afternoon."

"Do you know who I am?"

The little girl was hesitant. "I'm not sure."

He felt his heart stop. He had just died a death, seeing the blankness in her eyes, hearing the wariness in her voice. He had been on so many raids over the first three years of her life. Grief numbed him.

He started to tell her who he was but what was the point?

"If you see Aruns, would you tell him to hurry please?" his oldest daughter said. "We really want to go swimming."

He spent the next half hour searching the village for his wife. He took his broadsword with him. She was nowhere about. And then Ierna appeared again, eager to conjoin trouble. "If you look by the brook to the west you may find them. They spend much time there."

And so it was he found them. He climbed a tree that overlooked the brook where the two lovers sat. She played the flute, and it was beautiful. And Aruns sang, it was more beautiful still.

He had to turn his head away when Aruns took Epona in his arms and kissed her. He could smell and taste and feel Epona in his own arms—as she had been when she loved him. A madness overtook him and he climbed down from the tree and drew his broadsword and started to walk through the long grasses to the bank of the brook.

And then stopped himself.

What would happen to the girls if he killed their mother and her lover? Who would take care of them?

He slid his broadsword back into its sheath and walked away from the brook, back into the forest once again, the sunlight glowing here and there on the huge boles of ancient trees, larksong and sweetwind momentarily cooling his anger. Aruns could talk to the beasts of the forest, he was sure of it.

Just as Aruns could paint and Aruns could sing and Aruns could make love to Epona. Aruns was who he used to be. And thinking that, not even larksong nor sweetwind could cool or solace him.

He went back to the bank of the brook and slew them both with his great slashing bloody sword. He beheaded Aruns and carried his head back to the village and nailed it to the front of Aruns' hut.

And was then fallen upon by the elders of the village, who locked him in a hut and prepared for trial.

Celtic law was strict and simple. You could not kill another simply because he had committed adultery with your mate. That was the law and on a sunny morning, the elders read the law as Valerius stood before them. The entire village was ringed behind, eager to know what punishment the elders would hand down. Executions were always fun to watch.

And it looked as if there might well be an execution until Brein, the most celebrated of all the village warriors, told of the toll that two ceaseless years of raiding took on the raiders themselves. While not all the elders appreciated the activities of the warriors, the elders had to admit that without them the village would be far poorer—and might not be able to exist.

The crowd found this a reasonable argument and began to chant for Valerius' freedom. The elders knew they dare not go against the crowd. The warriors had long wanted to pack the council with their own members and get rid of the elder tribunal and this—if they ordered Valerius' death—would be a fine opportunity.

The elders spent two hours in their hut and then emerged and announced that Valerius was free to rejoin the raiders again.

There was rejoicing for the rest of the day, led by Valerius' father, who made no secret of the fact that he was proud of his son for slaying both an unfaithful wife and an interloper like Aruns.

Valerius went to Semona, the woman who had volunteered to raise his daughters. He asked to see them but Semona said that they did not want to see him ever again. She saw his grief and took his arm and said in the way of wise older women that she felt someday their attitude would change, that they would understand how a madness had fallen upon him and that he was sorry for what he had done. And it was then he realized—though of course he would not say this to Semona—that he did not feel sorry at all. Did not the true warrior right wrongs? And had this situation not been wrong for a true warrior to endure? He thanked her and went away.

A week later, Valerius was part of a raiding party that went deep into Caesar-held territory. He killed with a particular rage that day, and when a young girl ran in front of his horse, he bent down and cleaved her head off with his broadsword, and he did not feel half so bad as he'd imagined he would.

BRIGHT STREETS OF AIR

Nina Kiriki Hoffman

Nina Kiriki Hoffman has been pursuing a writing career for fifteen years and has sold more than 150 stories, two short story collections, two novels: The Thread that Binds the Bones, *winner of the Bram Stoker award for best first novel, and* The Silent Strength of Stones, *one novella,* Unmasking, *and one collaborative young adult novel with Tad Williams,* Child of an Ancient City. *Currently she almost makes a living writing scary books for kids.*

IN THIS war of words, my best friend Jessamine has all the advantages. She speaks faster than I, and with more heat.

I set a pansy-decorated teacup in front of her on my kitchen table, then take my place across from her. Westering sun strikes through the window on a bowl of oranges, lifting the true color out of them in a way no other intensity of light can do. Light silvers the cobwebs near the ceiling, too; I hadn't realized how long it's been since I dusted. I'm an indifferent housekeeper, but I always have cookies.

A plate of chocolate chip cookies sits between us on the yellow tabletop. I baked them this morning. I love that smell.

I curl my hands around my teacup, treasuring its

warmth. The tea I have chosen for myself is smoky and black, with gunpowder notes. Jessamine has chamomile, as she usually does.

As I reach into my pocket to take out the fossilized spell I just found in the hills, Jessamine extracts her palmtop computer from her purse, sets it on the table by her teacup, and flips up the lid so she can stare at the tiny screen. Electronic light the color of foxfire glows on her face. "Wait'll you hear this one, Ellowyn," she says. "My best yet. And . . ."

I lay my spell on the table. It looks unimpressive. They usually do. Just another river-rounded sandstone egg, fine-grained but unremarkable brown, though my fingertips itch from the sparks of potential in it.

"You won't believe what it does," says Jessamine.

It is too much to hope that she will be excited by my find. She never is. She has no interest in the past. Her favorite word is *upgrade*.

"What is it this time?" I ask. "A formula for shrinking parked cars so more can fit into available space? A spell to make everybody's clocks run just fast enough that people will arrive on time wherever they go? Something to make your VCR understand the exact right moment to start and stop recording so you never lose the first few seconds of a program?"

"Better," she says.

"You've debugged the Internet?"

She bites her lip. Okay, maybe I shouldn't have guessed that big. "Less global than that," she says.

"But your spells are always global."

"I made this one especially for you." She sips her tea.

Tingles of apprehension creep up my back. I don't like her even *considering* tailoring a spell for me. We have been friends for ages—since the days of cobblestone roads and horse-drawn vehicles, since men delivered ice and milk to one's home. We have watched each other's choices all these years and had our own thoughts.

We come together for tea every week. Jessamine casts her spells out into the world and I cast mine, and we sometimes work at cross purposes, but we try not to cancel each other out. I don't always approve of what she's doing, and I know she doesn't care much about my concerns either, but we almost never speak aloud our doubts. Censoring each other is not something we do.

"Plus, I have a new delivery system," Jessamine says, smiling down at her tiny computer. "Infrared data transfer."

She is speaking a language I have no desire to learn.

She taps the screen with a small black stylus, angles the back of the computer toward me, and a red light strobes into my eyes.

It hurts.

Blinking does not stop its invasion. I can see the light even through my eyelids, and I feel old and paper-thin for the first time in a long while.

What is she ensorcelling me with? Does she *want* to hurt me? Weaken me? Kill me? Only because I'm not sure I like the devicing of this century in all its manifest glory?

I collapse back in my chair, feeling like a marionette with cut strings. The pulsing pain of the red light ceases. For a moment all I feel are myriad aches, screeches from muscles that haven't scolded me in years.

My mind falls open, like a flower forced by time-lapse photography to bloom.

Then Jessamine's true assault begins. Snowing down on my unguarded edges, the structure of her reasons, the imprint of her influences, the chemistry of her choices. My mind lies quiet as her beliefs and impulses press down on it, and then I understand everything about her.

I feel her delight and terror in everything newest and next. Her burnished curiosity that wants to poke copper fingers everywhere. Her impatience with anything slower than she.

Her buried fear that if she sits still long enough so many things will catch up to her.

I crank open my eyelids and stare across the table at my friend, and then I *am* my friend. Her desires shape and restrict me; her joy flares through me and her fears gnaw at my heart. Falling gold and scarlet leaves of memory drift against a celadon green backdrop that is the edge of her consciousness. I can touch any leaf and tumble into one of our yesterdays.

I pick one, let it rest on my palm. It flattens against the skin, a damp silken kiss.

Sixty, seventy years ago. I am back in Brooklyn in the middle of a sweltering summer, and Jessamine and I are sitting side by side on steps in front of a brownstone, holding ice cream cones, mine strawberry and hers chocolate. Except I remember this moment from my own memory, too, and I had the chocolate cone. The ice cream melts faster than we can lick it, flowing down across our fingers, cool and sticky. In this moment we are only girls together without thought, lost in delicious taste, sweating and sticking to each other without caring, reaching across to offer tastes of each others' cones.

It is a moment most like this present one in how close we feel to one another.

I blink and I am back in my own head. Yet the whole tapestry of Jessamine's thoughts and motivations still weaves through my mind, inextricably tangled, forcing me to filter past it. I cannot tell where she begins and I end, and I feel hopelessly confused.

Jessamine has come around the table and is standing over me. "Are you all right?" she asks, her amber eyes staring into mine. She leans forward, presses her palm to my forehead. "Ellowyn? Are you all right?"

I shudder deep and long. Webs of foreign feelings drape my thoughts, feelings not my own, feelings that force me to feel them. Thoughts I don't want to own flicker through my brain.

I stare at my kitchen with stark clarity, see the careless stains on the cupboard doors, dustmice under the outthrust cabinets, spiderwebs in the corners, scratches in the dishes, all the things I don't mind because I don't wear my glasses in the house. There is that smell of orange peels rotting in the bag under the sink. I never notice that; I don't mind mold; things are only doing what they are supposed to do, everything changing into other things across time. But now this odor affronts me.

"Ell? That spell wasn't supposed to hurt you! Ell?" Jessamine grips my shoulder.

I try to cast the invasion out of my mind, but it is knitted and knotted too tightly to me. I struggle to reclaim myself. Everywhere in me are shards of someone else.

I feel my age. I let out a long breath and stop fighting, and all of Jessamine snaps into place within me. I feel . . . brisk. I sit upright. I gulp tea. Its smoky taste no longer pleases me, but I know I don't want chamomile either.

"Are you all right?" Jessamine asks for the fiftieth time, perhaps. Why should I pay attention to her when she is already inside me?

"Leave me alone," I say. I rise and go to the cupboard, find a tea called Plantation Mint that I usually share with my neighbor James when we play gin rummy on Sunday night and watch *60 Minutes*.

That'll do. I drop a teabag into a new mug. I put the kettle on the stove and turn on the burner. (Where's the microwave? Oh. I don't have one. Tomorrow I'll get one.) I run water into the sink until it's hot. I dump soap and sponges in, and then I begin to scrub.

It is odd. I wear glasses for distance, and Jessamine doesn't. I never knew what she saw when she looked at my house, and I never tell her what I think about her chrome and glass furniture or her love of plastic fabrics. A guest doesn't criticize the host's house no matter how long they have known each other.

"Ell?" Jessamine shakes my shoulder. "Stop it. What are you doing?"

There is dust everywhere. Housekeeping has never been my strong point. I scrub a film of ancient cat vomit off the linoleum and fight with myself. To care, or not to care? *Well,* says Jessamine in my head, *simplest if we spell it away, and that way both of us can relax.*

I sit back, drop the sponge on the floor. My hands flash through a series of mudras. I feel the dust and dirt shifting away to somewhere it can be more comfortable, and my house becomes a strange sacred space outside of the normal world where things will not stain it. Jessamine is happy here.

I, Ellowyn, feel as though I've sliced off my roots.

From the living room come the screams of three different cats. I jump up and run there and see that the couch where they usually lie in a furry heap is repelling them. They scramble in air, trying to swim to safety, but the table repels them, and the carpet. They float, claws extended, an inch above the ground. Their cries become more frantic.

"What did I do? What did you do?" I cry, snatching at my frantic cats, who cling and claw and screech.

"Damn, I forgot about cats. This is a people-only house now," my internal Jessamine says with my mouth.

"Well, stop it! Change it back! Stop it!" I am talking to myself.

"You'll have to free the hands." My second voice is an approximation of Jessamine's, higher and more forceful than my own.

I am supporting Sprite's hind legs with my right hand. Fleet clings to my shoulders, and Dobro stands on my left forearm, his paws wrapped around my upper arm. They all moan, an eerie, ascending sound like the end of the world.

"What happened?" Jessamine asks from behind me. Her voice is thin with fright.

I turn and force Sprite and Fleet into her arms. "Your silly spell," I say in my own voice, "your silly banish-dust, repel-pests, eternal-stain free spell has turned my house into a tomb." Hands freed, I shape the mudras again in reverse order, stumbling a little because this is not my usual spell method. The Jessamine overlay in my mind prompts me, sighing all the while. She craves cleanliness that is close to hermetic, and now I know why all the way down to my bones. I can remember the apartment where Jessamine lived before we met, filth and cockroaches and rotting food, her mother's older sister spreading pestilence and chaos everywhere around her in a way that Jessamine did not learn until later was magical.

Such stains, set deep into her image of her childself. Such a compulsion to escape them.

I shape my hands around the final mudra, and my roots regrow; the house is connected to the everyday world once again. The cats, still moaning, drop to the floor and vanish into their safest hiding places.

Jessamine is crying. We both go to the bathroom to put Neosporin on our bleeding scratches and to spell for healing. "Ellowyn, what happened?" Jessamine says.

"You should know," I say. "It was your spell."

"It wasn't supposed to work this way!"

"What did you imagine it would do?" Now, from my view of the inside of her mind, I know what the spell was: a spell of total understanding. I can even ferret out her thinking about it, why she devised it: she is lonely in her passions, and she only wanted me to appreciate them more than I do. We have been getting together for years. We are best friends. Yet, there has been this film between us, areas we have kept separate from each other where we might clash, and finally her frustration about this place where she is still and always alone built to the bursting point.

And, in her straightforward Jessamine way that sometimes frightens me, she reached for what looked like the best solution. *Make* me understand.

"I thought maybe you'd *listen* to me," she says.

I stare at a particularly long cat scratch on my arm and listen to the conflict in my head. My body needs protection. I dab some antibiotic ointment on my index finger and look at the red edges of my wound. My Ellowyn self has sympathy for the microorganisms that have found this entrance into blood heaven, the ones I am about to kill. My Jessamine self is appalled that I even hesitate. I smooth the ointment along the scratch and sigh.

"How can I hear you now?" I ask. "I have voices in my head."

Her nose is pink with stifled tears. "I'll uncast it. I'm so sorry. I didn't know it would work like this."

"You can't uncast it," I say, because I know how carefully she built it, and which of the ingredients are permanent. I stare at my face in the mirror, and two people look out of my eyes. I fear that once the Jessamine inside me has time to look around and analyze things, she will gradually send more and more of my true self to sleep and happy dreams until she is all that is conscious in me.

I hate this thought. Fighting has never been my strength, though.

I get the Band-Aids down from the cupboard, and, moving with uncharacteristic determination, slap them onto myself and Jessamine where they will do the most good. Jessamine's pathological hatred of infection spells out of me as I work. I don't even think as

I mouth these words. I know they have been a mantra for her over the years.

Cats, part of me thinks with disgust. Horrible messy things. No more events like this! We have to get rid of them!

Horror curls through me. The cats are my companions, my friends. They greet me when I return from anywhere. We all live our separate lives in this shared space, and intercept each other for caresses. I love them.

In my head, Jessamine apologizes for her thought, but I know she still thinks it. Finally I understand why the cats never come into the kitchen while Jessamine is visiting me. She has a repel spell for all animals. She cannot rid herself of the conviction that they carry disease.

No. I can't live like this.

We head back to the kitchen. I make yet another cup of tea, this time English Breakfast, fully loaded with caffeine. While the water heats, I take Jessamine's little computer, tap the screen with the stylus to find the spell-processing program, scroll through the spell she constructed. It is just as I remembered: Jessamine exact, Jessamine elegant, all parts interlocking so tightly that I can't get a fingernail in to split it apart. What about transmission errors? I check the data-sent log, and it says SENT OK. Frowning, I set the computer on the table and discover Jessamine staring at me, her face pale.

"What?" I say.

"You know how to use it," she murmurs, and then I feel the backlash, the Jessamine in my head reflecting the other Jessamine's outrage at someone even touching this computer, her precious friend, making it do tricks without asking.

"Oh, this makes me tired," I say. I make my tea and slam the kettle down on the burner, denting its edge, full of rage and fatigue from fighting this self forced on me.

I sit.

I see the egg-shaped spell, golden as earth, that I found in the hills, and a sweet taste touches my tongue.

Before my interior Jessamine can stop me—I had no idea that she had these shudders under her skin all the time, worries always that edges are not clean, that touch is not safe—I cradle the spell in my hands. Comfort seeps into me. This spell's history isn't entirely clear to me. I only know someone cast it a long time ago, and that it worked beautifully, so beautifully that the earth reached up and made it into treasure in memory of its power. No spell that hurts anyone ever gets pearled like this.

Part of me wants to fling the ugly, dirty thing from me, banish it from the house. The other part turns the spell over and traces the glyph of welcome on the grainy sandstone surface. Answering warmth wakes under my fingertip. The spell is joyous with its own power. I cup my hands around it and taste its flavor, waiting for the spell to tell me what it does. Juicy sourgrass stems, cinnamon, wheatbread, green grapes—a harvest spell, of sorts.

Harvest.

What would I plant? What reap?

This experience of having the Other inside me. Already planted. Already grown and flowered. Fruit, unbearable fruit. Can I harvest it now and lay it away?

I stroke the spell, trace some glyphs of inquiry into it. The Jessamine in my head watches, quiet, not protesting.

The red warmth of wine answers my touch. The spell accepts my alterations.

"Will you go quietly?" I ask.

"Oh, yes," she says with my mouth. And past all her fears and worries, I feel the great flood of love she feels for me, the gratitude and exasperation and choked delight and longing, the leaves of so many shared memories, laughter and starlight and wonder, times we pushed each other away but came back, times we asked hard questions and stayed for hard answers, times we surprised each other.

For a moment I think, I can live with this.

Then she says, "Let go, Ell. You can't live with me. You know it and I know it."

It is her hand in my hand that lifts the stone to my mouth, her lips in my lips that press the opening glyph into the spell's skin.

The rock melts. The spell opens. Shimmering gold and green light weaves around me, and I see orchards flowering with spring rain, leafing out green with summer's sun, sturdy and strong from earth, air, water, sunfire, all mixed with each fruit's own signature. Jessamine grows strong and ripe inside me. For a little while I am afraid that I will be cast into dreams indeed, leaving Jessamine alone in my head.

She grows more, basking in the light, too big now to be contained. I cry aloud as pain flashes through me, and then she is reft from me.

When my eyes clear, I hold a perfect black plum in my hands, and Jessamine is gone from my head.

She stares across the table at me. "What happened?" she whispers, pale and frightened.

"It's all right," I say. The spell is gone and I send gratitude after it. I set the plum on the table. I look at the cookies on the plate and sigh with happiness, blessing my singular state. "Don't ever do that again."

She picks up her computer, turns it so I can see the spell on the screen. She selects the entire document and hits the delete button. The spell vanishes.

"Take it off the flashcard too," I say.

Her eyes widen, but she opens the memory storage card and removes the spell from that as well.

It doesn't matter. If she really wants to, she can

reconstruct the spell from scratch. I know better than ever how her mind works now. Anything she spent so much time crafting is etched into her brain.

"I love you," I say. "But I don't want to be you."

She shakes her head. "I understand."

"You don't," I say. "You don't want to." I push the plum and it rolls all the way across the table to stop in front of her. "But if you want to know what it was like to be you inside of me, taste this."

She picks up the plum and stares at me. I remember two girls sitting on a front stoop in Brooklyn. I remember us walking along a seaside street on a misty evening, things silvered with street light and damp, the only warmth her hand in mine.

Sometimes I want never to see her again.

Sometimes I'm so angry with her I want to scream.

She's my best friend in all the world.

She raises the plum to her mouth and takes a bite.

HELL'S BANE

Jane Lindskold

*Unbidden, New Mexico keeps creeping into much
of Jane Lindskold's recent work, including her most
recent novel* Changer *and, of course, this short
story. A full-time writer, her novels include* When
the Gods Are Silent *and* Donnerjack, *written in col-
laboration with Roger Zelazny. She lives just down
the street from Rinconada Canyon with her husband, archaeologist Jim Moore, and assorted
small animals.*

IN THE city where I live there's a nightclub whose
bottom level is a direct annex of Hell.

Now, hold on, I know I've told you about this before[1] and I'm not going to repeat myself—or not
much, anyhow. The club's called the Double Decker.
After my first—and only—visit there, I didn't expect
it to stay open longer than a couple more weeks.

That was spring term. This is fall and things are
here in Albuquerque are getting pretty freaky.

It started with the billboards. I drive over to the
University of New Mexico, where I'm starting my ju-

[1]See "Hell's Mark" in *Wizard Fantastic,* edited by Martin H.
Greenberg, DAW Books.

nior year, just about every day, either for classes or to hang out with my friends.

There's a group of six of us who've been through Hell together: Danny, Cindy, William, Pedro, Madeleine, and me.

Vanessa is still one of us, but she graduated at the end of the spring term, Honors in English, and went off to get her Masters, and probably her Ph.D., in Literature at some California school. She's learning Italian, 'cause she's decided that she wants to read Dante's *Divine Comedy* in the original—especially *The Inferno*.

Well, we've all been marked by that trip to the Double Decker.

On this particular day, I'm not thinking about Hell—or not really—well, I sort of am—but that's because of Danny. He's older than I am, several years, at least, since I'm a junior and he's been a senior at least three times. And he's very handsome, with longish brown hair, melting brown eyes, and a way of smiling that just gives you the shivers—or something that feels a lot like the shivers.

I'm thinking about Danny as I'm driving down I-40, wondering if you get sent to Hell for lustful thoughts and hoping like anything that you don't because I've been there and I really don't want to go back. Then I realize that the billboard I'm passing is completely insane.

It's a fancy advertisement for Taos, a town about two and a half hours north of here, known mostly for its artsy people and its skiing. In the winter the billboard has a little electronic gizmo that tells you how many inches of snow are available for sliding around on. In the fall, like now, it just tries to make you wish for winter, so you'll make reservations ahead of time.

You know the type of picture: happy, smiling, good-looking Anglos, swooshing (or whatever they call it) through sparkling powdery snow. I've seen the like so many times before that usually I don't even notice the picture. Today I can't miss it.

There are the good-looking Anglos, all right, dressed in their expensive snowsuits, but the snow they're swooshing on is dotted with red—blood red. The man is down, headfirst in a drift. Given the angle his body's torqued at you don't have to be my *curandera* mama to know that his neck is broken. The woman with him has it worse. She's impaled on her ski poles, hanging up there in the air, screaming.

The picture is so good you can almost hear the sound.

I nearly lose control of my old sedan, but I manage to pull it straight. I'm shaking so bad, I don't look around to see what the other drivers think of this novel new marketing ploy. A little corner of my brain wonders if some rival ski basin, like Purgatory up in Colorado, bought the billboard.

Getting to campus, I find parking just in time to sprint to my class. Fortunately, it doesn't demand a lot of my attention, so I get through without making too big a fool of myself. Then I go looking for the gang.

Luck is with me and I find them all hanging together in one of the outdoor plazas. Everyone except Pedro is sitting on the stairs. He's standing, neat and compact, his Van Dyke beard freshly trimmed, dressed in slacks, button-down shirt, and, wonder of wonders, a tie, telling some story that's holding them so rapt they don't even see me hurrying to join them.

Seeing them there in the warm September sunshine, I feel ashamed of my panic. I'll still find a way to tell them all about what I saw, but I'll keep my cool. This resolve lasts all of thirty seconds, right up until I hear what Pedro is saying:

". . . and so I'm coming out of the hospital from visiting my grandmama, going down Gibson and I pass that big thing the public art program put up a couple of years ago—the old dark blue Chevy way up in the air on the tiled arch, you know?''

Danny nods, "The Chevy on a Stick, sure.''

"Sí," Pedro says. "But that car sure don't want to be on a stick anymore. The wheels are spinning and the headlights are flashing. Music, too, that old song,'' he hums a few bars, " 'Low Rider.' ''

"By the Zombies,'' Will says. "I think.''

Going to Hell was good for Will. He's gained confidence and no longer looks like such a geek. Spending the summer on the staff of some New Age camp in upstate New York didn't hurt. They only served vegetarian food, so his skin cleared up and, oddly, he gained some weight and muscle. Cindy says he's cute now, but I can't see him for Danny.

"That's the song,'' Pedro agrees. "That car isn't a low-rider, but it's bopping away on its arch like it wants to be one, cruising the strip with the *amigos,* looking for pretty girls.''

He sees me then and smiles greeting. *"Hola,* Lucia. *Como 'stas?''*

Pedro, like me, is from a local Hispanic family, but, unlike me who had love to fill in where there wasn't money, he didn't have money and his family didn't have much love. His older brother, Juan, who Pedro just about worshiped, died in a gang fight late last spring—just after the thing with Hell. Losing him made Pedro wild for a while, but Danny saved him by helping him realize that Juan's fate was his own responsibility. The only problem with the cure is that Pedro now wants to go completely straight and to him that means having a girl . . . well, a girl like me.

Sometimes, as I look at him, not overly tall but full of *machismo* and with brains enough to win a four year academic scholarship, I wish I could be what he wants me to be. I just don't know if I'm ready to settle down.

"Hey," I say by way of general greeting. "Did I just hear what I thought I heard?"

"You did," Pedro says with that smile he saves for me. "I barely made it here on time for class. There was a major accident. Four cars. Ambulances, cops, traffic backed up."

I cut in excitedly. "That's too weird! Your story reminds me of something that I saw on my way to school."

I tell them all about the billboard, relieved that I'm not cracking up. When I finish, Cindy frowns. She's mellowed a lot since she went into counseling last spring, but just because she's stopped envying everyone else doesn't mean that she's much less competitive. Now that Vanessa has graduated, Cindy's determined to take over as leader of our little band.

Hey, it's her senior year. I don't mind. Anyhow, Danny's the leader in my heart.

So Cindy, brushing back her soft blonde hair with one hand, looks serious and says in The Voice of Authority: "Have any of the rest of you seen anything?"

Unspoken is "Or is this something cooked up by our two Hispanic *compadres*?"

I hear it and ignore it. Cindy isn't bigoted. She's just overly sensitive to the existence of any group to which she can't belong. Pedro bristles, but a look from Danny calms him down.

Madeleine shyly raises one hand. She may be a sophomore now, but since we haven't recruited anyone new, she's still the baby of the group and Cindy intimidates her.

"I think I've got something," she says softly.

Cindy gestures for her to go on, but Madeleine hesitates a moment more before speaking, absently stroking the feathers of a blue-gray finch that has perched on her plump forefinger.

"Yesterday I went to the zoo," Madeleine says at

last, "for my internship. You know the big statue of the wolf out front?"

She waits until we all nod.

"I thought I heard it growling. I turned to face it, kinda startled, you know, and I thought it tried to wag its tail. It wasn't growling anymore, either, just whining a 'come and play with me whine.' "

She pauses again, but no one says anything. I figure everyone is thinking what I'm thinking. If anyone could tell what a wolf is whining, it would be Madeleine.

"Anything else?" Danny coaxes, speaking to Madeleine much as I've heard her speak to a timid animal. She nods.

"You know how the zoo is full of art: statues, murals, relief sculptures. All day, whenever I went past one of them I'd glimpse movement out of the corner of my eye or just almost hear something. When I looked at it straight on," she shrugs, "nothing."

"Interesting," Cindy says, still playing group moderator, "anyone else?"

Danny and Will both shake their heads. Cindy traces the twists of the Celtic knotwork "bracelet" tattooed around her right wrist before continuing:

"And I haven't seen anything either. I wonder why you three have and we haven't?"

"Have you been off-campus?" I ask. In reply I get three "nos." "That may be it. We all know that the main campus is in a protected zone. Maybe what we should do is wait until classes are over and then go for a tour of the city."

We compare notes and find that by two o'clock everyone but Danny will be done for the day. Danny has a later class, but he doesn't mind cutting. That's part of the reason that he's never finished his degree.

So two-thirty finds us all piling into the big Impala that Pedro inherited from Juan. Juan had planned to low-rider it, but hadn't had the chance, a thing for

which I am immensely grateful. He had found the time
to repaint it, though, so we go touring in a vehicle
painted dark purple with sparkly gold flames licking
down the sides.

Oh well.

I hope to sit next to Danny, but Pedro wants me
up front, so I end up between him and Cindy. We
start on I-25, then cross at the Big I to I-40 so I can
show everybody my billboard. They're appropriately
impressed.

Public artwork provides more of a challenge. I
mean, it's everywhere in Albuquerque, but who ever
thinks about where it is? You just take it for granted.
Old Town is the obvious place to start since there are
the two dinosaurs out in front of the Natural History
Museum and the sculpture garden alongside the Albuquerque Museum.

After Old Town, we cruise by the Chevy on a Stick
and past several murals, down to the new Botanical
Park and Aquarium, and then all the way up to Tram-
way to look at the mother bear and cub in Bear Canyon Arroyo.

What started out as a fact-finding mission rapidly
turns into a sort of treasure hunt with no prize except
the dubious one for spotting the next deviation from
reality as we know it. It gets creepy at times.

The mother bear growls at us until Madeleine
soothes her. The long duster on the cowboy near the
Albuquerque Museum flaps in the wind—though there
isn't any wind. His horse paws the pedestal with an
eager hoof, making the ringing sound of metal against
metal. The bronze lady seated on the park bench—
the one who's so lifelike that people sometimes ask if
she minds before they sit down next to her—is rooting
through her purse, looking for something.

And the dinosaurs scare me out of my mind. Only
one's a carnivore—a T-Rex or something—the other's
a triceratops (I think). Watching them move, tails

shifting, jaws opening so you get a really good look at those enormous teeth, I feel like a mouse confronting a lion.

William and Cindy go inside to see if any of the other displays are affected and when they come out they are whiter than God ever intended them to be.

And those are the mild transformations. The more abstract art looks all out of focus, like it's searching for meaning. That makes me queasy, but far worse is what has happened to the billboards and murals. Wherever possible, the picture has mutated into something violent or obscene. Marketing slogans change, too. Sometimes the letters have just been switched around so that "Hotel" becomes "To Hel."

In other cases, the jingles have been changed to something similar to the original but twisted. A billboard proclaiming "Make it a Santa Fe Weekend!" now reads "Make it an Auto de Fe Weekend!" and the altered illustration leaves no doubt in my mind just how gross that could be.

By the time we're refilling the Impala's gas tank, we're sure that something odd is going on—not just something odd, something sinister.

"What I don't quite get," Will admits, once we've adjourned to a convenient Blake's Lotta Burger, "is just who can see this? It isn't everyone or there'd be something on the news."

"Or riots in the streets," Pedro agrees, "but except for maybe a few more accidents than normal we have seen *nada.*"

"Is it just us then?" Madeleine asks. She's had the most mixed reaction of any of us. On the one hand, she doesn't care for the more violent manifestations; on the other she's getting a kick out of seeing animals freed from their metal and stone.

"No," Danny says, his voice eddying calm like ripples from a pebble tossed in a pool, "I don't think so. It's more like we see clearly what other people only glimpse from the corners of their eyes. When they look at it straight it vanishes."

"That makes sense," I agree. "We're all magically talented. At the Double Decker, we saw the gateway to Hell when most of the patrons didn't."

"What worries me," Madeleine puts in, "is that whatever's doing this is definitely getting stronger. When I was at the zoo yesterday, *I* was just seeing things out of the corners of my eyes. Today I had no trouble. What will happen tomorrow?"

"That's the question, Maddie," Danny says.

Cindy interrupts, bossy as usual. "I think that Lucia is onto something. The effect is just like the one at the club except it's more widespread."

"Lots more," Pedro agrees. "Like a whole city."

Cindy nods. "Still, there may be a link. I think we should check out the Double Decker tonight. If we find a connection we take our information right to Madame A. and Lord Whatsis."

Madame Alexandria and Lord Whatsis are the Craft names of the two top members of the High and Mighty here in Albuquerque. Like our absent Vanessa, they are Wiccans. I'm not surprised that Cindy thinks of consulting them before she things of consulting, say, my mom, who is a *curandera* and could be part of the High and Mighty if her family and her practice left her time.

Madame Alexandria and Lord Whatsis have been tutoring Cindy in various forms of the Art ever since she took her initial ranking in the middle of this past summer. She showed a strong talent for conjuration, but strong subsidiary talents as well.

More importantly, at least to Madame Alexandria and Lord Whatsis, Cindy's Talent isn't strongly allied with any one tradition. That means that the Wiccans have a chance of scooping her up and, since they do lots of group rituals, an extra body is always welcome.

Pedro sets down the French fry he'd been about

to eat, preparatory to arguing, but I forestall him by speaking first. I don't really *want* my mom brought into this, not if I can help it.

"That's a good idea, Cindy," I say quickly. "Do you want to consult them now?"

Cindy looks so gratified that I'm agreeing with her that I feel like a creep. You see, even after Cindy went into therapy, I was the one she had the hardest time coming to terms with. My ranking is CW6, the highest ranking ever given since the current system started being used. Cindy, by contrast, is a G4, a very high rating—generalists are always valued—but not close to mine. What made Cindy more comfortable with me was when I confided in her (after swearing her to deepest secrecy) that ever since we left Hell I've been scared of my Power.

You see, it's not really mine, it's sort of a loaner and I don't know what the interest rate on the loan is and I'm scared to find out.

All Mom knows is that I've got more power than I know how to use. She keeps trying to push me in certain directions. Knowing what I do about the source of my power (something only the other members of the Seven know) I'm nervous about steering it any way at all, so I haven't told Mom anything. If she knew, she'd probably try to put me away in a convent. I'm just not ready for that, and I'm scared that's going to be the price.

Looking at Danny, incredibly handsome in jeans and his omnipresent black leather jacket, I know I won't ever be ready to pay that price—I'm just not cut out to be a virgin saint.

Cindy's answering my question now, after pausing to give it some real consideration, another sign of how she's changed. Before she would have snapped off an answer, any answer, just to show you that you couldn't get one over on her.

"Lucy, I'd like to know more before we bring them

in. They don't take us," (read "me"), "as seriously as I'd like. If we could prove the connection between the Double Decker and these manifestations, then they would have to take us seriously."

William (who has tried to stay vegetarian after his summer indoctrination but keeps backsliding) says around his mouthful of cheeseburger: "Cindy's right. Madame A. and I have clashed a couple of times because I've kept my word to Lucy and won't tell the High and Mighty just how we got out of Hell. She's even hinted that we made up all or part of our adventure—or that we had help we aren't admitting to—so that we'd seem more important. I'd rather do more investigating on our own."

Danny nods. "Cool with me. Hate the idea of going back there, though."

"Me, too," Madeleine shivers. "But like Vanessa said last time, we've got to hang together or hang separately."

Pedro reaches over and squeezes my hand. "And you, Lucia? Are you certain that you should do this thing?"

I pat his hand in what I hope is a sisterly fashion.

"I'm with the rest on this. I really don't want to go running to Mom. Anyhow, Cindy and Will are right. The High and Mighty have been downplaying our report. If they took us seriously, they would have closed the club months ago. I've only got one modification to suggest."

"Oh?" Cindy doesn't even look affronted that I'm not following her blindly. "Tell."

"Let's e-mail Vanessa before we go. That way if we don't make it back, someone will know why."

That evening, I tell Mom that I'm going out and might not be back until late. She looks at me as if she's going to demand an explanation, then doesn't. Maybe she's just practicing patience, but I don't rule out that she might have seen a few strange things herself over the past couple of days.

When I come down from my room all dressed up, she opens her mouth then shuts it. Clearly I'm not pulling an all-nighter, not in the lace-trimmed dress with the flounced skirt I bought for Cousin Teresa's wedding. I can see her considering what to ask.

"See you later, Mama."

(Lord! I haven't called her "Mama" since I was five. What's wrong with me? Could I be scared?)

"Good night, Lucia. Be careful."

"I will."

She smiles then and I leave, thanking my patron saint that Dad is on the early morning shift at Rainbo Bakery and has already gone to bed. Especially since he won't see them clearly, all the recent manifestations have made him uneasy. The last thing he would want is for his little girl to go out at night.

By pre-arrangement, we meet at the UNM campus and pile into Pedro's car. Like me, everyone's dressed to go clubbing, but there isn't that feeling of fun and excitement that had filled us the first time we went thrill seeking at the Double Decker.

Although dressed in one of the expensive spandex outfits she favors, Cindy looks like she's spent more time meditating than on her attire. Her jewelry consists of a variety of amulets—some bogus, some genuine. Madeleine has done the unthinkable and arrived without even one pet, not even a squirrel or ferret to make a fur collar for her dress. The three guys look sharp in variations of standard guy clothes, but serious. I admire their courage in showing up at all.

Danny's talent is for healing, Pedro's for divination, and Will's for doing past life regressions, not exactly the magic you'd want to bring into a potential fight. Madeleine, at least, can charm the fiercest beast. Cindy's conjuration abilities let her pull off some surprising things and me . . . well, last time I just boosted everyone else's talents as needed. I sincerely hope that's all I'm needed for this time since I'm scared to try anything else.

It's a Tuesday night, so you'd think the parking lot at the Double Decker would be pretty empty, but we have no such luck. Nearly every parking space in the blacktopped lot is taken and cars line the side streets in blatant violation of traffic codes.

Even though at this altitude most of the daytime heat vanishes with the setting sun, the September evening is still pleasant. People are hanging out near the cars, checking each other out. The neon lights from the Double Decker's sign glitter back from the fancy hologram plastic bracelets that indicate you've paid admission to the club.

This is gathered in the blink of an eye as Pedro is pulling the Impala into a just vacated parking space and getting cursed out by some skinheads in an RV that probably cost as much as a year's tuition at a private college.

Normally, the six of us would have delighted in an argument, but tonight we have a bigger problem and our battlefield is just across the parking lot.

You know how on a hot day you can see the heat shimmer off the pavement like it's a living thing? Well, that's kind of how it is when we look at the Double Decker Club. We can hardly see the lines of the building because of the evil that radiates from its walls, flowing up and consolidating into clouds that drift off into the night, glowing with faint luminosity.

"That must be how the art and all got contaminated," Danny says, shoving his hands deeper into his jacket pockets. "Who knows what else is soaking it up?"

Cindy nods. "But we need more proof. This can be dismissed as more of our tall tales. C'mon!"

We go, though I for one am not very happy. If we

can see the emanations of Hell's evil, can the minions of Hell see the glow of Heaven? That could have some serious ramifications . . . especially for me.

But I go because I'm not going to turn tail in front of my buddies, because I know that the others are braver knowing that I—super-powerful Lucia—am at their side.

We stride into the wedge-shaped entry foyer like we carry engraved invitations. This time the desk where the beauty in the Bob Mackie gown had stood is untenanted.

"Guess there's no cover charge tonight," Will says, sounding so confident that we all take heart. "Good. I've been spending my summer money too fast."

Pedro, who had been our guide the first time we came here, takes point once more. The door onto the catwalk that frames the dance floor below is invitingly open, but he checks around the corners before motioning the rest of us through.

"It's clear," he says. Then he points down, "Too damn clear."

There's no need to guess at his meaning. Tonight, to the accompaniment of a heavy metal beat, Hell has ventured up from the nether regions and is playing havoc with the patrons.

I don't want to get too gross, so I'll leave the details to your imagination, but down there every one of the Seven Deadly Sins is being practiced and most of those practitioners are very practiced at what they're doing. Nor are they restricting themselves to those seven neat little categories. Cruelty in many forms is rampant.

In a word, it is Hell.

Madeleine crumples in shock, probably at what is being done to a hutch full of cute pink-eyed bunny rabbits. Pedro catches her before she hits the floor, but only because he sees the portent of her falling before it happens.

His own eyes are wide with horror at what is being done to a young man flung over the bar. I suppose it is a version of Lust, but it's called other things, too, and it's illegal in most of the fifty states.

I reached for Danny's arm and find him already holding Cindy. Her gaze is fastened on a woman who is being treated as Crassus was by the Parthians, but in this woman's case they aren't stopping with pouring the molten gold down her throat.

Will, bless him, is the only one who keeps any presence of mind and he's watching the door by which we had entered.

"Folks," he calls, warningly. "We'd better get out of here while we can. Those guys who were bugging us by the Impala are coming in and I don't think they want to talk."

I glance over my shoulder and see what he means. At least six big skinheads are pushing through the door. The guy in the lead is swinging a chain against his thigh. The one behind him is tossing a tire iron from hand to hand. Already they have blocked our exit.

"Fine," Cindy says, seeing the question in my eyes as she turns in response to Will's warning. "We go up and out through the restaurant. There must be a fire exit or something."

The club's called the Double Decker, not because of the level into Hell which, after all, most people don't know about, but because there's a restaurant on the level above the nightclub. Cindy's idea is good, but Madeleine shakes her head.

"No go," she says, pointing up. "Look!"

We do and that's when we realize that flames are raging where there had once been fancy tables and elegant waiters.

"It could be an illusion," Pedro offers hesitantly.

"Do you want to risk it?" Danny counters.

"But that leaves only one way out," Madeleine says,

and to her credit she is already heading that way. "Down."

Skinheads at our heels, we charge down the spiral stairway, bouncing against the thin metal railings in our haste.

Fearing that we'll escape, the skinhead in the lead snags his chain in Cindy's long hair. Pulled up short like a lassoed heifer, she screams.

Pain flaring in her blue eyes, she wheels around, her right palm extended like a traffic cop signaling a stop.

"Damn you!" she yells. "That hurts!"

Fire bursts from her hand, red fire like the hellfire that burns in the restaurant above us. It sticks to the man's face and he falls to the floor, clawing at the little gobbets that cling to his lips and nose.

Shocked, Cindy staggers back a few paces, nearly falling off the stair, the chain still tangled in her hair.

"Oh God!" she cries. "I didn't mean . . ."

Danny grabs her, hustles her along. "Baby, he can't hear reason just now. Let's get out of here and call an ambulance."

Cindy nods and the chain clanks, tangling through the railing like a living thing. To free her, Pedro whips out Juan's old switchblade and slices through her hair.

Will and Madeleine head toward the exit door, an exit that on a more normal night, would have stood open to let in some fresh air and provide a place for the smokers to hang out.

Tonight the door is closed and barred in direct contravention of the sign that reads "This Door to Be Kept Unlocked During Business Hours."

A couple of tough guys in leather vests and lots of attitude lean against it, just daring us to try to leave that way. One's black, one's white, but they're both wearing those really ugly chin beards that have become fashionable all of a sudden.

"I'm scared," Madeleine whimpers, biting down hard on her lip. "And I'm kind of tired of this, too."

Squaring her shoulders, plump and pale in her party dress, she marches up to the two men.

"Excuse me," she says firmly. "I'd like to leave and you're blocking the door."

The white guy grins. "Yeah? Well, we're using the door."

Maddie shows an amazing amount of what in a guy gets called *cojones*. "To rest your fat butts. Well, that figures. You're too damn dumb to figure out how to turn a doorknob."

The remaining four of us come trooping up just in time to hear this amazing exchange.

"What's with Madeleine?" I mutter.

Danny shakes his head slowly, "Wrath, too, is one of the Seven Deadly Sins. Something's reached out and grabbed her, just like it grabbed Cindy's magic. We've got to get her out of here before she gets hurt."

Maddie hears him and spins, her normally placid features contorted with rage. "Getting us out of here is exactly what I'm trying to do," she snarls. "Since you're so smart."

She doesn't make much sense, but since when has an infuriated person made sense? Trusting his gift for bringing calm and healing wherever he goes, Danny reaches for her.

"Come here, Maddie. Cool off."

But there's something wrong. I look at him in puzzlement.

Normally Danny is all soft lines—not that he's fat—not at all! He just slouches, leans against things, his jacket loose and kind of bulgy, like leather jackets are. His T-shirts or flannel shirts are always too big and his jeans faded and soft, never crisp and pressed.

Now he's standing tall and straight, his posture that of an military commander or an SS trooper. Even his leather jacket seems to fit better. His chin is thrust out, his shoulders thrust back, and his smile, normally sleepy and gentle, has a cunning twist to it. He knows he has a gift, a gift that grants him power over the emotions of weaker mortals.

Pride.

Pride faces Wrath to the amusement of the two door guards and neither one seems likely to back down. How long is it going to take for one of the other Sins to grab hold and pull?

If I let down my guard in the slightest I become acutely aware of a hot buffet set over to one side and feel Gluttony tug on my belly, reminding me that dinner was several hours ago. Sloth reminds me it's late. Surely no one would mind if I went over and sat on those pillows in the corner. I'm awfully tired.

I dig the nails of my right hand into the palm of my left, hoping the pain will clear my head and feel Wrath entering through that door.

"Oh, God," I pray, almost unconsciously, reverting to the formulas of my childhood, "tell me what to do!"

Immediately a sweet voice whispers inside my head and I see a vision of white wings. *"Open yourself to me. I will help."*

Panicked, I close my mind to the vision, terrified that the hellions will see the glow of Heaven through my skin. Certainly Will has, for he looks at me in concern.

"Do you need my help, Lucy?" he asks, no pride in his tone, just memory of the first time he helped me brings the source of my powers to the surface.

"No!" I insist. "I'm under control."

"Right," he says doubtfully. "Let's see what we can do about luring those guards away from the door."

That's a good idea. Behind us, the skinheads have gotten into a brawl with some of the other patrons, but I have a feeling it won't be long before they remember us.

Cindy puts herself between Madeleine and Danny, keeping our little animal lover from clawing out her would-be rescuer's eyes.

After a hurried consultation, Will and Pedro start performing bits of fairground magic for the two door guards. In a completely serious tone of voice, Will tells the big black guy how he was Shaka Zulu in a previous life. Pedro, meanwhile, produces a pouch of runestones from his jacket pocket and has the white guy toss them. Step by step, they draw them from the door.

I catch Pedro's worried gaze and know that he's counting on me to get the door open when it's clear. I think I see reproach in his eyes, too, as if he's wondering why I'm just standing there in my newest dress, doing nothing but watching.

Whether the reproach is in his eyes or in my heart, the effect is the same. As soon as the door is clear I rush in and shove up the bar. Mercifully, it swings outward. Dropping the bar, I push hard, so hard that I stumble out into the cool night air, amazing a couple sitting on a car and sharing a joint.

"Hey . . ." the guy begins in a tone of mild reproach, then he sees inside the club and forgets what he was about to say.

Ignoring his muttered, "Wow!" I turn back toward the others.

"Come on!" I yell. "Get out of there!"

The clear air seems to have broken the spell holding Madeleine and Danny. They stop in mid-motion, amazed to find themselves separated only because Cindy has a hand pressed to each of their breastbones. Will stops weaving tales of past wonders for the black fellow (I hear him saying something about pharaohs in ancient Egypt), and Pedro gathers up his runestones and drops them into his pouch.

Everything is going wonderfully until the white guy picks a stray runestone from the floor.

"Buddy," he says to Pedro in the friendliest tone imaginable. "You missed one." Then he tosses it overhand toward the bar.

The stone smashes several glasses, stopping the fun the group clustered around the bar is having with the young man. The young man lifts his head, revealing a face handsome in a tough way and terribly familiar: Pedro's brother, Juan.

Pedro screams. "Juanito!" and runs *back* into the damn club.

Cindy turns, flinging out her hands as if conjuring a net or rope to pull him back. I see the white lines flow from her fingertips, see them get tangled into themselves, morph into an octopus that starts tugging her into its embrace. Madeleine is about to try her stuff on the octopus when suddenly I stop being afraid.

I have had enough.

"Okay!" I shout to God and Heaven. "Do with me according to your will!"

That does it. Something swells inside of me, something as powerful as all the evil in that club. It explodes outward filling the club with white light, creating a cyclone that spins hard and fast, sealing the gateway to Hell—forever, I hope.

In the process there's screams both from the infernal and from the spectators, jets of multicolored light, and lots of confusion. We get away in the midst of it. All of us, even Pedro who is sobbing like a baby. It takes most of the night and all of Danny's gift to convince him that he hasn't failed Juan and left him to the torments of Hell.

But that doesn't finish it.

When we wake up the next morning, the volcanoes to the west of town are smoking and the city of Albuquerque is in a panic unequaled in all of its history. All residents with the least bit of power are being driven nearly mad by Things glimpsed out of the corners of their eyes. The rest are in a real hurry to get out of Dodge before the volcanoes blow, not in the least comforted by news bulletins that insist that there is no way that those three old cones could have any new fire.

The Mayor gets on radio and television to explain that it is all a prank—just like the time in the 1950s when some smart-alecks carried old tires up to the top and set them on fire. His speech doesn't do any good. It does less than any good when someone on his staff leaks out a report that the Mayor is going to leave the Duke City by helicopter.

I'd spent the night with the others at Danny's campus apartment, too wired to go home. Before the phones go dead, I manage to call my mom and assure her I'm safe.

"Lucia," she says urgently, "I have heard from the High and Mighty. No one can get into Albuquerque. Our resident members were out of town at a conference and even they cannot get back. Our colleagues in the neighboring Pueblos are doing their best to help, but for now we're on our own."

"Thanks, Mom," I say. "Stay close to home and keep the family safe. We'll deal with this. I love you all."

I hang up before she can ask me how or what "this" is. The phones go dead soon after, saving me from having to explain. That's a good thing, because our theory sounds shaky, even to me.

Our guess is that when my Power sealed the portal to Hell last night, the evil that had already emanated forth remained free. Needing a place to concentrate, it settled on the volcanoes, since in almost any mythology you'd care to name volcanoes have been considered gateways to the underworld.

Whether those three elderly volcanoes are really active or are only creating the illusion of activity is a pretty moot point. Just the smoke is causing panic and rioting. The evil that men do, added to the evil released from Hell, is transforming our city into Hell on Earth.

I pass on my mom's message to the others and they look pretty somber. I think that up to this point we'd still been viewing our role as recon for the High and Mighty. Learning that there will be no help from that quarter is scary.

Will says hesitantly, "I guess we're on our own, but I sure think we're going to need somebody else. Even with Lucy's help, we barely made it out of the club last night."

"My *help*?" I ask, my voice shrill. I swallow and continue sullenly. "Let's face it. The situation's worse since we acted, since *I* acted, whatever it was I did."

Danny reaches out and hugs me, but although I feel calmer I take no comfort in his embrace. I know it's what he'd do for any of us. I so want to be special to him.

"You tried," Danny says gently.

"I didn't," I say, admitting what I know is true. "I didn't try. I tried not to do. In the end, I just surrendered and let God and Santa Lucia use me—and look what a mess they made of it. That *I* made of it. Oh, hell!"

I slide off the sofa, onto the floor, crying softly, tears running hot and wet down my cheeks, spotting the oversized T-shirt Danny had loaned me for a nightshirt.

"I never asked for this," I sob. "I liked having Power until I found out I was channeling a saint. I don't want it now. God's expecting too much of me. What he expected from Jesus was almost too much for Jesus, and I'm not Jesus. I'm just me."

My friends listen to this outburst with incredible patience considering that the sounds of sirens, car horns, shouts, and screams keep invading our sanctuary. If we raise the shade and look west we see three pillars of black smoke, ugly and thick with soot, against the deep blue sky of a New Mexico September.

And all I do is sit on the floor and cry. When I

stop, Cindy tilts up my chin so that I have to look at her.

"Lucy, did it ever occur to you that maybe God and Saint Lucia never wanted you to be anything other than yourself?"

I meet her blue eyes and see no mockery in them, no cleverness, just wisdom born out of her own battles with self-rejection and fears of inadequacy.

"I'm no shrink," Cindy continues, "but I know that not so long ago I was my own worst enemy. Facing that helped me deal with my problems and, incidentally, to focus my Power. Don't get mad at me, sister, but I think that now you are *your* own worst enemy. This 'saint power' is the same stuff you delighted in before. It's the same power you used to make fools of the High and Mighty when they tested you."

She grins at me. "Madame Alexandria told me all about your test as an example of how I *shouldn't* behave. The power hasn't changed, Lucy, but you have. Don't get what you can do all mixed up with what you've been catechized to expect of saints. From what I remember, some of them were rogues and others were warriors and others were just plain folks."

"Cindy," I say, wiping my eyes, "you were worth going to Hell for, you know that? Okay. I'll do my best to stop moping and start helping. Where do we start?"

"West," Pedro says, looking up from the complicated divinations he's been working at the kitchen table. "I've tried over and over again to refine the answers, but it keeps repeating one thing: 'Go West, young man.' "

"Well," says Madeleine, trying hard to sound brave, "I guess that's obvious enough. West we go."

Back in the Impala, with Danny driving so that Pedro can try to refine his reading, we head toward the part of the city called the West Mesa. A friend once explained to me that technically the mesa isn't a proper mesa, just a lava flow that stopped, leaving a high terrace. Usually I can ignore that fact. Today with the volcanoes getting stoked to blow, I can't forget that this time the lava would course over that terrace and go splashing down right onto people's houses.

We don't see any other vehicles on westbound I-40 until we get to the last couple of exits. Some west side residents have obviously decided to brave a pass by the volcanoes in the hope that once they are in the open country farther west they'll be safer than those poor souls caught in eastbound traffic.

Exiting at Paseo del Volcan, we head north, past the truck stop, past the ball field, past signs for the Double Eagle airfield. We're slowing onto the rutted dirt road that leads toward the volcanoes when a young man in mirrored shades gets out of a Park Service vehicle and signals for us to turn around.

"I'm sorry," he says, "but the park is closed today."

He even smiles as if aware how stupid this incredibly mundane statement sounds with the volcanoes puffing behind him, but the set of his jaw is firm and I know that there will be no arguing with him. This is a brave man, staying by his post despite a firm belief that he will be among the first to die when the volcanoes erupt.

The rest must sense this, too, and perhaps the sight of other official vehicles blocking the road in a makeshift barrier does its part in convincing us to retreat.

"What do we do now?" Danny says as he turns us around.

Pedro looks up from his runestones.

"Those volcanoes are still messing up my readings," he apologizes, "but once for my anthropology course I went to see the petroglyphs in Rinconada Canyon. I think that from there we could climb to the top of the mesa and walk to the volcanoes."

Cindy nods. "That's as good a plan as any."

Pedro says to Danny. "Drive east to the Unser exit,

then north. The park is at Saint Josephs Street. We just have to pray that there are no guards there to stop us."

"I'll handle the praying," I quip, trying not to feel queasy. "That sounds like my department."

Whether or not my prayers do the job is anybody's guess, but when we get to Rinconada Canyon, no one's there. Leaving the Impala in the dirt parking lot, we hike up a path in the sand.

The day is warm and pleasant now that the sun is getting high. Jagged chunks of basalt, mostly a dark gray-brown verging into black, are to our right as we hike into the canyon. Basalt's not a really pretty rock, but the patterns left by the gas bubbles that were trapped when the lava was molten are interesting. To our left is a broad meadow, full of wildflowers, beyond that, the southern wall of the canyon.

One of New Mexico's many quirks is that there are more native plants that flower in the fall than in the spring. Asters, sunflowers, spectacle pod, and mallow brighten the pale green of the sagebrush, saltbrush, rabbitbrush, and lots of other brushes I don't know the names of with purple, yellow, white, and orange.

The deeper we walk into the canyon, the harder it is to remember that we're on a dangerous mission. The high walls hide our view of the western horizon and since most of us are searching for petroglyphs, it's easy to find an excuse not to look up and see the smudge of smoke to the west.

"There's one," Cindy calls out, pointing to a big rock. "It looks like a hand."

"There's a snake on the rock next to it," Madeleine adds, "and a bear's paw and a spiral and a sun."

"What's that?" Will asks, pointing to some squiggles.

Pedro shrugs, "Doodling?"

"On solid rock?" Will, hardheaded in some areas

as befits a math and economics major, frowns. "I don't think so."

"Ritual markings, then," Pedro says, grinning as he uses the standard anthropological catchall. "Those look like cloud symbols. The spirals may indicate a journey or a whirlwind.

"To be honest," Pedro continues, "no one knows what many of the petroglyphs are. Even when the picture is obvious, we don't know what it means. All we know is that what these pictures stood for was important enough that long ago people came here and pecked them into the smooth sides of the rocks."

I must not be the only one who finds Pedro's lecture a pleasant distraction because Danny asks: "I don't get it. How can we recognize a picture and not know what it means?"

Pedro nods approvingly. "Good question. Okay, look there, what's that?"

Obediently, Danny looks. "A round circle with markings in it and some lines around it."

"That's a shield figure," Pedro explains, "like a man with a shield. We can guess that, but we don't know if that shield is a prayer for protection or a prayer for success in war or maybe somebody's signature—like heraldry in the Middle Ages."

Madeleine nods. "But surely a duck," she points to one, "is a duck, or a snake a snake."

"Maybe, but in some modern Indian cultures a snake is a symbol for rain," Pedro responds. "Think about it. You know the 'universal' symbols used on crosswalks?"

We all nod, never pausing in our steady trudging toward the western wall of the canyon. Sand doesn't make for easy walking and already my calves ache. Cindy's quiet, trying to hide that she's nursing a slightly turned ankle. Danny notices, though, and we pause long enough for him to do a laying on of hands.

"Okay," Pedro continues. "We see that picture of

a person walking and we know it means 'Walk.' What might someone from the future see, especially without the context of crosswalks?"

"Just a picture of a man," Will answers eagerly. "It's like numbers or mathematical symbols. They mean something only if you know what they mean. Otherwise they're just funny marks."

He looks at the closest groups of petroglyphs with new respect. "There could be some very powerful magic here."

"I wish we could tap it," I am saying when a macaw flies out of the rocks and lands on Madeleine's shoulder.

It's the craziest bird I've ever seen: not really a bird, just a white outline of a bird with the basalt still showing in the middle. Though it's not well drawn, you can tell from the shape of its head and curve of its beak that it's a macaw, not a duck, like the one that waddles out a moment later.

Pedro clears his throat. "You were saying, Lucia?"

"I . . ."

More petroglyphs are emerging now, and not just animals. We'd seen the masks pecked into the rock, eyes indicated by rectangles or sometimes just lines, more lines for mouth and nose. They'd been interesting there, but seeing them float toward us now, unconnected to a body is pretty creepy. So are the foot- and handprints. The former walk through the sand like they're being left by the Invisible Man. The latter join thumbs and flap toward us using their fingers as ungainly wings.

In this context, the shield figures are something of a relief, even though many of the round-bodied figures lack a head and have nothing more than thin lines to indicate arms and legs. A couple of more complete figures join them. One rubbery limbed fellow reminds me of a Martian, since his head is topped with what look like antennae. Another is clearly a ceremonial dancer, dressed in a mask and kilt not unlike what I've seen depicted on the kachina dolls sold in Old Town.

Like the macaw, these are drawings. They don't swing arms and legs or flap wings as they silently close around us, yet, as with some of the artwork we saw during our tour the previous day, there is a slight sense of motion.

The Kachina Dancer and the Martian seem to be the leaders of the group, for the other petroglyphs fall back to let them through.

"We're done for," Will moans. "Hell's gotten the art here, too!"

Madeleine says hesitantly. "I don't think so. I don't feel scared."

That's quite a pronouncement since at this moment she is half-buried in petroglyph critters.

There are birds on her shoulders and outstretched arms, even a duck on her head. Snakes are coiling up her legs and bear paws minus the bear are tromping around her. There are even some things that might be sheep (but could just as easily be deer or armadillo) rubbing against her torso. Something I'd be willing to swear is a coyote is wagging its stick-and-line tail appreciatively, looking for a chance to join the pileup.

"You're a braver woman than I, Gunga Din," Danny says, brows raised. "Are they telling you anything?"

Madeleine frowns and pushes back a duck. "I get the feeling that *they're* scared, scared of the volcanoes erupting and wiping them out. They want our help."

"Great."

We stare blankly at each other and then at the gathering of petroglyphs. There's a lot of them here and, leaving out Madeleine's menagerie, many of them are plenty martial.

Cindy pulls at her recently shortened hair. "They need our help," she muses, "and we were saying earlier that we can't tackle this alone. Maybe we can help each other."

"Lucia did say," Pedro adds, "just before the macaw came, that she wished we could tap the magic stored here. A wish is a sort of prayer, I think. Maybe this is an answer to her prayer."

"You mean," I say doubtfully, "that I did this?"

"No, *querida*," he shakes his head vigorously, "but maybe your wish enabled them to rise up and show us they are here and friendly."

"Sort of friendly," Danny contradicts, for a shield figure is poking him with its spear. "Or at least sort of impatient."

"Let's keep walking toward the volcanoes," Cindy decides, "and see if the petroglyphs follow us."

Follow us they do, and our army grows as we go deeper into the canyon. So does the petroglyphs' mobility. The Kachina Dancer and the Martian lead the way, dancing a summons that brings more petroglyphs out from the basalt. The critters carry Madeleine like a princess, but the rest of us must hurry along, feet slipping on the sand. At the canyon's deepest point, we begin the climb to the top, scrabbling up the broken basalt like we're climbing a giant's stair.

As we hustle along, Cindy gives orders. "I'll be ready to conjure stuff for attack or defense as needed.

"Lucia, try to strengthen the petroglyphs just like you strengthened each of us in the Inferno. Madeleine, encourage those animals to do something more useful than jittering around. Danny, you're First Aid. Pedro, you figure out which of the volcanoes we need to concentrate our attack on. Will . . ."

Will shrugs. "Not much use for past life regressions. I'll keep an eye out for trouble. I expect there will be plenty."

Despite my new resolve to trust my Power, I feel a pang of the old doubt, and protest, "But, Cindy, my

Power is Christian in origin. These petroglyphs belong to a non-Christian tradition."

"Don't be so medieval," Cindy says. "You know God isn't restricted by human categories. Prayers are prayers no matter who speaks them. The people who made these petroglyphs are long gone, but their prayers remain."

Pedro glances over. "And maybe those people are not so long gone, Lucia. Didn't you tell me that your grandfather was Hopi?"

I nod.

"And we know full well that the conquistadors intermarried with *los Indios* for a long time. I doubt that there is one Hispanic in all New Mexico without Indian blood, nor one Indian without Hispanic."

Danny grins his warm, sleepy grin. "Yeah. No matter what the UFO fans like to think, people don't just disappear. They move on, marry into new groups, make new alliances. I once heard an archeologist say that the Anasazi didn't vanish, they just moved down the road to the nearest pueblo."

"So we bring the magic of our ancestors," Pedro says, "to this new battle, protecting both their sacred things and our future."

I grin, relieved, feeling as if the wool that has been wrapped around my soul has finally been pulled off. At last, I can see Santa Lucia for who she is—Holy Lucy, Holy Light.

"Let's go!" I say and with this simple prayer that light blossoms from my heart and fills us all—humans and picture people alike.

The change in the petroglyphs is the most striking. They fill out, gain dimension and motion, though they never quite stop looking like pictures. The points on spears and arrows look sharp now, and the eyes in the faces move and the mouths shape somber greetings.

I find myself thinking that the Kachina Dancer does look something like Grandpa Hopi did in pictures my father has of him as a young man. The Martian now is clearly a man wearing a mask with protruding decorations, not antennae. He still looks rubbery around the joints, though, and when he leans down to help me up to the top of the mesa his arm elongates to reach me.

The blue sky is full of clouds where there had been none before and I realize that some of the former squiggly lines have claimed their places as thunderheads. The snakes balance on their tails as real snakes never do and when they stretch upward lightning crackles in reply.

My friends are changed, too. Danny strides along beside Madeleine, helping her instill courage in the animals. Eyes shining from within, they communicate easily with the animals.

Will has accepted a spear from a shield figure and walks between two of these warriors, acting as a scout. Cindy discusses tactics with the Kachina Dancer. Then Pedro, in the midst of a whirlwind of spirals, calls out:

"Go for the middle volcano. That's where the Hell power is concentrated."

Cindy nods thanks. "The Leader here says we have two choices. We can attempt to banish Hell back where it belongs or we can seal it into the volcano."

"We banish it, of course," Madeleine says firmly, "so it can't threaten us again."

"That will be the harder fight," Cindy warns, but none of us wimps out and that's a good thing, because at that moment of decision Hell unleashes its fury.

First the cone of the middle volcano cracks and a thin line of red hot lava oozes forth. There's a funny smell in the air that I barely register as poisonous gas before the petroglyph winds disperse it. Shifting ash clouds the sky and hot bombs of lava thud around us.

"Hell's pulling out all the stops," Danny mutters.

"I don't think this is exactly how my geology prof said a volcano worked."

He lopes over to where a shield figure has been partially shattered by a lava bomb and, amazingly, his power is able to heal the rock. Then I don't have any more time to sightsee because the fight is upon us.

My memories of the battle are the intimate kind: dodging falling stuff, ducking when a poorly aimed lightning bolt gets too close, leaping over clawing hands that emerge from cracks in the shaking ground.

Every so often, I catch a glimpse of one of my buddies and we seem to be holding our own. Still, without the petroglyphs we never would have crossed that mile or so of mesa top and gotten to the volcanoes.

The Martian stays by me the whole way and somewhere along our journey I realize that he is somebody very holy, a priest or maybe even a god. I also realize, without knowing quite how, that it's going to be up to the two of us to banish Hell's power. Despite hellish voices screaming horrid things at me, I sit on my doubts and immerse myself in the glory of the Light.

Getting to the volcano top leaves me scraped and bruised, but basically intact. The Martian has lost one of his antenna, but is otherwise fine. The two of us stand there on trembling ground, trying to concentrate our power, and Hell fights back with all it's got, but our allies are right there to protect us.

When hot gases burst from the ground, whirlwinds blow them away. When darkness shrouds us, miniature suns and stars glow golden and bright. When lava bursts forth right under our feet, Cindy conjures an ice floe to freeze it solid.

I seize the Martian's rubbery hand and squeeze it tight. I don't know who he prays to, but I'm sure our prayer is the same. I imagine a cool clean wind racing through the volcano's hot interior and chasing out the infernal emanations. We tap a spring deep beneath the basalt and bring water to flush the evil that lurks in rock crevices and hidden gullies.

Once driven out, the infernal emanations are fair game for our warriors. Wind and lightning net them, spears and arrows pin them, rain and sunlight disperse their evil until it is no more.

When the battle is over, we hurry back to the canyon with our allies, not wanting anyone to find us at the volcanoes.

As we retrace our steps, one by one, the petroglyphs return to their places on the rocks. By the time we get to the trailhead, only the macaw remains. After a final loop around Madeleine's head, it flies into the rock and is gone.

All of us look pretty battered, but Danny has power enough to mend our wounds. With a sudden inspiration I wave my hands and we are clean and freshly dressed.

"Not bad, Lucy," Cindy says, fingering her newly restored hair. "Not bad at all."

I grin, knowing she's not just talking about her hair, feeling a Light inside of me, a Light that I pray will illuminate all my days. I've been worried about the interest on that God's loan and I'm beginning to get a feeling for what it will be.

It's not going to be simple, making decisions for myself rather than letting precedent or catechism or tradition do it for me but, fresh from one battle, I'm ready for the next.

THE FATAL WAGER

A RETELLING OF
AN IRISH MYTH
Elizabeth Ann Scarborough

*Elizabeth Anne Scarborough won a Nebula Award
in 1989 for her novel* The Healer's War, *based on
her experiences as an Army nurse in Vietnam. She
has collaborated on four books with Anne McCaf-
frey, three novels and one anthology,* Space Opera.
Her most recent novel is The Godmother's Web,
*which uses Native American folklore as a backdrop.
She lives in Washington with four cats.*

WHEN folk think of war witch, they tend to think of
the Morrigan or of her sister, the one who appears as
the Ban Sidhe. But the truth of it is, the Morrigan is
but the eldest of three dark sisters, known as the
Babd. She's a bitter one, is the Morrigan, for she was
once the love of a High King and when he died, so
did the loving part of her. Ever since, though she has
lusted often enough, her true love has been the thrill
of battle and the death rattle is only the sweet nothing
she cares to hear.

Her youngest sister was not so hard, though. Macha
was still full of the hope and idealism of youth. Her
hair was red and long, her form willowy and slender,
she was graceful as a doe but could run more fleetly

than any deer; aye, more fleet was she than an arrow's flight. She delighted in her youth, her beauty, her own grace and speed, and she longed for a man to delight in it too—and made the mistake of saying so to her elder sister.

"Don't wish for *that* too hard," the Morrigan said. "Men are short lived and most of them false. They care more for their honor and their bonds with each other than any will care for you."

"You've not been with them all," Macha replied. "The men of Ulster, your own chosen warriors many a time, are strong and handsome, and some are very good husbands indeed. Take that Crummnac now, he who lost his wife only recently, and him left with two wee children, he was a good and kind husband. It twists my heart to hear him weep with loneliness."

"Go to him then, if you think so. Play wife to the man and see what it gets you. I'll wager that within the year he'll betray you. Of course, if he knows you're a mighty goddess, he'll treat you accordingly for what he can get out of you so to make the wager fair you can't tell him who you are. In fact, it's best you say as little as possible. Otherwise he's sure to guess."

But Macha shook her head. "I can pretend to be like any mortal woman and I've seen how he is with those he loves. I'll win your wager easily. So long then, elder sister, I'm off to chance my luck."

And so she waited until twilight when the widower Crummnac, who was a farmer, would walk across his fields up into the woods to go hunting.

Macha didn't want to go right up to the man, you see, she wanted to give him a bit of time to admire her—oh, she had no doubt she was admirable. Those ancient goddesses, there was nothing shy about them, so she ran circles around him as he walked, enjoying the feeling of him watching her. She outran his dogs and the deer they chased, she outran the hare and ran faster than the birds could fly. She jumped the streams without needing the stepping stones, and played tag with the trees until at last Crummnac yelled, "Stop! Who are you?"

She did not answer but she followed him home. She swept his hearth and washed his dishes, baked some bread and made a good stew with what meat was left from his last hunting expedition, since she had distracted him too much to catch a thing on the most recent. She wiped the noses of his children and put them to bed, and when it was time for him to go to his bed, she followed him in, dropped her dress to her feet, and stood until he lifted the blanket for her. She did not have long to stand there shivering.

They were very happy indeed together, despite the Morrigan's *geas* that Macha could not speak to her man unless it was something very important. The truth was, he was like many of his countrymen and liked to speak so much himself that he thought her highly intelligent and well informed and a fascinating conversationalist when she said not a word. And since, though a humble farmer, he himself was actually highly intelligent, well-informed, and if not an excellent conversationalist, at least an excellent storyteller, besides which he was kind and considerate, as she had already noticed, she grew to love him more with each passing day.

She was sure the Morrigan had been wrong about betrayal. The man could not do enough for her and that was a fact.

And then came the day, after a few months of such bliss, when she had something very important indeed to tell him and the children. "I'm to have a baby," she said.

He was overjoyed as were the children, who made an extra effort to be helpful around the house. He fairly broke his back with the planting and hunting and harvesting bringing in food for them all for the winter, and in his spare time he carved beautiful figures of deer and boar, horse and hare, which he sold to buy a cow. The cow slept in the little room next to the one the family lived in, where her warmth could add to the fire's to keep them warm, and their fire could warm her as well in the winter and all of them could remember that men and beasts were not without relationship to one another. With the arrival of the cow, there would be milk for all, three children being known to consume so much more food than two.

But Macha grew much larger than expected. Her belly grew rounder and rounder and protruded further and further until it equaled nearly half the length of her, and herself a tall woman. "I am having two babies, husband," she told him, speaking for the second time only. "Twins.'

"Ah, well, that explains it then," he said, and gave her a rather awkward embrace.

If she did not lose her grace, neither did she go running in the woods for sport any longer, but stayed inside weaving, spinning, and knitting in preparation for the coming of the twins.

One day, as she was lining the cradle with a soft blanket she had woven while Crummnac told her stories of his days in the service of the king, Conner MacNessa, who should come knocking at the door but a messenger from the king himself.

Not knowing who it was, Crummnac opened the door cautiously, his dirk in hand, and stepped outside while his family listened from within the stone walls of their house.

The rider did not dismount. "Good day and good health to you, Crummnac," he said.

"And to you as well," the farmer replied, still cautiously. This was a man younger than himself and Crummnac had not been with the king for several years and did not recognize the fellow.

"The king has acquired the fastest chariot horses in

all of Ireland preparatory to the upcoming war. He's giving a great party and he wants you to come."

"It's an honor to be asked," Crummnac said, though he was worried that the party would happen when his new wife was bearing their children. But he said nothing because when the king asks someone to come to a party, it's not just a social invitation, it's a command performance.

"When will it be?" he asked.

"Tomorrow. Be there by noon," the rider said. "I'll see you there, then. I'm off to invite the others now."

"Farewell till then," Crummnac said politely.

"And to yourself," the man replied and was gone.

When Crummnac returned inside, the peace in his little house had gone as if war had broken out within the walls. Macha fretted and paced, fretted and paced, and she would not say what the matter was. The other children cried and clung to their father.

"I have to go, *acushla*," he said to his wife. "You can go with me if you like—I could borrow a cart."

"No!" she said, speaking for the third time. And now, what she had to say was very important indeed, though she did not know why, but the dread was as huge in her as her babies. "No, I will not go and you must not even tell them about me. No one but you and the children know I am here and until our babes are born, no one *may* know I am here. You stay at your party and if all goes well, you will be home in time for the birth and even if you're not, I should manage well enough."

She said it with such certainty that his mind was much relieved and he set out the next morning for the party. It was not far to the king's fort. No one wished to live too far from the protection of their overlord in those days and it was but a few hours walk. He was thinking there might be vendors there, perhaps he could do a carving and trade for something pretty for his woman.

Though they had not long been together, the farther he walked, the more he missed her, the more he thought of how remarkable she was and how lucky he was. And being human, the more he wanted to tell other men how lucky he was, so that they would envy and admire him for having had the love of not only one, but two wonderful women in his lifetime.

But his wife had said he must say nothing and he had promised and he fully meant to keep his word.

The king greeted him personally, as if he were a brother, and Crummnac was glad of that because the king had been a bit peeved with him the last time they were together. The king had not wanted him to leave his service, for in his time Crummnac had been the best judge of horses in all of Ulster, though now he owned not even a single steed. And also, Crummnac's first wife, Sorcha, had been the king's elder sister's daughter, too close a kin for the king himself to take to wife, but Crummnac and Sorcha both knew the king had wanted to, and had he not been distracted by another woman things might not have gone as happily for the couple as they had. But all of that seemed forgotten as Conner MacNessa clapped his old friend on the back and called for strong drink to be brought to them both. For a time, they drank and spoke of what had happened since the old times for a while, and then the king said, "It's time for the race now. And I will show my prize off to you."

He took Crummnac to see his horses, two beautiful black beasts they were, shining and snorting and full of spirit, with slender strong legs and graceful arched necks that put Crummnac in mind of the grace of his wife.

Every time his cup was empty, the king called for it to be refilled and after a bit, he didn't have to call. A servant followed them around with a golden vessel full of the fermented drink and the cups did not get even half empty before they were filled again. At one time, this would not have affected Crummnac very much because, as a soldier, he had been used to the drink. But on his farm, he drew water from the clear stream that ran behind his house or fresh milk from the new cow, and with two children to feed had neither milk nor grain to waste on fermenting for drink.

He quickly felt his head begin to spin, his feet to tangle, and his tongue to loosen.

The races began. The beautiful chariot horses raced all of the other horses at the party. First the king's relatives and highborn friends raced their chariots and horses with the king's new steeds, but all were easily bested. The other horses looked clumsy and slow, but then, they *were* clumsy and slow. Most of them were not bred for racing chariots, but for battle in wartime and the plow or riding in peacetime. Horses were far too dear to have special ones for each occasion. Only the king could afford that luxury.

Conner grew drunk on victory and pride as well as the drink as his new black steeds defeated first the chariot horses, then every other horse there.

"There's not a thing in Ireland can touch them!" the king boasted. "Have you ever seen anything so fast as they are, Crummnac? Come now, you never have, have you, man?"

Crummnac nearly fell over when the king pounded him on the back in his enthusiasm. "Now that you mention it, sire, I have. For horses, they're fast enough, but my wife, now, she'd run circles around them, as she did the hares and deer when I first saw her."

"What wife is that?" the king asked, and as drink will do to a man's mood, it changed him from merry and exultant to angry and petulant. "Sorcha is dead a long year now. I didn't know you had another wife." The king's face was red and a throbbing vein stood out beneath his eye. "Why did you not bring her here as I commanded?"

"Well, sire, you didn't say she was to come and she's heavy with child at the moment and not fit for travel."

"Still, you say, she's faster than my horses?" the king asked.

"When I met her she was faster than anything I've ever seen," Crummnac said, "But now she's with child, as I said and . . ."

"If she's faster than my horses, I must see her run against them," the king said and there was a wicked stubborn gleam in his eye that made Crummnac wish he'd cut out his own tongue before he'd broken his word to his wife and told the king about her.

"Oh, no, sire, she couldn't run *now*. She's about to bear twins."

"Then you lied to me?" the king demanded. "She's either faster than my horses or she isn't, which is it to be?"

Crummnac tried to be reasonable, to explain that while she had been so fast when he first met her, she was no longer able to run. Indeed, she should not run for the sake of her life and that of her unborn babies, but the king would hear nothing he said, and this time, when he clapped him on the back, the king sent Crummnac sprawling into a pile of manure, and with a jerk of his thumb, had his soldiers take Crummnac in custody.

"My men will go and fetch this wife of yours and we'll see how fast she is," he said. "If she's that fast, maybe she should pull my chariot instead of my horses. We'll have her race against them and see if you're lying or not."

Crummnac was fast in the grip of two of the king's men and too drunk to stand, too ashamed to do anything but weep.

Macha was in her herb garden when the king's men rode up, their horses all lathered and themselves sweating as well from the heat of the day and the

races they'd run earlier in it. Macha knew her time
was very near and was looking for the flowers and
leaves that would ease her labor pains and help the
babes be born safely and quickly. She had no time to
find them, however, when the men rode right up to
her, trampling her careful plantings.

"You're to come with us, wife of Crummnac,"
they said.

"Oh, no, I couldn't," she said easily enough, for her
sister's *geas* did not include talking to men other than
her husband. "As you can see, I'm about to have a
baby. Besides, there are the two wee ones here at
home."

"We'll take them along too, but come you must at
the king's command," said the first rider. His companion gathered the frightened children up on his horse
and the man who spoke to Macha, grabbed her beneath her swollen breasts and above her swollen belly
and pulled her up in front of him on the horse. She
was so big he almost could not reach the reins.

During the ride to the king's fort, Macha's labor
began but the sight of her did not move Conner
MacNessa to kindness, to pity, or to anything but
scorn. Crummnac, sagging between two of the king's
warriors, took one agonized look at his poor pregnant
wife as she was tossed down from the horse to lie at
the feet of the king like a bundle of laundry. Crummnac could not meet her eyes but looked away,
weeping.

Macha felt like weeping herself. The Morrigan, her
sister, had been right about the Ulstermen. For all of
the love and work they had shared, Crummnac had
betrayed her and told the king of her, for how else
would Conner MacNessa have come to know? From
the sneer on the king's face, she knew she had been
right to fear his knowledge of her. There was anger
in that sneer, and desire as well, but not an ounce of
respect for her condition, nor compassion.

"I haven't seen you around here before," the king said, lifting her chin with his fist to stare into her face. "No matter. Your husband tells me you are the fastest creature he's even seen. He says you are faster than my new chariot horses. I cannot believe it. You will race with my horses and we'll see who's the fastest."

"Sire, I am in labor with twins!" she said. "Have mercy! If I run now it will kill me and perhaps my children. I cannot."

Conner MacNessa's mouth twisted cruelly. "If you can't, then your husband has lied to his king and I'll have him put to death, slowly. And his children as well. Either you run, or they die." He pretended to soften and said, "It's too bad for you that you're about to spawn offspring for my old servant, but it's fair after all. You're fresh and my horses have been racing all day."

With a heaviness greater even than that in her belly, Macha rose and turned, and with something of her old grace, lined up with the front feet of the horses.

The king gave the signal and they were off. Macha was slower than she had been, but still, to the amazement of both Crummnac and the king, faster than the black horses who lagged three of their own lengths behind her until she suddenly doubled over with birth pangs and cried out.

The king set his own dagger at the throat of Crummnac's little daughter so that her stepmother could see. His nod to Macha clearly said, "continue, or she dies."

With a scream, Macha let her pain thrust her forward as if she were flung from a giant fist. The black horses had caught up with her in the meantime but now, as the pain released her, she sprang forward and outdistanced them until another pain overtook her. This time she did not look at the king and she did not pause but, incredibly, once more used the pain to catapult herself forward. A few more paces ad she was at the finish line.

The horses were far behind her, exhausted and all but broken from their exertions of the day. Crummnac had been watching and could not believe what he saw, and was filled with more fear and dread of his wife than he was of Connor MacNessa, for he was fully sober now, and he knew that no mortal woman could do what she had done.

But as soon as her foot crossed the finish line that had been furrowed in the field, Macha screamed, and the front of her skirt, which had been kilted up above her knees, blossomed with bright red blood. She fell to the ground screaming, and as Connor began to stroll toward her, Crummnac broke from his captors and began to run.

But he was too late. Women who had been standing near the finish line aided Macha, bringing forth first one boy, and then another, but Macha's red blood did not cease to flow, roused as it had been by her running.

Crummnac reached her side at the same time as the king, who stood staring down at her with a heartless haughtiness at her blood and sweat and the hair plastered to her face, head, and shoulders.

As she looked up at them, Crummnac knew she was dying, for her eyes were already seeing beyond them both.

"For your cruelty to me during my time, Connor MacNessa, I lay a curse upon you and all the men of Ulster that during *your* greatest time of need, you will feel as weak as I did today and you will suffer the pangs of a woman in labor." And with that, Macha left her husband, her new sons, Ulster, and the world of men, to return to her sister the Morrigan and pay her debt.

Conner MacNessa was a fool, but only up to a point. On hearing the curse, he knew, as did all his men, that the dying woman was a mortally offended goddess. No one else could have run the race that she did, deliver healthy twins, and die with a curse on her lips.

He had her buried where she lay and built a great cairn around her, a small mountain where he built a new fort so that he could see his enemies coming for miles away. To belatedly do honor to Macha's superhuman feat, the king ordered that the hill be called Emain Macha—the twins of Macha. As for the twins themselves, that is another story.

Connor MacNessa needed the view from Emain Macha. In fact, he needed all the advantage he could get, for, as he found in the next battle, her curse came true. When the enemy was upon them, the men of Ulster collapsed with the pains of labor and were weak as women. The Morrigan and her sisters, in the guise of great crows, laughed and drank their blood, feasted on their flesh, and plucked out their eyes. Had it not been for the Ulsterwomen, all would have been killed, or enslaved, or driven from their own lands. During this time did the great woman warrior Scathach come forward to lead her people in battle.

And it's to her we send you now, my son, our little hound, you not born of Ulster, you not bound by Macha's curse. Go to the woman warrior and she will teach you the battle skills you lack, that you and she and her women will be the saving of our land, all but lost to a king's pride and foolishness and the curse of an outraged goddess.

'WARE THE SLEEPER

Julie E. Czerneda

Canadian author Julie E. Czerneda lives by a forest with her family, indulging in rocketry and canoeing whenever possible. Her first SF novel, A Thousand Words for Stranger, *was published in 1997 by DAW Books. Her latest work,* Beholder's Eye, *has just been released, and the sequel to* Thousand, Ties of Power, *will be released in June, 1999. A biologist by training and inclination, Julie has also written science and other texts. "'Ware the Sleeper" is her first fantasy fiction.*

THERE were bones where the children played: small, smooth pieces perfect for game markers on the black sand, and long shards Skalda remembered using for fence posts around imaginary horses. The tides washed them here, along with links from shattered chain mail and futile bits of armor.

She regarded them now as portents: *May my enemies' bones keep you company,* she wished them.

"You're certain about this, Dir Agnon," this from Rathe, the priest-warrior from the Hinter Islands. His fleet lay in safety in the cove whose calm waters defined the near edge of the children's playground. *Safety won too late,* Skalda thought sadly, looking out over the sun-sparkled water at that handful of ships, masts split by spells of lightning, crews decimated by sendings of thirst and wasting disease.

They'd come here to huddle behind the great, untested fleet of the Circle Cove, to be nursemaided and told it wasn't their fault, that nothing anyone could do would succeed against the Enemy. *Which might well be true.*

"Certain? When are any of us certain these days, Dir Rathe?" Agnon offered in his soft, careful voice. As priest-adviser to the secular rulers of the Cove and the outlying island clusters, he was magnificently noncommittal at any given time. A virtue in times of slow, peaceful prosperity; a dangerous paralysis in this time of utter peril. Skalda stared out to the narrow, mist-filled opening that led to the open ocean until her eyes ached from the water's glare.

"Dir Skalda sounded quite sure of this course in our Council. And why else are we here today, with them?" Rathe pointed a bone-thin finger at the brightly clad group near their feet. The ten children, daughters and sons collected from each of the Noble Houses, were equally oblivious to the presence of adults or to portents of doom, half-arguing and half-laughing in dispute over a shell. Their shrill voices rose into the still morning air like the piping of shorebirds.

Skalda was not too old to remember playing in this very spot. The unremitting debates and meaningless conspiracies wearied her soul as the trials and failures of ancient magic had stolen her youth. Skalda knew herself to be skin stretched over bone, the once-elegant lines of her face etched in resemblance to her grandmother, not her mother. She did not know, nor would she warm to the thought, that others would argue her beauty had only been fired by turmoil as clay takes on the perfect glaze of porcelain after its time in the hearth. It was her people's fate that mattered, not the cost of their salvation.

"I am sure we have no other options left to us, comrades," Skalda answered calmly. "Let us choose and speedily. No amount of magic will delay the tides for more argument. We've little margin as it is to assure the *Mariner's Pride* safe passage over Blood Reef."

She looked back at the children playing amid the bones of their elders' hopeless war and prepared to make her own selection. When Rathe would have simply picked the nearest two to be done with it, Skalda touched the scarred chain mail of his sleeve and shook her head. His eyes were as haunted as she knew hers would appear.

The parchments, fragile with age and imperfectly translated, were clear on this point of the Summoning Spell at least. The payment for their salvation would be the blood of six innocents. That the blood should be royal and willing, not stolen from the arms of common folk, was Skalda's answer to her conscience.

* * *

Shafts of sunlight disappeared, reappeared; they filled at times with motes of life, golden suspended dust, then at others reflected silver as the great flocks swam through their columns, dancing with the light.

I was content thus, to gaze upward through the lens of my eye into the living magic of my world, my place, and see only that which belonged here. I felt the surge of waves over the crust of my side, reading there the approach of storms, the tug of moon and sun—events distant yet intimate. I slept, as some life reckoned this state of consciousness. It was as true a description as any; since I needed nothing and need do nothing.

If this is sleep, I sometimes wondered, struck by some particular beauty above me or caught by starlight through a rare clarity of ocean, *perhaps I dream the world.*

* * *

Fortress and fantasy, Skalda thought as she took one lingering, hungry look at her home before climbing the ramp onto the *Mariner's Pride* later that afternoon. The Circle Cove was a perfect shaping of black hard stone, the inward-facing surface of its mountainous sides etched by generations of artists into towers of breathtaking loveliness, decked with flower-laden balconies and terraces rich with green life; the outward sides carved by the ocean herself into equally fantastic shapes. The water within was the deepest, clearest blue, framed by beaches of soft black sand. Despite the grim reality of the Enemy's spread into almost all the territory once ruled from this place, the citizens continued their peacetime ways: floating scented candles on the still waters each night and tossing flower petals from their balconies to grace the decks of the mighty ships each morning.

The *Mariner's Pride* had left her crew behind, a sullen group of Leeward Islanders distrustful of dry land and the mysterious ways of priests. *Sullen was perhaps an unjust term,* Skalda corrected herself. The Leewards were the farthest south of the immense archipelago of islands within the rule of the Circle Cove, an afterthought of six volcanic rocks curled out into the icy current of the Palagar Sea. The folk who clung to those rocks were tough and self-reliant, proud of their hardship and uncomfortable in the warm caress of the Cove. Distant as the Leewards were from main routes of trade, they weren't far enough to escape the wrath pouring eastward from the mainland. This rare ship, hold filled with pink-fleshed fish and warrel pelts, had made her long journey as much for news of the Enemy's advance as for cloth and fruit.

With the God's blessing, Skalda thought, *she might carry home news of the Enemy's defeat.* Not only was the *Pride* no warship, her sturdy, clean lines and low profile had little in common with any other vessel now bobbing to the rise and fall of the Cove: the perfect choice for this journey where speed and secrecy could be the most potent weapons of all.

Captain Bocknek, a small, rotund man built much like his ship, had been understandably dismayed to have his beauty conscripted by the priesthood the moment the *Pride* kissed the dock—dismayed, yet resolute in insisting she wouldn't sail without him. Skalda had watched him oversee the hasty off-loading of cargo and crew, creating order of the necessary confusion and protest. He had stood quietly by as strangers came on his ship, seeming reassured by the quick comments of those who would crew the *Pride*. He had definitely been startled as the children came aboard, eyes half closed in trance, hands held gently.

Skalda noted without surprise how the Leeward Captain then remained on deck, refusing to even step below to his cabin where the children, soothed by spells of sleep and forgetfulness, rested on the softest of mattresses.

For this voyage, priests would crew the *Pride*: novices and warriors, in rank from sedir to dir, selected from scanty enough ranks not for their knowledge of the sea—they all, even the sleeping children, had that—but for the reliability of their magic. The spell they would attempt tomorrow was twofold, containing both summoning and aiming. There could be no margin for error, no chance to hesitate, fear failure, and stop. Skalda had not needed the ancient parchments' warnings or the worries of her fellow dir-priests to make that plain.

Besides, what good would a second try be? The massive fleet of the Enemy was moving inexorably closer. Why should it stop now, when nothing they had sent against it had made the slightest difference?

* * *

"We'll just make the tide, Dir Skalda, Dir Rathe," said Captain Bocknek as he joined them at the rail.

Overhead, the sails snapped as the breeze began, spelled by the sedir-priests below whose talents were sufficient for this (steady wind being the most useful magic to their seafaring kind and thus the first essential learning). The tiny wind caught at the canvas edges then began to swell the sheets themselves.

Now that his ship was alive on the sea, her deck swaying lightly underfoot, Captain Bocknek had assumed a slight swagger to his walk Skalda believed was quite unconscious and, from his reputation, deserved. "Wouldn't have wanted to wait any longer. This girl's not one to like her belly scraped on rock, no, sir."

Rathe's nostrils flared and he looked down at the little seaman as though trying to fathom why he, dir-priest and former commander of a fleet of warships, was being chatted with like some fisherfolk on his way to the rich hunting of the Banks offshore. Skalda leaned back against the railing, careless of her fine robes on the damp, cold wood, and almost smiled. Instead, she drew in a deep breath through her nostrils, relishing the salt and fish tang to the air, the tar-stink of fresh caulking. "We appreciate you holding at the dock for us, Captain," she said graciously. "And be sure we also value your fine ship."

Captain Bocknek's nut-brown skin darkened even further under the bristles of his sparse beard. "'Course, 'course," he muttered. "Dir Skalda. I wasn't implying other, you know."

"Have you taken her after baskers in the deep south, Captain?" she asked absently, looking to the passageway ahead, its gap wide enough to pass three of the Circle Cove fleet's largest galleys abreast. The opening was protected by twin towers manned ceaselessly by priest-warriors, dir and so capable of calling rock-falls on intruders. Their magic was a last resort, since catapults and burning oil were always aimed and ready. Despite the war with the Enemy, despite bones drifting in on tides she suspected the Enemy sent to appall them with its message that not even the blessed Depths were safe, none had ever assailed this port. *Some here,* thought Skalda, *slept well at night.* She was not one of them.

As always, preparing to leave the Circle Cove and its protection, she felt both exhilaration and foreboding. On this journey, she suspected her exhilaration was simply that of freedom from the endless debates, the weeks of searching musty records for any hint of a weapon; her fear had a more rational source. Those protecting cliffs curved outward just enough to conceal an ambush, should the Enemy's sea skills be able to hold ships within the crashing surf beyond. *Let them try,* Skalda thought, feeling a surge of welcome defiance. For all their sakes, this ship must not be stopped.

The Captain's reply drew her back to the moment. "Baskers for sure, Dir Skalda, but sail further south? Not damn likely, excuse me, even if the fish were willing to climb in the holds. The Enemy was scouting those parts long before their bows dipped into the Hinter Island Sound. Dir Rathe knows that."

"Dir Rathe knows it is time to go below and continue our preparations," that worthy snapped, walking away, then forced to catch and steady himself with one hand as the *Pride* entered the channel and rose cheerfully to meet the incoming swells.

"Dir Rathe," Skalda informed the offended Captain in a low voice, "also knows this deck will surely be splashed as we pass between the Cove's arms."

Captain Bocknek's eyes met and held hers with unexpected directness. She realized Rathe's rudeness hadn't bothered him after all. He reached out as if to touch her arm. "Dir Skalda. I confess I'm not—comfortable—" words seemed to fail him, and his face paled suddenly, as if seeing a whirlpool ahead into which he was about to plunge. "Forgive my impertinence, Dir Skalda. But I worry about the children.

The hazards of this journey. They looked so young when you brought them on board. And they sleep."

Skalda found she had no comfort to offer him. His eyes went dull as he looked into hers and understood. "Like that, it is," Bocknek said in a voice oddly free of bitterness. "As well they sleep, then. Would we all could."

* * *

Men rained down on me one day. I watched them come, limbs given grace by the ocean, armor glinting in the sun as it dragged the bodies to me. The great flocks, startled apart by the disruption, disappeared beyond my crust. Moments later, they coyly returned to start their feast. Blood clouded the water beyond my eye, but it was a temporary blindness. I had seen all this before.

* * *

They practiced below decks, rehearsing ritual none understood and, truth be told, none trusted. Skalda's urgings from the beginning had been to follow the Summoning Spell without modification, including use of the archaic language forms used in the parchments. Agnon, chant-master and their best authority on the older tongues, coached them all in the proper accents and subtle inflections. It had been many ages since this Spell had been cast. If it ever had been.

When they rested, Rathe expressed all their doubts. "This Summoning. It promises to sweep our foes from the sea, to guarantee utter and uncontestable victory. Explain to me then, if it ever truly worked before, how could our Enemy have rebuilt its fleets?"

"There may have been another Enemy," Agnon answered, his voice a gentle salve to counter Rathe's outburst. "It was certainly long ago."

Captain Bocknek sent word down. They would reach the Blood Reef at sunset, coinciding with the highest tide of the season in this place: safety for his ship's keel but most importantly, the appointed hour for the Spell.

Skalda sipped from a mug of mulled wine, thanking the sedir-priest who brought it warm to her hands. It was cold below deck, cold and redolent of the *Pride*'s former cargo.

There was no luxury in the *Pride,* beyond that given the sleeping children, and no food for any of them until the deed was done. She noticed the others drank cautiously as well, valuing the heat in their empty bellies but keeping their thoughts cool and directed. "If you have another plan for our salvation, Dir Rathe," she observed quietly, "we'd all be grateful. Since you are the only one of us here to contest the Enemy's forces directly in battle, perhaps you believe the Circle's Fleet is equipped to defeat them at sea?"

There were six of them around the crude table, all dir-priests. Of the six, she, Rathe, and Agnon would bear the action of the Spell, casting it over the Blood Reef. There was a second for each of them, a source of strength if any faltered, replacement if any were killed. For herself, Dir Clefta, a grim, silent man from the Hinter Isles. His community had been the first to abandon their homes to the Enemy's newest assault; he and three sedir priests managed to protect their few ships as they fled to the Circle Cove. Dir Segon would stand at Rathe's back; she, though young, was already considered heir apparent to Skalda's own place in the council. *It is dangerous to risk her here,* Skalda thought with regret, but she no longer believed in safe refuge, even for her promising apprentice. Agnon would rely on the solid good sense of his own brother, Dir Agnar—theirs being one of very few family pairings within the priesthood. Their harmony drew more strength to their magic than either possessed alone.

Strength? Experience? We have those, Skalda said to

herself, gazing at each in turn, collecting a somber reply of determined, if anxious, looks. *Let's hope we also have the blessing of the Depths and Her Quiet God on this ancient magic as well.*

There had been soul-searching and argument far beyond Rathe's cynical, albeit reasonable, doubts. While magic had been the tool of priests since records were first kept, that tool had evolved with their society's growth and change. Today's magic was precise, well-schooled, applied by specialists. The older magic had been larger in scope and far bloodier in cost. She had only to think of the wind filling the *Pride's* sails to capacity. Legends held that wind was once summoned by sacrifice, and once summoned, tore across the waves with the random fury of a cyclone to destroy all in its path.

Skalda had deliberately sought the fabled, deadly old magic, once reports were confirmed that the Enemy—no, she would not keep them faceless—the P'okukii were about to crush the Island states once and for all.

Had it only been in her parents' lifetime that the P'okukii traded peacefully for the riches of the sea? The mainlanders had little in common with the island folk, relying on a halting trade tongue to deal with the ships calling at their poorly maintained ports. Neither side had been interested in learning more about the other. The first of many misjudgments, Skalda and many other islanders realized too late. For while they learned the P'okukii feared invasion from some mysterious eastward land—a fear the more widely traveled islanders dismissed as superstition—they had not appreciated the depth of that fear. After all, who would take seriously a people who refused to step from the land?

Suddenly, like a nightmare, all that had changed. In one night, traders had been forced to flee from every mainland port, some barely escaping with their lives, all bringing word of a transformed nation, its inhabitants boiling with fear and rage. The cause was unclear—some spoke of evil portents in the night sky, others babbled of soothsayers crying out that the doom of the P'okukii was coming, the doom from the east.

The immense resources of the P'okukii were turned to the ocean they feared. Ports were fortified; shipbuilding went on at a feverish pace. The bemused islanders watched from a distance, returning to trade among themselves until the P'okukii settled back to sanity. They didn't see how the Circle Cove and its string of islands were all that lay between the P'okukii and their fear. There was no warning of what was to come.

For during Skalda's childhood, the P'okukii flooded seaward in a vast fleet consisting of more and larger ships than the islands together possessed. All that saved them was the caution of an enemy new to the sea. The Enemy was fearful, their sorcerers grappling with the chanciness of land spells over water, their commanders inexperienced. The islands of the Circle Cove defended themselves in surprise, expecting offers of reconciliation, resumptions of trade.

What they received was unending war. At first, it was an even conflict, the sea knowledge of the islanders and their priests more than a match despite the superior numbers of their foe. Then, slowly, island after island began to fall, their inhabitants forced to flee or die. But the Enemy, while never embracing the ocean, learned her ways. Their sorcerers grew deadly, gaining spells stripped from the minds of dir priests captured before they could perform the d'yet—ritual suicide. Somehow the battle magic of the islanders, the blessing of the Depths and her Quiet God, proved even more effective in the hands of unbelievers.

There were, Skalda sighed, *never guarantees on what offended deity.*

*   *   *

" 'Ware Ships!" The cries from the crow's nest pulled them all on deck, only those keeping the wind in the *Pride*'s sails ignoring the alarm. Skalda whispered a seeing spell. Muttered echoes rippled from either side and behind as the multitude of priests did the same. The Captain steadied his telescope. He needed no magic to witness the swarm darkening the horizon.

Rathe and other survivors hadn't exaggerated, Skalda thought with regret as her vision focused on the wavy line of painted prows and tossing masts. This wasn't a fleet—it was as if an entire nation had armed and launched itself on to the sea. *Why do they think us such a threat?* she wondered sadly. The very old tales held rumors of a decisive battle centuries ago, long before the days of record-keeping, one in which the island states gained their freedom from the mainland. But battles, successful or otherwise, seemed unlikely to spawn such hate and fear as this. *Unless,* she thought uneasily, *it was how that battle was won.*

"Why are they here, Dir Skalda?" It was Captain Bocknek pulling at her elbow urgently. "There is nothing in this direction worth attacking. Just the deserted Outer Islands and then the open ocean. They've gone right past the Cove!"

Segnon's clear, young voice held the slightest shiver as she drew the conclusion they all feared. "The Blood Reef. They have learned about the Summoning Spell. They mean to stop us."

"Or to use it themselves," Skalda said flatly. She deliberately turned her back on that threat and raised her voice so it soared over the murmurs and speculations filling the deck. "Put on all the sail the *Pride* carries. Dir-priests. Spells of warding. Protect the hull and the sedir-priests. We must not be hindered. We will not be stopped. For the Cove!"

"For the Cove!" they chanted back, eyes afire with

purpose, gnarled hands rising as one with smooth young fists to accept her challenge.

The *Pride* drove her prow fast and deep into the oncoming waves. Skalda stayed well away from the railing now. She had no right to risk herself so close to her duty. Wind whipped her hair free of its knot, lashing her cheeks.

" 'Ware! The Blood Reef! 'Ware below!" came the cry heartbeats later. Priests scrambled to drop the *Pride*'s sails. The Enemy fleet had already halved the distance between them; now its ships were close enough for shouts to carry, close enough for protection spells to be tested by the magic of sorcerers. So far, only those in the crow's nest had been harmed, caught in the boundary between forces, screaming as they were blinded. An early victory for their Enemy.

The *Pride* settled into position above the Blood Reef. There was a sudden hush of sound and breath. All knew it would be only moments before they were within the range of more mundane weaponry, against which the sturdy whip had no defense.

"Wake the children," Skalda said calmly.

* * *

A finger of darkness scratched the crystalline sky above me, a moving finger casting its shadow and more into my sight. Six forms detached from it, drifting down to me in synchrony and sacrifice. In their wake, I could hear the old words.

The Summoning.

The forms, small and devoid of armor, fell closer. The flocks converged, undeterred by blessing or purpose. Blood stained my vision, refusing to diffuse into the ocean as it should. Instead, it flowed down to me, coated me, entered my mouth tasting of innocence shed for rage's sake.

At last!

If I had slept, this was the moment I awoke.

* * *

"It's working!" shouted a voice, panic-fringed rather than triumphant. *Something was happening,* Skalda amended to herself, bracing as the deck of the *Pride* shifted under an ocean seeming to rise under their feet. A barrel came loose and rolled; sedir-priests jumped to dodge it.

The water lifted impossibly alongside them, with no wind, no swell to explain it. The Enemy fleet was caught as well, cries of alarm ringing over the strange silence of the sea. Only the noises of human and ship broke against it.

The *Pride* began to slip down the side of a watery mountain, the movement so delicate and deceptively slow the Captain let go his death's grip on the wheel and simply stared, openmouthed, at what was becoming plain.

For it wasn't a wave rising to loom beside them. It was the Blood Reef itself, its coral-crusted bulk shedding water in a fall leagues long as it rose beyond the ocean's grip, the roar enough to drown out any screams. Fish drowned, caught by spurs and outcrops of stony growth, imprisoned helplessly in the air. Other things were caught as well: bits of bone and flesh, swords and armor, a child's robe.

Skalda found it strange that over the din of the waterfall she could still hear Dir Agnon losing his mulled wine beside her.

She clung to the rail, more to hold what was human than because the ship was unsteady. The waterfall ended, replaced by a single loud whoof of air as whatever they had summoned expelled its first breath.

"What is it?" breathed Clefta, his hand still tight on her shoulder. "I expected a storm, maybe a great wave . . ."

Skalda shook her head, then realized she did know

just as what looked like a promontory to one end of the floating reef turned to regard her through a gleaming black and yellow eye easily as tall as the *Pride*'s mast.

"It's the Quiet God," she whispered, "roused to war."

* * *

Vision sharpened and added the plane of horizon, distracting with its promises of *far* and *new*. I sought the Summoners. *There*. There must be three.

* * *

"There must be three," Skalda said, repeating from the parchment.

"Yes, yes. Three to Summon," Rathe added, moving to stand beside her and Agnon. His voice held the same mixture of pride and horror they likely all felt. It was one thing to pray daily and interpret blessings—quite another to wake a god and wait.

"Three to Aim," Skalda said in the same stunned whisper, tearing her eyes from that one great eye to seek out the scattered but formidable fleet of their Enemy. "But how? 'Each to become an Eye' the parchment said. What do we do?"

"Sweet Depths," breathed a voice behind her. She couldn't recognize it and didn't turn to see. Her question was answered as the huge, awesome head turned fully toward them. There were two more eyes, similar in size to the first, opening slowly as coral cracked away from their lids to splash in the water below.

"Quickly!" Skalda ordered, her voice cold and steady. A shame her insides were the opposite, but that was a distant problem. "Ready the skiff!"

"Remind me not to be near you when you are wrong," Rathe said, his eyes fever-bright. He undid the sword belted low around his hips and let it drop to the deck, an instinctive and accurate disarming, Skalda decided, following suit. Agnon had no weapon beyond his wit. He looked as though he'd prefer to pick up one of the deadly blades himself.

The Enemy fleet, perhaps reassured by what appeared to be merely a new island, had begun to reorganize. Catapults fired test shot, thumping into the ocean just distant from the *Pride*. "Hurry," Skalda urged the others, moving first to the rail.

Captain Bocknek himself took her arm to guide her into the small boat. She looked into his face, astonished to see not fear but rather a grim pride. "Make it a good trade, Dir Skalda," he said quietly, for her ear only.

"Get the *Pride* home," she replied as evenly. "Tell them what you see."

Agnon and Rathe climbed down into the boat with her. None of them sat, finding their balance as their partners on the *Pride* guided them to their fate with the gentlest of breezes.

As if fully aware of what was happening, the Quiet God slid closer, until the wooden prow of the small boat grated delicately against a cheek of dying coral and sponge. Something held them rock steady; glancing down Skalda thought she could make out an immense ridge of coral disappearing below.

Skalda concentrated on setting one sandaled foot ahead of the other, the rhythm like that of a bride's procession. Ahead waited the soft darkness of an eye larger than herself, a darkness she knew was her future, one final payment for her people's rescue.

The end of the boat, and the world she knew. Skalda had traveled from her body in magical learnings, had swum beyond light's reach in the ocean, and known the dream plain. This great eye was another doorway, she convinced herself. A last deep breath, and she stepped through its dark disc, into the warm, black core.

WELCOME, SUMMONER, throbbed reality.

* * *

Expansion. I flowed around instincts and passions, explored terrors and lusts, searching for the common purpose of the Summons. There.

Destruction.

Was that all?

* * *

Her hands and touch, her mouth and breath were no more; almost worse, her legs prickled as though asleep. Skalda gained then lost all sense of herself repeatedly. Finally, she refused the effort and focused on what was here—sight.

And such sight. As part of the Quiet God's eye she could see the regrouping of the Enemy fleet; at a thought, that vision sharpened so she could see the foreign shape of their sails and swords, the exotic pallor of their skin. Otherwise, they were men and women like any others she had known. The realization was disquieting. Never had she considered them so.

If she relaxed her vision, glints appeared on the periphery of the immense lens: Rathe and Agnon, she knew without understanding how. She concentrated, trying to ignore fear and wonder—neither were helpful—and focused on uttering a spell without a tongue.

The effort drained her but was not forbidden. A link was forged between the dir-priests, as well as their host.

Skalda . . . she felt her name, wrapped in vibrations that identified the source as Agnon. *What are we? Are we dead?*

We are the Aim, Rathe stated, less voice than a pressure on what once was skin.

YOU ARE THE AIM, agreed some vastness. I HAVE BEEN SUMMONED. WHERE MUST I GO?

The minds of the dir-priests focused in an instant.

There was no sense of motion, yet the Enemy fleet seemed to leap closer.

Skalda's view also included the *Pride* as she ran, sails full to bursting. Behind her, a coral-crusted flipper tossed the little boat aside, planks scattering over the water like so many sticks.

* * *

I accepted their guidance, almost blind in this drier, brighter world. Their rage had a color, hate another. Fear for self was there. As was regret. I'd felt all of this before.

They aimed me at frail crafts filled with men and I obeyed, my passage sending more to the Depths, carried down by their armor, limbs given grace by the water, to enrich the great flocks below.

* * *

WHERE DO I GO? boomed that incessant voice, not impatient, Skalda could tell, but rather a plea like a plaintive cry from a child. She still shuddered over the ease with which the P'okukii fleet had been swept from the ocean. Their magic, their weapons, and their numbers had availed them nothing. The war begun in one night had ended in one battle, without contest.

Almost. There'd been one attempt at defense and one loss. A harpoon had penetrated a great eye. Agnon's presence was gone.

There'd been no pain along their link. Only a shared, skewed view of the harpooner, lips drawn back in a rictus, his skin so white his face was already a skull, the desperate eyes black pits.

She could scarcely believe it was done. What she *could* believe was how many were now in the Depths. It was as if she'd had to look into each and every face as they died, share their fear and horror. None sought the sea willingly. Was it worse for the P'okukii to die here, away from their beloved land?

No matter the cost. It was done and their people were safe once more. Or were they?

WHERE DO I GO? wailed the God.

She had tried the Spell of Departing; they'd have been fools to summon the deadly old magic without being able to dispel it again. But Agnon was no longer there to support her. Skalda could accept her own ending—would be glad of it. Rathe, she discovered to her horror, had found a home for his hate and a reason to continue.

Kill them!

WHERE DO I GO?

She couldn't keep out their punishing demands. Rathe's response was a matching crescendo of torment. *To their ports! Crush their homes as they crushed mine. Kill them all!*

No, Skalda objected, horrified. *The Enemy is defeated. The Cove is safe.*

SAFE?

Almost instantly, her memories of home were exposed like shells on a beach, carved free from sand by the icy winds of winter. She could somehow see each one as it was torn from her: views of the moon through the arched windows of her bedroom, tall to the child she'd been; breathless glimpses of the royal barges from a hiding place high on her aunt's balcony; the cool, musty darkness of the underground passages interrupted only by spells of light; the prismed beauty of fireworks overhead as she swam in the warmth of the cove. Memory after memory—a torrent pouring away from her.

Then, as abruptly, nothing. Skalda wept without tears or eyes, feeling the loss of her home more intimately than the loss of her physical form, the longing to return so intense she knew with horror it wasn't hers alone. The Quiet God felt it too.

It was a feeling and intention Rathe didn't share. *To their ports,* he insisted, rage coloring his presence so Skalda felt she looked through heat shimmers as she watched the empty ocean ahead.

This, she realized suddenly, was why there had to be three to Summon and Aim. With just two of them left, there was no consensus, no clear voice to guide the God. She wondered how long it would take them to drive the God insane.

* * *

The pain was new, a novelty I would as soon excise from my body. All I could do was close the damaged eye. My flippers drove into the water, there being no reason given to stop moving. My lips cracked open, shedding even more coral. Warm ocean flowed over them, healing, soothing, reminding me of greater things than now and here and me.

But the Summoning locked me to the surface where I could not seek them.

* * *

Skalda . . . Skalda

Once, more than once, she'd dozed over the parchments; the stuffy room and hours of close reading making a poor combination. Each time, she woke not fully aware, her eyes glued shut until she rubbed them free of sleep, her mind slow to rouse from its subconscious exploration of the words of the Great Spell. This might be one of those times, she thought, on the edge of a dream.

Skalda.

Her name drew her back to reality, a reality encompassing the loss of friends, the agonizing defeat of an Enemy, and the sure knowledge of her own doom.

Rathe, she replied unwillingly, but aware that even his insanity was more human than anything else here.

He seemed unexpectedly calm, almost reasonable, as if this was one of their innumerable practice sessions in the Council Chamber. *They foresaw this, you know* he said to her. *The P'okukii foresaw it all.*

The soothsayers and portents. Their fear of the east and superstition. Skalda would have wept if she could. Rathe was right. The Summoning Spell had been cast before—she knew it now. The Quiet God had risen at their whim and blood, destroying their Enemy so that the island states could grow and flourish. They had forgotten, attributing lifetimes of prosperity and peace to long ago human heroes and human magic. But the P'okukii, terrified of the sea, terrified of the east, had the more accurate memories.

In a sense it didn't matter, Skalda thought. Many things in the world moved in vast cycles, unnoticed until one's life was ground into insignificance by storms, famine, or drought. That they had had a part in this one was merely proof that the Depths showed her power however she chose.

We must end this, she urged Rathe, unsure how much he could or would understand.

We shall. We must kill them all, he replied, still calm, still reasonable until she realized what he meant.

* * *

I burned. The sunlight lost its beauty without the lens of ocean. Fish, large and small, tossed themselves ahead of my wake without recognition. The Summoners fought constantly, their purposes bright and conflicting. When they dreamed, I had no peace, only longings for a place. The Cove.

* * *

THE COVE. The darkness confused her only briefly as the longing woke her. Skalda focused and saw stars spilled overhead. Stars she knew.

Rathe, she wailed. *It's taken us home!*

Kill them all, he sang. *More gifts for the Gods.*

KILL.

No! But her protest wasn't helping. She could sense confusion. Alone, she wasn't strong enough to overcome Rathe's madness.

There was another way. Skalda tightened her awareness of herself, of her plan until she could hardly see or feel anything else.

* * *

The entrance of the Cove was narrow. I struggled through the rocky barrier, heaving myself half out of the warm sea with reluctance, driven.

Look! Look there!

The Aiming was imperative. I turned my head upward in time for the mass of jagged stone to smash into the side of my head. PAIN.

Skalda . . . bless you . . . sang a dying voice, softly.

Then I could no longer see the color of rage. I could no longer see at all.

Except through one eye.

* * *

Without Rathe, the Spell of Departing would work, Skalda knew. Yet she hesitated. The Quiet God waited too, stopping up the channel into the Cove. The ships within looked like a school of tiny fish startled by a shark, scattering at random as galleys rowed, others with sails filling with bespelled wind.

The balconies? They were filled with people as well as flowers, equally beautiful and as still. They were waiting too.

WHERE DO I GO?

Where you will be safe, she thought, sharing its desperate weariness, its need for peace.

WILL I BE ALONE?

No, she promised, releasing all claim on that world outside. As she did, she found she owned it as never before.

* * *

Shafts of sunlight disappeared, reappeared; they filled at times with flower petals, twirling downward. At night, the stars were doubled by closer, smaller flames, floating above us to outline the dark hulls of ships.

We were content thus, to gaze upward through the great lens of our eye into the living magic of this place and see that which belonged here. The great flocks came, seeking the richness of the new reef, dancing silver in the light. Others swam among them, taking as was their need, sometimes just to dance as well.

If this is sleep, we sometimes wondered, surprised by bursts of fireworks, or touched by children's play, *perhaps we dream the world.*

A MATTER OF HONOR

Josepha Sherman

*Josepha Sherman is a fantasy writer and folklorist
whose latest titles are the dark urban fantasy novel
Son of Darkness and the folklore volume Merlin's
Kin: World Tales of the Hero Magicians. She has
also published over 125 short stories and articles,
including works in anthologies such as Black Cats
and Broken Mirrors, Zodiac Fantastic, and Return of
the Dinosaurs.*

JEZHAR, Queen of Qurtan, a slender woman with
the long, glossy black hair and tapering dark eyes of
her people, sat in her sun-dappled garden. All around
her, the roses had opened, a blaze of color the exact
red of her silky tunic, filling the soft air with sweet-
ness, and somewhere nearby a peacock was trum-
peting his presence to all the world under a blue so
pure it made the heart ache.

And there before her, Jezhar's advisers droned on and
on about the war. The utterly stalemated war, she
thought wearily.

Two years now, the queen mused, and what had
Gerhan of Zhal accomplished in his would-be conquest of Qurtan? He'd gotten as far as the northern
border, yes, but no farther, blocked by the mountains
and her own mountain-bred troops. He couldn't still

be hot with the flame of conquest; by now, surely, it was nothing but sheer stubbornness holding him there.

Yes, and what have I accomplished? Two years, and I still haven't gotten him away from the northern border. Two years, and the provinces continue to suffer his occupation, and my people—yes, and his—go right on dying.

The peacock was still screaming, and for a moment, Jezhar wanted to scream with him out of sheer frustration. Lives lost, villages razed—for what? What in the name of all holiness was the point of all this? Gerhan didn't *need* her lands; for all she knew, after two years, he didn't even *want* her lands, but he simply couldn't figure out how to back down.

And I can't exactly go and tell him. Bah, I can't even trouble his dreams any longer.

Jezhar sprang to her feet, and the advisors hastily scrambled up, following like so many nervous chicks as she paced through the garden. So many flowers in bloom, such a wonderfully blue sky—no place for war, no time for war—

And when, her mind asked dourly, *was* it time?

She stopped short at a far-too familiar sound: the rumbling of wheels mixed with the moans of men in pain. There, just beyond the low garden wall, wagons were bringing in the latest casualties. Leaving the advisers to follow or not as they chose, Jezhar hurried out of the garden to see what could be done.

Gods, gods, so many wounded lying here in the great courtyard that had been turned into a hospital, so many dying . . .

She stopped by the side of one aging, weather-worn soldier whose arm had been severed.

"Majesty!" he gasped, and tried to salute, but she shook her head.

"I cannot restore the arm," she told him, honestly and frankly, as an honorable soldier deserved. But,

her hand resting on the jagged stump, her eyes closed,
Jezhar willed smooth healing on it . . .

She staggered, backed away, gasping. But the soldier was staring at her in awe. "Doesn't hurt," he
murmured. "Majesty, it doesn't hurt."

*And what good have I worked? He was a career
soldier, now he has nothing.* "Have someone mark
down your name," Jezhar told him wearily. "Something will be done for you."

She moved on to a warrior so young the sight of
him made her heart ache. Magic told her, even before
she saw the terrible wound in his side and smelled the
too-familiar reek, *no.* This one could not survive. But
Jezhar could at least take his hand, heedless of the
dust and blood, could at least will his pain away. He
looked up at her, wide-eyed, the faintest of smiles on
his face.

"Dying . . . ?"

"Yes."

"Yes," he echoed softly, staring up at her, asking
without words.

I cannot!

But the soothing she'd put on him wouldn't last
long enough. As the first flare of returning pain blazed
in the boy's eyes, Jezhar stilled his heart. His life slid
away, his death shivering along her nerves.

No more, no more.

But how could she stop now? There were those who
could be helped, the man with the shattered leg she
could restore, the warrior with the terrible gash down
his face she could knit up again.

There were others, the too badly hurt, the ones who
pleaded with her for ease, for death . . . those whose
deaths recoiled on her, the feel of them terrified or
joyous or just . . . resigned.

Her advisers caught up with her at last, her hair
half-free of its long braid, her tunic stained a darker
red, her body trembling with fatigue.

"Majesty, you must rest."

"Yes. I know that. And I . . . I know you all blame me."

That sparked the expected storm of protestations, some of it probably even genuine. Jezhar let it go on for a few moments, then held up a weary hand.

"Of course you blame me. And were I in your place, were I . . ." She hesitated, hunting for a tactful word, "ordinary, I would be blaming me, too: An enchanter, a wielder of great magics—why does she not destroy the enemy with one mighty spell?"

"No, Queen Jezhar!"

"We do not wonder that at all!"

"We know that cannot be done."

Oh, it could. Jezhar knew she could, indeed, cast a battle spell powerful enough to shred the flesh from the bones of every warrior in Gerhan's army.

Then, of course, she would die as well, as the death agonies of all those warriors recoiled on her. Jezhar bit her lip, trying not to look at the wounded all around her. It wasn't fear of death, or rather, of dying, not after having felt it so many times through others. And it was honorable to die for one's country, yes— but not if it left that country without a ruler and with envious rivals like King Nurhad at Qurtan's east flank. Her death would only mean more warfare.

That was the true reason for hesitation, wasn't it?

The advisers were still protesting, trying to comfort her. "You have already done more than could be expected. Did your magics not block the Urbaid Pass?"

Indeed. Which will, as a result of my rockslides, be closed to trade for years. Was that worth it?

And the unseasonable storm I brought down on Gerhan's troops slowed them down and, no doubt, made them miserable for a time, but not miserable enough to force them out. And that same storm also flooded out several of my people's farms so that they had no harvest.

*I don't dare try creating disease, not unless I want to
destroy a good many of my own troops as well, yes,
and risk sickening myself with the backlash as well—
oh, holiness, what good am I?*

"I will go there myself," Jezhar told them all
shortly. "Let my troops see my presence."

"To the battlefield? B-but, Queen Jezhar, you can't!
The danger—"

"Is very real, yes, I know that. But it's just as real
for our troops, and for the farmers and merchant cara-
vans Gerhan's been looting for the last two years."

"Please, Your Majesty, the sorcerers—"

"Do you think that I don't know about them, too?"

Gerhan had hired the nearly useless creatures half
a year ago, and that he hadn't slain them for not pro-
ducing results said something for his self-restraint.

Still, ineffectual though they were, lately the sorcerers did seem to be focusing enough Power to block
her mind-sendings to Gerhan. That meant, unfortunately, that they were also focused enough to sense
her presence if she attempted any spells within their
reach.

"They cannot sense what isn't being used," Jezhar
said, and smiled a weary smile at her advisers'
confusion.

But then she straightened in alarm. "Vendrat!"

The merchant-spy staggered forward to fall at Jezhar's feet, more in exhaustion than reverence. Blood
stained his robes and matted his hair, but the look he
gave her as he straightened was steady enough.

"Majesty. He has it. The *Tentrac Book*."

Her first wild thought was astonishment that Gerhan could read. Her second was utter horror. "Vendrat. Are you quite sure?"

"Majesty, it bore the threefold spiral on the
binding."

Jezhar sank back against a wall, eyes shut. Gods,
not this, not this, too! The *Tentrac,* that most potent

book of magic, had recently been stolen from its place in the holy sanctuary—and the *Tentrac,* being as powerful as it was, screened itself from magical scrying so she'd been unable to locate it.

At least there was this much: Gerhan either hadn't let his hireling sorcerers see the book, or else he'd had them slain. If they, even with their small talents, held the *Tentrac,* Qurtan would already have felt its force.

Not all that comforting. Oh yes, the book's spells were at their strongest in the hands of a skilled magician, but even an amateur could read a spell. And those of the *Tentrac* could be cast in part, with deadly effect, by anyone with sufficient will. An amateur such as Gerhan, who had certainly proved himself strong-willed enough during this war. Sooner or later, he would manage to—

Gods, and he'd have no magical judgment at all, no knowledge of what he might unleash!

I can't do this.

No? Out of honor, she must. There was no one else with sufficient skill.

Jezhar paced restlessly, plotting . . . yes . . . the advisers weren't going to like this . . . but then, she need not tell them everything . . .

And did she have the courage for this?

Excellent question.

"Now I *must* go," Jezhar told her advisers, and to her pleasure, her voice was steady. "Ah, don't look so grim! I have a plan." *And you, my friends, shall hear only part of it.*

Oh, she'd had a plan, indeed, Jezhar thought a few days later, bent low over her straining horse's neck and trying not to look back over her shoulder yet again. Unfortunately this wasn't it!

That she'd eluded her men and gone off on her private hunt, yes, that much had gone right. But that she'd then run into a patrol of Gerhan's men—aie, call it the Luck of the Perverse.

At least her pursuers couldn't have recognized the Queen of Qurtan in this bedraggled desert warrior. But that wasn't keeping them from the chase. Did they think her a spy? Or were they merely bored enough to go after anything that ran? Particularly something, Jezhar realized as her long braid whipped free of its binding, that might be female.

Does Gerhan know they're risking his precious horses like this? If they lose but one, he'll have their heads for it.

The irony of it was that she could stop them all with one spell—oh, yes, and in the process announce her presence to Gerhan and his cursed sorcerers. Weak they might be, but with the *Tentrac Book* behind them . . .

At least, Jezhar thought wryly, she'd kept herself warrior-fit, since a wise queen prepared herself for anything.

Even being hunted through the mountains like a—

Jezhar's horse suddenly stumbled on the rough footing, falling forward. The queen catapulted over its head and hurtled down a rocky slope in a cloud of dust and pebbles. Jezhar fought frantically, clawing at the gravel, trying to dig in her toes, anything to stop her slide, because there was a cliff at the bottom of the slope, and she—

—had stopped with a breathtaking thud, there on a narrow ledge at the very edge of the cliff. Jezhar had one terrifying glance down, then began warily backing away, staggering back to her feet, realizing only then that her desert robes had been torn half off her.

Someone laughed. Stifling a sigh, Jezhar turned to find, as she'd expected, that one of the warriors had followed her down—the easy way. The Luck of the Perverse holding true, she'd fallen down the steepest part of the slope; the warrior had, instead, strolled down the shallowest part.

"Well now, I was right," he drawled as Jezhar hastily knotted her torn clothing back together. "You are a woman. And such a pretty one, too! Too bad you're on the wrong side."

Without warning, he threw himself at her, hurling them both off their feet.

You idiot, are you trying to kill us both?

No. Killing her, judging from his eyes as he struggled to pin her under him, was the last thing on his mind. A quick glance up showed that the other soldiers had dismounted and were watching from the top of the slope. Waiting their turns?

Not in all the Seven Hells! Jezhar silently told them.

She went utterly limp, and heard the man laugh a little uncertainly. His hands loosened their grip on her wrists ever so slightly and Jezhar lunged up from the waist, bringing her palm flashing forward, slamming it into his nose with all her force. The soldier howled, staggering to his feet, hands over his face, blind to everything but the pain in his nose, and for a second, seeing him perilously close to the edge of the cliff, Jezhar thought of just letting him fall.

No. As he teetered, she grabbed his shoulder, pulling him back. "Not yet," she told him, breathless enough for her voice to sound properly coarse. "And you, all you up there, I'm coming up, so no 'mistakes' with bows or knives, hear?"

Half-dragging the man, who still had both hands clamped over his bloody nose, she struggled back up the slope. The soldiers were still on foot, their horses behind them.

Foolish mistake.

Guessing that the soldier with the most arrogant expression was the leader, Jezhar snarled, "So, what in the Seven Hells was all that chasing about?"

Startled, he blustered, "No enemy of—"

"What makes you think I'm an enemy? Hells, no! I'm not a spy, either!"

She moved boldly forward, Bloody Nose in tow, then twisted, spun, used her momentum to send Bloody Nose crashing into the leader. In the second's confusion, she jumped blindly at the nearest horse, landing broadside as the animal shied, then frantically pulling herself into the saddle. Reins, where were the—yes!

"I'm no spy!" she shouted. "I'm a horse thief!"

Part of her was utterly astonished at herself, part of her was terrified. But Jezhar shouted, and kicked her mount into a gallop, right through the other horses— the riderless horses that, being herd animals, followed with hers.

My army! Jezhar thought breathlessly, as she and they thundered down the pass.

Now would be a sensible time to hunt for her own men, now would be a sensible time to just get out of here—

Honor never had been sensible. Jezhar, biting her lip, turned her horse away from safety, toward where her spies had told her Gerhan was still camped. That she was being watched from the cliffs on either side, oh, no doubt about it. That no one was going to risk loosing arrows or spears at one woman and so many valuable horses, no doubt about that, either.

The land was opening up, the cliffs giving way to the rocky plains where battle after battle had been fought. Good land for earthquakes, part of her mind noted, all those broken rocks evidence of past violence. She could work a spell—

To shake the earth? To kill an army and herself with them?

No. I can't. I can't.

And current violence, she thought, human violence, was just as bloody as anything the earth could create. Heart pounding, Jezhar rode through rank after rank

of Gerhan's soldiers, sick to see how many remained.
An earthquake—

No! There is another way. There must be.

Men scrambled hastily out of the way of the horses,
then stood staring after her: After so long a stalemate,
they probably welcomed any break in the routine.

But someone was finally shouting orders, and soldiers were forming a living barricade, waving down
the horses. Jezhar instinctively pulled back on the
reins, too sharply, bringing her mount to a flashy, up
on its hind legs, stop. She lost her balance, flew off
sideways, landed on her feet with a jarring thump—
ha, I meant to do that!—and said breathlessly, "I'm
here to see Gerhan."

"Are you?" a scar-faced, weather-worn officer
drawled. "As what? We don't need any more camp
followers."

"Hells no! If I were one of those, think I'd have
brought him a gift?"

"Of his own horses?"

"Could have sold them. To the other side. That's
what I need to tell him. About the other side.
About . . . her. She knows about It. Tell him just that:
She knows he's got the book."

He clearly hadn't a clue as to what she meant, but
she'd been just cryptic enough. "Wait," he snapped.

Jezhar slid a wary glance sideways, trying not to
flinch at the thought of being one woman alone in an
enemy camp. "Not going anywhere," she said
truthfully.

But now that she was standing still, she could
sense . . . ah, they had their wounded, too, their
dying . . . and their anguish tore at her. Enemies or
no, these were no monsters, only men in pain.

You can do nothing for them, save pity them.

But before she could do or say anything perilous,
the soldier returned. "Follow," he said curtly.

Not the slightest sign of any sorcerers. Of course

not. As she'd guessed, Gerhan, with the *Tentrac* in his possession, had disposed of them.

"There."

A tent. It would be a tent, and with one flap drawn dramatically back like something out of the old tales. But the tents in those tales had all been woven of silk glittering with gold. This one was common burlap dingy with mud.

And inside stood . . . No, there was nothing dingy about Gerhan. Jezhar had never seen him up close, merely in dream-images that never quite told the real-world truth. Her first thought was a foolish: *But he doesn't look like a warlord.*

And how should a warlord appear? This man, not quite of middle years, was fit enough, wiry rather than heavily muscled, his dark hair streaked ever so slightly with gray. Not an unattractive man, with wide, strong cheekbones. A drooping mustache hid much of a wry mouth and strong chin, and his eyes, darker even than her own, revealed nothing but utter weariness. And for another foolish moment, Jezhar longed to say, *Then just go home! Nothing's keeping you here. Just go home and end all this.*

"You have news for me." His voice was thick with his Eastern accent.

"About a certain . . . well, call it a book, yes." Jezhar forced herself to swagger forward, like someone with nothing in her mind but reward and maybe a bit of fun along the way. "She does know you've got the thing."

"How would you know that? And, for that matter, who are you?"

"Me? No one. Nobody notices just one more woman in a palace."

He gave the most terse of chuckles. "True enough. Go on."

"And as to how I know what I know—hells, everyone in the palace knows what the book looks like:

spiral thing on the cover, right?" She caught Gerhan's not-quite repressed start and continued, "Well, I heard her say it, didn't know I was listening. She knows you've got it, all right. And you bet she and her people, they're trying to figure out a way to get it back."

"And so you came here. Why?"

Why, indeed? Jezhar let her voice go suddenly grim, utterly serious. "I am a healer." True enough. "I see all those folks in pain because of the war, I want to help them. But I—she—she won't let me. Doesn't want anyone, you know . . ."

"Sharing her glory?"

"You got it! You don't know what it's like, so much pain and you knowing you could do something, if only—I couldn't stand it, had to heal, didn't matter who."

"Really." Not by the slightest trace of emotion did Gerhan show if he believed that. "Come."

He led her out behind the tent, out to where—

Jezhar stopped short, stunned by the sudden wave of pain. Here lay the wounded she had dimly sensed before, now seen and heard and felt with nothing between their anguish and her mind.

Gerhan was watching her closely. "Heal them."

How could she not? Overwhelmed by the misery, Jezhar suddenly could no longer see anything of *them*, anything of *enemy*. These were only souls in torment, souls crying out to her for an aid she could deliver, and she moved blindly through their ranks, reaching out here to weave torn flesh back together, there to knit broken bones whole . . .

Jezhar stopped again, dazed and shaking with fatigue, not certain where she was, staring blankly at a row of what at first seemed merely drying racks.

But hanging from those racks were men. Or those who had once been men. So terribly torn and charred were they that they barely seemed—

The sorcerers! Jezhar knew that in a shocking flash of Power. *Of course. Gerhan no longer needed them.*

One at least was still, horribly, alive. His mind touched hers, knowing instantly who and what she was, and Jezhar heard without words, *Kill us.*

She felt the terrible, terrible weariness, stronger by now even than pain, the weariness of one kept too long from rest. And what could she say in return but a whispered, "Yes."

Pain shocked through her—Gerhan! Gerhan had slapped her. "You are not to touch those," he warned her grimly.

"But . . . they can't harm you . . ."

Another slap, staggering her. "You are not to touch them!"

His hand closed with bruising force about her arm, dragging her back with him to his tent. There, too drained and shaken to stand, Jezhar sank to a cushion, staring up at him in dazed confusion. He returned the stare, utterly without expression.

"Those men failed me," he told her.

"But they can do you no more harm. Surely you could show them the mercy of—"

"Mercy," Gerhan said, "is a costly thing. I cannot afford it."

And you, Jezhar thought through her haze of weariness, *are hiding something.*

There was more here than a warlord's discipline or injured pride. She prodded her exhausted brain. Why would he need those tortured souls alive . . .

Yes, most surely there was a reason! Before it could be used, the *Tentrac Book* must be mastered, and for a man without magic of his own . . .

No wonder you don't want to kill them! You're drawing on their Power, using their slow death to add to the force. And that means . . . that means you are almost ready to take on the Tentrac's *Power as well.*

*But not yet, you cannot control it yet! The weapon will
become the master.*

Right now, she was too weary to think of that, too
weary to think about what he might or might not do
with her.

*Nothing just now . . . unless he likes his
women . . . limp . . .*

Evidently, Jezhar thought, waking alone in darkness, he did not. Instead, Gerhan had dumped her
here in . . . ah, yes, in the corner of his tent, presum-
ably to make use of her, one way or another, when
she woke.

Except that now his snoring and her wariest of mental touches told her that Gerhan was fast asleep
himself.

*Just the two of us in here. Guards outside, of course,
but still . . .*

Did he trust her that greatly? Or hold her in such
contempt? After all, Gerhan had no reason to think
her anything more than a common-born healer.

Or was he simply that secure in his budding
sorceries?

Jezhar hesitated a long moment, wondering, studying him. Asleep, Gerhan looked even less like the war
leader who would have conquered her land; he was
merely a man, one caught in a snare of . . .

Of honor, Jezhar realized with a little shock. He
could, out of honor, no more retreat than she could
yield.

But she could end this here and now. One swift
burst of magic would kill him in his sleep.

Oh, yes, Jezhar answered herself, *kill him. Then try
to get out of this camp alive. Honor is one thing, but
do you really wish slow martyrdom as well?*

And if she killed him now, she'd be leaving the
Tentrac Book hidden here, somewhere, for anyone
to find.

Hidden for the moment, at any rate.

Very, very warily, Jezhar opened her senses, knowing that the cursed book was quite able, for all its non-life, to alert its current possessor. And she felt . . .

Not the book. The sorcerer, the one still conscious enough to call to her, *Kill us* . . .

His weary agony shivered through her, quivering in every nerve. Unbearable for any healer, unbearable. Even while her rational self was screaming at her for a fool, Jezhar stole from the tent. The guards, after a quick glance inside to be sure their master was unhurt, let her pass; one woman alone in a war camp wasn't going very far.

Far enough. As far as the dying men on their racks. The sorcerer's mind brushed hers. *Yes?*

"Yes."

The weariest wisp of ironic humor touched her: That after all this war, all this hate, mercy should come not at his own hands, but at those of his utter enemy.

"I am not your enemy," Jezhar whispered. "Not now. And magic makes us kin." Her terrified inner voice was screaming to her, *No, you cannot take their deaths upon you! They will kill you!*

But these men were in such terrible pain, such wrongness and, out of honor, there was nothing to do but add gently, "Rest, kinsman."

Jezhar reached out to him, to the other anguished, dying sorcerers, and stopped their hearts. Their deaths enfolded her, but not as waves of hate or horror but as . . . as grateful caresses, warm against her mind . . .

The shock of pain like a mental slap was all the more stunning for the contrast. Jezhar whirled to see Gerhan standing with the *Tentrac Book* in his arms. And magic, raw and unformed, swirled about them both. In another moment, he would use it, try to use it, and it would blaze free, wild, deadly, without any limits or controls—

"I did not give you leave!" Gerhan shouted, and now his dark eyes burned with an insane power. Gone, as suddenly as that, was all trace of the calm, weary war leader; only the madness of the magic remained, and Jezhar felt the smallest pang of regret for the man he'd been, the man he might have become.

"I know," she said in utter resignation. "I did what I must. And now, too, I do what I must."

She had waited almost too long. But she could no longer be afraid, she could no longer hide behind a wall of honor.

She could not longer pretend to be anything but the magician she truly was.

And if I must die for my people, so be it.

Jezhar reached into herself, into her mind and will. No time to focus fully, no time for anything but this: As Gerhan flung open the *Tentrac Book* and shouted out the beginning of a spell, Jezhar flung her will down into the land about her, calling, pulling, all the long years of war, all the stupid, senseless deaths behind her, calling with her, with all her might, saying, *Now, yes, release!*

The Power answered, agony tearing free within her, far more than she had ever expected. Jezhar screamed—

And, as though answering her pain with a great roar of tortured rock, the earth shook. Jezhar was hurled sideways off her feet, landing amid dust and flying bits of stone, all about her the terrified screams of men and beasts.

Again the earth shook, and again, tearing itself asunder, and she saw one quick, terrible glimpse of rock opening under Gerhan and the *Tentrac Book,* then snapping together again over them with harsh finality. Death surrounded her, death upon death, engulfing her, drowning her . . .

But she was all at once cushioned in warmth, sheltered by the sorcerers she had freed, and beyond them was a dim sense of all the others to whom she'd shown that final mercy. Jezhar knew this could not be reality. She must surely be dying as well.

"Greetings, kinsmen," she heard herself say.

And then . . .

Nothing.

Something!

Light, and hard stone bruising her side, and something warm on her cheek—

Jezhar woke with a shriek, and the horse that had been nuzzling her shied away, only to stand staring at her.

She sat up very slowly, aching in mind as well as body, looking about in horror. The whole landscape was changed, cliffs crumbled and new ridges raised. Where Gerhan's army had been camped . . .

How many have I slain I, who call myself healer? Yes, and how many slain that I, just the day before, did heal?

At least there were some survivors. No longer an army, merely battered, bewildered men without a leader. Jezhar thought of the finality of that rock snapping shut on Gerhan, and shuddered. There he and the *Tentrac Book* lay entombed, and there let them stay.

Carefully, she got to her feet, and the men shied away from her like that startled horse. They had, after all, seen her call forth the earthquake.

"Go home," Jezhar told them with as much magical force as she could muster. "Out of honor, just go home."

They could easily have slain her. She was too utterly worn to fight. But so were they. Without a word to her or each other, walking or riding whatever horses they could catch, they began their retreat.

But Jezhar tensed at the sudden sound of hoofbeats, thinking, *Ah no, not this. Not a new attack.*

But the riders were her own astonished men, and Jezhar waved them down.

"No. Do not follow. They are no longer a threat.

"B-but, M-majesty! What happened here?"

What, indeed? "The war," Jezhar, Queen of Qurtan said wearily, "is over."

WARLORD

Michelle West

Michelle West is the author of The Sacred Hunter *duology,* The Broken Crown, *and* The Uncrowned King, *all published by DAW Books. She reviews books for the on-line column* First Contacts, *and less frequently for* The Magazine of Fantasy & Science Fiction. *Other short fiction by her appears in* Black Cats and Broken Mirrors, Elf Magic, *and* Olympus.

HE CAME down from the mountain on the day the sun rose between its peaks in a curtain of orange and crimson, a gesture of near-forgotten glory. He had some wealth with him, and in some quantity, although he had taken care to make certain it was easily carried and easily hidden. He dressed for the weather, although the cold never bothered him, and carried a pack—empties—that observers might believe had once been filled with supplies. He wore no obvious weapons, although he might have chosen to arm himself with a sword had he taken the Southward pass; in the Dominion, a weapon defined the status of a man, and he was not above vanity, although the sword was no true weapon. He had his birthright, and with it, he had destroyed whole armies. Those fires were not banked.

It was time, again; time, but still too early.

He had woken the previous day, and the day before it, from the nightmare that had haunted his life for so many years not it had become, in some fashion, his closest companion—the only companion he was allowed. At dusk, having thrown off sleep by a monumental act of either will or cowardice, he would be wreathed in old ghosts, and the blood on his hands would glisten darkly as he listened to old cries.

The ghosts drove him for years, and as always, he had retired to the finery of his mountain confines to wait out their long decline. Half-mad when he arrived—always that—clothing rent and torn, blood across his chest, his hands, and the length of his face not covered by untended beard, he would plunge through the mystical wards that separated his mountain vastness from the cold, the wind, the snow, and the presence of any other man.

There, surrounded by the finery of lifetimes, awash in the reflection of magelight against crystal, gold and silk, he would recover from his wounds.

But the deepest of the wounds seldom left completely.

As a younger man, his rage had fuelled the healing; as a younger man, it had been easier to foist the import—and impact—of his actions upon his enemies and allies. *If,* he would reason, *they had not attacked* or *If they had done as they were ordered . . .*

But he was younger then. The pain was easier to twist into rage, and rage was by far the more comfortable. Unfortunately, with age came a certain understanding, a certain self-knowledge, and a distinct self-loathing. A man so enraged was an easy pawn, and he intensely disliked being the servant of any other man.

Intensely.

But he was tired.

And the dreaming was different, this morn. Different because it had followed the course of three nights, unchanging; different in that the ghosts of the dead were escorted, were called back, by the visage of a woman in robes of blue.

He disliked gods on principle; they were, of a type, rulers, and made of men—men and their own flesh and blood—groveling servants. And they, in their time, had destroyed more than his life by their curse and their geas, by the edicts they had *no right* to pronounce upon him. It was no surprise that he recognized the hand of a god in the figure of the woman.

"It is time," she said, her voice low and deep, yet still loud enough to be heard clearly over the terrified accusations of his dead, all his dead. "The battle that you've trained for all your life is about to start. They will find you; they have always found you in the past."

He could not make out her face in the folds of cloth that framed it. Shadows, there. Darkness of her own.

"And am I a pawn," he said stiffly, "to be ordered into a life I've chosen to leave?"

"You have never," she replied, "chosen to leave it. Never." And so saying, she pulled a glowing orb from the confines of her sleeves. "Or perhaps you do not remember your beginnings."

He lifted his hands. Pulled back. He knew what the orb was, although it had been a long, long time since he had seen one.

"You are weary," she said, as the light faded, as the implied attack ceased. "And I understand weariness. Will you not, at last, face the truth?"

"I have tried," he said bitterly.

"Have you?"

"I have lost everything that I have ever cared for. I have surrendered all, again and again. And I am still as you see me. I am still as I *was*."

"Perhaps," she replied softly, "it is time to seek the truth of that fact. Go North, and East. Seek service."

"Have I not served in my time?"

Her eyes were violet ice; he saw them, saw the hint

of pale, icy cheek, the hint of moving lips in shadowed faces. "You have never served any master but yourself. After all these years, do you not understand that truth?"

The first night, he might ignore the words, although he heard the truth in them clearly. And the second night. But the third night, he accepted the sign of Fate, he stirred himself, and left his mountain fortress far earlier than he would have chosen to otherwise depart it: The loss was still fresh, and the pain still too close, and the voice and face of the woman he had loved was still locked in accusation and madness whenever his memory was unkind enough to return to her.

"The life of those who serve is not an easy life, and if lived correctly—and it will be, by those of you who finish your apprenticeship—it is not a life of glory." The man who spoke paused a moment. Frowned. "I realize," he added stiffly, "that you are in your first year here. Manners, however, are not the preserve of the well-taught; they are a *requirement* within the guild halls."

It was a threat, of course, and it worked; the unruly, unacceptable, thoroughly disgraceful lot of boys that the guildmaster had seen fit to send him fell silent as they contemplated life outside of the future employment the guild offered.

And that was the problem.

They saw it was a *job,* and while it was that, it was also more, this gifting of service, this dedication of life. It was a vocation.

Most of these boys wouldn't make it past their first year. If they somehow managed that, it was unlikely they'd persevere beyond the first year of their apprenticeship. They were like young weeds, and it was his task to strengthen the garden; he'd grown used to the job over the years.

The door swung open, exposing his students to the

faint noise of the hall. Just what they needed. Another distraction.

"Sir?"

Ellerson frowned at the familiar young man. When
the boy didn't cringe, the old man assumed it *was*
important. He put on his this-had-better-be-good expression—although when he taught it was never that
far away from his real one—and nodded at the
interruption.

"I expect," he said, as he walked across the room,
"that you will be ready for the history test when we
resume."

Although the classrooms in the guild hall were modest, the building itself hosted rooms that only the finest
of the Ten's mansions could boast; it was to these that
clients came with their requests, seeking the service of
a domicis. Most had temporary needs, and often of an
exceedingly dull and transitory nature; they wished to
impress a certain group of the right people for a certain season.

Ellerson was a practical man; he understood that
the guild prestige derived partly from the money that
men and women such as that were prepared to spend
for the sake of appearances, and he treated them with
courtesy and deference. But it was not in his nature
to accept their offers.

Truthfully, it was not in his nature to accept many;
he was of an age where he felt his service was suspect,
and he had taken a well-deserved retirement after the
lingering death of his last master.

All of which should have been beside the point, and
none of which usually was. When he was summoned
at all, he was offered a task by the guildmaster, and
one refused the guildmaster only rarely. Always at
some risk.

He found the door ajar. Waited a moment to see
just how formal Akalia was being. But no attendant

peered out; no one waited to greet him in the stuffy uniforms that younger journeymen were forced to endure when Akalia was entertaining clients of money and power.

Ellerson grabbed the door's authoritative handle and pulled it open.

"Ah, Ellerson. We were waiting for you. Please, come in." Akalia frowned slightly, pursing her well-weathered lips. Ellerson noted the expression, but he was frowning as well.

There was a man sitting in the armchair in front of Akalia's ancient desk. The desk itself was spotless—hardly its usual state—and there was a decanter and three cut crystal glasses which were reserved only for the finest of the patriciate.

Or at least those who considered themselves among the finest. Ellerson had met many, many such men and women in his life. He had also offended quite a few.

"Before you start," Akalia said quietly, raising a palm in a gesture that was part command part surrender, "let me say that I realize that you are a) retired and b) far too curmudgeonly to be asked to serve a member of the minor or major nobility even if you weren't."

The man in the chair raised a dark brow in an otherwise perfect face. It was too perfect by half for Ellerson's liking; too haughty and too well-formed, umblemished by the heat of the sun or a day's honest labor. It was also completed by the finest clothing he had seen in perhaps five years—give or take a year for the Princess Royale—and a modest collection of rings which, thrown together were the only quirky thing about the man. They were not fine, the rings, or rather, not all of them were; they were a mishmash of styles and materials that clashed rather than complemented.

"Ellerson," Akalia said, looking dowdy and unkempt by the unavoidable visual comparison to her visitor.

Ellerson stiffened; he couldn't help it. Instinct shored up his shoulders, his chin, the line of his nose. "How may I be of assistance?"

"You might start," she said, just slightly less stiffly, "by being less formal. This is not an interview, Ellerson. This man is not a prospective master." *And if he were, I'd never invite you to meet him without several days of coaxing and preparation first.* The unspoken sentence was several degrees louder than the spoken one, and followed by a brief, perfect frown. She was good at that; she, too, taught unruly boys.

"Ah." Ellerson relaxed. Slightly. "Your pardon. Akalia knows I'm retired, but occasionally seems to forget. I am Ellerson of the guild. Whom do I have the privilege of addressing?"

The man rose. "Avandar," he replied. "Avandar Gallais." He did not bow; nor did he extend a hand. But there was a warming of expression that might not be missed if one were paying careful attention.

Ellerson waited; the time passed. At last, Akalia cleared her throat. "Avandar Gallais," she said quietly, speaking to Ellerson, although the older man hadn't taken his eyes off the visitor, "has come to . . . join the guild."

"Impossible," Ellerson said flatly.

"Impossible?" the visitor said, raising a dark brow. "I have failed at very little that I have attempted in my life, in spite of opposition."

"You see what I mean, Akalia?"

"Ellerson—"

"And I have offered, of course, to pay for the privilege of being taught the . . . guild's vocation. Service, I believe."

"Akalia."

"Your guildmaster seemed to think that my money was good, and my intent not obviously damaging."

"*Akalia,* may I speak with you in private?"

"No," Avandar Gallais replied, "I do not believe it would be suitable. I am . . . unused to having my future discussed when I am not present to mount my own defense."

Ellerson said, coldly, "I-was-not-speaking-to-you. Should you, for reasons that completely escape me—and should any sane teaching member of *this* guild—find your *petition* accepted, you will have to endure far worse than merely being discussed when you are not, as you put it, able to mount your own defense. Do I make myself clear?"

The air literally crackled.

Akalia's face dropped into her hands.

Ellerson's face froze into rigid, unpleasant lines. "If that is supposed to impress me," he said, "it fails. You are certainly not the only mage domicis—or would-be one—to cross this threshold. Certainly the most arrogant, and the least suitable, but not the only, and not the first. Now, if you are at all serious, I have two words of advice for you: *Get out.*"

To his surprise—and judging from her apprehensive expression, Akalia's—Avandar Gallais did just that. Slowly, to be sure, and with an icy stillness that spoke of barely-checked anger. But he went.

"Why?"

As the guest absented himself, Akalia relaxed. "Why what?"

"Why do you want to accept him? There is no possible way that service is any part of that man's calling. Forcing others to service—and quite probably unpleasantly—yes. But serving? Taking a master and making that life the only life? Akalia, not even you can believe this."

"No," she said softly. "I don't." She rose, then, and went to the windows nested between ancient, very fine shelves.

"He reeks of power. It clings to hi in every possible way. Had he come to request the services of a guild member, there are three I would immediately suggest. I would also inform the three, should they choose to apply, that I would consider their chances of surviving their service to be vanishingly small."

Akalia nodded absently.

"Akalia, I find your lack of response distressing."

"I concur," she said, again quietly.

"We have enough trouble finding acceptable students among the desperate rabble that come seeking some skill for employment. Would you put a man of this nature in this classroom?"

"No."

"Then?"

She turned to face him, eyes hard. "I would pull you from your classroom, Ellerson, and I would put him entirely in your care."

"If he's going to learn *in* the guild, he'll follow the guild procedures. Is that clear? The students have to be housebroken; I don't care how old they think they are. Akalia—" Ellerson stopped. "It's not just the money."

"No."

"And it's not his status. You don't recognize his name either."

"No."

"Then what? If you're going to saddle me with this task—a task, mind, that I think will be impossible to succeed at—I will at least be offered the courtesy of truth."

"I had a dream, Ellerson," she whispered. "I had a dream, three times."

He lifted a hand to his face. "Gods," he muttered. "You're going to make the next four years of my life miserable for the sake of superstition."

"Yes."

He didn't bother to ask her what she would do if

he refused. "Very well. Avandar, you may return," he said, quietly and dryly, to the empty air.

Avandar Gallais stepped into the room.

"And if I catch you doing that again, I'll throw you out of the guild myself. I am your teacher, and if you are here to learn, you *will* learn. If it kills us both."

Avandar raised a brow. "It won't," he said at last.

Unfortunately, Ellerson could hear the unspoken part of Avandar's sentence as easily as he could Akalia's.

Avandar attended classes. That was the first calamity.

At about the time the tabletop beneath his hands began to sizzle and blacken—causing an offending young adolescent to think better of his comments about age and stupidity—Ellerson had already decided two things. First, that the classroom was not the suitable place for a man of Avandar's abilities, and second, that Avandar was perhaps not as familiar with the laws of Averalaan as one grew used to assuming everyone was.

He excused Avandar, continued teaching the class, and when that was finished, dismissed the boys under his tutelage as if, indeed, he dealt with mages every day.

After that, he sought Avandar out.

The new students were given quarters within the guild halls; rooms with a bed, a window which varied in size depending upon whether or not the boy in question was expected to live on his own or in a grouping of such young creatures, and the usual shelves and desk that had endured for so long they were proof that carpenters really were forces unto themselves.

Avandar had been granted a privilege reserved for few first year students: A room of his own. And given the depth of the black singe marks on wood that seemed to have melted beneath his spread palms, Ellerson considered it wise. Certainly wiser than when Akalia had first suggested it.

He knocked.

Avandar opened the door.

"I suppose you know why I'm here."

He stepped out of the way, letting Ellerson into the admittedly tiny space before closing the door upon them both. "Yes."

"*You* are a man. *He* is a boy."

"He is a lucky boy," Avandar replied coldly. "In my youth I lost many . . . friends who learned the lesson he survived."

"Mockery is not considered a capital offense."

Silence.

Ellerson walked over to the pristine bed. "I'm old," he said, by way of preamble, "And I refuse to have this conversation standing up." He sat. Avandar did not; instead he walked moodily over to the window and turned half toward it. His profile was a shadow with elements of color; he looked neither in nor out. Significant, that.

"Why are you here?"

"To learn how to serve."

It was not quite what Ellerson had expected to hear. "What do you think that means?"

Avandar turned toward him; his face was haloed by a sunlight harsh enough to shadow his features completely. Ellerson kept the smile off his face, wondering if Avandar had chosen his place by the window for just that purpose. *My eyes aren't what they used to be,* he thought; *but I don't need to see your face. I can hear enough of you in the words.*

"To suborn my will," the shadow said. "To suborn my will to another's. To take orders with grace. To live in the shadow and glory of another man while taking credit for nothing." Northern winters were warmer than his words. "To stand in shadow."

"Avandar Gallais," Ellerson said, his voice oddly gentle, "this is not the quest of a man of your nature, of your stature. I understand what you *think* you will learn from the guild. What I don't understand is *why* you want to learn it."

"Why is not your concern."

"Why is the only concern I will have for the next four years. Most boys come searching for money. The balance come because they're young and insecure and they'd rather attach themselves to greatness than take the risk of becoming great themselves. Some come because taking orders is easier than thinking of orders to give; some because they think the domicis are well-paid house servants. Pedigreed. Expensive.

"In our first interviews, we attempt to discern the why; to place the boys where they are likely to have the most success in questioning their own motives. Not," he added dryly, "that at this age there is much success in that.

"But you—you are a man who has attained his power."

Ellerson straightened his shoulders. "You realize that we have no writ to protect you from accusations of rogue magery."

"There are . . . mages among the domicis?"

Ellerson shrugged. "Being domicis does not convey immunity from the illegal use of magic."

"This is not public property."

"No. I see you have some inkling of the laws that you are breaking. Let me make it clear: There will be *no* unauthorized use of magic in these halls. Another such incident—even one—and you will find no teacher."

Silk rustled as Avandar Gallais—if that was indeed his name—brought his arms up across his chest.

"Why are you here?"

"I will not answer that."

"Very well. Tomorrow we will avoid the classroom.

I have errands to run on behalf of the guild; you will accompany me."

"As . . . errand boy?"

"As that, yes. I do not find your method of dress appropriate for the station you are to assume. If you have difficulty choosing the correct clothing, you may come to my quarters after dinner."

The man nodded.

Ellerson knew he'd burn in the Hells for eternity before asking for help.

Averalaan was not a small city. It was not, in the estimation of most Imperial travelers, a city at all; it was a vast island of humanity, folding in and farther in upon itself, that harbored *everything* anyone might desire to see in a lifetime. Magery; money; the famed bardic College of Senniel; the Holy Isle upon which *Avantari* rose, circled by the three most important cathedrals in the land; Southern silks and Northern furs, exotic spices, gems, and the work of Makers.

The trees here were taller than all trees but those found in the deepings, where men seldom traveled, and if they were surrounded by cobbled stone and man-made stalls, by house and horse and cart and dog and donkey, they were no less grand for exposure.

Avandar Gallais did not condescend to notice them. Which meant either that he had visited the Common before—which Ellerson doubted—or that he refused to display the weakness of awe to anyone. It was interesting.

As they walked—more slowly than Avandar would have liked, judging from his slightly sour expression—Ellerson observed. Not Avandar, but rather the people who moved out of his way. Women stopped, or stared at him from under the shadow of umbrella or awning; some very few gawped, but not even the young were moved to act foolish. Men also moved;

the elderly and the wise. Young boys pretended not to notice him.

There were men who smelled of power, and Avandar was one of them.

A domicis.

Ellerson put a hand up to his forehead to massage the wrinkles from it. They were unbecoming.

In four years we hope to accomplish what with a young man? Civility, for one. A better understanding of the life of a domicis. A clear acceptance of the value of service, and of what service itself must mean.

This man did not need to learn civility; he understood it, and would practice it or not as flawlessly as he probably practiced his magic. If. Ellerson thought that a month would be long enough, and four years too short a time, to teach him what service *meant*.

He was lost in the thought. As teacher, and not domicis, he took the luxury of such reflection. He would remind himself of this later.

But something caught his attention: the tone of Avandar Gallais' voice.

"And I tell you, ADarias, that you have approached the *wrong* man. Do I make myself clear?"

"You are not the mage who calls himself AGallais?"

"Have I not just said so?"

"Three times." A man wearing House Darias colors drew himself up to his full height. "Three times. I seldom give a man a chance to lie to my face three times. But I am in . . . a tolerant mood." He lifted an arm, this House crested man.

Something was wrong with the gesture. It was innately foreign. But the Houses were not constrained in who they chose as members; The Ten did not birth their family; they adopted it, choosing merit instead of bloodline to carry the name. At least that was the theory.

Four men stepped out of the crowd. They, too, wore

Darias crests, but again, the crests were odd. More significant—much more significant—were the swords they unsheathed.

Ellerson cursed.

The Common was crowded. Too crowded for a fight of this nature. He himself had barely mastered the use of a sword—if master was a word that applied to his ability to lift a blade without losing fingers or toes to it—and he carried no weapon.

But he thought they might brazen or at least speak their way out of the difficulty until he saw the expression on Avandar's face.

A cool, an icy, smile. A gesture of welcome, almost of relief.

"I will tell you, again, ADarias, that you are making a mistake. You are seeking a man. I am not that man. Let us say that in theory you are incapable of making such an irresponsible mistake. Let us say, as your ego decides, that I am, for whatever reasons of my own, lying to you.

"If I were the man you were seeking, and I refused your request—a request which you have not made and which I have not heard—what do you think the wisest course of action would be?"

Ellerson couldn't see the ADarias' face. But he could hear, in the reply, the same chilly pleasure, the same recognition, that marred Avandar's features.

"This, of course." He lifted his arms again, and this time there was no mistaking the utter wrongness of the gesture. Ellerson was a man who had learned over time to trust his instincts. He *moved*. "While I admit a certain surprise at your foolish reluctance, there really is only one course of action, Warlord. We couldn't leave you alive to join our enemies."

Magic.

Fire.

Death.

*   *   *

The battlefield was alive with magic. The winds carried it. The fires burned with it. The swords—drawn under a sun not quite bloodied by its fall—reflected its light, glowing and burning where they struck. All around him, in the fresh air of a bloody spring dusk, the dying screamed, their words an accusation, a cacophony of voices that he could not recognize, they'd been twisted so badly by pain and fear.

The trees cast long shadows where they still stood; many of their thick, ancient trunks had been splintered by the movement of earth, sudden and sharp, beneath their great roots. He felt it coming, a distinct, a distant, surge of power beneath his feet. Bodies flew to either side, a press of momentary flesh, stilled where it fell— or swallowed by turning earth.

He smiled. Sometimes he chose to play games with his enemies. Sometimes he pretended to give them the advantage; sometimes he let them see fear where none existed. They were fools; they believed in their own power although they had heard—they had all heard— of *his*.

But today, he felt no such desire. Enough of toying. He had come to the city to cleanse himself of war, and the war had come—as it always came—to him. This time, it wore the guise of an old, old foe, and an older ally: Demon. *Kialli* and its kin; one greater, four lesser. Had he so chosen, he could have seen them from miles away, and, in truth, had he suspected their presence so strongly, he would have called the power forth instead of letting it slumber so uneasily.

But it woke; it always woke. That was his curse and his gift.

"Impressive," the *kialli* said.

"Indeed," Avandar replied, cool now. He lifted his hands, palms up. No one would have mistaken the gesture for a surrender. His fingers snapped down, making fists of his hands. The four lesser demons snapped just as easily, spraying blood—then nothing at all—into the crackling air.

The *kialli* lord drew his blood-red sword; its flames were dull in the harsh light Avandar's magic cast.

"I tell you now," the would-be servant said coolly, "that I have no battle with you. I am here for my own purposes, and until you cross them you are of no interest whatever to me.

"It is the last chance I will give you; you are insignificant otherwise. But choose, and choose quickly."

The *kialli* were creatures of power and arrogance; there really was very little choice to be made. They closed, warrior-mage and demon, and where they touched they could not be seen for the crackle and glow of brilliant light. The earth thundered beneath them, the winds howled, the air snapped with lightning.

And when it was over, when the maelstrom had cleared, Avandar Gallais stepped out of the floating dust and the shattered ruin of the Common ground. He was not unblooded; he granted the *kialli* some respect for that. But he was, as always, undefeated. As always.

He had come down from the mountains too early.

He had known it when he left them, driven North by the ghosts of the dead and three dark dreams. But the dead had become tricky over the passage of centuries; they waited until the battlefield loomed around him, then snuck out of the shadows and debris, finding bodies, lingering in the whimpering screams of the dying.

He found the boy that way.

Found him bleeding to death, his chest a puckered, blackening wound that would not hold until a healer could be found. Young boy, not more than four years old, and beside him, arms broken on impact, his mother or grandmother. Hard to tell; the magic had scarred her face completely. The boy was not wild

with pain, nor yet with fear, but he was wild with the
desolation of abandonment, and no magic that
Avandar Gallais possessed—or had ever possessed—
would bring back the dead.

He should not have touched the child. That was his
first mistake. But his body had given in to the glory
of the fight and the satisfaction of the kill; it was sati-
ated now, and other things had room to play.

He knelt by the boy. Reached out for him, his long
sleeves sticky with blood that had not been shed in
decades. *This* blood, his own, he was not used to
seeing. But the boy's blood—the blood of others, had
become his life. *Was* his life.

In the foreign, Weston tongue, the boy cried out for
his mother. Avandar Gallais spoke a few words, a few
comforting words of enchantment, and then, after a
second's pause, snapped the child's neck cleanly.

He had done it countless times before, but he had
always had time to recover; had given himself that
much. The ghosts were so *strong* in these streets. Almost without thought, he held the child's corpse to his
chest, tucking the lolling head beneath his chin.

There, in the dimming day, Avandar Gallais began
to weep.

And it was weeping that Ellerson of the guild of
the domicis found him.

They did not speak.

Ellerson, because he could think of nothing at all
to say at the sight of a child in the broken city streets,
and Avandar for his own reasons.

The magi were summoned. The magi arrived.

The witnesses—the few that had somehow stayed
the scene *and* survived it—were unclear about what
had happened. They had seen men wearing the awkward crest of Darias, they had seen another man,
taller and prouder of bearing, and they had seen the
earth break, the sky rain fire, the trees snap like kin-

dling on a hot, dry day. Not that the port city had many of those.

Ellerson's duty was to the guild, and not to the magi; to the guild, and not to the magisterial guards. He did not speak, except once, and that was to say that in his considered opinion as a longtime member of the Domicis guild, the House Colors that the five men wore were so sloppily put together they were obviously forgeries. That much was true.

Avandar said nothing. He rose as a witness, spoke as a witness, lied as a witness. The magi who had come to question him took his name and his occupation—apprentice guildsman—with some surprise, but the surprise was clearly not one of recognition.

"Come along, Avandar," Ellerson said, when the magisterial guards were finished questioning him. "It is time, I think, to go home."

Avandar looked up, beyond the fringe of Ellerson's remaining hair; looked South. He staggered to his feet, looking once over his shoulder at the unknown child the magisterial guards were bearing away on a simple cot.

"No," Ellerson said softly, "not South. To the guild, apprentice." He was gentle. He had not thought to be gentle with this man. "We go to the guild. Come. Follow me." Even in gentleness, he could not bring himself to touch his student.

Avander pulled himself up to his full height, as if stung by the softness of Ellerson's tone. He followed.

Every life you take will become yours, Warlord. It's power, although not its knowledge, will be your strength.

And what price? What price will I pay for this gift? I am a man, and I will not give up my life to night or darkness in order to prolong it. I will not feed like an animal upon my own kind; I will not play kialli *games or dance* Ariani *dances.*

Do you think you do not prey upon your kind even now? No, do not answer. You are wiser than I thought you would be—an interesting sign. I cannot confer eternal night; I cannot change your essential nature. If you fear either from me, be easy. That is not my intent.

What is your intent?

To give you immortality, Warlord. War is an interest of mine, and you will keep it alive.

He woke to a darkened room. His arms ached. His chest hurt. The stench of the dead was in his nostrils, and to breathe he must rise, must seek the open air. The bed he left behind; his step to the window was almost, but not quite, flight. He threw the latches off, pushed the window up, sought the open air. The dream was thick and heavy, and he had seen it often enough that he knew what would follow.

He would stand, at the foot of a god, waiting.

The mists of the halfworld where god and man might meet, if not as equals, then not quite as slave and master, would be thick with a life of their own, sensuous and disturbing. They had never seemed so immediate before; it was almost as if his answer would make him part of them, part of their dominion. His first intimation of immortality.

That, part of the dream he could face. But what followed was harder.

He was almost grateful for the knock at the door.

"Come," he said, knowing that Ellerson would bring light with him; knowing that he would stop at the threshold a moment before stepping across and closing the door behind him. Knowing that he would come alone.

"Avandar."

"I . . . often have trouble sleeping."

"I rarely do."

"That does not surprise me." He lifted a hand to touch the peak of the window frame. "It was perhaps . . . to attain such easy sleep that I came to you." He turned; the light that Ellerson carried was a muted, simple lamp.

"My turn to stand behind the light, and you in it, is that it?" the domicis asked quietly.

"Even so."

"Tell me."

"There is not much to tell."

"You killed that child."

He turned away again. "I have seen enough of the dying, old man. That child was already dead. I spared him a few minutes of isolation, fear, pain. You would have done the same had he been a dog."

"Yes. Had he been a dog." The night was harsh. "You killed the five men."

"They would have killed me."

"True enough. But your battle killed some thirty people, at best count."

"So few?" The windows were airless. "I have killed thousands, in my time."

"In *your* time," Ellerson replied. "Not on *mine*." He set the lamp down. "Tell me why you've come, Avandar Gallais, and I will do what I can to help you. Refuse, and I will likewise refuse. This was a game, to me, and I repent of it; it is now clear that I have accepted a task whose failure will be too costly. I can step back, or I can go forward.

"I am prepared to wash my hands and step back."

Avandar Gallais stepped into the darkness and stared a long time at the older—at the younger—man's face. "You are not what I expected, Ellerson of the domicis. I will tell you what I may tell you. If it is enough, it is enough."

Ellerson stood quietly, seeking to take no comfort by seating himself. He was, in his way, like the mountains that Avandar Gallais called home.

He spoke first of his dream. He had thought to be interrupted, but Ellerson did not offer him that comfort, except to say, almost dryly. "You accepted, of course."

"I was a younger man," Avandar replied, as if that was answer enough. In a way, it was. "Younger," he said, "and less sure of my power." His hands, shadowed, were still visible in the night of small room and single window. "I am sure, now, of nothing but power."

"You aren't a god."

"No. But if I killed no other men in my life, I would live as long as one. As far as I've been able to determine, the length of life is year for year: One potential year of their life for one actual year of my own.

"I said I did not wish to feed upon my own, but I have, and if I do not hunger for their lives, I hunger for the thing that takes it most: war. Dominion." His hands dropped. "I had an Empire, of a sort, when I chose to accept the god's offer.

"And an Empress, a woman of beauty and power in her own right, a partner of consequence." This, then, was the second part of the dream, the part that defined his existence, that made him understand the mercy of gods. "She was fair, Ellerson, as your Northern snows; the sun could not bite her. Her hair was dark, the blue-black of night, and her eyes were dark as well; nothing cold at all about them. She was as tall as I, harder and more determined, and she had turned her talent and her energy to the study of magery so that she might be my equal." He laughed bitterly. "*My* equal. I indulged her shamelessly. She was the jewel in the crown; the crown itself." He looked into the dim light, the old man's stiff face. "I tell you this because I am a fool, and I am too new from loss. I will kill you if I hear it spoken of, because it will have to have come from you."

"If I choose to accept you, Avandar, what you say will be as close to sacred as words can be."

Truth, there. "And if not?"

"If not, I will take your words as a confidence between a lord and the man who has chosen, for this single night, to serve him as only one of the domicis can do."

That surprised him. He was silent a long while, unsure of whether or not the silence was due his wife or this strange man, "She was the first kill," he said at last.

Ellerson said nothing.

"She knew what I had done. I do not know how, but I assume the god's servants told her. Did I tell you that she was like the fires themselves? Hot, scorching, blistering—sudden in her anger and her fury, sudden in her love. She felt betrayed; she felt abandoned to mortality by me, by the only man she had chosen to love.

"She came to me in fury, and she—who had honed her talent at my side and knew better than any what my weaknesses were, attempted to destroy me. I tried to speak to her. To speak with her—she was beyond reason. A day, two days, and we might have spoken and had peace of one sort or another, but there was no peace offered.

"I did not intend to kill her."

"But you did."

"Worse, Ellerson. When she died, I *felt* it. The life that left her, the magery that had been her pride—and mine—came to me as if they were swords and I was the only sheath they had ever known. I had doubled my life span, and my power, in a single blow.

"But she was not just any woman. She was of an old, old line, and had in her the blood of the firstborn. It was not above her to place a curse upon the gift that had been given me. *You have chosen victory over love,* she said, *and this is what it will buy you: eternity. You will come to curse it, for you will hold* nothing *that you value until the day you choose another man's cause over your own. As you have conquered, so must you serve.*

He did not kneel; did not sit. But the stiffness left him. The nightmare of her death, her slack, blistered face, the shock and the anger melting into hurt and denial. Nights that he could not leave the dream quickly enough he still woke screaming at the feel of her life bleeding into his. He had tried so hard to stop it.

But his pride was part of his power; he could not scream in front of this old man. He spoke instead, quickly, to cover the pain, to pass over it. "She was the first of six wives who attempted to take my life. It . . . makes a man cynical about love and the fair sex."

"Did you kill them all?"

"No. Not after her. But I didn't love them either; not that way. In the case of my wives—or my children—I let executioners deal with their deaths. I could not quite bring myself to claim them."

"Your children?"

"Sons, mostly. They tired of a father's Imperial grip, and as my life would extend infinitely beyond theirs, they saw no better way to free themselves. I will admit that I had some sympathy for them; they were young men much like I had once been.

"I built Empires, and after a while, I left them. To my sons, to their sons. Once in a while to my daughters. But it pales, as time passes. We live—we who are mortal—in a world of 'ifs.' Imagine, Ellerson, that you have finally lived the perfect life.

"I chose to absent myself from war for a time— albeit a short time—and to find a woman who might be wife not to the Warlord, but to a soldier, a common man who had cunning and strength to recommend him. It was not a guise that suited me well, but I wore it. And I found such a woman, and I lived with her.

I joined the army of the man who ruled the city in which we lived; it was long ago.

"War came." He was silent. "She was lost to the war; my son was lost to it. I remained. I conquered. I made my enemies pay, and with every life I took, the time of my return to her—to any of the people I loved—grew more distant.

"Was I a good man? What does the word mean? I have never understood it, and I understand it less and less with time. In my youth I did things that I could not speak to you of; I am not proud of them now, but I do not judge them, and those injured are so long dead it is hard to believe that any other judge exists. But I am not what I was.

"It is tiring, to watch every person you love wither and die. Whether they die attempting to take your life, or die because you have chosen to join battle— and I have chosen many battles, and I have held many of my children as they lie insensate with pane, unaware of me, of my presence—they die and I remain. I am *tired*, Ellerson. I have come this way to fulfil her curse and have peace.

"I tried. I tried it on my own. I lived what I thought was a life of service. Three lives. It was not, apparently, enough. And it came to me that I did not understand service; that I could not understand the conditions of her curse enough to be free of it. I had heard of this . . . unusual guild long before you were born, and I had thought to recover from my last life and come to you here for instruction."

"You've come here to learn enough to die?"

Avandar smiled softly. "Not the way I would have worded it, had you offered me the choice, but yes, I believe that is what I said."

"You realize," Ellerson said quietly, "that the magi would kill for the opportunity to speak with you. That the historians would stand in line, beg and plead for years on end, for a chance to listen to what you might say."

"I would speak to them in tongues that have long since died," Avandar replied, "if I spoke at all. There is some history that is better left buried; I would bury my own if I could. Will you aid me?"

Ellerson was quiet. "I cannot answer you tonight, except to say this: I may not be able to give you the peace you desire, but if it is in my power, I will point you in the right direction."

Pride.
Pride was the root of all great falls, in both story and religious text. In that ground where old religions faltered and fell into the realms only children now knew, it was a sin so often warned of that the children themselves had lost the sense of its grandeur and its greatness; in their language it was a crime much like theft."

But Ellerson was no longer contained by childhood. He stood in the darkened classroom, framed by door, the lamp's oil burning dangerously low. After a moment, he walked through the door to the room that was his preserve, his territory, his hallowed ground. He paused in front of a desk that still held the scorched and blackened marks of two palms.

Closing his eyes a moment, he listened to the tenor of Avandar Gallais' voice. How could a man such as he learn the value of service when in truth he had never done anything but rule? Even in this, his desire was his own, a thing apart from a master or mistress.

And what had Akalia seen, in the Three Dreams that had driven her to accept what was plainly otherwise unacceptable?

I am too old for this, he thought, and set the lamp in the cradle of burned wood.

He knew what he would do, of course. Because he could still hear the man's voice breaking, and breaking

again, like water against the seawall, the new corpse
of a child held ragged against chin and chest.

"Service in the guild is not the service offered by a
servant, or a guard, or even a Southern oathguard.
The Chosen of Terafin, who lay down their lives, and
make of their lives their duty, are not—could not be—
domicis. Do you understand this?"

"No."

The one good thing about Avandar: He was honest
to a fault. Ellerson could understand how a man of
his nature had somehow stood still for long enough to
learn the art of magery. His focus was astonishing.

"To be willing to die for a cause is *not* what the
heart of service is about. Young men scattered across
the globe throw their lives away—uselessly and use-
fully—on a daily basis. They neither know, nor understand, the heart of service; they offer themselves, and
they are accepted." Here, the sun cast a shadow. It
had taken Ellerson the better part of two weeks before he was willing to appear in public with Avandar
Gallais again.

But the days were long and lovely, and he found
this student so oppressive he almost had to get up and
walk around to escape the sensation of being caged
with a hungry beast. Avandar himself did not seem to
mind the interruption, although he did not appear to
understand it.

"First," Ellerson said, as they walked by the seawall,
a place where few people ventured, "there is the matter of inclination, *I* am not a man interested in serving power."

"And yet you are with me."

"I will teach you, but teaching has different con-
straints. I would never serve a man of your nature."

"Why?"

"You are a man of power, Avandar, and service to
power is its own responsibility. I am not willing to

become what I would have to become to be useful to you."

"And what have you served, then?"

"This is not about *me,* and the question is therefore impertinent—but I will answer it. I have served merchants in my time, in particular three who sought to achieve some status within the patriciate. They were not well-bred, but they were cunning and they were decent enough."

"And you taught them manners, one presumes?"

"That and more, although they did not hire me to teach them." He shrugged. "I cannot speak of them further; it is part of the code. But I have been hired on contract, I have fulfilled my contract, and I have returned to the guild."

"I do not understand."

"No, I suppose you don't. There are two ways to offer service. The first is for a term: a year is usually the shortest, and five the longest. The second is for the life of the master—or the mistress—who requests a domicis. These are always people of power." He looked down at the sea, which was oddly still beneath their feet.

"Why do you make the distinction?"

"A domicis must protect his master and mistress, and that protection takes many forms. He must be aware of their needs, sensitive to them, and able to respond by either presence or absence, without the need for formal spoken word. He must understand what they desire when they themselves *do not understand it,* and this is one of the most difficult things a domicis learns to do.

"It is part of our art, to understand people." He turned to look at Avandar Gallais. "You were called Warlord; you understand people in a fashion, but I would say, given your long years of experience, that you actually understand less than the students who remain with the guild after the first three years of their lessons."

It did not surprise him when Avandar Gallais bristled. He wondered, almost idly, if the man would melt the stone beneath his hands.

The stone did not melt. After an uneasy moment, Avandar Gallais spoke again. "Pretend for a moment that I am such a student. That I have been judged ready and worthy. To whom would you . . . display me?"

He will never be ready for this. "A person of power, Avandar. A man or a woman who has need of the talent you display—a man or woman who can take the flow of your power and bend it to their life without being so bent by it they lose *that* life."

"In other words," the mage said, showing a humor that always surprised Ellerson, "no one."

The days grew longer; grew shorter; grew longer again. There were no more mages, no more attacks; the streets had become so safe that Ellerson—had he been a different man—might have forgotten what he had witnessed in the Common.

But two things happened to change that.

The first was a visit from an old student. An old student who had, as so many did, sought service to a woman of power, and who had been found acceptable by The Terafin herself—the most powerful woman in the realm, after the Kings. He was curious; he was always curious when his students returned to him seeking either advice or favor. Morretz was not a man who did either.

"Morretz," he said, as he took a seat. "Akalia says you have an unusual request?" He was suspicious of an unusual request Akalia placed before him, but he was not suspicious of Morretz.

"Very."

"You know I've retired from all of this nonsense."

"Of course."

"Which is why you had Akalia call me in, not time for more than a quick change of clothing and a hasty gathering of personal items?"

"Not precisely."

"Then tell me. Precisely."

"The Terafin wishes to hire you, for a contracted period, not for life. You will have a wing of the House proper, and it will be your domain; you may choose your own servants, if those provided do not meet your approval, and you will, of course, be given a generous budget out of which to operate. You will be offered the sum of not less than two thousand crowns for a period which may be as short as two days and as long as two years."

"Two *thousand* crowns? That is rather a lot. Am I to serve some nefarious criminal?"

"Ellerson, The Terafin might not be aware of your particular choices in masters, but I am—I assure you that we would not house a nefarious criminal under your care"

"The patriciate is composed of them."

"However," Morretz continued, knowing him well, "we would certainly not shy away from asking you to serve a petty criminal."

"I beg your pardon?"

"A girl. Possibly of age, but most likely fourteen or fifteen by her size and look." Pause. "She came off the street of the older holdings. With her den."

"Akalia, *tell me*."

Akalia looked *old*. She lifted her head and met his eyes with a fraction of her usual vigor. "That girl," she said softly, "needs you."

"More of your dreaming nonsense."

"No, Ellerson; part of the original. I am tired of this, in a way even you would find difficult to understand." She rose. "But Avandar Gallais was sent to us for a reason." She frowned "Morretz saw him. He was not particularly pleased to renew the acquaintance."

"He didn't mention—"

"Don't ask him. And don't ask me."

"I cannot possibly accept the care of this girl—although I admit my curiosity and my inclination are both piqued—while having the care of Avandar Gallais."

"No."

"And you would let me take service to the girl?"

"Yes."

"Why, Akalia?"

"You must answer that for yourself. Will you do as I have asked?"

"He will not be pleased."

"No, but he will accept it. I have already seen to that."

Teaching was a type of service; Ellerson acknowledged this in one corner of his mind. One corner of all he had left for it. The Terafin manse—the manse upon the Holy Isle itself—was in fine condition, but the wing was run in a way not to his liking, and setting it straight, with the required frosty tact, had taken concentration, energy, and speed.

But he was up to a task of that nature, and when his new master arrived, he was ready for her. Ready, and not ready, prepared and unprepared. She was, as Morretz had said, a girl not quite fifteen by the look of her, but beneath the wild fringe of humidity-curled hair, and above the bruised circles that ringed them, her eyes were bright and sharp; free from the hard edge that the street often put there.

He bowed formally, and she stared at him as if he were a different form of life. He was. "I am Ellerson," he said. He waited a moment, and then added, "I am the domicis."

Pride was such folly; it was clear that she had no idea what the word meant. And he was heartily tired, at that moment, of attempting to explain it. When one of the unruly young men at her back called for food with manners that would have embarrassed soldiers of the field, he led the way. Time to teach them all that they needed to know later. For now, food, shelter, the hint of home.

What had this to do with Avandar?

Nothing. Ellerson was here as domicis, and it was almost a pleasure to let the responsibility of Avandar recede. He had this one, this Jewel Markess, and she was a child that he could see the possibility in.

A day later, a day, and he had the answer to a question he wished he had not asked.

A day, the girl with her den, her den in the silence of shock that magic often leaves in its wake, the word *demon* whispered but never spoken aloud. He sat with them in the darkness of an evening around, of all things, a kitchen table. And he knew, when they spoke, that what he had to offer them would not be enough.

But he watched this girl, this Jewel, speak. He watched her speak to the white-haired boy, Angel, the dark-haired boy, Carver—children who were not quite children. Watched her struggle with her own fear in order to calm theirs.

You are a leader, he thought, as a face framed by the lamplight he would come to understand she best loved sank toward the tabletop, *and you will be a person of power.*

The Henden that year was dark; the darkest month that Ellerson had even known, and he had known many. He had not had word from Avandar Gallais in the three months leading up to it, and wondered, as he advised and guided the young Jewel Markess, if

Avandar Gallais and the Guild of the Domicis were still together.

He was fond of the girl, but more than that, he could see that the power that she would take was fast coming, faster than he would have liked. *I have never served a man or a woman of power,* he thought, *but you, Jewel Markess, are the first one that I will regret walking away from.* Almost, he did not. He was fond of her, as he had never been fond of a master; her sharp temper and salty language aside, she was a mistress worthy of service, one not aiming for power, but destined for it nonetheless. And when she had it, would she even understand what it meant? Would she know how to protect it, how to nurture it, how to remain true to herself while wearing it?

Those things, he could teach her. But he had come to understand that he could not keep her alive in the deadly world of House Politics for long enough that she might learn.

This is why you sent me, Akalia, he thought. And he returned in secret to the Domicis Guild. Akalia was waiting for him.

"Well?" she asked softly.

"Yes," he replied.

"She is, I hear, a young girl."

"Yes. Young for her station, old for her age."

"Would you give her to Avandar?"

The old man laughed. "Not easily, no. But I would say that they will be evenly matched in their fashion. She is not a girl, Akalia, she is—"

The door swung open. Avandar Gallais strode into the room. It was expected, at least by Ellerson. "You have found me a master," he said, with a terrible confidence.

"I told you," Ellerson said, "Never to do that again."

"And I might play at apologies, Ellerson. But I have waited three lifetimes. I do not wish to wait a fourth.

Come. You have found me a master, and she is a master of power; I will take what I am offered. *Now.*"

Ellerson and Akalia exchanged a single glance, and the glance spoke volumes. But the old man remembered how that imperious voice could break, and he saw the young woman who he thought might not survive the House itself without the aid of a powerful and completely trusted domicis; he rose.

She was going to hate him. To hate them both.

"Very well, Avandar Gallais," he said softly. "But I must warn you now to be careful; she is not what you expect, and she will judge you for the next decade by what you do when you first meet."

When he left the Domicis Guild for what he hoped was the final time, he carried very little with him. But he carried history, and history was heavy.

The old man walked beside him almost stiffly.

"You are worried," he said, because he understood Ellerson that well.

"Yes."

"Why?"

"This girl—she's not what you expect."

"I have seen many women, and many girls, in my time. You have already said that she is a master who requires *my* service. What else should I know?

"You are not ready to serve, Avandar. I do this with misgivings, but I feel that—for reasons I cannot explain, either to myself or to you—you will be of aid to each other in the years to follow.

"She is . . . young. She is not—" Ellerson fell silent. "Avandar, remember: first impressions." He paused. "It is not our way to discuss our masters. I feel, however, that I should warn you—"

But the words were like gnats; he brushed them aside. The sea wind carried the tang, the taste of freedom. He walked quickly, and Ellerson walked slowly, and together, by dint of ruffled compromise, they reached the Terafin Manse at more or less the same time.

Avandar Gallais was shocked.

To see the girl—for she was a girl, no more—seated uncomfortably before Ellerson, her eyes half-filled with defiant tears, was perhaps the most disappointing event in his life. To hear Ellerson speak to her, as if she were somehow a weak child, was worse. But to know, to *know* that this was to be his fate—to serve *this*—was almost more than he could bear.

He would have left the room, but The Terafin's domicis, Morretz, was present. They had met before; clashed before. The younger man had, of course, lost. He was an enemy, if one beneath notice, and Avandar did not show defeat or weakness in the face of an enemy. He stood his ground.

But he could not believe that this . . . urchin . . . was to be his *master*. He rebelled against it, until the power within him made more noise than the speech of the people around him.

No. Wait. Think. He took a breath. The power sometimes drove him, and *he* was its master, not the other way around. Ellerson had tried to tell him something about this girl; he had not listened. He listened now, trying to sort out the buzz of half-remembered words. Minutes passed before the right ones returned to him.

She has the sight. It had been centuries, longer, since he had encountered that power, but it had always intrigued him. Perhaps something could be salvaged from the ruin of his plan.

Turning to The Terafin, he said coldly, "This is the one?"

"Yes."

"Good."

He let the power go; it jumped from the skin of his

gently pointed fingertips in a fan of light and fire toward the girl.

Who was not thee to greet it. He heard drawn sword; heard the crackle of Morretz' magic, saw the stiffening of The Terafin's fine features. And he smiled.

"That," The Terafin said icily, "was unnecessary."

"For you, yes," Avandar replied, turning to the only person in the room who would normally be worthy of his attention. "But it is not you who will devote your life to the services of this one."

She was close to refusing him that opportunity; he saw it clearly in the frost of her unchanged face. He was not used to explaining any of his actions. But he swallowed his pride. Turned to the girl who was even now lifting herself from the carpets beneath the large, expensive table that graced this library. "My apologies." He turned back to The Terafin, gauging her reaction.

Morretz spoke; he replied. It was an insignificant exchange; The Terafin's reaction was the only one that counted.

He was therefore extremely surprised when something struck him on the shoulder. Something sharp, hard, with enough of an edge to bruise, although not enough to draw blood. Eyes widening, he turned in the direction of the missile, his gaze sweeping groundward for just long enough to note that what had hit him was, in fact, a simple book.

She stood there, defiant, bristling, her cheeks flushed with anger and just a hint of triumph. He saw her age, and he saw beyond her age, and he thought: *No, I have been here before, and I will not do this.* For her eyes were dark and of fire, and he had thought her unworthy of notice until that moment. Now, he thought her beautiful.

It hurt him.

"It seems," The Terafin said, her voice as smooth

and neutral as his would have been under similar circumstance, "that you are not the only one to test, Avandar."

"No," he said softly, seeing now some of what Ellerson must have seen in this young woman, this Jewel Markess ATerafin. "Just the only one to fail. Your pardon, little one." He was only slightly surprised when she bristled at the term of almost affection. "Terafin, I accept your contract. I will serve this one."

The Terafin raised a brow slightly, and then nodded. "Jewel, this is Avandar Gallais. He is of the Domicis and has come to fulfil the obligation that Ellerson felt he could not."

"W-what?"

"I am," Avandar said gravely, "your domicis."

"I won't have him!"

The Terafin's voice chilled several degrees. "You will. This interview is at an end." She turned, sweeping out of the room, followed by Morretz and the Chosen who attended her always.

Jewel was left in her wake, flat-footed, deflated. He had seen that before. Knew that in her, it wouldn't last long.

What am I doing? He almost turned and followed The Terafin out. Because he recognized in Jewel something that, in time, he might come to love. And he loathed the loving because it was the source of all grief, all loss, all damage.

She turned to him. Mutinous. Certain—as he was certain—that she had no choice but to follow her Lord's dictate. "*You* serve *me*, is that clear?"

"Oh, absolutely," he replied, speaking through slightly clenched teeth, as was his habit when someone attempted to give him an order. Something he would have to change; one of many things. He would try. That was all he could do.

Perhaps this would be the lifetime. Perhaps this would be his salvation. And perhaps it would be a waste of his time. He had time. He told himself that, staring down at her face. He had time. She, on the other hand, willful, defiant, *foolish* in the certainty age lent her, might not. He understood why power was needed, what he didn't understand, given her outburst, was how Ellerson thought she would survive to attain any rank or stature. she stank of the sincerity that led most easily to death.

And that, perversely, was what he would like best in her.

"You will listen to me in emergencies; you will do as I say and you will allow me to protect you as I see fit."

"Don't even start," she replied, her teeth on edge.

The magic came, rose at the tone of her arrogant little voice.

She snorted, as if she could see it, and see what lay beneath it. She probably could.

A guard came to lead her away, and she allowed it; they had their battles laid out before him in a grid-work that he could see more clearly than she.

He thought about his conversations with Ellerson; he could not see a clear path from them to this girl. But there was something here; he was almost afraid to touch it. Love? Perhaps. Or perhaps something more precious still.

That night, the mountains rose in the distance of dreams. He rose with them, taking to air as he seldom did in these latter centuries.

The woman who had sent him from the mountain paths met him halfway up, her robes a billowing dark-ness that might be mistaken for cloud if seen from below. "Avandar Gallais," she said quietly.

"You have the advantage."

"I will not always have it, and you have advantage enough. Forgive me if I wait before making my formal introduction. You have come farther than I thought you would."

"Do you think," he said, because it was a dream, and it was not a nightmare, and the ghosts were miraculously silent in the shadowed night, "that I will walk far enough?"

"Who can say? You are a warrior, and in service, you are *still* a warrior." She bowed her head. "I have served my life under the geas of a god, and it is only to end the geas that I continue the service."

"My god is a dead god."

"Mine is not."

"I see." He turned away from her. "Do they stop screaming, the dead? Do they rest in peace, do they slumber? Do they . . . forgive?"

When he turned, she was gone; he was alone in the night air.

But her voice at the distance of dream's edge, of waking, said, *You will have the opportunity to ask that question yourself.*

And for a moment, before the day broke, before life called him back to its endless demands, he felt a tremulous peace.

TEN FOR THE DEVIL

Charles de Lint

Charles de Lint is a full-time writer and musician who presently makes his home in Ottawa, Canada with his wife MaryAnn Harris, an artist and musician. His most recent novels are Someplace to Be Flying *and* Trader. *For more information about his work, visit his website at <http://www.cyberus.ca/~cdl>.*

"ARE YOU sure you want off here?"

"Here" was in the middle of nowhere, on a dirt county road somewhere between Tyson and Highway 14. Driving along this twisty back road, Butch Crickman's pickup hadn't passed a single house for the last mile and a half. If he kept on going, he wouldn't pass another one for at least a mile or so, except for the ruin of the old Lindy farm and that didn't count, seeing as how no one had lived there since the place burned down ten years ago.

Staley smiled. "Don't you worry yourself, Butch."

"Yeah, but—"

Opening the passenger door, she jumped down onto the dirt, then leaned back inside to grab her fiddle case.

"This is perfect," she told him. "Really."

"I don't know. Kate's not going to be happy when she finds out I didn't take you all the way home."

Staley took a deep breath of the clean night air. On her side of the road it was all Kickaha land. She could smell the raspberry bushes choking the ditches close at hand, the weeds and scrub trees out in the field, the dark rich scent of the forest beyond it. Up above, the stars seemed so close you'd think they were leaning down to listen to her conversation with Butch. Somewhere off in the distance, she heard a long, mournful howl. Wolf. Maybe coyote.

"This *is* home," she said. Closing the door, she added through the window, "Thanks for the ride."

Butch hesitated a moment longer, then sighed and gave her a nod. Staley stepped back from the pickup. She waited until he'd turned the vehicle around and started back, waited until all she could see was the red glimmer of his taillights through a thinning cloud of dust, before she knelt down and took out her fiddle and bow. She slung the case over her shoulder by its strap so that it hung across her back. Hoisting the fiddle and bow up above her shoulders, she pushed her way through the raspberry bushes, moving slowly and patiently so that the thorns didn't snag on her denim overalls.

Once she got through the bushes, the field opened up before her, ghostly in the starlight. The weeds were waist high, but she liked the brush of stem and long leaf against her legs, and though the mosquitoes quickly found her, they didn't bite. She and the bugs had an understanding—something she'd learned from her grandmother. Like her music.

The fiddle went up, under her chin. Tightening the frog on the bow, she pulled it across the strings and woke a sweet melody.

Butch and Kate Crickman owned the roadhouse back out on the highway where Staley sat in with the house band from time to time, easily falling into what-

ever style they were playing that night. Honky-tonk.
Western swing. Old-timey. Bluegrass. The Crickmans
treated her like an errant daughter, always worried
about how she was doing, and she let them fuss over
her some. But she played coy when it came to her
living accommodations. They wouldn't understand.
Most people didn't.

Home was an old trailer that used to belong to her
grandmother. After Grandma died, Staley had gotten
a few of the boys from up on the rez to move it from
her parents' property on the outskirts of Tyson down
here where it was hidden away in the deep woods.
Strictly speaking, it was parked on Indian land, but
the Kickaha didn't mind either it or her being here.
They had some understanding with her grandmother
that went way back—Staley didn't know the details.

So it was a couple of the Creek boys and one of
their cousins who transported the trailer for her that
winter, hauling it in from the road on a makeshift sled
across the snowy fields, then weaving in between the
older growth, flattening saplings that would spring
back upright by the time spring came around again.
There were no trails leading to it now except for the
one narrow path Staley had walked over the years,
and forget about a road. Privacy was absolute. The
area was too far off the beaten track for hikers or
other weekend explorers, and come hunting season
anyone with an ounce of sense stayed out of the rez.
Those boys were partial to keeping their deer, par-
tridge, ducks, and the like to themselves, and they
weren't shy about explaining the way things were to
trespassers.

Round about hunting season Staley closed up the
trailer and headed south herself. She only summered
in the deep woods. The other half of the year she was
a traveling musician, a city girl, making do with what
work her music could bring her, sometimes a desert
girl, if she traveled far enough south.

But tonight the city and traveling were far from her mind. She drank in the tall night sky and meandered her way through the fields, fiddling herself home with a music she only played here, when she was on her own. Grandma called it a calling-on music, said it was the fiddle sending spirit tunes back into the otherworld from which it had first come. Staley didn't know from spirit music and otherworlds; she just fancied a good tune played from the heart, and if the fiddle called up anything here, it was that. Heart music.

When she got in under the trees, the music changed some, took on an older, more resonant sound, long low notes that spoke of hemlock roots growing deep in the earth, or needled boughs cathedraling between the earth and the stars. It changed again when she got near the bottle tree, harmonizing with the soft clink on the glass bottles hanging from its branches by leather thongs. Grandma taught her about the bottle tree.

"I don't rightly know that it keeps unwelcome spirits at bay," she said, "but it surely does discourage uninvited visitors."

Up in these hills everybody knew that only witches kept a bottle tree.

A little farther on Staley finally reached the meadow that held her trailer. The trailer itself was half-hidden in a tangle of vines, bookended on either side by a pair of rain barrels that caught spill off from the eaves. The grass and weeds were kept trimmed here, not quite short enough to be a lawn, but not wild like the fields along the county road.

Stepping out from under the relative darkness cast by the trees, the starlight seemed bright in contrast. Staley curtsied to the scarecrow keeping watch over her little vegetable patch, a tall, raggedy shape that sometimes seemed to dance to her music when the wind was right. She'd had it four years now, made it herself from apple boughs and old clothes. The second summer she'd noticed buds on what were supposed to be dead limbs. This spring, the boughs had actually blossomed and now bore small, tart fruit.

She stood in front of it for a long moment, tying off her tune with a complicated knot of sliding notes, and that was when she sensed the boy.

He'd made himself a nest in the underbrush that crowded close up against the north side of her clearing—a goosey, nervous presence where none should be. Staley walked over to her trailer to lay fiddle and bow on the steps, then carefully approached the boy's hiding place. She hummed under her breath, a soothing old modal tune that had first been born somewhere deeper in the hills than this clearing. When she got to the very edge of her meadow, she eased down until she was kneeling in the grass, then peered under the bush.

"Hey, there," she said. "Nobody's going to hurt you."

Only it wasn't a boy crouching there under the bushes.

She blinked at the gangly hare her gaze found. It was undernourished, one ear chewed up from a losing encounter with some predator, limbs trembling, big brown eyes wide with fear.

"Well, now," Staley said, sitting back on her haunches.

She studied the animal for along moment before reaching carefully under the branches of the bush. The rabbit was too scared or worn out—probably both—to do much more than shake in her arms when she picked it up. Standing, she cradled the little animal against her breast.

Now what did she do with it?

It was round about then she realized that she and the rabbit weren't alone here in the clearing. Calling on music, she thought and looked around. Called up the rabbit, and then something else, though what she couldn't say. All she got was the sense that it was something old. And dangerous. And it was hungry for the trembling bundle of fur and bone she held cradled in her arms.

It wasn't quite all the way here yet, hadn't quite managed to cross over the way its prey had. But it was worrying at the fabric of distance that kept it at bay.

Staley had played her fiddle tunes a thousand times, here in her meadow. What made tonight different from any other?

"You be careful with this music," Grandma had told her more than once. "What that fiddle can wake in your chest and set you to playing has lived over there behind the hills and trees forever. Some of it's safe and pretty. Some of it's old and connects a straight line between you and a million years ago. And some of it's just plain dangerous."

"How do you know the difference?" she'd asked.

Grandma could only shake her head. "You don't till you call it up. That's why you need to be careful, girl."

*   *   *

Staley Cross is about the last person I expect to find knocking on my apartment door at six A.M. I haven't seen her since Malicorne and Jake went away—and that's maybe three, four years ago now—but she looks about the same. Straw-colored hair cut short like a boy's, the heart-shaped face, and those big green eyes. Still fancies those denim overalls, though the ones she's wearing over a white T-shirt tonight are a better fit than those she had on the last time I saw her. Her slight frame used to swim in that pair.

I see she's still got that old Army surplus knapsack, hanging on her back, and her fiddle case is standing on the floor by her feet. What's new is the raggedy-ass rabbit she's carrying around in a cloth shopping bag, but I don't see that straightaway.

"Hey, William," she says when I open the door on her, my eyes still thick with sleep. "Remember me?"

I have to smile at that. She's not easy to forget, not her nor that blue fiddle of hers.

"Let's see," I say. "Are you the one who went skinny-dipping in the mayor's pool the night he won the election, or the one who could call up blackbirds with her fiddle?"

I guess it was Malicorne who told me about that, how where ravens or crows gather, a door to the otherworld stands ajar. Told me how Staley's blue spirit fiddle can play a calling-on music. It can call up the blackbirds and open that door, and it can call us to cross over into the otherworld. Or call something back to us from over there.

"Looks like it's not just blackbirds anymore," she tells me.

That's when she opens the top of her shopping bag and shows me the rabbit she's got hidden away inside. It looks up at me with its mournful brown eyes, one ear all chewed up, ribs showing.

"Sorry looking thing," I say.

Staley nods.

"Where'd you find it?"

"Up yonder," she says. "In the hills. I kind of called him to me, though I wasn't trying to or anything." She gives me a little smile. " 'Course I don't try to call up the crows either, and they still come with no nevermind."

I nod like I understand what's going on here.

"Anyway," she goes on. "The thing is, there's a boy trapped in there, under that fur and—"

"A boy?" I have to ask.

"Well, I'm thinking he's young. All I know for sure is he's scared and wore out and he's male."

"When you say boy . . . ?"

"I mean a human boy who's wearing the shape of a hare. Like a skinwalker." She pauses, looks over her shoulder. "Did I mention that there's something after him?"

There's something in the studied casualness of how she puts it that sends a quick chill scooting up my spine. I don't see anything out of the ordinary on the street behind her. Crowsea tenements. Parked cars. Dawn pinking the horizon. But something doesn't set right all the same.

"Maybe you better come inside," I say.

I don't have much, just a basement apartment in this Kelly Street tenement. I get it rent-free in exchange for my custodial duties on it and a couple of other buildings the landlord owns in the area. Seems I don't ever have any folding money, but I manage to get by with odd jobs and tips from the tenants when I do a little work for them. It's not much, but it's a sight better than living on the street like I was doing when Staley and I first met.

I send her on ahead of me, down the stairs and through the door into my place, and lock the door behind us. I use the term "lock" loosely. Mostly it's the idea of a lock. I mean I'm pushing the tail end of fifty and I could easily kick it open. But I still feel a sight better with the night shut out and that flimsy lock doing its best.

"You said there's something after him?" I say once we're inside.

Staley sits down in my sorry excuse for an armchair—picked it out of the trash before the truck came one morning. It's amazing the things people will throw away, though I'll be honest, this chair's had its day. Still I figured maybe a used up old man and a used up old chair could find some use for each other and so far it's been holding up its end of the bargain. I pull up a kitchen chair for myself. As for the rabbit, he sticks his head out of the cloth folds of the shopping bag and then sits there on the floor looking from me to Staley, like he's following the conversation. Hell, the way Staley tells it, he probably can.

"Something," Staley says.

"What kind of something?"

She shakes her head. "I don't rightly know."

Then she tells me about the roadhouse and her friend dropping her off near home. Tells me about her walk through the fields that night and finding the rabbit hiding in the underbrush near her trailer.

"See, this calling-on's not something I do on purpose," she explains when she's taken the story so far. "But I got to thinking, if I opened some door to who knows where, well, maybe I can close it again, shut out whatever's chasing Mr. Rabbitskin here."

I raise my eyebrows.

"Well, I've got to call him something," she says. "Anyway, so I got back to playing my fiddle, concentrating on this whole business like I've never done before. You know, being purposeful about this opening doors business."

"And?" I ask when she falls silent.

"I think I made it worse. I think I let that something right out."

"You keep saying 'you think.' Are you just going on feelings here, or did you actually see something?"

"Oh, I saw something, no question there. Don't know what it was, but it came sliding out of nowhere, like there was a door I couldn't see standing smack in the middle of the meadow and it could just step through, easy as you please. It looked like some cross between a big cat and a wolf, I guess."

"What happened to it?" I ask.

She shakes her head. "I don't know that either. It ran off into the forest. I guess maybe it was confused about how it got to be here, and maybe even where here is and all. But I don't think it's going to stay confused. I got only the one look at its eyes and what I saw there was smart, you know? Not just human smart, but college professor smart."

"And so you came here," I say.

She nods. "I didn't know what else to do. I just

packed my knapsack and stuck old Mr. Rabbitskin here in a bag. Grabbed my fiddle and we lit a shuck. I kept expecting that thing to come out of the woods while we were making our way down to the highway, but it left us alone. Then, when we got to the blacktop, we were lucky enough to hitch a ride with a trucker all the way down to the city."

She falls quiet again. I nod slowly as I look from her to the rabbit.

"Now don't get me wrong," I say, "because I'm willing to help, but I can't help but wonder why you picked me to come to."

"Well," she says. "I figured rabbit-boy here's the only one can explain what's what. So first we've got to shift him back to his human skin."

"I'm no hoodoo man," I tell her.

"No, but you knew Malicorne maybe better than any of us."

"Malicorne," I say softly.

Staley's story notwithstanding, Malicorne had to be about the damnedest thing I ever ran across in this world. She used to squat in the Tombs with the rest of us, a tall horsey-faced woman with—and I swear this is true—a great big horn growing out of the center of her forehead. You've never seen such a thing. Fact is, most people didn't, even when she was standing right smack there in front of them. There was something about that horn that made your attention slide away from it.

"I haven't seen her in a long time," I tell Staley. "Not since we saw her and Jake walk off into the night."

Through one of those doors that Staley and the crows called up. And we didn't so much see them go, as hear them, their footsteps changing into the sounds of hoofbeats that slowly faded away. Which is what Staley's getting at here, I realize. Malicorne had some kind of healing magic about her, but she was also one of those skinwalkers, those who change from something mostly human into something not even close.

"I just thought maybe you'd heard from her," Staley said. "Or you'd know how to get a hold of her."

I shake my head. "There's nobody you can talk to about it out there on the rez?"

She looks a little embarrassed.

"I was hoping I could avoid that," she says. "See, I'm pretty much just a guest myself, living out there where I do. It doesn't seem polite to make a mess like I've done and not clean it up on my own."

I see through what she's saying pretty quick.

"You figure they'll be pissed," I say.

"Well, wouldn't you be? What if they kicked me off the rez? I love living up there in the deep woods. What would I do if I had to leave?"

I can see her point, though I'm thinking that friends might be more forgiving than she thinks they'll be. 'Course, I don't know how close she is to the folks living up there.

I look down at the rabbit who still seems to be following the conversation like he understands what's going on. There's a nervous look in those big brown eyes of his, but something smarter than you'd expect of an animal, too. I lift my gaze back up to meet Staley's.

"I think I know someone we can talk to," I say.

* * *

The way William had talked him up, Staley expected Robert Lonnie to be about two hundred years old and, as Grandma used to describe one of those old hound dogs of hers, full of piss and vinegar. But Robert looked to be no older than twenty-one, twenty-two—a slender black man in a pin striped suit, small-boned and handsome, with long delicate fingers and wavy hair brushed back from his forehead. It was only when you took a look into those dark eyes of his that you got the idea he'd a been a place or two ordinary folks didn't visit. They weren't so much haunted as haunting; when he looked at you, his gaze didn't stop at the skin, but went all the way through to the spirit held in there by your bones.

They tracked him down in a small bar off Palm Street, found him sitting at a booth in the back, playing a snaky blues tune on a battered old Gibson guitar. The bar was closed and except for a bald-headed white man drying beer glasses behind the bar, he had the place to himself. He never looked up when she and William walked in, just played that guitar of his, picked it with a lazy ease that was all the more surprising since the music he pulled out of it sounded like it had to come from at least a couple of guitars. It was a soulful, hurting blues, but it filled you with hope, too.

Staley stood transfixed, listening to it, to him. She felt herself slipping away somewhere, she couldn't say where. Everything in the room gave the impression it was leaning closer to him, tables, chairs, the bottles of liquor behind the bar, listening, *feeling* that music.

When William touched her arm, she started, blinked, then followed him over to the booth.

William had described Robert Lonnie as an old hoodoo man and Staley decided that even if he didn't know a lick of the kind of mojo she was looking for, he still knew a thing or two about magic—the musical kind, that is. Lord, but he could play. Then he looked up, his gaze locking on hers. It was like a static charge, that dark gaze, sudden and unexpected in its intensity, and she almost dropped her fiddle case on the floor. She slipped slowly into the booth, took a seat across the table from him and not a moment too soon since her legs had suddenly lost their ability to hold her upright. William had to give her a nudge before she slid farther down the seat to make room for him. She hugged her fiddle case to her chest, only dimly aware of William beside her, the rabbit in its bag on his lap.

The guitarist kept his gaze on her, humming under his breath as he brought the tune to a close. His last chord hung in the air with an almost physical presence and for a long moment everything in the bar held its breath. Then he smiled, wide and easy, and the moment was gone.

"William," he said softly. "Miss."

"This is Staley," William said.

Robert gave her a considering look, then turned to William. "You're early to be hitting the bars."

"It's not like you think," William said. "I'm still going to AA."

"Good for you."

"Well," William said. "Considering it's about the only thing I've done right with my life, I figured I might as well stick with it."

"Uh-huh." Robert returned his attention to Staley. "You've got the look of one who's been to the crossroads."

"I guess," Staley said, though she had no idea what he meant.

"But you don't know who you met there, do you?"

She shook her head.

Robert nodded. "That's the way it happens, all that spooky shit. You feel the wind rising and the leaves are trembling on the trees. Next thing you know, it's all falling down on you like hail, but you don't know what it is."

"Um . . ." Staley looked to William for guidance.

"You've just got to tell him like you told me," William said.

But Robert was looking at the shopping bag on William's lap now.

"Who've you got in there?" he asked.

Staley cleared her throat. "We were hoping you could tell us," she said.

William lowered the cloth sides of the bag. The rabbit poked its head up, raggedy ear hanging down on one side.

Robert laughed. "Well, now," he said, gaze lifting to meet Staley's again. "Why don't you tell me this story of yours."

So Staley did, started with Butch dropping her off on the county road near her trailer late last night and took the tale all the way through to when she got to William's apartment earlier this morning. Somewhere in the middle of it the barman brought them a round of coffee, walking away before Staley could pay him, or even get out a thanks.

"I remember that Malicorne," Robert said when she was done. "Now she was a fine woman, big horn and all. You ever see her anymore?"

William shook his head. "Not since that night she went off with Jake."

"Can you help me?" Staley asked.

Robert leaned back on his side of the booth. Those long fingers of his left hand started walking up the neck of his guitar and he picked with his right, soft, a spidery twelve-bar.

"You ever hear the story of the two magicians?" he asked.

Staley shook her head.

"Don't know what the problem was between them, but the way I heard it is they got themselves into a longtime, serious altercation, went on for years. In the end, the only way they were willing to settle it was to duke it out the way those hoodoo men do, working magic. The one'd turn himself into a 'coon, the other'd become a coonhound, chase him up some tree. That treed 'coon'd come down, 'cept now he's wearing the skin of a wildcat." Robert grinned. "Only now that coonhound, he's a hornet, starts in on stinging the cat. And this just goes on.

"One's a salmon, the other's an otter. Salmon becomes the biggest, ugliest catfish you ever saw, big

enough to swallow that otter whole, but now the otter's a giant eagle, slashing at the fish with its talons.
Time passes and they just keep at it, changing skins—
big changes, little changes. One's a flood, the other's
a drought. One's human, the other's a devil. One's
night, the other's day. . . .

"Damnedest thing you ever saw, like paper-scissors-
rock, only hoodoo man style, you know what I'm saying? Damnedest thing."

The whole time he talked, he picked at his guitar,
turned the story into a talking song with that lazy
drawl of his, mesmerizing. When he fell silent, it took
Staley a moment or two to realize that he'd stopped
talking.

"So Mr. Rabbitskin here," she said, "and that other
thing I only caught half a glimpse of—you're saying
they're like those two magicians?"

"Got the smell of it to me."

"And they're only interested in hurting each
other?"

"Well, now," Robert told her. "That'd be the big
thought on their minds, but you've got to remember
that hoodoo requires a powerful amount of nourish-
ment, just to keep the body up to fighting strength.
Those boys'll be hungry and needing to feed—and I'm
guessing they won't be all that particular as to what
they chow down on."

Great, Staley thought. She shot the rabbit a sour
look, but it wouldn't meet her gaze.

"Mr. Rabbitskin here," she said, "won't eat a thing.
I've tried carrots, greens, even bread soaked in
warm milk."

Robert nodded. "That'd tempt a rabbit, right
enough. Problem is, what you've got here are creatures that are living on pure energy. Hell, that's probably all they are at this point, nothing but energy
gussied up into a shape that makes sense to our eyes.
They won't be eating food like we do. So far as that

goes, the way they'd be looking at it, we probably *are* food, considering the kind of energy we've got rolling through us."

The rabbit, docile up to now, suddenly lunged out of William's lap and went skidding across the smooth floor, heading for back door of the bar. William started after it, but Robert just shook his head.

"You'll never catch it now," he said.

"Are you saying that rabbit was feeding on me somehow?" William asked.

"I figure he was building up to it."

Staley stared in the direction that the rabbit had gone, her heart sinking. This whole situation was getting worse by the minute.

"So these two things I called over," she said. "They're the hoodoo men from your story?"

Robert shrugged. "Oh, they're not the same pair, but it's an old story and old stories have a habit of repeating themselves."

"Who won that first duel?" William asked.

"One of 'em turned himself into a virus and got the other too sick to shape a spell in reply, but I don't know which one. Doesn't much matter anyway. By the time that happened, the one was as bad as the other. Get into that kind of a state of mind and after awhile you start to forget things like kindness, decency . . . the fact that other people aren't put here in this world for you to feed on."

Staley's heart sank lower.

"We've got to do something about this," she said. "I've got to do something. I'm responsible for whatever hurt they cause, feeding on people and all."

"Who says it's your fault?" Robert wanted to know.

"Well, I called them over, didn't I? Though I don't understand how I did it. I've been playing my music for going on four years now in that meadow and nothing like this has ever happened before."

Robert nodded. "Maybe this time the devil was listening and you know what he's like. He purely hates anybody can play better than him—'specially if they aren't obliged to him in some way."

"Only person I owe anything to," Staley said, "is my Grandma and she was no devil."

"But you've been at the crossroads."

Staley was starting to understand what he meant. There was always something waiting to take advantage of you, ghosts and devils sitting there at the edge of nowhere where the road to what is and what could be cross each other, spiteful creatures just waiting for the chance to step into your life and turn it all hurtful. That was the trouble with having something like her spirit fiddle. It called things to you, but unless you paid constant attention, you forgot that it can call the bad as well as the good.

"I've been a lot of places," she said.

"You ever played that fiddle of yours in one?"

"Not so's I knew."

"Well, you've been someplace, done something to get his attention."

"That doesn't solve the problem I've got right now."

Robert nodded. "No, we're just defining it."

"So what can I do?"

"I don't know exactly. Thing I've learned is, if you call up something bad, you've got to take up the music and play it back out again or it'll never go away. I'd start there."

"I already tried that and it only made things worse."

"Yeah, but this time you've got to jump the groove."

Staley gave him a blank look.

"You remember phonograph records?" Robert asked.

"Well, sure, though back home we mostly played tapes."

Robert started to finger his guitar again, another spidery twelve-bar blues.

"Those old phonograph records," he said. "They had a one-track groove that the needle followed from beginning to end—it's like the habits we develop, the way we look at the world, what we expect to find in it, that kind of thing. You get into a bad situation like we got here and it's time to jump the groove, get someplace new, see things different." He cut the tune short before it could resolve and abruptly switched into another key. "Change the music. What you hear, what you play. Maybe even who you are. Lets you fix things and the added bonus is it confuses the devil. Makes it hard for him to focus on you for a time."

"Jump the groove," Staley repeated slowly.

Robert nodded. "Why don't we take a turn out to where you've been living and see what we can do?"

* * *

I call in a favor from my friend Moth who owns a junkyard up in the Tombs and borrow a car to take us back up to Staley's trailer. "Take the Chevette," he tells me, pointing out an old two-door that's got more primer on it than it does original paint. "The plates are legit." Staley comes with me, fusses over Moth's junkyard dogs like they're old pals, wins Moth over with a smile and that good nature of hers, but mostly because she can run through instrumental versions of a couple of Boxcar Willie songs. After that, so far as Moth's concerned, she can do no wrong.

"This guy Robert," she says when we're driving back to the bar to pick him up. "How come he's so fixed on the devil?"

"Well," I tell her. "The way I heard it, a long time ago he met the devil at a crossroads, made a deal with him. Wanted to be the best player the world'd ever seen. 'No problem,' the devil tells him. 'Just sign here.'

"So Robert signs up. Trouble is, he already had it

in him. If he hadn't been in such a hurry, with a little time and effort on his part, he would've got what he wanted and wouldn't have owed the devil a damn thing."

Staley's looking at me, a smile lifting one corner of her mouth.

"You believe that?" she says.

"Why not? I believed you when you told me there was a boy under the skin of that rabbit."

She gives me a slow nod.

"So what happened?" she asks.

"What? With Robert? Well, when he figured out he'd been duped, he paid the devil back in kind. You can't take a man's soul unless he dies, and Robert, he's figured out a way to live forever."

I watch Staley's mouth open, but then she shakes her head and leaves whatever she was going to say unsaid.

" 'Course," I go on, "it helps to stay out of the devil's way, so Robert, he keeps himself a low profile."

Staley shakes her head. "Now that I can't believe. Anybody hears him play is going to remember it forever."

"Well, sure. That's why he doesn't play out."

"But—"

"I'm not saying he keeps his music to himself. You'll find him sitting in on a session from time to time, but mostly he just plays in places like that bar we found him in today. Sits in a corner during the day when the joint's half empty and makes music those drunks can't ever forget—though they're unlikely to remember exactly where it was that they heard it."

"That's so sad."

I shrug. "Maybe. But it keeps the devil at bay."

Staley's quiet for a while, doesn't say much until we pull into the alley behind the bar.

"Do you believe in the devil?" she asks before we get out of the car.

"Everybody's got devils."

"No, I mean a real devil—like in the Bible."

I sit for a moment and think on that.

"I believe there's good in the world," I tell her finally, "so yeah. I guess I've got to believe there's evil, too. Don't know if it's the devil, exactly—you know, pointy horns, hooves, and tail and all—but I figure that's as good a name as any other."

"You afraid of him?"

"Hell, Staley. Some days I'm afraid of everything. Why do you think I spent half of my life looking for oblivion in a bottle?"

"What made you change?"

I don't even have to think about that.

"Malicorne," I tell her. "Nothing she said or did—just that she was. I guess her going away made me realize that I had a choice: I could either keep living in the bottom of a bottle, and that's not living at all. Or I could try to experience ordinary life as something filled with beauty and wonder—you know, the way she did. Make everyday something special."

Staley nods. "That's not so easy."

"Hell, no. But it's surely worth aiming for."

* * *

William drove, with Staley riding shotgun and Robert lounging in the back, playing that old Gibson of his. He worked up a song about their trip, a sleepy blues, cataloging the sights, tying them together with walking bass lines and bottleneck solos. Staley had made this drive more times than she could count, but all those past trips were getting swallowed by this one. The soundtrack Robert was putting to it would forever be the memory she carried whenever she thought about leaving the city core and driving north up Highway 14, into the hills.

It took them a couple of hours after picking Robert up at the bar to reach that stretch of country road closest to Staley's trailer. The late afternoon sun was in the west, but still high in the summer sky when Staley had William pull the Chevette over to the side of the road and park.

"Can we just leave the car like this?" William asked.

Staley nodded. "I doubt anybody's going to mess with it sitting here on the edge of Indian land."

She got out and stretched, then held the front seat up against the dash so that Robert could climb out of the rear. He kicked at the dirt road with his shoe and smiled as a thin coat of dust settled over the shiny patent leather. Leaning on the hood of the car, he cradled his guitar against his chest and looked out across the fields, gaze tracking the slow circle of a hawk in the distance.

"Lord, but it's peaceful out here," he said. "I could listen to this quiet forever."

"I know what you mean," Staley said. "I love to travel, but there's nowhere else I could call home."

William wasn't as content. As soon as he got out of the car, a half-dozen deerflies dive-bombed him, buzzing round and round his head. He waved them off, but all of his frantic movement did was make them more frenzied.

"What's the matter with these things?" he asked.

"Stop egging them on—all it does is aggravate them."

"Yeah, right. How come they aren't in your face?"

"I've got an arrangement with them," Staley told him.

They weren't bothering Robert either. He gave the ones troubling William a baleful stare.

" 'Preciate it if you'd leave him alone," he told them.

They gave a last angry buzz around William's head, then zoomed off down the road, flying like a fighter squadron in perfect formation. William followed their retreat before turning back to his companions.

"Nice to see some useful hoodoo for a change," he said.

Robert grinned. "It's all useful—depending on which side of the spell you're standing. But that wasn't hoodoo so much as politeness. Me asking, them deciding to do what I asked."

"Uh-huh."

Robert ignored him. "So where's this trailer of yours?" he asked Staley.

"Back in the woods—over yonder."

She led them through the raspberry bushes and into the field. Robert started up playing again and for the first time since they'd met, Staley got the itch to join him on her fiddle. She understood this music he was playing. It talked about the dirt and crushed stone on the county road, the sun warm on the fields, the rasp of the tall grass and weeds against their clothes as they walked in single file towards the trees. Under the hemlocks, the music became all bass and treble, roots and high boughs, the midrange set aside. But only temporarily.

When they reached the bottle tree, Staley glanced back. William gave the hanging bottles a puzzled look, but Robert nodded in apparent approval. His bottle-neck slide replied to the clink of glass from the bottle tree, a slightly discordant slur of notes pulled off the middle strings of the Gibson.

The bluesman and Grandma would've got along just fine, she decided.

Once they came out from under the trees, they could walk abreast on the shorter grass. Robert broke off playing when Staley gave her scarecrow a little curtsey by way of greeting.

"How well do you know that fellow?" he asked.

Staley smiled. "About four years—ever since I put him up."

"The clothes were yours?"

She nodded.

"And you collected the wood for his limbs?"

She nodded again. "Why are you asking all these questions?"

"Because he's halfway alive."

"You mean the branches sprouting?"

"No, I mean he's got the start of an individual spirit, growing there in the straw and applewood."

Staley regarded the scarecrow in a new light. Now that it had been pointed out, she could feel the faint pulse of life in its straw breast. Sentient life, not quite fully formed, but hidden there as surely as there'd been a boy hidden in the raggedy hare she'd lost in the city.

"But, how . . . ?" she began, her voice trailing off.

Robert turned in a slow circle, taking in the whole of the meadow. Her trailer, the vegetable garden.

"You've played a lot of music in here," he said. "Paid a lot of attention to the rhythms of the meadow, the forest, how you and your belongings fit into it. It's got so's you've put so much hoodoo in this place I'm surprised you only ever called over those two feuding spirits."

William nodded. "Hell, even I feel something."

Staley did, too, except it was what she always felt when she was here.

"I thought it was home I was feeling," she said.

"It is," Robert said. "But you've played it up so powerful it's no wonder the devil took notice."

Staley shot a glance at her scarecrow which made Robert smile.

"Oh, he's more subtle than that," he told her. "He's going to come up at you from the backside, like pushing through a couple of feuding spirits to wreak a little havoc with the things you love." He gave her fiddle case a considering look. "You know what you've got to do."

Staley sighed. "Jump the groove."

"That's right. Break the pattern. Don't give the devil something he can hold on to. Nothing's easier to trip a body up than habits and patterns. Why do you think the Gypsy people consider settling down to be so stressful? Only way they can rest is by traveling."

"You're saying I should go? That I've got to leave this place?"

Robert raised an eyebrow. "You a Romany girl now?"

"No."

"Then find your own groove to jump."

Staley sighed again. Intellectually, she understood what Robert was getting at. But how to put it into practice? She played the way she played because . . . well, that was the way she played. Especially here, in this place. She took the music from her surroundings, digging deeper and deeper into the relationships between earth and sky, forest and meadow, her trailer and the garden and the tattered figure of the scarecrow watching over it all. Where was she supposed to find a music still true to all of this, but different enough to break the pattern of four summers immersed in its quiet joys and mysteries?

"I don't know if I can do it," she said.

"You can try," Robert told her.

"I suppose. But what if I call something worse over?"

"You didn't call anything over. Those spirits were sent."

Staley shook her head. "This fiddle of Grandma's plays a calling-on music—I can hear it whenever I play."

"I don't deny that," Robert said. "But you've got to put some intent into that call, and from what you've been telling me, you didn't intend to bring anything over last night."

"So when those blackbirds gather to her fiddling," William said, "it's because she's invited them?"

Robert shrugged. "Crows and ravens are a whole different circumstance. They live on the outside of where we are and they learned a long time ago how to take advantage of the things we do, making their own hoodoo with the bits and pieces we leave behind."

That made sense to Staley. She'd never deliberately called up the blackbirds, but they came all the same. Only not here. That was why she'd always thought it was safe to play whatever she wanted around the trailer. She'd seen them from time to time, mostly going after her garden, or sneaking off with a bit of this or that for their nests, but they didn't gather here. The closest roost was out by the highway.

She glanced at Robert to find his gaze on her, steady but mild. She wanted to say, How do I know the devil's not being so subtle that he's persuading me through you? But they'd been talking long enough. And whatever else Robert was, she doubted he was the devil.

Kneeling on the grass, she cracked open her fiddle case. Took out her bow, tightened the frog, rosined the hairs. Finally she picked up the blue spirit fiddle her grandmother had given her and stood up again. She ran a finger across the strings. The E was a touch flat. She gave its fine tuner a twist, and tried again. This time all four strings rang true.

"Here goes nothing," she said, bringing the fiddle up under her chin.

"Not like that," Robert told her. "Dig a little with your heart before you start in on playing. You can't jump the groove until you know where it's at."

True, she thought.

William gave her an encouraging nod, then walked over to the trailer and sat down on the steps. After a moment Robert joined him, one hand closed around the neck of his guitar, damping the strings.

Staley took a breath and let it out, slow. She held the fiddle in the crook of her arm, bow dangling from her index finger, and closed her eyes, trying to get a feel of where the meadow was today, how she fit into it. She swayed slightly where she stood. Toe on heel, she removed one shoe, then the other, digging through the blades of grass with her bare toes until she was in direct contact with the earth.

What do I hear? she thought. What do I feel?

Woodpecker hammering a dead tree limb, deeper in the woods. The smell of grass rising up from by her feet. Herbs from the garden, mint, basil, thyme. The flutter and sweet chirps of chickadees and finches. A faint breeze on her cheek. The soft helicopter approach of a hummingbird, feeding on the purple bergamot that grew along the edge of the vegetable and herb beds. The sudden chatter of a red squirrel out by the woodpile. Something crawling across her foot. An ant, maybe. Or a small beetle. The hoarse croak of a crow, off in the fields somewhere. The sun, warm on her face and arms. The fat buzz of a bee.

She knew instinctively how she could make a music of it all, catch it with notes drawn from her fiddle and send it spiraling off into the late afternoon air. That was the groove Robert kept talking about. So where did she go to jump it?

The first thing she heard was what Robert would do, bottleneck slides and bass lines, complicated chord patterns that were both melody and rhythm and sounded far simpler than they were to play. But while she could relate to what his take would be—could certainly appreciate it and even harmonize with it— that music wasn't hers. Following that route wouldn't be so much jumping her own groove as becoming someone else, being who they were, playing the music they would play.

She had to be herself, but still play with a stranger's hand. How did a person even begin to do that?

She concentrated again on what this place meant to her, distilling the input of sounds and smells and all to their essence. What, she asked herself, was the first thing she thought of when she came back here in the spring from her winter wanderings? She called up the fields in her mind's eye, the forest and her meadow, hidden away in it, and it came to her.

Green.

Buds on the trees and new growth pushing up through the browned grasses and weeds that had died off during the winter. The first shoots of crocuses and daffodils, fiddlehead ferns and triliums growing in the forest shade.

She came here to immerse herself in a green world. Starting in April when the color was but a vague hue brushing the landscape through to deep summer when the fields and forest ran riot with verdant growth. Come September when the meadows browned and the deciduous trees began to turn red and gold and yellow, that was when she started to pack up the trailer, put things away, ready her knapsack, feet itchy to hit the road once more.

Eyes still closed, she lifted her fiddle back up under her chin. Pulling her bow across the strings, she called up an autumn music. She put into it deer foraging in the cedars. Her scarecrow standing alone, guarding the empty vegetable and herb beds. Geese flying in formation overhead. Frosts and naked tree limbs. Milkweed pods bursting open and a thousand seeds parachuting across the fields. Brambles that stuck to the legs of your overalls.

She played music that was brown and yellow, faded colors and grays. It was still this place. It was still her. But it was a groove she didn't normally explore with her music. Certainly not here. This was her green home. A green world. But all you had to do was look under the green to see memories of the winter past. A fallen tree stretched out along the forest floor, moss-covered and rotting. A dead limb poking through the leaves of a tree, the one branch that didn't make it through the winter. The browned grass of last autumn, covered over by new growth, but not mulch yet. And it wasn't simply memories. There were shadowings of the winter to come, too, even in this swelter of summer and green. She wasn't alone in her annual migrations south, but those that remained were already beginning their preparations. Foraging, gathering. The sunflowers were going to seed. There were fruits on the apple trees, still green and hard, but they would ripen. The berry bushes were beginning to put forth their crop. Seeds were forming, nuts hardening.

It was another world, another groove.

She played it out until she could almost feel a change in the air—a crispness, dry and bittersweet. Opening her eyes, she turned to look at the trailer. Is this what you meant? she wanted to ask Robert. But he wasn't there. She took bow from strings and stood there, silent, taking it all in.

Robert and William were gone, and so was the summer. The grass was browned underfoot. The fruit and leaves from her scarecrow's apple limbs were fallen away, the garden finished for the year.

What had she done now? Called up the autumn? Lost a few months of her life, standing here in her meadow, playing an unfamiliar music?

Or had she called herself away?

She knew nothing of the otherworld except for what people had told her about it. Grandma. Malicorne. A man named Rupert who lived in the desert, far to the south. Beyond the fact that spirits lived there who could cross over into our world, everything they had to say about the place was vague.

Right now, all she knew was that this didn't feel

like her meadow so much as an echo of it. How it
might appear in the otherworld.

The place where the spirit people lived and her fiddle had come from.

Grandma had told her it was a place sensible people
didn't go. Rupert had warned that while it was easy
to stray over into it, it wasn't so easy to leave behind
once you were there.

How could this have happened? How—

Movement startled her. She took a step back as a
hare came bounding out of the woods to take refuge
under her trailer. A moment later a large dog burst
into the meadow, chasing it. The dog rushed the
trailer, bending low and growling deep in its chest as
it tried to fit itself into the narrow space. Giving a
sudden yelp, it scrabbled away as a rattler came sliding
out from under the trailer. The snake took a shot at
the dog, but the dog had changed into a mongoose,
shifting so fast Staley never saw it happen. The mongoose's teeth clamped on the rattler, but it, too, transformed, becoming a boa constrictor, fattening,
lengthening, forcing the mongoose's jaws open, wrapping its growing length around the smaller mammal's
body, squeezing.

Staley didn't need a lot of considering time to work
out what was going on here. Maybe she'd fiddled herself over into the otherworld, but it was obvious that
she'd also pulled those two hoodoo men along with
her when she'd come.

"Hey, you!" she cried.

The animals froze, turned to look at her. She was
a little surprised that they actually stopped to listen
to her.

"Don't you have no *sense*? she asked them. "What's
any of this going to prove?"

She looked from one to the other, trapped by the
dark malevolence in their eyes and suddenly wished
she'd left well enough alone. What business was it of

hers if they killed each other? She'd gotten them back here where they belonged. Best thing now was that they forgot she ever existed.

For a long moment she was sure that wasn't going to happen. It was like playing in a bar when a fight broke out at the edge of the stage. The smart musician didn't get involved. She just stepped back, kept her instrument safe, and let them work it out between themselves until the bouncer showed up. Trouble was, there was no bouncer here. It was just the three of them and she didn't even have a mike stand she could hit them with.

She didn't know what she'd have done if they'd broken off their own fight and come after her. Luckily, she didn't have to find out. The mongoose became a sparrow and slipped out of the snake's grip, darting away into the forest. A half second later a hawk was in pursuit and she on her own again. At least she thought she was.

A low chuckle from behind her made her turn.

The newcomer looked like he'd just stepped down out of the hills, tall and lean, a raggedy hillbilly in jeans and a flannel shirt, cowboy boots on his feet. There were acne scars on his cheeks and he wore his dark hair slicked back in a ducktail. His eyes were the clearest blue she could ever remember seeing, filled with a curious mix of distant skies and good humor. He had one hand in his pocket, the other holding the handle of a battered, black guitar case.

"You ever see such foolishness?" he asked. "You think they'd learn, but I reckon they've been at it now for about as long as the day is wide."

Staley liked the sound of his voice. It held an easy-going lilt that reminded her of her daddy's cousins who lived up past Hazard, deep in the hills.

She laughed. "Long as the day is wide?" she asked.

"Well, you know. Start to finish, the day only holds

so many hours, but you go sideways and it stretches on forever."

"I've never heard of time running sideways."

"I'm sure you must know a hundred things I've never heard of."

"I suppose."

"You new around here?" he asked.

Staley glanced back at her trailer, then returned her gaze to him.

"In a manner of speaking," she said. "I'm not entirely sure how I got here and even less sure as to how I'll get back to where I come from."

"I can show you," he told her. "But maybe you'd favor me with a tune first? Been a long time since I got to pick with a fiddler."

The thing that no one told you about the otherworld, Staley realized, is how everything took on a dreamlike quality when you were here. She knew she should be focusing on getting back to the summer meadow where Robert and William were waiting for her, but there just didn't seem to be any hurry about it.

"So what do you say?" he asked.

She shrugged. "I guess. . . ."

* * *

I'm already feeling a little dozy from the sun and fresh air when Staley begins to play her fiddle. It doesn't sound a whole lot different from the kinds of things she usually plays, but then what do I really know about music? Don't ask me to discuss it. I either like it or I don't. But Robert seems pleased with what she's doing, nodding to himself, has a little smile starting up there in the corner of his mouth.

I can see his left hand shaping chords on the neck of his guitar, but he doesn't strum the strings. Just follows what she's doing in his head, I guess.

I look at Staley a little longer, smiling as well to see

her standing there so straight-backed in her overalls, barefoot in the grass, the sun glowing golden on her short hair. After a while I lean back against the door of the trailer again and close my eyes. I'm drifting on the music, not really thinking much of anything, when I realize the sound of the fiddle's starting to fade away.

"Shit," I hear Robert say.

I open my eyes, but before I can turn to look at him, I see Staley's gone. It's the damnedest thing. I can still hear her fiddling, only it's getting fainter and fainter like she's walking away and I can't see a sign of her anywhere. I can't imagine a person could run as fast as she'd have to disappear like this and still keep playing that sleepy music.

When Robert stands up, I scramble to my feet as well.

"What's going on?" I ask him.

"She let it take her away."

"What do you mean? Take her away where?"

But he doesn't answer. He's looking into the woods and then I see them too. A rabbit being chased by some ugly old dog. Might be the same rabbit that ran off on us in the city, but I can't tell. It comes tearing out from under the trees, running straight across the meadow toward us, and then it just disappears.

I blink, not surely I actually saw what I just saw. But then the same thing happens to the dog. It's like it goes through some door I can't see. There one minute, gone the next.

"Well, she managed to pull them back across," Robert says. "But I don't like this. I don't like this at all."

Hearing him talk like that makes me real nervous.

"Why?" I ask him. "This is what we wanted, right? She was going to play some music to put things back the way they were. Wasn't that the plan?"

He nods. "But her going over wasn't."

"I don't get it."

Robert turns to look at me. "How's she going to get back?"

"Same way she went away—right?"

He answers with a shrug and then I get a bad feeling. It's like what happened with Malicorne and Jake, I realize. Stepped away, right out of the world, and they never came back. The only difference is, they meant to go.

"She won't know what to do," Robert says softly. "She'll be upset and maybe a little scared, and then he's going to show up, offer to show her the way back."

I don't have to ask who he's talking about.

"But she'll know better than to bargain with him," I say.

"We can hope."

'We've got to be able to do better than that," I tell him.

"I'm open to suggestions."

I look at that guitar in his hands.

"You could call her back," I say.

Robert shakes his head. "The devil, he's got himself a guitar, too."

"I don't know what that means."

"Think about it," Robert says. "Whose music is she going to know to follow?"

* * *

The stranger laid his guitar case on the grass and opened it up. The instrument he took out was an old Martin D-45 with the pearl inlaid "CD MARTIN" logo on the headstock—a classic, prewar picker's guitar.

"Don't see many of those anymore," Staley said.

"They didn't make all that many." He smiled. "Though I'll tell you, I've never seen me a blue fiddle like you've got, not ever."

"Got it from my grandma."

"Well, she had taste. Give me an A, would you?"

Staley ran her bow across the A string of her fiddle and the stranger quickly tuned up to it.

"You ever play any contests?" he asked as he finished tuning.

He ran his pick across the strings, fingering an A minor chord. The guitar had a big rich sound with lots of bottom end.

"I don't believe in contests," Staley said. "I think they take all the pleasure out of a music."

"Oh, I didn't mean nothing serious. More like swapping tunes, taking turns 'till one of you stumps the other player. Just for fun, like."

Staley shrugged.

" 'Course to make it interesting," he added, "we could put a small wager on the outcome."

"What kind of wager would we be talking about here?"

Staley didn't know why she was even asking that, why she hadn't just shut down this idea of a contest right from the get-go. It was like something in the air was turning her head all around.

"I don't know," he said. "How about if I win, you'll give me a kiss?"

"A kiss?"

He shrugged. "And if you enjoy it, maybe you'll give me something more."

"And if I win?"

"Well, what's the one thing you'd like most in the world?"

Staley smiled. "Tell you the truth, I don't want for much of anything. I keep my expectations low—makes for a simple life."

"I'm impressed," he said. "Most people have a hankering for something they can't have. You know, money, or fame, or a true love. Maybe living forever."

"Don't see much point in living forever," Staley told him. "Come a time when everybody you care about would be long gone, but there you'd be, still trudging along on your own."

"Well, sure. But—"

"And as for money and fame, I think they're pretty much overrated. I don't really need much to be happy and I surely don't need anybody nosing in on my business.

"So what about a true love?"

"Well, now," Staley said. "Seems to me true love's something that comes to you, not something you can take or arrange."

"And if it doesn't?"

"That'd be sad, but you make do. I don't know how other folks get by, but I've got my music. I've got my friends."

The stranger regarded her with an odd, frustrated look.

"You can't tell me there's nothing you don't have a yearning for," he said. "Everybody wants for something."

"You mean for myself, or in general, like for there to be no more hurt in the world or the like?"

"For yourself," he said.

Staley shook her head. "Nothing I can't wait for it to find me in its own good time." She put her fiddle up under her chin. "So what do you want to play?"

But the stranger pulled his string strap back over his head and started to put his guitar away.

"What's the matter?" Staley asked. "We don't need some silly contest just to play a few tunes."

The stranger wouldn't look at her.

"I've kind of lost my appetite for music," he said, snapping closed the clasps on his case.

He stood up, his gaze finally meeting hers, and she saw something else in those clear blue eyes of his, a dark storm of anger, but a hurting, too. A loneliness that seemed so out of place, given his easygoing manner. A man like him, he should be friends with everyone he met, she'd thought. Except . . .

"I know who you are," she said.

She didn't know how she knew, but it came to her, like a gauze slipping from in front of her eyes, like she'd suddenly shucked the dreamy quality of the otherworld and could see true once more.

"You don't look nothing like what I expected," she added.

"Yeah, well, you've had your fun. Now let me be."

But something her grandmother had told her once came back to her. "I tell you," she'd said. "If I was ever to meet the devil, I'd kill him with kindness. That's the one thing old Lucifer can't stand."

Staley grinned, remembering.

"Wait a minute," she said. "Don't go off all mad."

The devil glared at her.

"Or at least let me give you that kiss before you go."

He actually backed away from her at that.

"What?" Staley asked. "Suddenly you don't fancy me anymore?"

"You put up a good front," he said. "I didn't make you for such an accomplished liar."

Staley shook her head. "I never lied to you. I really am happy with things the way they are. And anything I don't have, I don't mind waiting on."

The devil spat on the grass at her feet, turned once around, and was gone, vanishing with a small *whuft* of displaced air.

That's your best parting shot? Staley wanted to ask, but decided to leave well enough alone. She gave her surroundings a last look, then started up fiddling again, playing herself back into the green of summer where she'd left her friends.

* * *

Robert's pretty impressed when Staley just steps out of that invisible door, calm as you please. We heard the fiddling first. It sounded like it was coming from someplace on the far side of forever, but getting closer by the moment, and then there she was, standing barefoot in the grass, smiling at us. Robert's even more impressed when she tells us about how she handled the devil.

After putting her fiddle away, she boiled up some water on a Coleman stove and made us a pot of herbal tea. We take it out through the woods in porcelain mugs, heading up to the top of the field overlooking the county road. The car's still there. The sun's going down now, putting on quite a show, and the tea's better than I thought it would be. Got mint in it, some kind of fruit.

"So how do I stop this from happening again?" Staley asks.

"Figure out what your music's all about," Robert tells her. "And take responsibility for it. Dig deep and find what's hiding behind the trees—you know, in the shadows where you can't exactly see things, you can only sense them—and always pay attention. It's up to you what you let out into the light."

"Is that what you do?"

Robert nodded. " 'Course it's different for me, because we're different people. My music's about enduring. Perseverance. That's all the blues is ever about."

"What about hope?"

Robert smiled. "What do you think keeps perseverance alive?"

"Amen," I say.

After a moment, Staley smiles. We all clink our porcelain mugs together and drink a toast to that.